⟨ S0-BJJ-844

Fantastic Tales of Time and Space

SIGNET DOUBLE SCIENCE FICTION:

The People of the Wind

and

The Day of Their Return

SIGNET Science Fiction You'll Enjoy

(0451)

☐ **THE REBEL WORLDS** by Poul Anderson. (090462—$1.75)
☐ **A CIRCUS OF HELLS** by Poul Anderson. (090454—$1.75)
☐ **DANCER FROM ATLANTIS** by Poul Anderson.
(078063—$1.50)
☐ **THE DAY OF THEIR RETURN** by Poul Anderson.
(079418—$1.50)
☐ **THE HORN OF TIME** by Poul Anderson. (113934—$1.75)
☐ **BIBBLINGS** by Barbara Paul. (089375—$1.75)
☐ **GREYBEARD** by Brian Aldiss. (090357—$1.75)†
☐ **KILLBIRD** by Zach Hughes. (092635—$1.75)
☐ **PRESSURE MAN** by Zach Hughes. (094980—$1.95)*
☐ **THUNDERWORLD** by Zach Hughes. (112903—$2.25)*
☐ **TIME GATE** by John Jakes. (078896—$1.25)
☐ **SUN DOGS** by Mark McGarry. (096207—$1.95)*
☐ **PLANET OF THE APES** by Pierre Boulle. (086325—$1.25)

*Price slightly higher in Canada
†Not available in Canada

Buy them at your local bookstore or use this convenient coupon for ordering.

THE NEW AMERICAN LIBRARY, INC.,
P.O. Box 999, Bergenfield, New Jersey 07621

Please send me the books I have checked above. I am enclosing $_____
(please add $1.00 to this order to cover postage and handling). Send check
or money order—no cash or C.O.D.'s. Prices and numbers are subject to change
without notice.

Name_____

Address_____

City _____ State _____ Zip Code _____
Allow 4-6 weeks for delivery.
This offer is subject to withdrawal without notice.

The People
of the Wind

and

The Day of
Their Return

by Poul Anderson

⊘

A SIGNET BOOK

NEW AMERICAN LIBRARY

TIMES MIRROR

The People of the Wind Copyright © 1973 by Poul Anderson

The Day of Their Return Copyright © 1975 by Poul Anderson

Acknowledgment
The Lines which close *The Day of Their Return* are from
"The English Way," copyright 1929 by Rudyard Kipling,
from *Rudyard Kipling's Verse:* Definitive Edition.
Reprinted by permission of Mrs. George Bambridge and
Doubleday & Company, Inc.

All rights reserved. Originally appeared in paperback as separate
volumes published by The New American Library, Inc.

 SIGNET TRADEMARK REG. U.S. PAT. OFF. AND FOREIGN COUNTRIES
REGISTERED TRADEMARK—MARCA REGISTRADA
HECHO EN CHICAGO, U.S.A.

SIGNET, SIGNET CLASSICS, MENTOR, PLUME, MERIDIAN AND NAL
BOOKS are published by The New American Library, Inc.,
1633 Broadway, New York, New York 10019

First Printing (Double Science Fiction Edition), October, 1982

1 2 3 4 5 6 7 8 9

PRINTED IN THE UNITED STATES OF AMERICA

The People
of the Wind

To *Edmond Hamilton* and *Leigh Brackett*
with thanks for many years of adventure

I

"You can't leave now," Daniel Holm told his son. "Any day we may be at war. We may already be."

"That's just why I have to go," the young man answered. "They're calling Khruaths about it around the curve of the planet. Where else should I fare than to my choth?"

When he spoke thus, more than his wording became bird. The very accent changed. He was no longer using the Planha-influenced Anglic of Avalon—pure vowels, r's trilled, m's and n's and ng's almost hummed, speech deepened and slowed and strongly cadenced; rather, it was as if he were trying to translate for a human listener the thought of an Ythrian brain.

The man whose image occupied the phone screen did not retort, "You might consider staying with your own family," as once he would have. Instead Daniel Holm nodded, and said quietly, "I see. You're not Chris now, you're Arinnian," and all at once looked old.

That wrenched at the young man. He reached forth, but his fingers were stopped by the screen. "I'm always Chris, Dad," he blurted. "It's only that I'm Arinnian too. And, and, well, if war comes, the choths will need to be prepared for it, won't they? I'm going to help— shouldn't be gone long, really."

"Sure. Good voyage."

"Give Mother and everybody my love."

"Why not call her yourself?"

"Well, uh, I do have to hurry . . . and it's not as if this were anything unusual, my heading off to the mountains, and—oh—"

"Sure," said Daniel Holm. "I'll tell them. And you

9

give my regards to your mates." The Second Marchwarden of the Lauran System blanked off.

Arinnian turned from the instrument. For a moment he winced and bit his lip. He hated hurting people who cared about him. But why couldn't they understand? Their kind called it "going bird," being received into a choth, as if in some fashion those who did were renouncing the race that begot them. He couldn't count how many hours he had tried to make his parents—make any number of orthohumans—see that he was widening and purifying his humanity.

A bit of dialogue ran through memory: "Dad, look, two species can't inhabit the same globe for generations without pretty deep mutual consequences. Why do you go sky-hunting? Why does Ferune serve wine at his table? And those're the most superficial symptoms."

"I know that much. Credit me with some fair-mindedness, hm? Thing is, you're making a quantum jump."

"Because I'm to be a member of Stormgate? Listen, the choths have been accepting humans for the past hundred years."

"Not in such flocks as lately. And my son wasn't one of them. I'd've . . . liked to see you carry on *our* traditions."

"Who says I won't?"

"To start with, you'll not be under human law any more, you'll be under choth law and custom. . . . Hold on. That's fine, if you're an Ythrian. Chris, you haven't got the chromosomes. Those who've pretended they did, never fitted well into either race, ever again."

"Damnation, I'm not pretending—!"

Arinnian thrust the scene from him as if it were a physical thing. He was grateful for the prosaic necessities of preparation. To reach Lythran's aerie before dark, he must start soon. Of course, a car would cover the distance in less than an hour; but who wanted to fly caged in metal and plastic?

He was nude. More and more, those who lived like him were tending to discard clothes altogether and use skin paint for dress-up. But everybody sometimes needed garments. An Ythrian, too, was seldom without a belt and pouch. This trip would get chilly, and he lacked feathers. He crossed the tiny apartment to fetch coverall and boots.

Passing, he glanced at the desk whereon lay papers of his work and, in a heap, the texts and references he was currently employing, printouts from Library Central. *Blast!* he thought. *I loathe quitting when I've nearly seen how to prove that theorem.*

In mathematics he could soar. He often imagined that then his mind knew the same clean ecstasy an Ythrian, aloft alone, must know in the flesh. Thus he had been willing to accept the compromise which reconciled him and his father. He would continue his studies, maintain his goal of becoming a professional mathematician. To this end, he would accept some financial help, though he would no longer be expected to live at home. The rest of what little income he required he would earn himself, as herdsman and hunter when he went off to be among the Ythrians.

Daniel Holm had growled, through the hint of a grin, "You own a good mind, son. I didn't want to see it go to waste. At the same time, it's too good. If 'tweren't for your birding, you'd be so netted in your books, when you aren't drawing a picture or writing a poem, you'd never get any exercise; at last your bottom would grow fast to your chair, and you'd hardly notice. I s'pose I should feel a little grateful to your friends for making their kind of athlete out of you."

"My chothmates," Arinnian corrected him. He had just been given his new name and was full of glory and earnestness. That was four years ago; today he could smile at himself. The guv'nor had not been altogether wrong.

Thus at thirty—Avalonian reckoning—Christopher Holm was tall, slender, but wide-shouldered. In features as well as build, he took after his mother: long head, narrow face, thin nose and lips, blue eyes, mahogany hair (worn short in the style of those who do much gravbelt flying), and as yet not enough beard to be worth anything except regular applications of antigrowth enzyme. His complexion, naturally fair, was darkened by exposure. Laura, a G5 star, has only 72 percent the luminosity of Sol and less ultraviolet light in proportion; but Avalon, orbiting at a mean distance of 0.81 astronomical unit in a period of 0.724 Terran, gets 10 percent more total irradiation than man evolved under.

He made the customary part-by-part inspection of his unit before he put arms through straps and secured buckle at waist. The twin cone-pointed cylinders on his back had better have fully charged accumulators and fully operating circuits. If not, he was dead. One Ythrian couldn't hold back a human from toppling out of the sky. A couple of times, several together had effected a rescue; but those were herders, carrying lassos which they could cast around their comrade and pull on without getting in each other's way. You dared not count on such luck. O God, to have real wings!

He donned a leather helmet and lowered the goggles which were his poor substitute for a nictitating membrane. He sheathed knife and slugthrower at his hips. There would be nothing of danger—no chance of a duel being provoked, since a Khruath was peace-holy—not that deathpride quarrels ever happened often—but the Stormgate folk were mostly hunters and didn't leave their tools behind. He had no need to carry provisions. Those would be supplied from the family stores, to which he contributed his regular share, and ferried to the rendezvous on a gravsled.

Going out the door, he found himself on ground level. Humans had ample room on Avalon—about ten million of them; four million Ythrians—and even here in Gray, the planet's closest approximation to a real city, they built low and widespread. A couple of highrises sufficed for resident or visiting ornithoids.

Arinnian flicked controls. Negaforce thrust him gently, swiftly upward. Leveling off, he spent a minute savoring the view.

The town sprawled across hills green with trees and susin, color-patched with gardens, that ringed Falkayn Bay. Upon the water skimmed boats; being for pleasure, they were principally sail-driven hydrofoils. A few cargo vessels, long shapes of functional grace, lay at the docks, loaded and unloaded by assorted robots. One was coming in, from Brendan's Islands to judge by the course, and one was standing out to the Hesperian Sea, which flared silver where the sun struck it and, elsewhere, ran sapphire till it purpled on northern and southern horizons.

Laura hung low in the empty west, deeper aureate than at midday. The sky was a slowly darkening blue; streaks of high cirrus clouds, which Arinnian thought of as breastfeathers, promised fair weather would continue. A salt breeze whispered and cooled his cheeks.

Air traffic was scant. Several Ythrians passed by, wings gleaming bronze and amber. A couple of humans made beltflights like Arinnian; distant, they were hardly to be told from a flock of slim leathery draculas which evening had drawn out of some cave. More humans rode in cars, horizontal raindrops that flung back the light with inanimate fierceness. Two or three vans lumbered along and an intercontinental liner was settling toward the airport. But Gray was never wildly busy.

High up, however, paced shapes that had not been seen here since the end of the Troubles: warcraft on patrol.

War against the Terran Empire— Shivering, Arinnian lined out eastward, inland.

Already he could see his destination, far off beyond the coastal range and the central valley, like a cloudbank on worldedge, those peaks which were the highest in Corona, on all Avalon if you didn't count Oronesia. Men called them the Andromedas, but in his Anglic Arinnian had also taken to using the Planha name, Weathermother.

Ranchland rolled beneath him. Here around Gray, the mainly Ythrian settlements northward merged with the mainly human south; both ecologies blent with Avalon's own, and the country became a checkerboard. Man's grainfields, ripening as summer waned, lay tawny amidst huge green pastures where Ythrians grazed their maukh and mayaw. Stands of timberwood, oak or pine, windnest or hammerbranch, encroached on nearly treeless reaches of berylline native susin where you might still glimpse an occasional barysauroid. The rush of his passage blew away fretfulness. Let the Empire attack the Domain . . . if it dared! Meanwhile he, Arinnian, was bound for Eyath—for his whole choth, of course, and oneness with it, but chiefly he would see Eyath again.

Across the dignity of the dining hall, a look passed between them. *Shall we wander outside and be ourselves?*

She asked permission to leave of her father Lythran and her mother Blawsa; although she was their dependent, that was mere ritual, yet rituals mattered greatly. In like fashion Arinnian told the younger persons among whom he was benched that he had the wish of being unaccompanied. He and Eyath left side by side. It caused no break in the slow, silence-punctuated conversation wherein everyone else took part. Their closeness went back to their childhood and was fully accepted.

The compound stood on a plateau of Mount Farview. At the middle lifted the old stone tower which housed the senior members of the family and their children. Lower wooden structures, on whose sod roofs bloomed amberdragon and starbells, were for the unwed and for retainers and their kin. Further down a slope lay sheds, barns, and mews. The whole could not be seen at once from the ground, because Ythrian trees grew among the buildings: braidbark, copperwood, gaunt lightningrod, jewelleaf which sheened beneath the moon and by day would shimmer iridescent. The flowerbeds held natives, more highly evolved than anything from offplanet—sweet small janie, pungent livewell, graceful trefoil and Buddha's cup, a harp vine which the breeze brought ever so faintly to singing. Otherwise the night was quiet and, at this altitude, cold. Breath smoked white.

Eyath spread her wings. They were more slender than average, though spanning close to six meters. This naturally forced her to rest on hands and tail. "Br-r-r!" she laughed. "Hoarfrost. Let's lift." In a crack and whirl of air, she rose.

"You forgot," he called. "I've taken off my belt."

She settled on a platform built near the top of a copperwood. Ythrians made few redundant noises; obviously he could climb. He thought she overrated his skill, merely because he was better at it than she. A misstep in that murky foliage could bring a nasty fall. But he couldn't refuse the implicit challenge and keep her respect. He gripped a branch, chinned himself up, and groped and rustled his way.

Ahead, he heard her murmur to the uhoth which had fluttered along behind her. It brought down game with admirable efficiency, but he felt she made too much fuss over it. Well, no denying she was husband-high. He didn't quite like admitting that to himself. (*Why?* he wondered fleetingly.)

When he reached the platform, he saw her at rest on feet and alatans, the uhoth on her right wrist while her left hand stroked it. Morgana, almost full, stood dazzling white over the eastward sierra and made the plumes of Eyath glow. Her crest was silhouetted against the Milky Way. Despite the moon, constellations glistered through upland air, Wheel, Swords, Zirraukh, vast sprawling Ship. . . .

He sat down beside her, hugging his knees. She made the small ululation which expressed her gladness at his presence. He responded as best he could. Above the clean curve of her muzzle, the great eyes glimmered.

Abruptly she broke off. He followed her gaze and saw a new star swing into heaven. "A guardian satellite?" she asked. Her tone wavered the least bit.

"What else?" he replied. "I think it must be the latest one they've orbited."

"How many by now?"

"They're not announcing that," he reminded her. Ythrians always had trouble grasping the idea of government secrets. Of government in any normal human sense, for that matter. Marchwardens Ferune and Holm had been spending more energy in getting the choths to cooperate than in actual defense preparations. "My father doesn't believe we can have too many."

"The wasted wealth—"

"Well, if the Terrans come—"

"Do you expect they will?"

The trouble he heard brought his hand to squeeze her, very gently, on the neck, and afterward run fingers along her crest. Her feathers were warm, smooth and yet infinitely textured. "I don't know," he said. "Maybe they can settle the border question peacefully. Let's hope." The last two words were perforce in Anglic rather than Planha. Ythrians had never beseeched the future. She too was bilingual, like every educated colonist.

His look went back skyward. Sol lay . . . yonder in the Maukh, about where four stars formed the horns . . . how far? Oh, yes, 205 light-years. He recalled reading that, from there, Quetlan and Laura were in a constellation called the Lupus. None of the three suns had naked-eye visibility across such an abyss. They were mere G-type dwarfs; they merely happened to be circled by some motes which had fermented till there were chemistries that named those motes Terra, Ythri, Avalon, and loved them.

"Lupus," he mused. "An irony."

Eyath whistled: "?"

He explained, adding: "The lupus is, or was, a beast of prey on Terra. And to us, Sol lies in the sign of a big, tame herd animal. But who's attacking whom?"

"I haven't followed the news much," she said, low and not quite steadily. "It seemed a fog only, to me or mine. What need we reck if others clashed? Then all of a sudden— Might we have caused some of the trouble, Arinnian? Could folk of ours have been too rash, too rigid?"

Her mood was so uncharacteristic, not just of Ythrian temperament in general but of her usually sunny self, that astonishment jerked his head around. "What's made you this anxious?" he asked.

Her lips nuzzled the uhoth, as if seeking consolation that he thought he could better give. Its beak preened her. He barely heard: "Vodan."

"What? Oh! Are you betrothed to Vodan?"

His voice had cracked. *Why am I shaken?* he wondered. *He's a fine fellow. And of this same choth, too; no problems of changed law and custom, culture shock, homesickness—* Arinnian's glance swept over the Stormgate country. Above valleys steep-walled, dark and fragrant with woods, snowpeaks lifted. Closer was a mountainside down which a waterfall stood pillarlike under the moon. A night-flying bugler sounded its haunting note through stillness. On the Plains of Long Reach, in arctic marshes, halfway around the planet on a scorching New Gaiilan savannah, amidst the uncounted islands that made up most of what dry land Avalon had—how might she come to miss the realm of her choth?

No, wait, I'm thinking like a human. Ythrians get around more. Eyath's own mother is from the Sagittarius basin, often goes back to visit. . . . Why shouldn't I think like a human? I am one. I've found wisdom, rightness, happiness of a sort in certain Ythrian ways;

*but no use pretending I'll ever be an Ythrian, ever wed
a winged girl and dwell in our own aerie.*

She was saying: "Well, no, not exactly. Galemate,
do you believe I wouldn't tell you of my betrothal or
invite you to my wedding feast? But he is a . . . a person
I've grown very fond of. You know I planned on staying single till my studies were finished." She wanted the
difficult, honored calling of musician. "Lately . . . well,
I thought about it a lot during my last lovetime. I grew
hotter then than ever before, and I kept imagining Vodan."

Arinnian felt himself flush. He stared at the remote
gleam of a glacier. She shouldn't tell him such things. It
wasn't decent. An unmarried female Ythrian, or one
whose husband was absent, was supposed to stay isolated
from males when the heat came upon her; but she was
also supposed to spend the energy it raised in work, or
study, or meditation, or—

Eyath sensed his embarrassment. Her laughter rippled and she laid a hand over his. The slim fingers, the
sharp claws gripped him tenderly. "Why, I declare you're
shocked! What for?"

"You wouldn't talk like that to—your father, a brother—" *And you shouldn't feel that way, either. Never.
Estrus or no. Lonely, maybe; dreamy, yes; but not like
some sweating trull in the bed of some cheap hotel room.
Not you, Eyath.*

"True, it'd be improper talk in Stormgate. I used to
wonder if I shouldn't marry into a less strict choth. Vodan, though— Anyhow, Arinnian, dear, I can tell you
anything. Can't I?"

"Yes." *After all, I'm not really an Ythrian.*

"We discussed it later, he and I," she said. "Marriage, I mean. No use denying, children would be a
terrible handicap at this stage. But we fly well together;
and our parents have been nudging us for a long time,
it'd be so good an alliance between houses. We've wondered if, maybe, if we stayed hriccal the first few years—"

"That doesn't work too well, does it?" he said as
her voice trailed off, through the bloodbeat in his ears.
"That is, uh, continual sex relations may not be how
Ythrians reinforce pair bonds, but that doesn't mean sex
has no importance. If you separate every lovetime, you,

you, well, you're rejecting each other, aren't you? Why not, uh, contraception?"

"No."

He knew why her race, almost if not quite uniformly, spurned that. Children—the strong parental instinct of both mates—*were* what kept them together. If small wings closed around you and a small head snuggled down alongside your keelbone, you forgot the inevitable tensions and frustrations of marriage as much as if you were a human who had just happily coupled.

"We could postpone things till I've finished my studies and his business is on the wing," Eyath said. Arinnian remembered that Vodan, in partnership with various youths from Stormgate, Many Thermals, and The Tarns, had launched a silvicultural engineering firm. "But if war comes—kaah, he's in the naval reserve—"

Her free arm went around his shoulder, a blind gesture. He leaned his weight on an elbow so he could reach beneath the wings to embrace her stiff body. And he murmured to her, his sister since they both were children, what comfort he was able.

In the morning they felt more cheerful. It was not in Ythrian nature to brood—not even as a bad pun, they giving live birth—and bird-humans had tried to educate themselves out of the habit. Today, apart from a few retainers on maintenance duty, Lythran's household would fly to that mountain where the regional Khruath met. On the way they would be joined by other Stormgate families; arrived, they would find other choths entirely. However bleak the occasion of this gathering was, some of the color, excitement, private business, and private fun would be there that pervaded the regular assemblies.

And the dawn was clear and a tailwind streamed.

A trumpet called. Lythran swung from the top of his tower. Folk lifted their wings until the antlibranch slits beneath stood agape, purple from blood under the oxygen-drinking tissues. The wings clapped back down, and back on high; the Ythrians thundered off the ground, caught an updraft, and rode it into formation. Then they flew eastward over the crags.

Arinnian steered close to Eyath. She flashed him a

smile and broke into song. She had a beautiful voice—it
could nearly be named soprano—which turned the skirls
and gutturals of Planha into a lilt. What she cataracted
forth on the air was a traditional carol, but it was for
Arinnian because he had rendered it into Anglic, though
he always felt that his tricks of language had failed to
convey either the rapture or the vision.

"Light that leaps from a sun still sunken
  hails the hunter at hover,
  washes his wings in molten morning,
  startles the stars to cover.
  Blue is the bell of hollow heaven,
  rung by a risen blowing.
  Wide lie woodlands and mountain meadows,
  great and green with their growing.
      But—look, oh, look!—
      a red ray struck
      through tattered mist.
      A broadhorn buck
      stands traitor-kissed.
      The talons crook.

"Tilt through tumult of wakened wind-noise.
  whining, whickering, whirly;
  slip down a slantwise course of currents.
  Ha, but the hunt comes early!
  Poise on the pinions, take the target
  there in the then of swooping—
  Thrust on through by a wind-wild wingbeat,
  stark the stabber comes stooping.
      The buck may pose
      for one short breath
      before it runs
      from whistling death.
      The hammer stuns.
      The talons close.

"Broad and bright is the nearing noontide.
  Drawn to dreamily drowsing,
  shut-eyed in shade he sits now, sated.
  Suddenly sounds his rousing.
  Cool as the kiss of a ghost, then gusty,

rinsed by the rainfall after,
breezes brawl, and their forest fleetness
lives in leafage like laughter.
  Among the trees
  the branches shout
  and groan and throw
  themselves about.
  It's time to go.
  The talons ease.

"Beat from boughs up to row through rainstreams.
Thickly thutters the thunder.
Hailwinds harried by lash of lightning
roar as they rise from under.
Blind in the black of clawing cloudbanks,
wins he his way, though slowly,
breaks their barrier, soars in sunlight.
High is heaven and holy.
  The glow slants gold
  caressingly
  across and through
  immensity
  of silent blue.
  The talons fold."

Avalon rotates in 11 hours, 22 minutes, 12 seconds, on an axis tilted 21° from the normal to the orbital plane. Thus Gray, at about 43° N., knows short nights always; in summer the darkness seems scarcely a blink. Daniel Holm wondered if that was a root of his weariness.

Probably not. He was born here. His ancestors had lived here for centuries; they arrived with Falkayn. If individuals could change their circadian rhythms—as he'd had to do plenty often in his spacefaring days—surely a race could. The medics said that settling down in a gravity field only 80 percent of Terra's made more severe demands than that on the organism; its whole fluid balance and kinesthesia must readjust. Besides, what humans underwent was trivial compared to what their fellow colonists did. The Ythrians had had to shift a whole breeding cycle to a different day, year, weight, climate, diet, world. No wonder their first several generations had been of low fertility. Nevertheless, they survived; in the end, they flourished.

Therefore it was nonsense to suppose a man got tired from anything except overwork—and, yes, age, in spite of antisenescence. Or was it? Really? As you grew old, as you neared your dead and all who had gone before them, might your being not yearn back to its earliest beginnings, to a manhome you had never seen but somehow remembered?

Crock! Come off that! Who said eighty-four is old? Holm yanked a cigar from his pocket and snapped off the end. The inhalation which lit it was unnecessarily hard.

He was of medium height, and stocky in the olive tunic and baggy trousers worn by human members of the Ythrian armed services. The mongoloid side of his descent showed in round head, wide face, high cheekbones, a fullness about the lips and the blunt nose; the caucasoid was revealed in gray eyes, a skin that would have been pale did he not spend his free time outdoors hunting or gardening, and the hair that was grizzled on his scalp but remained crisp and black on his chest. Like most men on the planet, he suppressed his beard.

He was wading into the latest spate of communications his aides had passed on to him, when the intercom buzzed and said: "First Marchwarden Ferune wishes discussion."

"Sure!" Holm's superior was newly back from Ythri. The man reached for a two-way plate, withdrew his hand, and said, "Why not in the flesh? I'll be right there."

He stumped from his office. The corridor beyond hummed and bustled—naval personnel, civilian employees of the Lauran admiralty—and overloaded the building's air system till the odors of both species were noticeable, slightly acrid human and slightly smoky Ythrian. The latter beings were more numerous, in reversal of population figures for Avalon. But then, a number were here from elsewhere in the Domain, especially from the mother world, trying to help this frontier make ready in the crisis.

Holm forced himself to call greetings right and left as he went. His affability had become a trademark whose value he recognized. *At first it was genuine,* he thought.

The honor guard saluted and admitted him to Ferune's presence. (Holm did not tolerate time-wasting ceremoniousness in his department, but he admitted its importance to Ythrians.) The inner room was typical: spacious and sparsely furnished, a few austere decorations, bench and desk and office machinery adapted to ornithoid requirements. Rather than a transparency in the wall, there was a genuine huge window, open on garden-scented breezes and a downhill view of Gray and the waters aglitter beyond.

Ferune had added various offplanet souvenirs and a bookshelf loaded with folio copies of the Terran classics that he read, in three original languages, for enjoyment. A smallish, tan-feathered male, he was a bit of an iconoclast. His choth, Mistwood, had always been one of the most progressive on Avalon, mechanized as much as a human community and, in consequence, large and prosperous. He had scant patience to spare for tradition, religion, any conservatism. He endured a minimum of formalities because he must, but never claimed to like them.

Bouncing from his perch, he scuttled across the floor and shook hands Terran style. "Khr-r-r, good to see you, old rascal!" He spoke Planha; Ythrian throats are less versatile than human (though of course no human can ever get the sounds quite right) and he wanted neither the nuisance of wearing a vocalizer nor the grotesquerie of an accent.

"How'd it go?" Holm asked.

Ferune grimaced. But that is the wrong word. His feathers were not simply more intricate than those of Terran birds, they were more closely connected to muscles and nerve endings, and their movements constituted a whole universe of expression forever denied to man. Irritation, fret, underlying anger and dismay, rippled across his body.

"Huh." Holm found a chair designed for him, sank down, and drew tobacco pungency over his tongue. "Tell."

Foot-claws clicked on lovely-grained wood. Back and forth Ferune paced. "I'll be dictating a full report," he said. "In brief, worse than I feared. Yes, they're scrambling to establish a unified command and shove the idea of action under doctrine into every captain. But they've no dustiest notion of how to go about it."

"God on a stick," Holm exclaimed, "we've been telling them for the past five years! I thought—oh, bugger, communication's so vague in this so-called navy, I'd nothing to go on but impressions, and I guess I got the wrong ones—but you know I thought, we thought a halfway sensible reorganization was in progress."

"It was, but it moulted. Overweening pride, bickering, haggling about details. We Ythrians—our dominant culture, at least—don't fit well into anything tightly centralized." Ferune paused. "In fact," he went on, "the most influential argument against trading our separate, loosely coordinated planetary commands for a Terran-model hierarchy has been that Terra may have vastly greater forces, but these need to control a vastly greater volume of space than the Domain; and if they fight us, they'll be at the end of such a long line of communication that unified action is self-defeating."

"Huh! Hasn't it occurred to those mudbrains on Ythri, the Imperium isn't stupid? If Terra hits, it won't run the war from Terra, but from a sector close to our borders."

"We've found little sign of strength being marshaled in nearby systems."

"Certainly not!" Holm slammed a fist on the arm of his chair. "Would they give their preparations away like that? Would you? They'll assemble in space, parsecs from any star. Minimal traffic between the gathering fleet and whatever planets our scouts can sneak close to. In a few cubic light-years, they can hide power to blow us out of the plenum."

"You've told me this a few times," Ferune said dryly. "I've passed it on. To scant avail." He stopped pacing. For a while, silence dwelt in the room. The yellow light of Laura cast leaf shadows on the floor. They quivered.

"After all," Ferune said, "our methods did save us during the Troubles."

"You can't compare war lords, pirates, petty conquerors, barbarians who'd never have gotten past their

stratospheres if they hadn't happened to've acquired practically self-operating ships—you can't compare that
bloody-clawed rabble to Imperial Terra."

"I know," Ferune replied. "The point is, Ythrian methods served us well because they accord with Ythrian nature. I've begun to wonder, during this last trip, if an
attempt to become poor copies of our rivals may not be
foredoomed. The attempt's being made, understand—
you'll get details till they run back out of your gorge—
but could be that all we'll gain is confusion. I've decided
that while Avalon must make every effort to cooperate,
Avalon must at the same time expect small help from
outside."

Again fell stillness. Holm looked at his superior, asso-
ciate, friend of years; and not for the first time, it came
to him what strangers they two were.

He found himself regarding Ferune as if he had never
met an Ythrian before.

* * * * * *

Standing, the Marchwarden was about 120 centimeters
high from feet to top of crest; a tall person would have
gone to 140 or so, say up to the mid-breast of Holm.
Since the body tilted forward, its actual length from muzzle through tail was somewhat more. It massed perhaps
20 kilos; the maximum for the species was under 30.

The head looked sculptured. It bulged back from a
low brow to hold the brain. A bony ridge arched down in
front to a pair of nostrils, nearly hidden by feathers, which
stood above a flexible mouth full of sharp white fangs
and a purple tongue. The jaw, underslung and rather delicate, merged with a strong neck. That face was domi-
nated by its eyes, big and amber, and by the dense,
scalloped feather-crest that rose from the brow, lifted
over the head, and ran half the length of the neck: partly
for aerodynamic purposes, partly as a helmet on the thin
skull.

The torso thrust outward in a great keelbone, which
at its lower end was flanked by the arms. These were not
unlike the arms of a skinny human, in size and appearance;
they lacked plumage, and the hide was dark yellow on
Ferune's, brown or black in other Ythrian subspecies. The
hands were less manlike. Each bore three fingers between
two thumbs; each digit possessed one more joint than its

Terran equivalent and a nail that might better be called a talon. The wrist sprouted a dew claw on its inner surface. Those hands were large in proportion to the arms, and muscles played snakishly across them; they had evolved as ripping tools, to help the teeth. The body ended in a fan-shaped tail of feathers, rigid enough to help support it when desired.

At present, though, the tremendous wings were folded down to work as legs. In the middle of either leading edge, a "knee" joint bent in reverse; those bones would lock together in flight. From the "ankle," three forward toes and one rearward extended to make a foot; aloft, they curled around the wing to strengthen and add sensitivity. The remaining three digits of the ancestral ornithoid had fused to produce the alatan bone which swept backward for more than a meter. The skin over its front half was bare, calloused, another surface to rest on.

Ferune being male, his crest rose higher than a female's, and it and the tail were white with black trim; on her they would have been of uniform dark lustrousness. The remainder of him was lighter-colored than average for his species, which ranged from gray-brown through black.

*   *   *   *   *   *

"Khr-r-r-r." The throat-noise yanked Holm out of his reverie. "You stare."

"Oh. Sorry." To a true-born carnivore, that was more rude than it was among omnivorous humans. "My mind wandered."

"Whither?" Ferune asked, mild again.

"M-m-m . . . well—well, all right. I got to thinking how little my breed really counts for in the Domain. I figure maybe we'd better assume everything's bound to be done Ythrian-style, and make the best of that."

Ferune uttered a warbling "reminder" note and quirked certain feathers. This had no exact Anglic equivalent, but the intent could be translated as: "Your sort aren't the only non-Ythrians under our hegemony. You aren't the only ones technologically up to date." Planha was in fact not as laconic as its verbal conventions made it seem.

"N-no," Holm mumbled. "But we . . . in the Empire, we're the leaders. Sure, Greater Terra includes quite a few home worlds and colonies of nonhumans; and a lot of individuals from elsewhere have gotten Terran citizenship; sure. But more humans are in key positions of every kind than members of any other race—fireflare, probably of all the other races put together." He sighed and stared at the glowing end of his cigar. "Here in the Domain, what are men? A handful on this single ball. Oh, we get around, we do well for ourselves, but the fact won't go away that we're a not terribly significant minority in a whole clutch of minorities."

"Do you regret that?" Ferune asked quite softly.

"Huh? No. No. I only meant, well, probably the Domain has too few humans to explain and administer a human-type naval organization. So better we adjust to you than you to us. It's unavoidable anyhow. Even on Avalon, where there're more of us, it's unavoidable."

"I hear a barrenness in your tone and see it in your eyes," Ferune said, more gently than was his wont. "Again you think of your son who has gone bird, true? You fear his younger brothers and sisters will fare off as he did."

Holm gathered strength to answer. "You know I respect your ways. Always have, always will. Nor am I about to forget how Ythri took my people in when Terra had rotted away beneath them. It's just . . . just . . . we rate respect too. Don't we?"

Ferune moved forward until he could lay a hand on Holm's thigh. He understood the need of humans to speak their griefs.

"When he—Chris—when he first started running around, flying around, with Ythrians, why, I was glad," the man slogged on. He held his gaze out the window. From time to time he dragged at his cigar, but the gesture was mechanical, unnoticed. "He'd always been too bookish, too alone. So his Stormgate friends, his visits there— Later, when he and Eyath and their gang were knocking around in odd corners of the planet—well, that seemed like he was doing over what I did at his age, except he'd have somebody to guard his back if a situation got sharp. I thought maybe he also would end enlisting in the navy—" Holm shook his head. "I didn't see till too late, what'd gotten in him was not old-fashioned fiddlefootedness. Then when I did wake up, and we quarreled about it, and he ran off and hid in the Shielding Islands for a year, with Eyath's help— But no point in my going on, is there?"

Ferune gestured negative. After Daniel Holm went raging to Lythran's house, accusations exploding out of him, it had been all the First Marchwarden could do to intervene, calm both parties and prevent a duel.

"No, I shouldn't have said anything today," Holm continued. "It's only—last night Rowena was crying. That he went off and didn't say goodbye to her. Mainly, she worries about what's happening to him, inside, since he joined the choth. Can he ever make a normal marriage, for instance? Ordinary girls aren't his type any more; and bird girls— And, right, our younger kids. Tommy's completely in orbit around Ythrian subjects. The school monitor had to come in person and tell us how he'd been neglecting to screen the material or submit the work or see the consultants he was supposed to. And Jeanne's found a couple of Ythrian playmates—"

"As far as I know," Ferune said, "humans who entered choths have as a rule had satisfactory lives. Problems, of course. But what life can have none? Besides, the difficulties ought to become less as the number of such persons grows."

"Look," Holm floundered, "I'm not against your folk. Break my bones if ever I was! Never once did I say or think there was anything dishonorable about what Chris was doing, any more than I would've said or thought it if, oh, if he'd joined some celibate order of priests. But I'd not have liked that either. It's no more natural for a man. And I've studied everything I could find about bird people. Sure, most of them have claimed they were happy. Probably most of them believed it. I can't help thinking they never realized what they'd missed."

"Walkers," Ferune said. In Planha, that sufficed. In Anglic he would have had to state something like: "We've lost our share, those who left the choths to become human-fashion atomic individuals within a global human community."

"Influence," he added, which conveyed: "Over the centuries on Avalon, no few of our kind have grown bitter at what your precept and example were doing to the choths themselves. Many still are. I suspect that's a major reason why several such groups have become more reactionary than any on the mother world."

Holm responded, "Wasn't the whole idea of this colony that both races should grant each other the right to be what they were?"

"That was written into the Compact and remains there," Ferune said in two syllables and three expressions. "Nobody has been compelled. But living together, how can we help changing?"

"Uh-huh. Because Ythri in general and Mistwood in particular have made a success of adopting and adapting Terran technology, you believe nothing's involved except a common-sense swap of ideas. It's not that simple, though."

"I didn't claim it is," Ferune said, "only that we don't catch time in any net."

"Yeh. I'm sorry if I— Well, I didn't mean to maunder on, especially when you've heard me often enough before. These just happen to be thin days at home." The man left his chair, strode past the Ythrian, and halted by the window, where he looked out through a veil of smoke.

"Let's get to real work," he said. "I'd like to ask specific questions about the overall state of Domain preparedness. And you'd better listen to me about what's been going on here while you were away—through the whole bloody-be-flensed Lauran System, in fact. That's none too good either."

III

The car identified its destination and moved down. Its initial altitude was such that the rider inside glimpsed a dozen specks of ground strewn over shining waters. But when he approached they had all fallen beneath the horizon. Only the rugged cone of St. Li was now visible to him.

* * * * * *

With an equatorial diameter of a mere 11,308 kilometers, Avalon has a molten core smaller in proportion than Terra's; a mass of 0.635 cannot store as much heat. Thus the forces are weak that thrust land upward. At the same time, erosion proceeds fast. The atmospheric pressure at sea level is similar to the Terrestrial—and drops off more slowly with height, because of the gravity gradient—and rapid rotation makes for violent weather. In consequence, the surface is generally low, the highest peak in the Andromedas rising no more than 4500 meters. Nor does the land occur in great masses. Corona, capping the north pole and extending down past the Tropic of Swords, covers barely eight million square kilometers, about the size of Australia. In the opposite hemisphere, Equatoria, New Africa, and New Gaiila could better be called large islands than minor continents. All else consists of far smaller islands.

Yet one feature is gigantic. Some 2000 kilometers due west of Gray begins that drowned range whose peaks, thrusting into air, are known as Oronesia. Southward it runs, crosses the Tropic of Spears, trails off at last not far from the Antarctic Circle. Thus it forms a true, hydrological boundary; its western side marks off the Middle Ocean, its eastern the Hesperian Sea in the northern hemisphere and the South Ocean beyond the equator. It supports a distinct ecology, incredibly rich. And thereby, after the colonization, it became a sociological phenomenon. Any eccentrics, human or Ythrian, could go off, readily transform one or a few isles, and make their own undisturbed existence.

The mainland choths were diverse in size as well as in organization and tradition. But whether they be roughly analogous to clans, tribes, baronies, religious communes, republics, or whatever, they counted their members in the thousands at least. In Oronesia there were single households which bore the name; grown and married, the younger children were expected to found new, independent societies.

Naturally, this extremism was exceptional. The Highsky folk in particular were numerous, controlling the fisheries around latitude 30° N. and occupying quite a stretch of the archipelago. And they were fairly conventional, insofar as that word has any meaning when applied to Ythrians.

*   *   *   *   *   *

The aircar landed on the beach below a compound. He who stepped out was tall, with dark-red hair, clad in sandals, kilt, and weapons.

Tabitha Falkayn had seen the vehicle descending and walked forth to meet it. "Hello, Christopher Holm," she said in Anglic.

"I come as Arinnian," he answered in Planha. "Luck fare beside you, Hrill."

She smiled. "Excuse me if I don't elaborate the occasion." Shrewdly: "You called ahead that you wanted to see me on a public matter. That must have to do with the border crisis. I daresay your Khruath decided that western Corona and northern Oronesia must work out a means of defending the Hesperian Sea."

He nodded awkwardly, and his eyes sought refuge from her amusement.

Enormous overhead, sunshine brilliant off cumulus banks, arched heaven. A sailor winged yonder, scouting for schools of piscoid; a flock of Ythrian shuas flapped by under the control of a herder and his uhoths; native pteropleuron lumbered around a reef rookery. The sea rolled indigo, curled in translucent green breakers, and exploded in foam on sands nearly as white. Trawlers plied it, kilometers out. Inland the ground rose steep. The upper slopes still bore a pale emerald mat of susin; only a few kinds of shrub were able to grow past those interlocking roots. But further down the hills had been plowed. There Ythrian clustergrain rustled red, for ground cover and to feed the shuas, while groves of coconut palm, mango, orange, and pumpernickel plant lifted above to nourish the human members of Highsky. A wind blew, warm but fresh, full of salt and iodine and fragrances.

"I suppose it was felt bird-to-bird conferences would be a good idea," Tabitha went on. "You mountaineers will have ample trouble understanding us pelagics, and vice versa, without the handicap of differing species. Ornithoids will meet likewise, hm?" Her manner turned thoughtful: "You had to be a delegate, of course. Your area has so few of your kind. But why come in person? Not that you aren't welcome. Still, a phone call—"

"We . . . we may have to talk at length," he said. "For days, off and on." He took for granted he would receive hospitality; all choths held that a guest was sacred.

"Why me, though? I'm only a local."

"You're a descendant of David Falkayn."

"That doesn't mean much."

"It does where I live. Besides—well, we've met before, now and then, at the larger Khruaths and on visits to each other's home areas and—We're acquainted a little. I'd not know where to begin among total strangers. If nothing else, you . . . you can advise me whom to consult, and introduce me. Can't you?"

"Certainly." Tabitha took both his hands. "Besides, I'm glad to see you, Chris."

His heart knocked. He struggled not to squirm. *What makes me this shy before her?* God knew she was attractive. A few years older than he, big, strongly built, full-breasted and long of leg, she showed to advantage in a short sleeveless tunic. Her face was snubnosed, wide of mouth, its green eyes set far apart under heavy brows; she had never bothered to remove the white scar on her right cheekbone. Her hair, cropped beneath the ears, was bleached flaxen. It blew like banners over the brown, slightly freckled skin.

He wondered if she went as casually to bed as the Coronan bird girls—never with a male counterpart; always a hearty, husky, not overintelligent worker type—or if she was a virgin. That seemed unlikely. What human, perpetually in a low-grade lovetime, could match the purity of an Eyath? Yet Highsky wasn't Stormgate or The Tarns —he didn't know—Tabitha had no companions of her own species here where she dwelt—however, she traveled often and widely. . . . He cast the speculation from him.

"Hoy, you're blushing," she laughed. "Did I violate one of your precious mores?" She released him. "If so, I apologize. But you always take these things too seriously. Relax. A social rite or a social gaffe isn't a deathpride matter."

Easy for her, I suppose, he thought. *Her grandparents were received into this choth. Her parents and their children grew up in it. A fourth of the membership must be human by now. And they've influenced it—like this*

*commercial fishery she and Draun have started, a strict-
ly private enterprise—*

"I'm afraid we've no time for gaiety," he got out.
"We've walking weather ahead."

"Indeed?"

"The Empire's about to expand our way."

"C'mon to the house." Tabitha took his arm and urged
him toward the compound. Its thatch-roofed timber dwell-
ings were built lower than most Ythrian homes and were
sturdier than they seemed; for here was scant protection
from Avalon's hurricanes. "Oh, yes," she said, "the empire's been growing vigorously since Manuel the First. But
I've read its history. How has the territory been brought
under control? Some by simple partnership—civilized nonhumans like the Cynthians found it advantageous. Some
by purchase or exchange. Some by conquest, yes—but always of primitives, or at most of people whose strength
in space was ridiculously less than Greater Terra's. We're
a harder gale to buck."

"Are we? My father says—"

"Uh-huh. The Empire's sphere approaches 400 light-
years across, ours about 80. Out of all the systems in
its volume, the Empire's got a degree of direct contact
with several thousand, we with barely 250. But don't you
see, Chris, we know our planets better? We're more compact. Our total resources are less but our technology's
every bit as good. And then, we're distant from Terra.
Why should they attack us? We don't threaten them, we
merely claim our rights along the border. If they want
more realm, they can find plenty closer to home, suns
they've never visited, and easier to acquire than from a
proud, well-armed Domain."

"My father says we're weak and unready."

"Do you think we would lose a war?"

He fell silent until they both noticed, through the soughing ahead, how sand scrunched beneath their feet. At last:
"Well, I don't imagine anybody goes into a war expecting to lose."

"I don't believe they'll fight," Tabitha said. "I believe
the Imperium has better sense."

"Regardless, we'd better take precautions. Home defense
is among them."

"Yes. Won't be easy to organize, among a hundred or more sovereign choths."

"That's where we birds come in, maybe," he ventured. "Long established ones in particular, like your family."

"I'm honored to help," she told him. "And in fact I don't imagine the choths will cooperate too badly—" she tossed her head in haughtiness—"when it's a matter of showing the Empire who flies highest!"

Eyath and Vodan winged together. They made a handsome pair, both golden of eyes and arms, he ocher-brown and she deep bronze. Beneath them reached the Stormgate lands, forest-darkened valleys, crags and cliffs, peaks where snowfields lingered to dapple blue-gray rock, swordblade of a waterfall and remote blink of a glacier. A wind sang *whoo* and drove clouds, which Laura tinged gold, through otherwise brilliant air; their shadows raced and rippled across the world. The Ythrians drank of the wind's cold and swam in its swirling, thrusting, flowing strength. It stroked their feathers till they felt the barbs of the great outer pinions shiver.

He said: "If we were of Arinnian's kind, I would surely wed you, now, before I go to my ship. But you won't be in lovetime for months, and by then I might be dead. I would not bind you to that sorrow for nothing."

"Do you think I would grieve less if I had not the name of widow?" she answered. "I'd want the right to lead your memorial dance. For I know what parts of these skies you like best."

"Still, you would have to lift some awkward questions, obligation toward my blood and so on. No. Shall our friendship be less because, for a while, you have not the name of wife?"

"Friendship—" she murmured. Impulsively: "I dreamt last night that we were indeed like humans."

"What, forever in rut?"

"Forever in love."

"Kh-h'ng, I've naught against Arinnian, but sometimes I wonder if you've not been too much with him, for too many years since you both were small. Had Lythran not taken you along when he had business in Gray—" Vodan saw her crest rise, broke off and added in haste: "Yes, he's your galemate. That makes him mine too. I only wanted to warn you . . . don't try, don't wish to be human."

"No, no." Eyath felt a downdraft slide by. She slanted herself to catch it, a throb of wings and then the long wild glide, peaks leaping nearer, glimpse through trees of a pool ashine where a feral stallion drank, song and rush and caress of cloven air, till she checked herself and flew back upward, breasting a torrent, every muscle at full aliveness—traced a thermal by the tiny trembling of a mountain seen through it, won there, spread her wings and let heaven carry her hovering while she laughed.

Vodan beat near. "Would I trade this?" she called joyously. "Or you?"

Ekrem Saracoglu, Imperial governor of Sector Pacis, had hinted for a while that he would like to meet the daughter of Fleet Admiral Juan de Jesús Cajal y Palomares. She had come from Nuevo México to be official hostess and feminine majordomo for her widowed father, after he transferred his headquarters to Esperance and rented a house in Fleurville. The date kept being postponed. It was not that the admiral disliked the governor— they got along well—nor distrusted his intentions, no matter how notorious a womanizer he was. Luisa had been raised among folk who, if strict out of necessity on their dry world, were rich in honor and bore a hair-trigger pride. It was merely that both men were overwhelmed by work.

At last their undertakings seemed fairly well along, and Cajal invited Sarocoglu to dinner. A ridiculous last-minute contretemps occurred. The admiral phoned home that he would be detained at the office a couple of hours. The governor was already on his way.

"Thus you, Donna, have been told to keep me happy in the teeth of a postponed meal," Saracoglu purred over the hand he kissed. "I assure you, that will not be in the least difficult." Though small, she had a lively figure and a darkly pretty face. And he soon learned that, albeit solemn, she knew how to listen to a man and, rarer yet, ask him stimulating questions.

By then they were strolling in the garden. Rosebushes and cherry trees might almost have been growing on Terra; Esperance was a prize among colony planets. The sun Pax was still above the horizon, now at midsummer, but leveled mellow beams across an old brick wall. The air was warm, blithe with birdsong, sweet with green odors that drifted in from the countryside. A car or two caught the light, high above; but Fleurville was not big enough for its traffic noise to be heard this far from the centrum.

Saracoglu and Luisa paced along graveled paths and talked. They were guarded, which is to say discreetly chaperoned. However, no duenna followed several paces behind, but a huge four-armed Gorzunian mercenary on whom the nuances of a flirtation would be lost.

The trouble is, thought the governor, *she's begun conversing in earnest.*

It had been quite pleasant at first. She encouraged him to speak of himself. "—yes, the Earl of Anatolia, that's me. Frankly, even if it is on Terra, a minor peerage. . . . Career bureaucrat. Might rather've been an artist—I dabble in oils and clays—maybe you'd care to see. . . . Alas, you know how such things go. Imperial nobles are expected to serve the Imperium. Had I but been born in a decadent era! Eh? Unfortunately, the Empire's not run out of momentum—"

Inwardly, he grinned at his own performance. He, fifty-three standard years of age, squat, running to fat, totally bald, little eyes set close to a giant nose, and two expensive mistresses in his palace—acting the role of a boy who acted the role of an *homme du monde!* Well, he enjoyed that once in a while, as he enjoyed gaudy clothes and jewels. They were a relaxation from the wry realism which had never allowed him to improve his appearance through biosculp.

But at this point she asked, "Are we really going to attack the Ythrians?"

"Heh?" The distress in her tone brought his head swinging sharply around to stare at her. "Why, negotiations are stalled, but—"

"Who stalled them?" She kept her own gaze straight ahead. Her voice had risen a note and the slight Espanyol accent had intensified.

"Who started most of the violent incidents?" he countered. "Ythrians. Not that they're monsters, understand. But they are predators by nature. And they've no strong

authority—no proper government at all—to control the
impulses of groups. That's been a major stumbling block
in the effort to reach an accommodation."

"How genuine was the effort—on our side?" she demanded, still refusing to look at him. "How long have
you planned to fall on them? My father won't tell me
anything, but it's obvious, it's been obvious ever since he
moved here—how often are naval and civilian headquarters on the same planet?—it's obvious something is
b-b-being readied."

"Donna," Saracoglu said gravely, "when a fleet of spacecraft can turn whole worlds into tombs, one prepares
against the worst and one clamps down security regula-
tions." He paused. "One also discovers it is unwise to let
spheres interpenetrate, as Empire and Domain have. I
daresay you, young, away off in a relatively isolated system
. . . I daresay you got an idea the Imperium is provoking
war in order to swallow the whole Ythrian Domain. That
is not true."

"What is true?" she replied bitterly.

"That there have been bloody clashes over disputed
territories and conflicting interests."

"Yes. Our traders are losing potential profits."

"Would that were the only friction. Commercial disputes are always negotiable. Political and military rival-
ries are harder. For example, which of us shall absorb the
Antoranite-Kraokan complex around Beta Centauri? One
of us is bound to, and those resources would greatly
strengthen Terra. The Ythrians have already gained more
power, by bringing Dathyna under them, than we like a
potentially hostile race to have.

"Furthermore, by rectifying this messy frontier, we can
armor ourselves against a Merseian flank attack." Saracoglu lifted a hand to forestall her protest. "Indeed, Donna,
the Roidhunate is far off and not very big. But it's growing at an alarming rate, and aggressive acquisitiveness is
built into its ideology. The duty of an empire is to provide
for the great-grandchildren."

"Why can't we simply write a treaty, give a *quid pro
quo*, divide things in a fair and reasonable manner?"
Luisa asked.

Saracoglu sighed. "The populations of the planets would
object to being treated like inanimate property. No gov-

ernment which took that attitude would long survive." He gestured aloft. "Furthermore, the universe holds too many unknowns. We have traveled hundreds—in earlier days, thousands—of light-years to especially interesting stars. But what myriads have we bypassed? What may turn up when we do seek them out? No responsible authority, human or Ythrian, will blindly hand over such possibilities to an alien.

"No, Donna, this is no problem capable of neat, final solutions. We just have to do our fumbling best. Which does *not* include subjugating Ythri. I'm the first to grant Ythri's right to exist, go its own way, even keep offplanet possessions. But this frontier must be stabilized."

"We—interpenetrate—with others—and have no trouble."

"Of course. Why should we fight hydrogen breathers, for example? They're so exotic we can barely communicate with them. The trouble is, the Ythrians are too like us. As an old, old saying goes, two tough, smart races want the same real estate."

"We can live with them! Humans are doing it. They have for generations."

"Do you mean Avalon?"

She nodded.

Saracoglu saw a chance to divert the conversation back into easier channels. "Well, there's an interesting case, certainly," he smiled. "How much do you know about it?"

"Very little," she admitted, subdued. "A few mentions here and there, since I came to Esperance. The galaxy's so huge, this tiny fleck of it we've explored. . . ."

"You might get to see Avalon," he said. "Not far off, ten or twelve light-years. I'd like that myself. The society does appear to be unusual, if not absolutely unique."

"Don't you understand? If humans and Ythrians can share a single planet—"

"That's different. Allow me to give you some background. I've never been there either, but I've studied material on it since getting this appointment."

Saracoglu drew breath. "Avalon was discovered five hundred years ago, by the same Grand Survey ship that came on Ythri," he said. "It was noted as a potential colony, but was so remote from Terra that nobody was interested then; the very name wasn't bestowed till long afterward. Ythri was forty light-years further, true, but much more attractive, a rich planet full of people vigorously entering the modern era who had a considerable deal to trade.

"About three and a half centuries back, a human company made the Ythrians a proposal. The Polesotechnic League wasn't going to collapse for another fifty years, but already anybody who had a functional brain could read what a cutthroat period lay ahead. These humans, a mixed lot under the leadership of an old trade pioneer, wanted to safeguard the future of their families by settling on out-of-the-way Avalon—under the suzerainty, the protection, of an Ythri that was not corrupted as Technic civilization was. The Ythrians agreed, and naturally some of them joined the settlement.

"Well, the Troubles came, and Ythri was not spared. The eventual results were similar—Terra enforced peace by the Empire, Ythri by the Domain. In the meantime, standing together, bearing the brunt of chaos, the Avalonians had been welded into one.

"Nothing like that applies today."

They had stopped by a vine-covered trellis. He plucked a grape and offered it to her. She shook her head. He ate it himself. The taste held a slight, sweet strangeness; Esperancian soil was not, after all, identical with that of Home. The sun was now gone from sight, shadows welled in the garden, an evening star blossomed.

"I suppose . . . your plans for 'rectification' . . . include bringing Avalon into the Empire," Luisa said.

"Yes. Consider its position." Saracoglu shrugged. "Besides, the humans there form a large majority. I rather imagine they'll be glad to join us, and Ythri won't mind getting rid of them."

"Must we fight?"

Saracoglu smiled. "It's never too late for peace." He took her arm. "Shall we go indoors? I expect your father will be here soon. We ought to have the sherry set out for him."

He'd not spoil the occasion, which was still salvageable, by telling her that weeks had passed since a courier ship brought what he requested: an Imperial rescript declaring war on Ythri, to be made public whenever governor and admiral felt ready to act.

IV

A campaign against Ythri would demand an enormous fleet, gathered from everywhere in the Empire. No such thing had been publicly seen or heard of, though rumors flew. But of course units guarding the border systems had been openly reinforced as the crisis sharpened, and drills and practice maneuvers went on apace.

Orbiting Pax at ten astronomical units, the Planet-class cruisers *Thor* and *Ansa* flung blank shells and torpedoes at each other's force screens, pierced these latter with laser beams that tried to hold on a single spot of hull for as long as an energy blast would have taken to gnaw through armor, exploded magnesium flares whose brilliance represented lethal radiation, dodged about on grav thrust, wove in and out of hyperdrive phase, used every trick in the book and a few which the high command hoped had not yet gotten into Ythrian books. Meanwhile the Comet- and Meteor-class boats they mothered were similarly busy.

To stimulate effort, a prize had been announced. That vessel the computers judged victorious would proceed with her auxiliaries to Esperance, where the crew would get a week's liberty.

Ansa won. She broadcast a jubilant recall. Half a million kilometers away, an engine awoke in the Meteor which her captain had dubbed *Hooting Star*.

"Resurrected at last!" Lieutenant (j.g.) Philippe Rochefort exulted. "And in glory at that."

"And unearned." The fire control officer, CPO Wa Chaou of Cynthia, grinned. His small white-furred body crouched on the table he had been cleaning after a meal; his bushy tail quivered like the whiskers around his blue-masked muzzle.

"What the muck you mean, 'unearned'?" the engineer-

39

computerman, CPO Abdullah Helu, grumbled: a lean, middle-aged careerist from Huy Braseal. "Playing dead for three mortal days is beyond the call of duty." The boat had theoretically been destroyed in a dogfight and drifting free, as a real wreck would, to complicate life for detector technicians.

"Especially when the poker game cleaned and reamed you, eh?" Wa Chaou gibed.

"I won't play with you again, sir," Helu said to the captain-pilot. "No offense. You're just too mucking talented."

"Only luck," Rochefort answered. "Same as it was only luck that threw such odds against us. The boat acquitted herself well. As you did afterward, over the chips. Better luck to both next time."

She was his first, new and shiny command—he having recently been promoted from ensign for audacity in a rescue operation—and he was anxious for her to make a good showing. No matter how inevitable under the circumstances, defeat had hurt.

But they were on the top team; and they'd accounted for two opposition craft, plus tying up three more for a while that must have been used to advantage elsewhere; and now they were bound back to *Ansa* and thence to Esperance, where he knew enough girls that dates were a statistical certainty.

The little cabin trembled and hummed with driving energies. Air gusted from ventilators, smelling of oil and of recycling chemicals. A Meteor was designed for high acceleration under both relativistic and hyperdrive conditions; for accurate placement of nuclear-headed torpedoes; and for no more comfort than minimally essential to the continued efficiency of personnel.

Yet space lay around the viewports in a glory of stars, diamond-keen, unwinking, many-colored, crowding an infinitely clear blackness till they merged in the argent torrent of the Milky Way or the dim mysterious cloudlets which were sister galaxies. Rochefort wanted to sit, look, let soul follow gaze outward into God's temple the universe. He could have done so, too; the boat was running on full automatic. But better demonstrate to the others that he was a conscientious as well as an easy-going officer. He turned the viewer back on which he had been using when the message came.

A canned lecture was barely under way. A human xenologist stood in the screen and intoned:

"Warm-blooded, feathered, and flying, the Ythrians are not birds; they bring their young forth viviparously after a gestation of four and a half months; they do not have beaks, but lips and teeth. Nor are they mammals; they grow no hair and secrete no milk; those lips have developed for parents to feed infants by regurgitation. And while the antlibranchs might suggest fish gills, they are not meant for water but for—"

"Oh, no!" Helu exclaimed. "Sir, won't you have time to study later? Devil knows how many more weeks we'll lie in orbit doing nothing."

"War may erupt at any minute," Wa Chaou said.

"And if and when, who cares how the enemy looks or what his love life is? His ships are about like ours, and that's all we're ever likely to see."

"Oh, you have a direct line to the future?" the Cynthian murmured.

Rochefort stopped the tape and snapped, "I'll put the sound on tight beam if you want. But a knowledge of the enemy's nature might make the quantum of difference that saves us when the real thing happens. I suggest you watch too."

"Er, I think I should check out Number Three oscillator, long's we're not traveling faster-than-light," Helu said, and withdrew into the engine room. Wa Chaou settled down by Rochefort.

The lieutenant smiled. He refrained from telling the Cynthian, *You're a good little chap. Did you enlist to get away from the domination of irascible females on your home planet?*

His thought went on: *The reproductive pattern—sexual characteristics, requirements of the young—does seem to determine most of the basics in any intelligent species. As if the cynic's remark were true, that an organism is simply a DNA molecule's way of making more DNA molecules. Or whatever the chemicals of heredity may be on a given world. . . . But no, a Jerusalem Catholic can't believe that. Biological evolution inclines, it does not compel.*

"Let's see how the Ythrians work," he said aloud, reaching for the switch.

"Don't you already know, sir?" Wa Chaou asked.

"Not really. So many sophont races, in that bit of space we've sort of explored. And I've been busy familiarizing myself with my new duties." Rochefort chuckled. "And, be it admitted, enjoying what leaves I could get."

He reactivated the screen. It showed an Ythrian walking on the feet that grew from his wings: a comparatively slow, jerky gait, no good for real distances. The being stopped, lowered hands to ground, and stood on them. He lifted his wings, and suddenly he was splendid.

Beneath, on either side, were slits in column. As the wings rose, the feathery operculum-like flaps which protected them were drawn back. The slits widened until, at full extension, they gaped like purple mouths. The view became a closeup. Thin-skinned tissues, intricately wrinkled, lay behind a curtain of cilia which must be for screening out dust.

When the wings lowered, the slits were forced shut again, bellows fashion. The lecturer's voice said: "This is what allows so heavy a body, under Terra-type weight and gas density, to fly. Ythrians attain more than twice the mass of the largest possible airborne creature on similar planets elsewhere. The antlibranchs, pumped by the wingstrokes, take in oxygen under pressure to feed it directly to the bloodstream. Thus they supplement lungs which themselves more or less resemble those of ordinary land animals. The Ythrian acquires the power needed to get aloft and, indeed, fly with rapidity and grace."

The view drew back. The creature in the holograph flapped strongly and rocketed upward.

"Of course," the dry voice said, "this energy must come from a correspondingly accelerated metabolism. Unless prevented from flying, the Ythrian is a voracious eater. Aside from certain sweet fruits, he is strictly carnivorous. His appetite has doubtless reinforced the usual carnivore tendency to live in small, well-separated groups, each occupying a wide territory which instinct makes it defend against all intruders.

"In fact, the Ythrian can best be understood in terms of what we know or conjecture about the evolution of his race."

"Conjecture more than know, I suspect," Rochefort remarked. But he found himself fascinated.

* * * * * *

"We believe that homeothermic—roughly speaking, warm-blooded—life on Ythri did not come from a reptilian or reptiloid form, but directly from an amphibian, conceivably even from something corresponding to a lungfish. At any rate, it retained a kind of gill. Those species which were most successful on land eventually lost this feature. More primitive animals kept it. Among these was that small, probably swamp-dwelling thing which became the ancestor of the sophont. Taking to the treetops, it may have developed a membrane on which to glide from bough to bough. This finally turned into a wing. Meanwhile the gills were modified for aerial use, into superchargers."

"As usual," Wa Chaou observed. "The failures at one stage beget the successes of the next."

"Of course, the Ythrian can soar and even hover," the speaker said, "but it is the tremendous wing area which makes this possible, and the antlibranchs are what make it possible to operate those wings.

"Otherwise the pre-Ythrian must have appeared fairly similar to Terran birds." Pictures of various hypothetical extinct creatures went by. "It developed an analogous water-hoarding system—no separate urination—which saved weight as well as compensating for evaporative losses from the antlibranchs. It likewise developed light bones, though these are more intricate than avian bones, built of a marvelously strong two-phase material whose organic component is not collagen but a substance carrying out the functions of Terra-mammalian marrow. The animal did not, however, further ease its burdens by trading teeth for a beak. Many Ythrian ornithoids have done so, for example the uhoth, hawklike in appearance, doglike in service. But the pre-sophont remained an unspecialized dweller in wet jungles.

"The fact that the young were born tiny and helpless—since the female could not fly long distances while carrying a heavy fetus—is probably responsible for the retention and elaboration of the digits on the wings. The cub could cling to either parent in turn while these cruised after food; before it was able to fly, it could save itself

from enemies by clambering up a tree. Meanwhile the
feet acquired more and more ability to seize prey and
manipulate objects.

"Incidentally, the short gestation period does not mean
that the Ythrian is born with a poorly developed nervous
system. The rapid metabolism of flight affects the rate of
fetal cell division. This process concentrates on laying
down a body pattern rather than on increasing the size.
Nevertheless, an infant Ythrian needs more care, and more
food, than an infant human. The parents must cooperate
in providing this as well as in carrying their young about.
Here we may have the root cause of the sexual equality
or near equality found in all Ythrian cultures.

"Likewise, a rapid succession of infants would be impossible to keep alive under primitive conditions. This
may be a reason why the female only ovulates at in-
tervals of a year—Ythri's is about half of Terra's—and
not for about two years after giving birth. Sexuality does
not come overtly into play except at these times. Then it
is almost uncontrollably strong in male and female alike.
This may well have given the territorial instinct a cultural
reinforcement after intelligence evolved. Parents wish to
keep their nubile daughters isolated from chance-met males
while in heat. Furthermore, husband and wife do not wish
to waste a rich, rare experience on any outsider.

"The sexual cycle is not totally rigid. In particular,
grief often brings on estrus. Doubtless this was originally
a provision of nature for rapid replacement of losses. It
seems to have brought about a partial fusion of Eros and
Thanatos in the Ythrian psyche which makes much of the
race's art, and doubtless thought, incomprehensible to man.
An occasional female can ovulate at will, though this is
considered an abnormality; in olden days she would be
killed, now she is generally shunned, out of dread of her
power. A favorite villain in Ythrian story is the male
who, by hypnosis or otherwise, can induce the state. Of
course, the most important manifestation of a degree of
flexibility is the fact that Ythrians have successfully
adapted their reproductive pattern, like everything else, to
a variety of colonized planets."

"Me, I think it's more fun being human," Rochefort
said.

"I don't know, sir," Wa Chaou replied. "Superficially

the relationship between the sexes looks simpler than in your race or mine; you're either in the mood or you're not, and that's that. I wonder, though, if it may not really be more subtle and complicated than ours, even more basic to the whole psychology."

"But to return to evolution," the lecturer was saying. "It seems that a major part of Ythri underwent something like the great Pliocene drought in Terra's Africa. The ornithoids were forced out of dwindling forests onto growing savannahs. There they evolved from carrion eaters to big-game hunters in a manner analogous to preman. The original feet became hands, which eventually started making tools. To support the body and provide locomotion on the ground, the original elbow claws turned into feet, the wings that bore them became convertible to legs of a sort.

"Still, the intelligent Ythrian remained a pure carnivore, and one which was awkward on land. Typically, primitive hunters struck from above, with spears, arrows, axes. Thus only a few were needed to bring down the largest beasts. There was no necessity to cooperate in digging pits for elephants or standing shoulder to shoulder against a charging lion. Society remained divided into families or clans, which seldom fought wars but which, on the other hand, did not have much contact of any sort.

"The revolution which ended the Stone Age did not involve agriculture from the beginning, as in the case of man. It came from the systematic herding, at last the domestication, of big ground animals like the maukh, smaller ones like the long-haired mayaw. This stimulated the invention of skids, wheels, and the like, enabling the Ythrian to get about more readily on the surface. Agriculture was invented as an ancillary to ranching, an efficient means of providing fodder. The food surplus allowed leisure for travel, trade, and widespread cultural intercourse. Hence larger, complex social units arose.

"They cannot be called civilizations in a strict sense, because Ythri has never known true cities. The mobility of being winged left no necessity for crowding together in order to maintain close relationships. Granted, sedentary centers did appear—for mining, metallurgy, and other industry; for trade and religion; for defense in case the group was defeated by another in aerial battle. But these

have always been small and their populations mostly floating. Apart from their barons and garrisons, their perma-
nent inhabitants were formerly, for the main part, wing-
clipped slaves—today, automated machines. Clipping was
an easy method of making a person controllable; yet
since the feathers could grow back, the common practice
of promising manumission after a certain period of diligent
service tended to make prisoners docile. Hence slavery
became so basic to pre-industrial Ythrian society that to
this day it has not entirely disappeared."

Well, we're reviving it in the Empire, Rochefort thought.
*For terms and under conditions limited by law; as a
punishment, in order to get some social utility out of the
criminal; nevertheless, we're bringing back a thing the
Ythrians are letting die. How more moral are we than
they? How much more right do we have?*

He straightened in his chair. *Man is my race.*

* * * * * *

A willowy blonde with the old-fashioned Esperancian
taste for simplicity in clothes, Eve Davisson made a pleas-
ing contrast to Philippe Rochefort, as both were well
aware. He was a tall, rather slender young man, his bearing athletic, his features broad-nosed, full-lipped, and regular, his hair kinking itself into a lustrous black coif over
the deep-brown skin. And he stretched to the limit the
tolerance granted officers as regards their dress uniforms
—rakishly tilted bonnet bearing the sunburst of Empire,
gold-trimmed blue tunic, scarlet sash and cloak, snowy
trousers tucked into low boots of authentic Terran beef-
leather.

They sat in an intimate restaurant of Fleurville, by a
window opening on gardens and stars. A live sonorist
played something old and sentimental; perfumed, slightly
intoxicant vapors drifted about; they toyed with hors
d'oeuvres and paid more serious attention to their cham-
pagne. Nonetheless she was not smiling.

"This world was settled by people who believed in
peace," she said. Her tone mourned rather than accused.
"For generations they kept no armed forces, they relied
on the good will of others whom they helped."

"That good will didn't outlive the Troubles," Rochefort
said.

"I know, I know. I shan't join the demonstrators, whatever some of my friends may say when they learn I've been out with an Imperial officer. But Phil—the star named Pax, the planet named Esperance are being geared for war. It hurts."

"It'd hurt worse if you were attacked. Avalon isn't far, and they've built a lot of power there."

Her fingers tightened on the stem of her glass. "Attack from Avalon? But I've *met* those people, both races. They've come here on trade or tour or— I made a tour there myself, not long ago. I went because it's picturesque, but was so graciously treated I didn't want to leave."

"I daresay Ythrian manners have rubbed off on their human fellows." Rochefort let a draft go over his palate, hoping it would tingle away his irritation. This wasn't supposed to be a political evening. "Likewise less pleasant features of the Ythrian personality."

She studied him through the soft light before she said low, "I get an impression you disapprove of a mixed colony."

"Well . . . in a way, yes." He could have dissembled, facilely agreed to everything she maintained, and thus improved his chances of bedding her later on. But he'd never operated thus; and he never would, especially when he liked this girl just as a person. "I believe in being what you are and standing by your own."

"You talk almost like a human supremacist," she said, though mildly.

"To the extent that man is the leading race—furnishes most of the leaders—in Technic civilization, yes, I suppose you'd have to call me a human supremacist," he admitted. "It doesn't mean we aren't chronically sinful and stupid, nor does it mean we have any right to oppress others. Why, my sort of people are the xenosophont's best friend. We simply don't want to imitate him."

"Do you believe the Terran Empire is a force for good?"

"On balance, yes. It commits evil. But nothing mortal can avoid that. Our duty is to correct the wrongs . . . and also to recognize the values that the Empire does, in fact, preserve."

"You may have encountered too little of the evil."

"Because I'm from Terra itself?" Rochefort chuckled. "My dear, you're too bright to imagine the mother system is inhabited exclusively by aristocrats. My father is a minor functionary in the Sociodynamic Service. His job caused us to move around a lot. I was born in Selenopolis, which is a spaceport and manufacturing center. I spent several impressionable years on Venus, in the crime and poverty of a planet whose terraforming never had been quite satisfactory. I joined the navy as an enlisted rating—not out of chauvinism, merely a boyish wish to see the universe—and wasn't tapped for pilot school for two-three years; meanwhile, I saw the grim side of more than one world. Sure, there's a cosmos of room for improvement. Well, let's improve, not tear down. And let's defend!"

He stopped. "Damn," he said frankly. "I'd hoped to lure you out of your seriousness, and fell into it myself."

Now the girl laughed, and raised her glass. "Let's help each other climb out, then," she suggested.

They did. Rochefort's liberty became highly enjoyable. And that was fortunate, because two weeks after he reported back from it, *Ansa* was ordered into deep space. Light-years from Pax, she joined the fleet that had been using immensity as a mask for its marshaling; and ships by the hundreds hurled toward the Domain of Ythri.

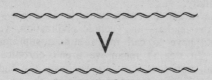

V

The conference was by phone. Most were, these days. It went against old Avalonian courtliness but saved time —and time was getting in mighty short supply, Daniel Holm thought.

Anger crackled through clearly enough. Two of the three holographs on the com board before him seemed about to climb out of their screens and into his office. No doubt he gave their originals the same impression.

Matthew Vickery, President of the Parliament of Man, wagged his forefinger and both plump jowls and said,

"We are not under a military regime, may I remind you in case you have forgotten. We, the proper civil government, approved your defense measures of the past several years, though you are aware that I myself have always considered them excessive. When I think of the prosperity that tax money, those resources, could have brought, left in private hands—or the social good it could have done in the public sector— Give you military your heads, and you'd build bases in the fourth dimension to protect us against an invasion from the future."

"We are always being invaded by the future," Ferune said. "The next part of it to arrive will not be pleasant."

Holm crossed his legs, leaned back, blew cigar smoke at Vickery's image, and drawled, "Spare us the oratory. You're not campaigning for re-election here. What's made you demand this four-way?"

"Your entire high-handedness," Vickery declared. "The overflow quantum was that last order, barring non-Ythrian ships from the Lauran System. Do you realize what a trade we do . . . not merely with the Empire, though that supports many livelihoods, but with unaffiliated civilizations like the Kraokan?"

"Do *you* realize how easy it'd be for the Terrans to get a robotic job, disguised, into low orbit around Avalon?" Holm retorted. "Several thousand megatons, touched off at that height when skies are clear, would set about half of Corona afire. Or it might be so sophisticated it could land like a peaceful merchantman. Consciousness-level computers aren't used much any more, when little new exploration's going on, but they could be built, including a suicide imperative. That explosion would be inside a city's force shields; it'd take out the generators, leaving what was left of the city defenseless; fallout from a dirty warhead would poison the whole hinterland. And you, Vickery, helped block half the appropriation we wanted for adequate shelters."

"Hysteria," the president said. "What could Terra gain from a one-shot atrocity? Not that I expect war, if only we can curb our own hotheads. But—well, take this ludicrous home-guard program you've instigated." His glance went toward Ferune and Liaw. "Oh, it gives a lot of young folk a fine excuse to swagger around, getting in people's way, ordering them arrogantly about, feeling important, and never mind the social as well as the fiscal cost of it. But if this navy we've been building and manning at your loud urging, by straining our production facilities and gutting our resources, if this navy is as advertised, the Terrans can never come near us. If not, who has been derelict in his duty?"

"We are near their sector capital," Ferune reminded him. "They may strike us first, overwhelmingly."

"I've heard that till I'm taped for it. I prefer to program myself, thank you." Vickery paused. "See here," he continued in a leveled tone, "I agree the situation is critical. We're all Avalonians together. If I feel certain of your proposals are unwise, I tell this to the public and the Parliament. But in the end we compromise like reasonable beings."

Ferune's face rippled. It was as well that Vickery didn't notice or wasn't able to read the meaning. Liaw of The Tarns remained expressionless. Holm grunted, "Go on."

"I must protest both your proceedings and the manner of them," Vickery said. "We are not under martial law, and indeed the Compact makes no provision for declaring it."

"Wasn't needed in the old days," Holm said. "The danger was clear and present. I didn't think it'd be needed now. The Admiralty is responsible for local defense and liaison with armed forces elsewhere in the Domain—"

"Which does *not* authorize you to stop trade, or raise a tin militia, or anything cutting that deeply into normal Avalonian life. My colleagues and I have endured it thus far, recognizing the necessity of at least some things. But today the necessity is to remind you that you are the servants of the people, not the masters. If the people want your policies executed, they will so instruct their legislative representatives."

"The Khruaths did call for a home guard and for giving the Admiralty broad discretion," Liaw of The Tarns said in his rustling voice. He was old, had frost in his feathers; but he sat huge in his castle, and the screen gave a background image of crags and a glacier.

"Parliament—"

"Is still debating," Holm interrupted to finish. "The Terran Imperium has no such handicap. If you want a legal formula, well, consider us to be acting under choth law."

"The choths have no government," Vickery said, red-
dening.

"What is a government?" asked Liaw, Wyvan of the
High Khruath—how softly!

"Why . . . well, legitimate authority—"

"Yes. The legitimacy derives, ultimately, no matter by
what formula, from tradition. The authority derives, no
matter by what formula, from armed force. Government
is that institution which is legitimized in its use of
physical coercion on the people. Have I read your human
philosophers and history aright, President Vickery?"

"Well . . . yes . . . but—"

"You seem to have forgotten for the moment that the
choths have been no more unanimous than your human
factions," Liaw said. "Believe me, they have been divided
and they are. Though a majority voted for the latest defense measures, a vocal minority has opposed: feeling,
as you do, President Vickery, that the danger has been
exaggerated and does not justify lifting that great a load."

Liaw sat silent for a space, during which the rest of
them heard wind whistle behind him and saw a pair of
his grandsons fly past. One bore the naked sword which
went from house to house as a summons to war, the other
a blast rifle.

The High Wyvan said: "Three choths refused to make
their gift. My fellows and I threatened to call Oherran on
them. Had they not yielded, we would have done so. We
consider the situation to be that grave."

Holm choked. *He never told me before!— Of course
he wouldn't have.* Ferune grew nearly as still on his bench
as Liaw. Vickery drew breath; sweat broke out on his
smoothness; he dabbed at it.

I can almost sympathize, Holm thought. *Suddenly getting bashed with reality like that.*

Matthew Vickery should have stayed a credit analyst instead of going into politics (Holm's mind rambled on, at
the back of its own shocked alertness). Then he'd have
been harmless, in fact useful; interspecies economics is often a wonderland in need of all the study anyone can give
it. The trouble was, on a thinly settled globe like Avalon,
government never had been too important aside from
basic issues of ecology and defense. In recent decades its
functions had dwindled still further, as human society

changed under Ythrian influence. (A twinge of pain.) Voting was light for offices that looked merely managerial. Hence the more reactionary humans were able to elect Vickery, who Viewed With Alarm the trend toward Ythrianization. (Was no alarm justified?) He had nothing else to offer, in these darkening times.

"You understand this is confidential," Liaw said. "If word got about, the choths in question would have to consider it a deathpride matter."

"Yes," Vickery whispered.

Another silence. Holm's cigar had burned short, was scorching his fingers. He stubbed it out. It stank. He started a new one. *I smoke too much,* he thought. *Drink too much also, maybe, of late. But the work's getting done, as far as circumstance allows.*

Vickery wet his lips. "This puts . . . another complexion on affairs, doesn't it?" he said. "May I speak plainly? I must know if this is a hint that . . . you may come to feel yourselves compelled to a *coup d'état*."

"We have better uses for our energies," Liaw told him. "Your efforts in Parliament could be helpful."

"Well—you realize I can't surrender my principles. I must be free to speak."

"It is written in the Compact," Ferune said, and his quotation did not seem superfluous even by Ythrian standards, " 'Humans inhabiting Avalon have the deathpride right of free speech, publication, and broadcast, limited only by the deathpride rights of privacy and honor and by the requirements of protection against foreign enemies.' "

"I meant—" Vickery swallowed. But he had not been years in politics for nothing. "I meant simply that friendly criticism and suggestions will always be in order," he said with most of his accustomed ease. "However, we certainly cannot risk a civil war. Shall we discuss details of a policy of nonpartisan cooperation?"

Behind the ready words, fear could still be sensed. Holm imagined he could almost read Vickery's mind, reviewing the full significance of what Liaw had said.

* * * * * *

How shall a fierce, haughty, intensely clannish and territorial race regulate its public business?

Just as on Terra, different cultures on Ythri at different

periods in their histories have given a variety of answers, none wholly satisfactory or permanently enduring. The Planha speakers happened to be the most wealthy and progressive when the first explorers arrived; one is tempted to call them "Hellenistic." Eagerly adopting modern technology, they soon absorbed others into their system while modifying it to suit changed conditions.

This was the easier because the system did not require uniformity. Within its possessions—whether these were scattered or a single block of land or sea—a choth was independent. Tradition determined what constituted a choth, though this was a tradition which slowly changed itself, as every living usage must. Tribe, anarchism, despotism, loose federation, theocracy, clan, extended family, corporation, on and on through concepts for which there are no human words, a choth ran itself.

Mostly, internal ordering was by custom and public opinion rather than by prescription and force. After all, families rarely lived close together; hence friction was minimal. The commonest sanction was a kind of weregild, the most extreme was enslavement. In between was outlawry; for some specified period, which might run as high as life, the wrongdoer could be killed by anyone without penalty, and to aid him was to incur the same punishment. Another possible sentence was exile, with outlawry automatic in case of return before the term was up. This was harsh to an Ythrian. On the other hand, the really disaffected could easily leave home (how do you fence in the sky?) and apply for membership in a choth more to their taste.

Now of course some recognized body had to try cases and hand down judgments. It must likewise settle interchoth disputes and establish policies and undertakings for the common weal. Thus in ancient times arose the Khruath, a periodic gathering of all free adults in a given territory who cared to come. It had judicial and limited legislative authority, but no administrative. The winners of lawsuits, the successful promoters of schemes and ordinances, must depend on willingness to comply or on what strength they could muster to enforce.

As Planha society expanded, regional meetings like this began to elect delegates to Year-Khruaths, which drew on larger territories. Finally these, in turn, sent their representatives to the High Khruath of the whole planet, which met every six years plus on extraordinary occasions. On each level, a set of presiding officers, the Wyvans, were chosen. These were entrusted with explication of the laws (i.e. customs, precedents, decisions) and with trial of as many suits as possible. It was not quite a soviet organization, because any free adult could attend a Khruath on any level he wished.

The arrangement would not have worked on Terra—where a version of it appeared once, long ago, and failed bloodily. But Ythrians are less talkative, less busybody, less submissive to bullies, and less chronically crowded than man. Modern communications, computers, information retrieval, and educational techniques helped the system spread planetwide, ultimately Domain-wide.

Before it reached that scale, it had had to face the problem of administration. Necessary public works must be funded; in theory the choths made free gifts to this end, in practice the cost required allocation. Behavior grossly harmful to the physical or social environment must be enjoined, however much certain choths might profit by it or regard it as being of their special heritage. Yet no machinery existed for compulsion, nor would Ythrians have imagined establishing any—as such.

Instead, it came slowly about that when a noncompliance looked important, the Wyvans of the appropriate Khruath cried Oherran on the offenders. This, carried out after much soul-searching and with the gravest ceremonies, was a summons to everyone in the territory: that for the sake of their own interests and especially their honor, they attack the defiers of the court.

In early times, an Oherran on a whole choth meant the end of it—enslavement of whoever had not been slaughtered, division of holdings among the victors. Later it might amount to as little as the arrest and exile of named leaders. But always it fell under the concept of deathpride. If the call to Oherran was rejected, as had happened when the offense was not deemed sufficient to justify the monstrosity of invasion, then the Wyvans who cried it had no acceptable alternative to suicide.

Given the Ythrian character, Oherran works about as well as police do among men. If your society has not lost morale, human, how often must you call the police?

None who knew Liaw of The Tarns imagined he would untruthfully say that he had threatened to rip Avalon asunder.

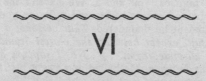

VI

Where the mighty Sagittarius flows into the Gulf of Centaurs, Avalon's second city—the only one besides Gray which rated the name—had arisen as riverport, seaport, spaceport, industrial center, and mart. Thus Centauri was predominantly a human town, akin to many in the Empire, thronged, bustling, noisy, cheerfully corrupt, occasionally dangerous. When he went there, Arinnian most of the time had to be Christopher Holm, in behavior as well as name.

Defense business now required it. He was not astonished at becoming a top officer of the West Coronan home guard, after that took its loose shape—not in a society where nepotism was the norm. It did surprise him that he seemed to be doing rather well, even enjoying himself in a grim fashion, he who had always scoffed at the "herd man." In a matter of weeks he got large-scale drills going throughout his district and was well along on the development of doctrine, communications, and supply. (Of course, it helped that most Avalonians were enthusiastic hunters, often in large groups on battues; and that the Troubles had left a military tradition not difficult to revive; and that old Daniel was on hand to advise.) Similar organizations had sprung up everywhere else. They needed to coordinate their efforts with the measures being taken by the Seamen's Brotherhood. A conference was called. It worked hard and accomplished as many of its purposes as one could reasonably hope.

Afterward Arinnian said, "Hrill, would you like to go out and celebrate? W-we may not have a lot more chances." He did not speak on impulse. He had debated it for the past couple of days.

Tabitha Falkayn smiled. "Sure, Chris. Everybody else will be."

They walked down Livewell Street. Her arm was in his; in the subtropical heat he was aware of how their skins traded sweat. "I . . . well, why do you generally call me by my human name?" he asked. "And talk Anglic to me?"

"We are humans, you and I. We haven't the feathers to use Planha as it ought to be used. Why do you mind?"

For a moment he floundered. *That personal a question . . . an insult, except between the closest friends, when it becomes an endearment. . . . No, I suppose she's just thinking human again.* He halted and swept his free hand around. "Look at that and stop wondering," he said. Instantly he feared he had been too curt.

But the big blond girl obeyed. This part of the street ran along a canal, which was oily and littered with refuse, burdened with barges, walled in by buildings jammed together, whose dingy façades reared ten or twelve stories into night heaven. Stars and the white half-disk of Morgana were lost behind the glare, blink, leap and worm-crawl of raw-colored signs. (GROG HARBOR, DANCE, EAT, GENUINE TERRAN SENSIES, FUN HOUSE, SWITCH TO MARIA JUANAS, GAMBLING, NAKED GIRLS, LOANS, BUY . . . BUY . . . BUY . . .) Groundbugs filled the roadway, pedestrians the sidewalks, a sailor, a pilot, a raftman, a fisher, a hunter, a farmer, a whore, a secretary, a drunk about to collapse, another drunk getting belligerent at a monitor, a man gaunt and hairy and ragged who stood on a corner and shouted of some obscure salvation, endless human seething, shrilling, chattering, through engine rumble, foot shuffle, raucousness blared out of loudspeakers. The air stank, dirt, smoke, oil, sewage, flesh, a breath from surrounding swamplands which would there have been a clean rotting but here was somehow made nasty.

Tabitha smiled at him anew. "Why, I call this fun, Chris," she said. "What else've we come for?"

"You wouldn't—" he stammered. "I mean, somebody like you?"

He realized he was gaping at her. Both wore thin short-sleeved blouses, kilts, and sandals; garments clung to wet bodies. But despite the sheen of moisture and the odor of female warmth that he couldn't help noticing, she stood as a creature of sea and open skies.

"Sure, what's wrong with once-in-a-while vulgarity?" she said, still amiable. "You're too puritan, Chris."

"No, no," he protested, now afraid she would think him naïve. "Fastidious, maybe. But I've often been here and, uh, enjoyed myself. What I was trying to explain was, uh, I, I'm proud to belong to a choth and not proud that members of my race elect to live in a sty. Don't you see, this is the old way, that the pioneers wanted to escape."

Tabitha said a word. He was staggered. Eyath would never have spoken thus. The girl grinned. "Or, if you prefer, 'nonsense,' " she continued. "I've read Falkayn's writings. He and his followers wanted not one thing except unmolested elbow room." Her touch nudged him along. "How about that dinner we were aimed at?" Numbly, he moved.

He recovered somewhat in the respectable dimness of the Phoenix House. Among other reasons, he admitted to himself, the room was cool and her clothes didn't emphasize her shape as they did outside.

The place had live service. She ordered a catflower cocktail. He didn't. "C'mon," she said. "Unbuckle your shell."

"No, thanks, really." He found words. "Why dull my perceptions at a happy moment?"

"Seems I've heard that line before. A Stormgate saying?"

"Yes. Though I didn't think they used drugs much in Highsky either."

"They don't. Barring the sacred revels. Most of us keep to the Old Faith, you know." Tabitha regarded him awhile. "Your trouble, Chris, is you try too hard. Relax. Be more among your own species. How many humans do you have any closeness to? Bloody-gut few, I'll bet."

He bridled. "I've seen plenty of late."

"Yeh. And emergency or no, doesn't it feel good? I wouldn't try to steer somebody else's life, of course, nor am I hinting it's true of you—but fact is, a man or woman who tries to be an Ythrian is a rattlewing."

"Well, after three generations you may be restless in your choth," he said, gauging his level of sarcasm as carefully as he was able. "You've knocked around quite a bit in human country, haven't you?"

She nodded. "Several years. Itinerant huntress, trapper, sailor, prospector, over most of Avalon. I got the main piece of my share in the stake that started Draun and me in business— I got that at assorted poker tables." She laughed. "Damn, sometimes it is easier to say things in Planha!" Serious: "But remember, I was young when my parents were lost at sea. An Ythrian family adopted me. They encouraged me to take a wandertime; that's Highsky custom. If anything, my loyalty and gratitude to the choth were strengthened. I simply, well, I recognize I'm a member who happens to be human. As such, I've things to offer which—" She broke off and turned her head. "Ah, here comes my drink. Let's talk trivia. I do get starved for that on St. Li."

"I believe I will have a drink too," Arinnian said.

He found it helpful. Soon they were cheerily exchanging reminiscences. While she had doubtless led a more adventurous life than he, his had not been dull. On occasion, such as when he hid from his parents in the surf-besieged Shielding Islands, or when he had to meet a spathodont on the ground with no more than a spear because his companion lay wing-broken, he may have been in worse danger than any she had met. But he found she was most taken by his quieter memories. She had never been offplanet, except for one vacation trip to Morgana. He, son of a naval officer, had had ample chances to see the whole Lauran System from sun-wracked Elysium, through the multiple moons of Camelot, out to dark, comet-haunted Utgard. Speaking of the frigid blue peace of Phaeacia, he chanced to quote some Homeric lines, and she was delighted and wanted more and asked what else this Homer fellow had written, and the conversation turned to books. . . .

The meal was mixed, as cuisine of both races tended increasingly to be: piscoid-and-tomato chowder, beef-and-shua pie, salad of clustergrain leaf, pears, coffee spiced with witchroot. A bottle of vintage dago gave merriment. At the end, having seen her indulge the vice before, Arinnian was not shocked when Tabitha lit her pipe. "What say we look in on the Nest?" she proposed. "Might find Draun." Her partner was her superior in the guard; she was in Centauri as his aide. But the choth concept of rank was at once more complex and more flexible than the Technic.

"Well . . . all right," Arinnian answered.

She cocked her head. "Reluctant? I'd've guessed you'd prefer the Ythrian hangout to anyplace else in town." It included the sole public house especially for ornithoids, they being infrequent here.

He frowned. "I can't help feeling that tavern is wrong. For them," he added in haste. "I'm no prude, understand."

"Yet you don't mind when humans imitate Ythrians. Uh-uh. Can't have it on both wings, son." She stood. "Let's take a glance into the Nest boozeria, a drink if we meet a friend or a good bard is reciting. Afterward a dance club, hm?"

He nodded, glad—amidst an accelerating pulse—that her mood remained light. While no machinery would let them take part in the Ythrian aerial dances, moving across a floor in the arms of another bird was nearly as fine, perhaps. And, while that was as far as such contact had ever gone for him, maybe Tabitha—for she was indeed Tabitha on this steamy night, not Hrill of the skies—

He had heard various muscular oafs talk of encounters with bird girls, less boastfully than in awe. To Arinnian and his kind, their female counterparts were comrades, sisters. But Tabitha kept emphasizing his and her humanness.

They took a taxibug to the Nest, which was the tallest building in the city, and a gravshaft to its rooftop since neither had brought flying gear. Uwalled, the tavern was protected from rain by a vitryl canopy through which, at this height, stars could be seen regardless of the electric lunacy below. Morgana was sinking toward the western bottomlands, though it still silvered river and Gulf. Thunderheads piled in the east, and a rank breeze carried the mutter of the lightning that shivered in them. Insectoids circled the dim fluoroglobe set on every table. Business was sparse, a few shadowy forms perched on stools before glasses or narcobraziers, a service robot trundling about, the recorded twangs of a steel harp.

"Scum-dull," Tabitha said, disappointed. "But we can make a circuit."

They threaded among the tables until Arinnian halted and exclaimed, "Hoy-ah! Vodan, ekh-hirr."

His chothmate looked up, plainly taken aback. He was seated at drink beside a shabby-plumed female, who gave the newcomers a sullen stare.

"Good flight to you," Arinnian greeted in Planha; but what followed, however automatic, was too obvious for anything save Anglic. "I didn't expect to find you here."

"And to you, good landing," Vodan replied. "I report to my ship within hours. My transport leaves from Halcyon Island base. I came early so as not to risk being detained by a storm; we've had three whirldevils in a row near home."

"You are yare for battle, hunter," said Tabitha at her most carefully courteous.

That's true, Arinnian thought. *He's ablaze to fight. Only . . . if he couldn't stay with Eyath till the last minute, at least I'd've supposed he'd've been in flight-under-moon, meditating—or, anyhow, at carouse among friends—* He made introductions.

Vodan jerked a claw at his attendant. "Quenna," he said. His informality was a casual insult. She hunched between her wings, feathers erected in forlorn self-assertion.

Arinnian could think of no excuse not to join the party. He and the girl seated themselves as best they could. When the robot rolled up, they ordered thick, strong New African beer.

"How blows your wind?" Tabitha asked, puffing hard on her pipe.

"Well; as I would like for you," Vodan answered correctly. He turned to Arinnian and, if his enthusiasm was a touch forced, it was nonetheless real. "You doubtless know I've been on training maneuvers these past weeks."

Yes. Eyath told me more than once.

"This was a short leave. My craft demands skill. Let me tell you about her. One of the new torpedo launchers, rather like a Terran Meteor, hai, a beauty, a spear! Proud I was to emblazon her hull with three golden stars."

"Eyath" means "Third Star."

Vodan went on. Arinnian glanced at Tabitha. She and Quenna had locked their gazes. Expressions billowed and jerked across the feathers; even he could read most of the unspoken half-language.

Yes, m' sweet, you long yellow Walker born, Quenna is what she is and who're you to look down that jutting snout of yours? What else could I be, since I, growing from cub to maiden, found my lovetimes coming on whenever I thought about 'em and knew there'd never be any decent place for me in the whole universe? Oh, yes, yes, I've heard it before, don't bother: "medical treatment; counseling."— Well, flabbyflesh, for your information, the choths don't often keep a weakling, and I'll not whine for help. Quenna'll lay her own course, better'n you, who're really like me . . . aren't you, now, she-human?

Tabitha leaned forward, patted one of those arms with no heed for the talons, smiled into the reddened eyes and murmured, "Good weather for you, lass."

Astounded, Quenna reared back. For an instant she seemed about to fly at the girl, and Arinnian's hand dropped to his knife. Then she addressed Vodan: "Better we be going."

"Not yet." The Ythrian had fairly well overcome his embarrassment. "The clouds alone will decide when I see my brother again."

"We better go," she said lower. Arinnian caught the first slight musky odor. At the next table, another male raised his crest and swiveled his head in their direction.

Arinnian could imagine the conflict in Vodan—dismiss her, defy her, strike her; no killing, she being unarmed— and yet that would be a surrender in itself, less to tradition than to mere conventionality— "We'll have to leave ourselves, soon's we finish these beers," the man said. "Glad to've come on you. Fair winds forever."

Vodan's relief was unmistakable. He mumbled through the courtesies and flapped off with Quenna. The city swallowed them.

Arinnian wondered what to say. He was grateful for the dull light; his face felt hotter than the air. He stared outward.

Tabitha said at length, softly, "That poor lost soul."

"Who, the nightflyer?" All at once he was furious. "I've met her sort before. Degenerates, petty criminals. Pray Vodan doesn't get his throat cut in whatever filthy crib she's taking him to. I know what must've happened here.

He was wandering around lonely, at loose ends, a mountaineer who'd probably never come on one like her. She zeroed in, hit him with enough pheromone to excite—ugh!"

"Why should you care? I mean, of course he's a friend of yours, but I hardly believe that pathetic creature will dare try more than wheedling a tip out of him." Tabitha drank smoke. "You know," she said thoughtfully, "here's a case of Ythrian cultural lag. They've been affected by human ideas to the point where they don't give their abnormals a quick death. But they're still not interested in sponsoring rehabilitation or research on cures, or in simple charity. Someday—"

He scarcely heard the last remark. "Vodan's to marry Eyath," he said through the interior grip on his gullet.

Tabitha raised her brows. "Oh? That one you mentioned to me? Well, don't you suppose, if she heard, she'd be glad he's gotten a bit of unimportant fun and forgetting?"

"It's not right! She's too clean. She—" Arinnian gulped. Abruptly he thought: *So why not take the risk? Now I need forgetting myself.* "Is the matter small to you?" he blurted. "In that case, let's us do the same."

"Hm?" She considered him for a while that grew. Lightning moved closer on heavy gusts. His rage ebbed and he must fight not to lower his eyes, not to cringe.

At last: "You are bitter for certain, aren't you, Chris?" A chuckle. "But likewise you're hopeful."

"I'm sorry," he got out. "I n-n-never meant disrespect. I wanted to give you a, an imaginary example—make you understand why I'm upset."

"I might resent your calling it imaginary," she smiled, though her tone had become more compassionate than teasing, "except I assume it wasn't really. The answer is no, thanks."

"I expected that. We birds—" He couldn't finish, but stared down into his mug until he lifted it for a quick, deep draft.

"What d'you mean, 'we'?" she challenged.

"Why, we . . . our generation, at least—"

When she nodded, her locks caught what illumination there was. "I know," she said gravely. "That behavior pattern, promiscuous as kakkelaks provided they don't much respect their partners, but hardly able to touch birds of the opposite sex. You're a bright lad, Chris; Avalonians aren't given to introspection, but you must have some idea of the cause. Don't you want a wife and children, ever?"

"Of course. I—of course. I will."

"Most of them will, I'm sure. Most of the earlier ones did eventually, when they'd come to terms with themselves. Besides, the situation's not universal. We birds do have this in common, that we tolerate less prying than the average human. So comparative statistics aren't available. Also, the problem has gotten conspicuous these days for no deeper reason than that the movement into the choths has begun snowballing. And, finally, Chris, your experience is limited. How many out of thousands do you know well enough to describe their private lives? You'd naturally tend to be best acquainted with your own sort, especially since we birds have gotten pretty good at picking up face and body cues."

Tabitha's pipe had gone out. She emptied it and finished: "I tell you, your case isn't near as typical as you think, nor near as serious. But I do wish that going bird didn't make otherwise sensible people lose years in thwarting themselves."

Anger pricked him again. What call had she to act superior? "Now wait—" he began.

Tabitha knocked back her beer and rose. "I'm headed for my hotel," she said.

He stared up at her. "What?"

She ruffled his hair. "I'm sorry. But I'm afraid if we continue tonight, we'll brew one cyclone of a squabble. I think too well of you to want that. We'll take another evening soon if you like. Now I aim to get into bed and have Library Central screen me some of that Homer stuff."

He couldn't dissuade her. Perhaps he took most umbrage at how calm his arguments left her. When he had bidden her a chill goodnight, he slouched to the nearest phoneboard.

The first woman he called was at work. Defense production was running at seven hours on, fifteen and the odd minutes off, plus overtime. The second female acquaintance said frantically that her husband was home if that

was the party he wanted; he apologized for punching a
wrong number. The third was available. She was overly
plump, chattered without cease, and had the brains of a
barysauroid. But what the chaos?

—He awoke about the following sunset. She was sweating in her sleep, breath stale from alcohol. He wondered
why the air had gone hot and sticky. Breakdown in the
conditioner? Or, hm, it'd been announced that if force
screens must be raised, the power drain would require
Environmental Control to shut off—

Force screens!

Arinnian jumped from bed. Rain had given way to low
overcast, but he glimpsed shimmers across that slatiness.
He groped through the dusty clutter in the room and
snapped on the holovid.

A recording played, over and over, a man's voice high-
pitched and his face stretched out of shape: "—war declared. A courier from Ythri has delivered the news in
Gray, that Terra has served notice of war."

〜〜〜〜〜〜〜〜〜〜〜〜〜

VII

〜〜〜〜〜〜〜〜〜〜〜〜〜

"Our basic strategy is simple," Admiral Cajal had explained. "I would prefer a simpler one yet: pitched
battle between massed fleets, winner takes all."

"But the Ythrians will scarcely be that obliging," Governor Saracoglu remarked.

"No. They aren't well organized for it, in the first place.
Not in character for them to centralize operations. Besides, they must know they're foredoomed to lose any
standup fight. They lack the sheer numerical strength. I
expect they'll try to maintain hedgehog positions. From
those they'd make sallies, harass, annihilate what smaller
units of ours they found, prey on our supply lines. We
can't drive straight into the Domain with that sort of
menace at our rear. Prohibitively costly. We could suffer

actual disaster if we let ourselves get caught between their inner and outer forces."

"Ergo, we start by capturing their advanced bases."

"The major ones. We needn't worry about tiny new colonies or backward allies, keeping a few ships per planet." Cajal gestured with a flashbeam. It probed into the darkness of a display tank, wherein gleamed points of luminance that represented the stars of this region. They crowded by thousands across those few scaled-down parsecs, a fire-swarm out of which not many men could have picked an individual. Cajal realized his talent for doing this had small intrinsic value. The storage and processing of such data were for computers. But it was an outward sign of an inner gift.

"Laura the nearest," he said. "Hru and Khrau further on, forming a triangle with it. Give me those, and I'll undertake to proceed directly against Quetlan. That should force them to call in everything they have, to protect the home star! And, since my rear and my lines will then be reasonably secure, I'll get the decisive battle I want."

"Um-m-m." Saracoglu rubbed his massive chin. Bristles made a scratchy sound; as hard as he had been at work, he kept forgetting to put on fresh inhibitor after a depilation. "You'll hit Laura first?"

"Yes, of course. Not with the whole armada. We'll split, approximately into thirds. The detached sections will proceed slowly toward Hru and Khrau, but not attack until Laura has been reduced. The force should be ample in all three systems, but I want to get the feel of Ythrian tactics—and, too, make sure they haven't some unpleasant surprise tucked under their tailfeathers."

"They might," Saracoglu said. "You know our intelligence on them leaves much to be desired. The problems of spying on nonhumans— And Ythrian traitors are almost impossible to find, competent ones completely impossible."

"I still don't see why you couldn't get agents into that mostly human settlement at Laura."

"We did, Admiral, we did. But in a set of small, close-knit communities they could accomplish nothing except report what was publicly available to see. You must realize, Avalonian humans no longer think, talk, even walk quite like any Imperial humans. Imitating them isn't

feasible. And, again, deplorably few can be bought.
Furthermore, the Avalonian Admiralty is excellent on security measures. The second in command, chap named
Holm, seems to have made several extended trips through
the Empire, official and unofficial, in earlier days. I understand he did advanced study at one of our academies. He
knows our methods."

"*I* understand he's caused not just the Lauran fleet but
the planetary defenses to be enormously increased, these
past years," Cajal said. "Yes, we must certainly take care
of him first."

—That had been weeks ago. On this day (clock concept in unending starry night) the Terrans neared their
enemy.

Cajal sat alone in the middle of the superdreadnaught
Valenderay. Communication screens surrounded him, and
humming silence, and radial kilometers of metal, machinery, weapons, armor, energies, through which passed several thousand living beings. But he was, for this moment,
conscious only of what lay outside. A viewscreen showed
him: darkness, diamond hordes, and Laura, tiny at nineteen astronomical units' remove but gold and shining, shining.

The ships had gone out of hyperdrive and were accelerating sunward on gravity thrust. Most were far ahead
of the flag vessel. A meeting with the defenders could be
looked for at any minute.

Cajal's mouth tightened downward at the right corner.
He was a tall man, gaunt, blade-nosed, his widow's peak
hair and pointed beard black though he neared his sixties.
His uniform was as plain as his rank allowed.

He had been chain-smoking. Now he pulled the latest
cigaret from a scorched mouth and ground it out as if it
were vermin. *Why can't I endure these final waits?* he
thought. *Because I will be safe while I send men to war?*

His glance turned to a picture of his dead wife, standing before their house among the high trees of Vera Fé.
He moved to animate but, instead, switched on a re-
corder.

Music awoke, a piece he and she had loved, well-nigh
forgotten on Terra but ageless in its triumphant serenity,
Bach's Passacaglia. He leaned back, closed his eyes and

let it heal him. *Man's duty in this life,* he thought, *is to choose the lesser evil.*

A buzz snapped him to alertness. The features of his chief executive captain filled a screen and stated, "Sir, we have received and confirmed a report of initial hostilities from Vanguard Squadron Three. No details."

"Very good, Citizen Feinberg," Cajal said. "Let me have any hard information immediately."

It would soon come flooding in, beyond the capacity of a live brain. Then it must be filtered through an intricate complex of subordinates and their computers, and he could merely hope the digests which reached him bore some significant relationship to reality. But those earliest direct accounts were always subtly helpful, as if the tone of a battle were set at its beginning.

"Aye, sir." The screen blanked.

Cajal turned off the music. "Farewell for now," he whispered, and rose. There was one other personal item in the room, a crucifix. He removed his bonnet, knelt, and signed himself. "Father, forgive us what we are about to do," he begged. "Father, have mercy on all who die. All."

"Word received, Marchwarden," the Ythrian voice announced. "Contact with Terrans, about 12 a.u. out, direction of the Spears. Firing commenced on both sides, but seemingly no losses yet."

"My thanks. Please keep me informed." Daniel Holm turned off the intercom.

"As if it were any use for me to know!" he groaned.

His mind ran through the calculation. Light, radio, neutrinos take about eight minutes to cross an astronomical unit. The news was more than an hour and a half old. That initial, exploratory fire-touch of a few small craft might well be ended already, the fragments of the vanquished whirling away on crazy orbits while the victors burned fuel as if their engines held miniature suns, trying to regain a kinetic velocity that would let them regroup. Or if other units on either side were not too distant, they might have joined in, sowing warheads wider and wider across space.

He spoke an obscenity and beat fist on palm. "If we could hypercommunicate—" But that wasn't practical. The

"instantaneous" pulses of a vessel quantum-jumping around
nature's speed limit could be modulated to send a message
a light-year or so—however, not this deep in a star's
distorting gravitational field, where you risked annihilation
if you tried to travel nonrelativistically—of course, you
could get away with it if you were absolutely sure of
your tuning, but nobody was in wartime—and anyhow,
given that capability, the Terrans would be a still worse
foe, fighting them would be hopeless rather than half
hopeless—*why am I rehearsing this muck?*

"And Ferune's there and I'm here!"

He sprang from his desk, stamped to the window and
stood staring. A cigar fumed volcanic between his teeth.
The day beyond was insultingly beautiful. An autumn
breeze carried odors of salt up from the bay, which
glittered and danced under Laura and heaven; and it bore
scents from the gardens it passed, brilliant around their
houses. North-shore hills lay in a blue haze of distance.
Overhead skimmed wings. He didn't notice.

Rowena came to him. "You knew you had to stay,
dear," she said. She was still auburn-maned, still slim and
erect in her coverall.

"Yeh. Backup. Logistic, computer, communications support. And maybe Ferune understands space warfare better,
but I'm the one who really built the planetary defense.
We agreed, months back. No dishonor to me, that I do the
sensible thing." Holm swung toward his wife. He caught
her around the waist. "But oh, God, Ro, I didn't think it'd
be this hard!"

She drew his head down onto her shoulder and stroked
the grizzled hair.

Ferune of Mistwood had planned to bring his own mate
along. Wharr had traveled beside him throughout a long
naval career, birthed and raised their children on the
homeships that accompanied every Ythrian fleet, drilled
and led gun crews. But she fell sick and the medics
weren't quite able to ram her through to recovery before
the onslaught came. You grow old, puzzlingly so. He
missed her sternness.

But he was too busy to dwell on their goodbyes. More
and more reports were arriving at his flagship. A pattern
was beginning to emerge.

"Observe," he said. The computers had just corrected the display tank according to the latest data. It indicated sun, planets, and color-coded sparks which stood for ships. "Combats here, here, here. Elsewhere, neutrino emissions reaching our detectors, cross-correlations getting made, fixes being obtained."

"Foully thin information," said the feathers and attitude of his aide.

"Thus far, aye, across interplanetary distances. However, we can fill in certain gaps with reason, if we assume their admiral is competent. I feel moderately sure that his pincer has but two claws, coming in almost diametrically opposite, from well north and south of the ecliptic plane . . . so." Ferune pointed. "Now he must have reserves further out. To avoid making a wide circuit with consequent risk of premature detection, these must have run fairly straight from the general direction of Pax. And were I in charge, I would have them near the ecliptic. Hence we look for their assault, as the pincers close, from here." He indicated the region.

They stood alone in the command bridge, broad though the chamber was. Ythrians wanted room to stretch their wings. Yet they were wholly linked to the ship by her intercoms, calculators, officers, crewfolk, more tenuously linked to that magnificence which darkened and bejeweled a viewscreen, where the killing had begun. Clangor and clatter of activity came faint to them, through a deep susurrus of power. The air blew warm, ruffling their plumes a little, scented with perfume of cinnamon bush and amberdragon. Blood odors would not be ordered unless and until the vessel got into actual combat; the crew would soon be worn out if stimulated too intensely.

Ferune's plan did not call for hazarding the superdreadnaught this early. Her power belonged in his end game. At that time he intended to show the Terrans why she was called after the site of an ancient battle on Ythri. He had had the Anglic translation of the name painted broad on the sides: *Hell Rock*.

A new cluster of motes appeared in the tank. Their brightnesses indicated ship types, as accurately as analysis of their neutrino emanations could suggest. The aide started. His crest bristled. "That many more hostiles, so soon? Uncle, the odds look bad."

"We knew they would. Don't let this toy hypnotize you. I've been through worse. Half of me is regenerated tissue after combat wounds. And I'm still skyborne."

"Forgive me, Uncle, but most of your fights were police actions inside the Domain. This is the *Empire* coming."

Ferune expressed: "I am not unaware of that. And I too have studied advanced militechnics, both practical and theoretical." Aloud he said, "Computers, robots, machines are only half the makers of a war-weird. There are also brains and hearts."

Claws clacked on the deck as he walked to the viewscreen and peered forth. His experienced eye picked out a glint among the stars, one ship. Otherwise his fleet was lost to vision in the immensity through which it fanned.

"A new engagement commencing," said the intercom.

Ferune waited motionless for details. Through his mind passed words from one of the old Terran books it pleasured him to read. *The fear of a king is as the roaring of a lion: whoso provoketh him to anger sinneth against his own soul.*

* * * * * *

Hours built into days while the fleets, in their hugely scattered divisions, felt for and sought each other's throats.

Consider: at a linear acceleration of one Terran gravity, a vessel can, from a "standing start," cover one astronomical unit—about 149 million kilometers—in a bit under fifty hours. At the end of that period, she has gained 1060 kilometers per second of velocity. In twice the time, she will move at twice the speed and will have spanned four times the distance. No matter what power is conferred by thermonuclear engines, no matter what maneuverability comes from a gravity thrust which reacts directly against that fabric of relationships we call space, one does not quickly alter quantities on this order of magnitude.

Then, too, there is the sheer vastness of even interplanetary reaches. A sphere one a. u. in radius has the volume of some thirteen million million Terras; to multiply this radius by ten is to multiply the volume by a thousand. No matter how sensitive the instruments, one does not quickly scan those deeps, nor ever do it with much accuracy beyond one's immediate neighborhood, nor know where a detached object is *now* if signals are limited to light speed. As the maddeningly incomplete hoard of data grows, not just the parameters of battle calculations change; the equations do. One discovers he has lost hours in travel which has turned out to be useless or worse, and must lose hours or days more in trying to remedy matters.

But then, explosively fast, will come a near enough approach at nearly enough matched velocities for a combat which may well be finished in seconds.

* * * * * *

"Number Seven, launch!" warned the dispatcher robot, and flung *Hooting Star* out to battle.

Her engines took hold. A thrum went through the bones of Philippe Rochefort where he sat harnessed in the pilot chair. Above his instrument panel, over his helmet and past either shoulder, viewscreens filled a quarter globe with suns. Laura, radiance stopped down lest it blind him, shone among them as a minikin disk between two nacreous wings of zodiacal light.

His radar alarm whistled and lit up, swiveling an arrow inside a clear ball. His heart sprang. He couldn't help glancing that way. And he caught a glimpse of the cylinder which hurtled toward *Ansa*'s great flank.

During a launch, the negagrav screen in that area of the mother vessel is necessarily turned off. Nothing is there to repulse a torpedo. If the thing makes contact and detonates— In vacuum, several kilotons are not quite so appallingly destructive as in air or water; and a capital ship is armored and compartmented against concussion and heat, thickly shielded to cut down what hard radiation gets inside. Nevertheless she will be badly hurt, perhaps crippled, and men will be blown apart, cooked alive, shrieking their wish to die.

An energy beam flashed. An instant's incandescence followed. Sensors gave their findings to the appropriate computer. Within a millisecond of the burst, a "Cleared" note warbled. One of Wa Chaou's guns had caught the torpedo square on.

"Well done!" Rochefort cried over the intercom. "Good show, Watch Out!" He rotated his detectors in search of the boat which must have been sufficiently close to loose that missile.

Registry. Lockon. *Hooting Star* surged forward. *Ansa*

dwindled among the constellations. "Give me an estimated time to come in range, Abdullah," Rochefort said.

"He seems aware of us," Helu's voice answered, stone-calm. "Depends on whether he'll try to get away or close in. . . . Um-m, yes, he's skiting for cover." (*I would too, for fair*, Rochefort thought, *when a heavy cruiser's spitting boats. That's a brave skipper who sneaked this near.*) "We can intercept in about ten minutes, assuming he's at his top acceleration. But I don't think anybody else will be able to help us, and if we wait for them, he'll escape."

"We're not waiting," Rochefort decided. He lasered his intentions back to the squadron control office aboard ship and got an okay. Meanwhile he wished his sweat were not breaking out wet and sour. He wasn't afraid, though; his pulse beat high but steady and never before had he seen the stars with such clarity and exactness. It was good to know he had the inborn courage for Academy psych-training to develop.

"If you win," SC said, "make for—" a string of numbers which the machines memorized—"and act at discretion. We've identified a light battleship there. We and *Ganymede* between us will try saturating its defenses. Good luck."

The voice clipped off. The boat ran, faster every second until the ballistics meters advised deceleration. Rochefort heeded and tapped out the needful orders. Utterly irrelevant passed through his head the memory of an instructor's lecture. "Living pilots, gunners, all personnel, are meant to make decisions. Machines execute most of those decisions, set and steer courses, lay and fire guns, faster and more precisely than nerve or muscle. Machines, consciousness-level computers, could also be built to decide. They have been, in the past. But while their logical abilities might be far in excess of yours and mine, they always lacked a certain totality, call it intuition or insight or what you will. Furthermore, they were too expensive to use in war in any numbers. You, gentlemen, are multipurpose computers who have a *reason* to fight and survive. Your kind is abundantly available and, apart from programming, can be produced in nine months by unskilled labor." Rochefort remembered telling lower classmen that it was three demerits if you didn't laugh at the hoary joke.

"Range," Helu said.

Energy beams stabbed. The scattered, wasted photons which burned along their paths were the barest fraction of the power within.

One touched *Hooting Star*. The boat's automata veered her before it could penetrate her thin plating. That was a roar of sidewise thrust. The interior fields couldn't entirely compensate for the sudden high acceleration. Rochefort was crammed back against his harness till it creaked, while weight underfoot shifted dizzyingly.

It passed. Normal one-gee-down returned. They were alive. They didn't even seem to need a patchplate; if they had been pierced, the hole was small enough for self-sealing. And yonder in naked-eye sight was the enemy!

With hands and voice, Rochefort told his boat to drive straight at that shark shape. It swelled monstrously fast. Two beams lanced from it and struck. Rochefort held his vector constant. He was hoping Wa Chaou would thus be able to get a fix on their sources and knock them out before they could do serious damage. *Flash! Flash!* Brightness blanked. "Oh, glorious! Ready torps."

The Ythrian drew nearer till the human could see a painted insigne, a wheel whose spokes were flower petals. *That's right, they put personal badges on their lesser craft, same as we give unofficial names. Wonder what that'n means.* He'd been told that some of their speedsters carried ball guns. But hard objects cast in your path weren't too dangerous till relative velocities got into the tens of KPS.

She fired a torpedo. Wa Chaou wrecked it almost in its tube. *Hooting Star*'s slammed home.

The explosion was at such close quarters that its fiery gases filled the Terran's screen. A fragment struck her. She shivered and belled. Then she was past, alone in clean space. Her opponent was a cloud which puffed outward till it grew invisible, a few seared chunks of metal and possibly bone cooling off to become meteoroids, falling away aft, gone from sight in seconds.

"If you will pardon the expression," Rochefort said shakily, "yahoo!"

"That was a near one," Helu said. "We'd better ask for antirad boosters when we get back."

"Uh-huh. Right now, though, we've unfinished business." Rochefort instructed the boat to change vectors.

"No fears, after the way you chaps conducted yourselves."

They were not yet at the scene when joyful broadcasts and another brief blossoming told them that a hornet swarm of boats and missiles had stung the enemy battleship to death.

VIII

Slowly those volumes of space wherein the war was being fought contracted and neared each other. At no time were vessels ranked. Besides being unfeasible to maintain, formations tight and rigid would have invited a nuclear barrage. At most, a squadron of small craft might travel in loose echelon for a while. If two major units of a flotilla came within a hundred kilometers, it was reckoned close. However, the time lag of communication dropped toward zero, the reliability of detection swooped upward, deadly encounters grew ever more frequent.

It became possible to know fairly well what the opponent had in play and where. It became possible to devise and guide a campaign.

Cajal remarked in a tape report to Saracoglu: "If every Ythrian system were as strong as Laura, we might need the whole Imperial Navy to break them. Here they possess, or did possess, approximately half the number of hulls that I do—which is to say, a sixth the number we deemed adequate for handling the entire Domain. Of course, that doesn't mean their actual strength is in proportion. By our standards, they are weak in heavy craft. But their destroyers, still more their corvettes and torpedo boats, make an astonishing total. I am very glad that no other enemy sun, besides Quetlan itself, remotely compares with Laura!

"Nevertheless, we are making satisfactory progress. In groundling language—a technical summary will be appended for you—we can say that about half of what remains to them is falling back on Avalon. We intend to follow them there, dispose of them, and thus have the planet at our mercy.

"The rest of their fleet is disengaging, piecemeal, and retreating spaceward. Doubtless they mean to scatter themselves throughout the uninhabitable planets, moons, and asteroids of the system, where they must have bases, and carry on hit-and-run war. This should prove more nuisance than menace, and once we are in occupation their government will recall them. Probably larger vessels, which have hyperdrive, will seek to go reinforce elsewhere: again, not unduly important.

"I am not underestimating these people. They fight skillfully and doggedly. They must expect to use planetary defenses in conjunction with those ships moving toward the home world. God grant, more for their sakes than ours, most especially for the sakes of innocent females and children of both races, God grant their leaders see reason and capitulate before we hurt them too badly."

The half disk of Avalon shone sapphire swirled with silver, small and dear among the stars. Morgana was coming around the dark side. Ferune remembered night flights beneath it with Wharr, and murmured, *"O moon of my delight that knows no wane—"*

"Hoy?" said Daniel Holm's face in the screen.

"Nothing. My mind drifted." Ferune drew breath. "We've skimpy time. They're coming in fast. I want to make certain you've found no serious objection to the battle plan as detailed."

The laser beam took a few seconds to flicker between flagship and headquarters. Ferune went back to his memories.

"I bugger well do!" Holm growled. "I already told you. You've brought *Hell Rock* too close in. Prime target."

"And I told you," Ferune answered, "we no longer need her command capabilities." *I wish we did, but our losses have been too cruel.* "We do need her firepower and, yes, her attraction for the enemy. That's why I never counted on getting her away to Quetlan. There she'd be just one more unit. Here she's the keystone of our configuration. If things break well, she will survive. I know the scheme is not guaranteed, but it was the best my staff, computers, and self could produce on what you also knew beforehand would be short notice. To argue, or modify much, at this late hour is to deserve disaster."

Silence. Morgana rose further from Avalon as the ship moved.

"Well . . ." Holm slumped. He had lost weight till his cheekbones stood forth like ridges in upland desert. "I s'pose."

"Uncle, a report of initial contact," Ferune's aide said.

"Already?" The First Marchwarden of Avalon turned to the comscreen. "You heard, Daniel Holm? Fair winds forever." He cut the circuit before the man could reply. "Now," he told the aide, "I want a recomputation of the optimum orbit for this ship. Project the Terran's best moves . . . from their viewpoint, in the light of what information we have . . . and adjust ours accordingly."

Space sparkled with fireworks. Not every explosion, nor most, signified a hit; but they were thickening.

Three Stars slammed from her cruiser. At once her detectors reported an object. Analysis followed within seconds—a Terran Meteor, possible to intercept, no nearby companions. "Quarry!" Vodan sang out. "Five minutes to range."

A yell went through the hull. Two weeks and worse of maneuver, cooped in metal save for rare, short hours when the flotilla dipped into combat, had been heavy chains to lift.

His new vector pointed straight at Avalon. The planet waxed; he flew toward Eyath. He had no doubts about his victory. *Three Stars* was well blooded. She was necessarily larger than her Imperial counterpart—Ythrian requirements for room—and therefore had a trifle less acceleration. But her firepower could on that account be made greater, and had been.

Vodan took feet off perch and hung in his harness. He spread his wings. Slowly he beat them, pumping his blood full of oxygen, his body full of strength and swiftness. It tingled, it sang. He heard a rustling aft as his four crewfolk did likewise. Stars gleamed above and around him.

Three representations occupied Daniel Holm's office and, now, his mind. A map of Avalon indicated the ground installations. The majority were camouflaged and, he hoped, he would have prayed if he believed, were unknown to the enemy. Around a holographic world globe, variegated motes swung in multitudinous orbits. Many stations had been established a few days ago, after being transported to their launch sites from underground automated factories which were also supposed to be secret. Finally a display tank indicated what was known of the shifting ships out yonder.

Holm longed for a cigar, but his mouth was too withered by too much smoke in the near past. *Crock, how I could use a drink!* he thought. Neither might that be; the sole allowable drugs were those which kept him alert without exacting too high a metabolic price.

He stared at the tank. *Yeh. They're sure anxious to nail our flagship. Really converging on her.*

He sought the window. While Gray still lay shadowy, the first dawnlight was picking out houses and making the waters sheen. Above, the sky arched purple, its stars blurred by the negagrav screens. They had to keep changing pattern, to give adequate coverage while allowing air circulation. That stirred up restless little winds, cold and a bit damp. But on the whole the country reached serene. The storms were beyond the sky and inside the flesh.

Holm was alone, more alone than ever in his life, though the forces of a world awaited his bidding. It would have to be his; the computers could merely advise. He guessed that he felt like an infantryman preparing to charge.

"There!" Rochefort shouted.

He saw a moving point of light in a viewscreen set to top magnification. It grew as he watched, a needle, a spindle, a toy, a lean sharp-snouted hunter on whose flank shone three golden stars.

The vectors were almost identical. The boats neared more slowly than they rushed toward the planet. *Odd,* Rochefort thought, *how close Ansa's come without meeting any opposition. Are they just going to offer token resistance? I'd hate to kill somebody for a token.* Avalon was utterly beautiful. He was approaching in such wise that on his left the great disk had full daylight—azure, turquoise, indigo, a thousand different blues beneath the intercurving purity of cloud, a land mass glimpsed green and brown and tawny. On his right was darkness, but moonlight shimmered mysteriously across oceans and weather.

Wa Chaou sent a probe of lightning. No result showed. The range was extreme. It wouldn't stay thus for long. Now Rochefort needed no magnification to see the hostile hull. In those screens it was as yet a glint. But it slid across the stellar background, and it was more constant than the fireballs twinkling around.

Space blazed for a thousand kilometers around that giant spheroid which was *Hell Rock*. She did not try to dodge; given her mass, that was futile. She orbited her world. The enemy ships plunged in, shot, went by and maneuvered to return. They were many, she was one, save for a cloud of attendant Meteors and Comets. Her firepower, though, was awesome; still more were her instrumental and computer capabilities. She had not been damaged. When a section of screen must be turned off to launch a pack of missiles, auxiliary energy weapons intercepted whatever was directed at the vulnerable spot.

Rays had smitten. But none could be held steady through an interval sufficient to get past those heavy plates. Bombs whose yield was lethal radiation exploded along the limits of her defense. But the gamma quanta and neutrons were drunk down by layer upon layer of interior shielding. The last of them, straggling to those deep inner sections where organic creatures toiled, were so few that ordinary medication nullified their effects.

She had been built in space and would never touch ground. A planetoid in her own right, she blasted ship after ship that dared come against her.

Cajal's Supernova was stronger. But *Valenderay* must not be risked. The whole purpose of all that armament and armor was to protect the command of a fleet. When word reached him, he studied the display tank. "We're wasting lesser craft. She eats them," he said, chiefly to himself. "I hate to send capital vessels in. The enemy seems to have much more defensive stuff than we looked for, and it's bound to open up on us soon. But that close,

speed and maneuverability don't count for what they
should. We must have sheer force to take that monster
out; and we must do that before we can pose any serious
threat to the planet." He tugged his beard. "S-s-so . . .
between them, *Persei, Ursa Minor, Regulus, Jupiter,* and
attendants should be able to do the job . . . fast enough
and at enough of a distance that they can also cope with
whatever the planet may throw."

Tactical computers ratified and expanded his decision.
He issued the orders.

Vodan saw a torpedo go past. "Hai, good!" he cried.
Had he applied a few megadynes less of decelerative
force, that warhead would have connected. The missile
braked and came about, tracking, but one of his gunners destroyed it.

The Terran boat crawled ahead, off on the left and
low. Vodan's instruments reported she was exerting more
sideways than forward thrust. The pilot must mean to
cross the Ythrian bows, bare kilometers ahead, loose a
cloud of radar window, and hope the concerted fire of
his beam guns would penetrate before the other could
range him. Since Ythrians, unlike Terrans, did not fight
wearing spacesuits—how could anybody not go insane after more than a few hours in those vile, confining things?
—a large hole in a compartment killed them.

The son-of-a-zirraukh was good, Vodan acknowledged
happily. Lumbering and awkward as most space engage-
ments were, this felt almost like being back in air. The
duel had lasted until Avalon stood enormous in the bow
screens. In fact, they were closer to atmosphere than was
prudent at their velocity. They'd better end the affair.

Vodan saw how.

He went on slowing at a uniform rate, as if he intended
presently to slant off. He thought the Terran would think:
*He sees what I plan. When I blind his radar, he will
sheer from my fire in an unpredictable direction. Ah,
but we're not under hyperdrive. He can't move at anything like the speed of energy beams. Mine can cover
the entire cone of his possible instantaneous positions.*

For that, however, the gun platform needed a constant
vector. Otherwise too many unknowns entered the equations and the target had an excellent chance of escaping.

For part of a minute, if Vodan had guessed right, the
Meteor would forego its advantage of superior mobility.
And . . . he had superior weapons.

The Terran might well expect a torpedo and figure he
could readily dispose of the thing. He might not appreciate
how very great a concentration of energy his opponent
could bring to bear for a short while, when all projectors were run at overload.

Vodan made his calculations. The gunners made their
settings.

The Meteor passed ahead, dwarfish upon luminous Avalon. A sudden, glittering fog sprang from her. At explosive speed, it spread to make a curtain. And it hid one
ship as well as the other.

Rays sliced through, seeking. Vodan knew exactly
where to aim his. They raged for 30 seconds.

The metal dust scattered. Avalon again shone enormous
and calm. Vodan ceased fire before his projectors should
burn out. Nothing came from the Meteor. He used magnification, and saw the hole which gaped astern by her drive
cones. Air gushed forth, water condensing ghost-white until it vanished into void. Acceleration had ended entirely.

Joy lofted in Vodan. "We've struck him!" he shouted.

"He could launch his torps in a flock," the engineer
worried.

"No. Come look if you wish. His powerplant took
that hit. He has nothing left except his capacitor bank.
If he can use that to full effect, which I doubt, he still
can't give any object enough initial velocity to worry us."

"Kh'hng. Shall we finish him off?"

"Let's see if he'll surrender. Standard band. . . . Calling
Imperial Meteor. Calling Imperial Meteor."

One more trophy for you, Eyath!

Hell Rock shuddered and toned. Roarings rolled inward. Air drifted bitter with smoke, loud with screams
and bawled commands, running feet and threshing wings.
Compartment after compartment was burst open to space.
Bulkheads slid to seal twisted metal and tattered bodies off
from the living.

She fought. She could fight on under what was left
of her automata, well after the last of the crew were
gone whose retreat she was covering.

Those were Ferune, his immediate staff, and a few ratings from Mistwood who had been promised the right to abide by their Wyvan. They made their way down quaking, tolling corridors. Sections lay dark where fluoro-panels and facings were peeled back from the mighty skeleton.

"How long till they beat her asunder?" asked one at Ferune's back.

"An hour, maybe," he guessed. "They wrought well who built her. Of course, Avalon will strike before then."

"At what minute?"

"Daniel Holm must gauge that."

They crowded into their lifeboat. Ferune took the controls. The craft lifted against interior fields; valves swung ponderously aside; she came forth to sight of stars and streaked for home.

He glanced behind. The flagship was ragged, crumpled, cratered. In places metal had run molten till it congealed into ugliness, in other places it glowed. Had the bombard-ment been able to concentrate on those sites where de-fenses were down, a megaton warhead or two would have scattered the vessel in gas and ashes. But the likelihood of a precise hit at medium range was too slim to risk a supermissile against her remaining interception capability. Better to hold well off and gnaw with lesser blasts.

"Fare gladly into the winds," Ferune whispered. In this moment he put aside his new ways, his alien ways, and was of Ythri, Mistwood, Wharr, the ancestors and the children.

Avalon struck. The boat reeled. Under an intolerable load of light, viewscreens blanked. Briefly, illumination went out. The flyers crouched, packed together, in bellow-ing, heat, and blindness.

It passed. The boat had not been severely damaged. Backup systems cut in. Vision returned, inside and out-side. Aft, *Hell Rock* was silhouetted against the waning luridness of a fireball that spread across half heaven.

A rating breathed, "How . . . many . . . megatons?"

"I don't know," Ferune said. "Presumably ample to dis-pose of those Imperials we sucked into attacking us."

"A wonder we came through," said his aide. Every feather stood erect on him and shivered.

"The gases diffused across kilometers," Ferune reminded. "We've no screen field generator here, true. But by the time the front reached us, even a velocity equivalent of several million degrees could not raise our temperature much."

Silence clapped down, while smaller detonations glittered and faded in deeper distances and energy swords lunged. Eyes sought eyes. The brains behind were technically trained.

Ferune spoke it for them. "Ionizing radiation, primary and secondary. I cannot tell how big a dose we got. The meter went off scale. But we can probably report back, at least."

He gave himself to his piloting. Wharr waited.

Rochefort groped through the hull of *Hooting Star*. Interior grav generation had been knocked out; freefalling, they were now weightless. And airless beyond the enclosing armor. Stillness pressed inward till he heard his heart as strongly as he felt it. Beads of sweat broke off brow, nose, cheeks, and danced between eyes and faceplate, catching light in oily gleams. That light fell queerly across vacuum, undiffused, sharp-shadowed.

"Watch Out!" he croaked into his radio. "Watch Out, are you there?"

"I'm afraid not," said Helu's voice in his earplugs, from the engine room.

Rochefort found the little body afloat behind a panel cut half loose from its moorings. The same ray had burned through suit and flesh and out through the suit, cauterizing as it went so that only a few bloodgouts drifted around. "Wa Chaou bought it?" asked Helu.

"Yes." Rochefort hugged the Cynthian to his breast and fought not to weep.

"Any fire control left?"

"No."

"Well, I think I can squeeze capacitor power into the drive units. We can't escape the planet on that, but maybe we can land without vaporizing in transit. It'll take a pretty fabulous pilot. Better get back to your post, skipper."

Rochefort opened the helmet in order to close the bulged-out eyes, but the lids wouldn't go over them. He secured the corpse in a bight of loose wire and returned forward to harness himself in.

The call light was blinking. Mechanically, conscious mainly of grief, he plugged a jack into his suit unit and pressed the Accept button.

Anglic, accented, somehow both guttural and ringing: "—Imperial Meteor. Are you alive? This is the Avalonian. Acknowledge or we shoot."

"Ack . . . ack—" Before the noise in his throat could turn to sobbing, Rochefort said, "Yes, captain here."

"We will take you aboard if you wish."

Rochefort clung to the seatback, legs trailing aft. It hummed and crackled in his ears.

"Ythri abides by the conventions of war," said the unhuman voice. "You will be interrogated but not mistreated. If you refuse, we must take the precaution of destroying you."

Kh-h-h-h . . . m-m-m-m. . . .

"Answer at once! We are already too nigh Avalon. The danger of being caught in crossfire grows by the minute."

"Yes," Rochefort heard himself say. "Of course. We surrender."

"Good. I observe you have not restarted your engine. Do not. We are matching velocities. Link yourselves and jump off into space. We will lay a tractor beam on you and bring you in as soon as may be. Understood? Repeat."

Rochefort did.

"You fought well," said the Ythrian. "You showed deathpride. I shall be honored to welcome you aboard." And silence.

Rochefort called Helu. The men bent the ends of a cable around their waists, cracked the personnel lock, and prepared to tumble free. Kilometers off they saw the vessel that bore three stars, coming like an eagle.

The skies erupted in radiance.

When ragged red dazzlement had cleared from their vision, Helu choked, *"Ullah akbar, Ullah akbar. . . .* They're gone. What *was* it?"

"Direct hit," Rochefort said. Shock had blown some opening in him for numbness to drain out of. He felt strength rising in its wake. His mind flashed, fast as those war lightnings yonder but altogether cool. "They knew we were helpless and had no friends nearby. But in spite of a remark the captain made, they must've forgotten to look out for their own friends. The planet-based weapons have started shooting. I imagine the missiles include a lot of tracker torpedoes. Our engines were dead. His weren't. A torp homed on the emissions."

"What, no recognition circuits?"

"Evidently not. To lash out on the scale they seem to be doing, the Avalonians would've had to sacrifice quality for quantity, and rely on knowing the dispositions of units. It was not reasonable to expect any this close in. The fighting's further out. I daresay that torp was bound there, against some particular Imperial concentration, when it happened to pass near us."

"Um." They hung between darkness and glitter, breathing. "We've lost our ride," Helu said.

"Got to make do, then," Rochefort answered. "Come."

Beneath his regained calm, he was shaken at what appeared to be the magnitude of the Avalonian response.

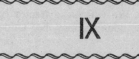

IX

When the boat had come to rest, thundering and shuddering ended, only bake-oven heat and scorched smells remaining, Rochefort let go of awareness.

He swam up from the nothing some minutes later. Helu stood over him. "Are you okay, skipper?" At first the engineer's voice seemed to come across a whining distance, and the sweat and soot on his face blurred into the haze which grayed all vision.

"Okay," Rochefort mumbled. "Get me . . . 'nother stimpill. . . ."

Helu did, with a glass of water that wrought a miracle on wooden tongue and parchment palate. "Hand of Fatima, what a ride!" he said unevenly. "I thought for certain we were finished. How did you ever get us down?"

"I don't remember," Rochefort answered.

The drug took hold, giving him back clarity of mind and senses, plus a measure of energy. He could reconstruct what he must have done in those last wild minutes. The ergs stored in the capacitors had not been adequate to kill the boat's entire velocity relative to the planetary surface. He had used them for control, for keeping the hull from being boiled off by the atmospheric friction that braked it. *Hooting Star* had skipped halfway around the globe on the tropopause, as a stone may be skipped over a lake, then screamed down on a long slant which would have ended in drowning—for the hole aft could not be patched, and a sealed-off engine room would have weighed too much when flooded—except that somehow he, Philippe Rochefort, had spotted (he recollected now) a chain of islands and achieved a crash landing on one. . . .

He spent a while in the awe of being alive. Afterward he unharnessed, and in their separate fashions he and Helu gave thanks; and they added a wish for the soul of Wa Chaou. By that time the hull had cooled to a point where they dared touch the lock. They found its outer valve had been torn loose when the boat plowed across ground.

"Good air," Helu said.

Rochefort inhaled gratefully. It was not just that the cabin was hot and stinking. No regeneration system on any spacecraft could do the entire work of a living world. This atmosphere that streamed to meet him smelled of ozone, iodine, greenery, flower fragrances; it was mild but brisk with breezes.

"Must be about Terran standard pressure," Helu went on. "How does a planet like this keep so much gas?"

"Surely you've met the type before," Rochefort said.

"Yes, but never stopped to wonder. Now that I've had the universe given back to me, I'd, uh, I'd like to know it better."

"Well, magnetism helps," Rochefort explained absently. "The core is small, but on the other hand the rotation is rapid, making for a reasonable value of H. Besides, the field has fewer charged particles to keep off, therefore fewer get by it to bounce off gas molecules. Likewise, the total ultraviolet and X radiation received is less. That sun's fairly close—we're getting about 10 percent more illumination than Terra does—but it's cooler than Sol. The energy distribution curve peaks at a lower frequency and the stellar wind is weak."

Meanwhile he sensed the gravity. His weight was four-fifths what it had been when the boat's interior field was set at standard pull. When you dropped sixteen kilos you noticed it at first—a bounciness, an exuberance of the body which the loss of a friend and the likelihood of captivity did not entirely quench—though you soon came to take the feeling for granted.

He stepped forth and looked around. Those viewscreens which remained functional had shown him this area was unpeopled. Inland it rose steeply. On the other side it sloped down to a beach where surf tumbled in a white violence whose noise reached him across more than a kilometer. Beyond, a syenite sea rolled to a horizon which, in spite of Avalon's radius, did not seem appreciably nearer than on Terra or Esperance. The sky above was a blue more bright and deep than he was used to. The sun was low, sinking twice as fast as on man's home. Its disk showed a bit larger, its hue was tinged golden. A sickle moon trailed, a fourth again the angular diameter of Luna seen from the ground. Rochefort knew it was actually smaller but, being close, raised twice the tides.

Occasional sparks and streaks blinked up there—monstrous explosions in space. Rochefort turned his mind from them. For him the war was presumably over. Let it be over for everybody, soon, before more consciousnesses died.

He gave his attention to the life encircling him. His vessel had gouged and charred through a dense mat of low-growing, beryl-green stuff which covered the island. "I suppose this explains why the planet has no native forests," he murmured, "which may in turn help explain why animal life is underevolved."

"Dinosaur stage?" Helu asked, watching a flock of clumsy winged creatures go by. They each had four legs; the basic vertebrate design on Avalon was hexapodal.

"Well, reptiloid, though some have developed features like hair or an efficient heart. By and large, they don't stand a chance against mammalian or avian life forms. The colonists had to do quite a lot of work to establish a stable mixed colony, and they keep a good deal of land reserved, including the whole equatorial continent."

"You've really studied them up, haven't you?"

"I was interested. And . . . seemed wrong to let them be only my targets. Seemed as if I ought to have some reality on the people I was going to fight."

Helu peered inland. Scattered shrubs and trees did exist. The latter were either low and thick or slim and supple, to survive the high winds that rapid rotation must often create. Autumn or no, many flowers continued in bloom, flamboyant scarlets and yellows and purples. Fruits clustered thick on several other kinds of plant.

"Can we eat local food?" Helu asked.

"Yes, of course," Rochefort said. "They'd never have made the success they did, colonizing, in the time they've had, if they couldn't draw on native resources. Some essentials are missing, assorted vitamins and whatnot. Imported domestic animals had to be revamped genetically on that account. We'd come down with deficiency diseases if we tried to eat Avalonian material exclusively. However, that wouldn't happen fast, and I've read that much of it is tasty. Unfortunately, I've read that much is poisonous, too, and I don't know which is which."

"Hm." Helu tugged his mustache and scowled. "We'd better call for somebody to come get us."

"No rush," said Rochefort. "Let's first learn what we can. The boat has supplies for weeks, remember. We just might be able to—" He stopped. Knowledge stung him. "Right now we've a duty."

Perforce they began by making a spade and pick out of scrap; and then the plant cover was tough and the soil beneath a stubborn clay. Sunset had perished in flame before they got Wa Chaou buried.

A full moon would have cast ample light; higher albedo as well as angular size and illumination gave it more than thrice the brilliance of Luna. Tonight's thin crescent was soon down. But the service could be read by two lamp-white companion planets and numberless stars. Most of their constellations were the same as those Rochefort had shared with Eve Davisson on Esperance. Three or four parsecs hardly count in the galaxy.

Does a life? I must believe so. "—Father, unto You in what form he did dream You, we commit this being our comrade; and we pray that You grant him rest, even as we

pray for ourselves. Lord have mercy, Lord have mercy,
Lord have mercy."

The gruesome little flashes overhead were dying away.

"Disengage," Cajal said. "Withdraw. Regroup in wide
orbits."

"But, but, Admiral," protested a captain of his staff,
"their ships—they'll use the chance to escape—disappear
into deep space."

Cajal's glance traveled from screen to screen on the
comboard. Faces looked out, some human, some nonhuman, but each belonging to an officer of Imperial Terra.
He found it hard to meet those eyes.

"We shall have to accept that," he told them. "What
we cannot accept is our present rate of losses. Laura is
only a prologue. If the cost of its capture proves such
that we have to wait for reinforcements, giving Ythri time
to reorganize, there goes our entire strategy. The whole
war will become long and expensive."

He sighed. "Let us be frank, citizens," he said. "Our
intelligence about this system was very bad. We had no
idea what fortifications had been created for Avalon—"

* * * * * *

In orbit, automated stations by the hundreds, whose
powerplants fed no engines but, exclusively, defensive
screens and offensive projectors; thus mortally dangerous
to come in range of. Shuttling between them and the
planet, hence guarded by them, a host of supply craft,
bringing whatever might be needed to keep the robots
shooting.

On the surface, and on the moon, a global grid of
detectors, launch tubes, energy weapons too immense for
spaceships to carry; some buried deep in rock or on the
ocean beds, some aboveground or afloat. The chance of a
vessel or missile getting through from space, unintercepted,
small indeed; and negafields shielding every vital spot.

In the air, a wasp swarm of pursuit craft on patrol,
ready to streak by scores against any who was so rash as
to intrude.

* * * * * *

"—and the defenders used our ignorance brilliantly.
They lured us into configurations that allowed those in-
strumentalities to inflict staggering damage. We're mouse-

trapped between the planet and their ships. Inferior though the enemy fleet is, under present circumstances it's disproportionately effective.

"We have no choice. We must change the circumstances, fast. If we pull beyond reach of the defenses, their fleet will again be outmatched and, I'm sure, will withdraw to the outer parts of this system as Captain K'thak has said."

"Then, sir?" asked a man. "What do we do then?"

"We make a reassessment," Cajal told him.

"Can we saturate their capabilities with what we've got on hand?" wondered another.

"I do not know," Cajal admitted.

"How could they do this?" cried a man from behind the bandages that masked him. His ship had been among those smashed. "A wretched colony—what's the population, fourteen million, mostly ranchers?—how was it possible?"

"You should understand that," Cajal reproved, though gently because he knew drugs were dulling brain as well as pain. "Given abundant nuclear energy, ample natural resources, sophisticated automatic technology, one needs nothing else except the will. Machines produce machines, exponentially. In a few years one has full production under way, limited only by available minerals; and an underpopulated, largely rural world like Avalon will have a good supply of those.

"I imagine," he mused aloud—because any thought was better than thought of what the navy had suffered this day—"that same pastoral economy simplified the job of keeping secret how great an effort was being mounted. A more developed society would have called on its existing industry, which is out in the open. The Avalonian leadership, once granted *carte blanche* by the electorate, made most of its facilities from zero, in regions where no one lives." He nodded. "Yes, citizens, let us confess we have been taken." Straightening: "Now we salvage what we can."

Discussion turned to ways and means. Battered, more than decimated, the Terran force was still gigantic. It was strewn through corresponding volumes of space, its units never motionless. Arranging for an orderly retreat was a major operation in itself. And there would be the un-

certainties, imponderables, and inevitable unforeseen ca-
tastrophes of battle. And the Avalonian space captains
must be presented with obvious chances to quit the fight
—not mere tactical openings, but a clear demonstration
that their withdrawal would not betray their folk—lest
they carry on to the death and bring too many Imperials
with them.

But at last the computers and underlings were at work
on details, the first moves of disengagement were started.
Cajal could be alone.

Or can I be? he thought. *Ever again? The ghosts are
crowding around.*

No. This debacle wasn't his fault. He had acted on
wrong information. Saracoglu— No, the governor was a
civilian who was, at most, peripherally involved in fact-
gathering and had worked conscientiously to help prepare.
Naval Intelligence itself—but Saracoglu had spoken sooth.
Real espionage against Ythri was impossible. Besides, Intelligence . . . the whole navy, the whole Empire . . . was
spread too thin across a reach too vast, inhuman, hostile;
in the end, perhaps all striving to keep the Peace of Man
was barren.

You did what you could. Cajal realized he had not done
badly. These events should not be called a debacle, simply
a disappointment. Thanks to discipline and leadership, his
fleet had taken far fewer losses than it might have; it
remained overwhelmingly powerful; he had learned les-
sons that he would use later on in the war.

Nevertheless the ghosts would not go away.

Cajal knelt. *Christ, who forgave the soldiers, help me
forgive myself. Saints, stand by me till my work is done.*
His look went from crucifix to picture. *Before everyone,
you, Elena who in Heaven must love me yet, since none
were ever too lowly for your love, Elena, watch over me.
Hold my hand.*

Beneath the flyers, the Middle Ocean rolled luminous
black. Above them were stars and a Milky Way whose
frostiness cut through the air's warmth. Ahead rose the
thundercloud mass of an island. Tabitha heard surf on its
beaches, a drumfire in the murmur across her face.

"Are they sure the thing landed here?" asked one of
the half-dozen Ythrians who followed her and Draun.

"Either here or in the sea," growled her partner. "What's the home guard for if not to check out detector findings? Now be quiet. And wary. If that was an Imperial boat—"

"They're marooned," Tabitha finished for him. "Helpless."

"Then why've they not called to be fetched?"

"Maybe their transmitter is ruined."

"And maybe they have a little scheme. I'd like that. We've many new-made dead this night. The more Terrans for hell-wind to blow ahead of them, the better."

"Follow your own orders and shut up," Tabitha snapped.

Sometimes she seriously considered dissolving her association with Draun. She had come to see over the years that he didn't really believe in the gods of the Old Faith, nor carry out their rites from traditionalism like most Highsky folk; no, he enjoyed those slaughterous sacrifices. And he had killed in duello more than once, on his own challenge, however much trouble he might have afterward in scraping together winner's gild for the bereaved. And while he seldom abused his slaves, he kept some, which she felt was the fundamental abuse.

Still—he was loyal and, in his arrogant way, generous to friends; his seamanship combined superbly with her managerial talents; he could be good company when he chose; his wife was sweet; his youngest cubs were irresistible, and loved their Kin-She Hrill who took them in her arms. . . .

I'm perfect? Not by a fertilizing long shot, considering how I let my mind meander!

They winged, she thrust above the strand and high over the island. Photoamplifier goggles showed it silver-gray, here and there speckled with taller growth; on boulders, dew had begun to catch starlight. (*How goes it yonder? The news said the enemy's been thrown back, but—*) She wished she were flying nude in this stroking, giddily perfumed air. But her business demanded coveralls, cuirass, helmet, boots. That which had been detected coming down might be a crippled Avalonian, but might equally well be — *Hoy!*

"Look." She pointed. "A fresh track." They swung about, crossed a ridge, and the wreck lay under them.

"Terran indeed," Draun said. She saw his crest and tail-feathers quiver in eagerness. He wheeled, holding a magnifier to his eyes. "Two outside. Hya-a-a-a-ah!"

"Stop!" Tabitha yelled, but he was already stooping.

She cursed the awkwardness of gravbelts, set controls and flung herself after him. Behind came the other Ythrians, blasters clutched to breasts while wings hastened their bodies. Draun had left his gun sheathed, had taken out instead the half-meter-long, heavy, crooked Fao knife.

"Stop!" Tabitha screamed into the whistle of split air. "Give them a chance to surrender!"

The humans, standing by a patch of freshly turned earth, heard. Their glances lifted. Draun howled his battle cry. One man yanked at a holstered sidearm. Then the hurricane was on him. Wings snapped around so it roared in the pinions. Two meters from ground, Draun turned his fall into an upward rush. His right arm swept the blade in a short arc; his left hand, on the back of it, urged it along. The Terran's head flew off the neck, hit the susin and horribly bounced. The body stood an instant, geysering blood, before it collapsed like a puppet on which the strings have been slashed.

"Hya-a-a-a-ah!" Draun shrieked. "Hell-winds blow you before my chothmates! Tell Illarian they are coming!"

The other Terran stumbled back. His own sidearm was out. He fired, a flash and boom in blackness.

Before they kill him too— Tabitha had no time for planning. She was in the van of her squad. The man's crazed gaze and snap shot were aimed at Draun, whose broad-winged shadow had not yet come about for a second pass. She dived from the rear, tackled him low, and rolled over, gripping fast. They tumbled; the belt wasn't able to lift both of them. She felt her brow slammed against a root, her cheek dragged abradingly over the susin.

His threshings stopped. She turned off her unit and crouched beside him. Pain and dizziness and the laboring of her lungs were remote. He wasn't dead, she saw, merely half stunned from his temple striking a rock. Blood oozed in the kinky black hair, but he stirred and his eyeballs were filled with starlight. He was tall, swarthy by Avalonian measure . . . people with such chromosomes generally settled beneath stronger suns than Laura. . . .

The Ythrians swooped near. Wind rushed in their quills.

Tabitha scrambled to her feet. She bestrode the Terran. Gun in hand, she gasped, "No. Hold back. No more killing. He's mine."

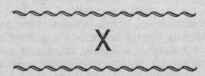

X

Ferune of Mistwood reported in at Gray, arranged his affairs and said his goodbyes within a few days.

To Daniel Holm: "Luck be your friend, First March-warden."

The man's mouth was stretched and unsteady. "You must have more time than—than—"

Ferune shook his head. The crest drooped ragged; most feathers that remained to him were lusterless white; he spoke in a mutter. His grin had not changed. "No, I'm afraid the medics can't stimulate regeneration in this case. Not when every last cell got blasted. Pity the Imperials didn't try shooting us full of mercury vapor. But you'd find that inconvenient."

Yes, you've more tolerance for heavy metals than humans do, went uselessly through Holm, *but less for hard radiation.* The voice trudged on: "As is, I am held together by drugs and baling wire. Most of those who were with me are already dead, I hear. But I had to get my powers and knowledge transferred to you, didn't I, before I rest?"

"To me?" the man suddenly couldn't hold back. "Me who killed you?"

Ferune stiffened. "Come off that perch, Daniel Holm. If I thought you really blame yourself, I would not have left you in office—probably not alive; anyone that stupid would be dangerous. You were executing my plan, and bloody-gut well it worked too, kh'hng?"

Holm knelt and laid his head on the keelbone. It was sharp, when flesh had melted from above, and the skin was fever-hot and he could feel how the heart stammered. Ferune shifted to handstance. Wings enfolded the man

and lips kissed him. "I flew higher because of you,"
Ferune said. "If war allows, honor us by coming to my
rite. Fair winds forever."

He left. An adjutant helped him into a car and took
him northward, to the woodlands of his choth and to
Wharr who awaited him.

"Permit me to introduce myself. I am Juan de Jesús
Cajal y Palomares of Nuevo México, commanding His
Imperial Majesty's naval forces in the present campaign.
You have my word as a Terran officer that the beam is
tight, the relays are automatic, this conversation will be
recorded but not monitored, and the tape will be classified
secret."

The two who looked out of the screens were silent, until
Cajal grew overaware of the metal which enclosed him,
background pulse of machinery and slight chemical taint
in the air blown from ventilators. He wondered what impression he was making on them. There was no way to
tell from the old Ythrian—Liaw? Yes, Liaw—who evidently represented civil authority. That being sat like a
statue of grimness, except for the smoldering yellow eyes.
Daniel Holm kept moving, cigar in and out of his mouth,
fingers drumming desktop, tic in the left cheek. He was
haggard, unkempt, stubbly, grimy, no hint of Imperial
neatness about him. But he scarcely seemed humble.

He it was who asked at length: "Why?"

"¿ Por qué?" responded Cajal in surprise. "Why I had a
signal shot down to you proposing a conference? To discuss terms, of course."

"No, this secrecy. Not that I believe you about it, or
anything else."

Cajal felt his cheeks redden. *I must not grow angry.*
"As you wish, Admiral Holm. However, please credit me
with some common sense. Quite apart from the morality
of letting the slaughter and waste of wealth proceed, you
must see that I would prefer to avoid further losses. That
is why we're orbiting Avalon and Morgana at a distance
and have made no aggressive move since battle tapered
off last week. Now that we've evaluated our options, I
am ready to talk; and I hope you've likewise done some
hard thinking. I am not interested in pomp or publicity.
Such things only get in the way of reaching practical

solutions. Therefore the confidential nature of our parley. I hope you'll take the chance to speak as frankly as I mean to, knowing your words need not commit you."

"Our word does," Holm said.

"Please," Cajal urged. "You're angry, you'd kill me were you able, nevertheless you're a fellow professional. We both have our duties, however distasteful certain of them may be."

"Well, get on with it, then. What d'you want?"

"To discuss terms, I said. I realize we three alone can't authorize or arrange the surrender, but—"

"I think you can," Liaw interrupted: a low, dry, harshly accented Anglic. "If you fear court-martial afterward, we will grant you asylum."

Cajal's mouth fell open. "What are you saying?"

"We must be sure this is no ruse. I suggest you bring your ships one at a time into close orbit, for boarding. Transportation home for the crews will be made available later."

"Do you . . . do you—" Cajal swallowed. "Sir, I'm told your proper title translates more or less into 'Judge' or 'Lawspeaker.' Judge, this is no time for humor."

"If you don't want to give in," Holm said, "what's to discuss?"

"Your capitulation, *por Díos!*" Cajal's fist smote the arm of his chair. "I'm not going to play word games. You've delayed us too long already. But your fleet has been smashed. Its fragments are scattered. A minor detachment from our force can hunt them down at leisure. We control all space around you. You've no possibility of outside help. Whatever might recklessly be sent from other systems would be annihilated in detail; and the admiralties there know it. If they go anywhere with what pitiful strength they have, it'll be to Quetlan." He leaned forward. "We'd hate to bombard your planet. Please don't compel us to."

"Go right ahead," Holm answered. "Our interceptor crews would enjoy the practice."

"But—are you expecting blockade runners to—to— Oh, I know how big a planet is. I know an occasional small craft could sneak past our detector grids, our patrols and stations. But I also know how very small such craft must be, and how very occasional their success."

Holm drew savagely on his cigar before he stabbed it into its smoke. "Yes, sure," he snapped. "Standard technique. Eliminate a space fleet, and its planet has to yield or you'll pound it into radioactive slag. Nice work for a man, that, hunh? Well, my colleagues and I saw this war coming years back. We knew we'd never have much of a navy by comparison, if only because you bastards have so much more population and area behind you. But defense— Admiral, you're at the end of a long line of communication and supply. The border worlds aren't geared to produce anything like the amount of stuff you require; it has to come from deeper in the Empire. We're *here*, set up to make everything necessary as fast as necessary. We can't come after you. But we can bugger well swamp whatever you throw at us."

"Absolutely?"

"Okay, once in a great while, by sheer luck, you doubtless could land a warhead, and it might be big and dirty. We'd weather that, and the home guard has decontamination teams. Chances of its hitting anything important are about like drawing three for a royal flush. No ship of yours can get close enough with an energy projector husky enough to pinken a baby's bottom. But there're no size and mass limits on our ground-based photon weapons; we can use whole rivers to cool their generators while their snouts whiff you out of our sky. Now tell me why in flaming chaos we should surrender."

Cajal sat back. He felt as if struck from behind.

"No harm in learning what conditions you meant to offer," Liaw said, toneless.

Face saving? Those Ythrians are supposed to be satanically proud, but not to the point of lunacy. Hope knocked in Cajal. "Honorable terms, of course," he said. "Your ships must be sequestered, but they will not be used against Ythri and personnel may go home, officers to keep their sidearms. Likewise for your defensive facilities. You must accept occupation and cooperate with the military government, but every effort will be made to respect your laws and customs, individuals will have the right to petition for redress of grievances, and Terran violators of the statutes will be punished as severely as Avalonian. Actually, if the population behaves correctly,

I doubt if a large percentage will ever even see an Imperial marine."

"And after the war?"

"Why, that's for the Crown to decide, but I presume you'll be included in a reorganized Sector Pacis, and you must know Governor Saracoglu is efficient and humane. Insofar as possible, the Empire allows home rule and the continuation of local ways of life."

"Allows. The operative word. But let it pass. Let us assume a degree of democracy. Could we stop immigrants from coming until they outvoted us?"

"Well . . . well, no. Citizens are guaranteed freedom of movement. That's one of the things the Empire is for. Confound it, you can't selfishly block progress just because you prefer archaism."

"There is no more to discuss. Good day, Admiral."

"No, wait! Wait! You can't—condemn your whole people to war by yourselves!"

"If the Khruaths and the Parliament change their views, you will be informed."

"But listen, you're letting them die for nothing," Cajal said frantically. "This frontier is going to be straightened out. You, the whole Domain of Ythri have no power to stop that. You can only prolong the murderous, maiming farce. And you'll be punished by worse peace terms than you could have had. Listen, it's not one-sided. You're coming into the Empire. You'll get trade, contact, protection. Cooperate now and I swear you'll start out as a chartered client state, with all the privileges that means. Within years, individuals will be getting Terran citizenship. Eventually the whole of Avalon could become part of Greater Terra. For the love of God, be realistic!"

"We are," said Liaw.

Holm leered. Both screens blanked.

Cajal sat for minutes, staring. *They can't have been serious. They can't.* Twice he reached toward his intercom. Have them called; maybe this was some childish insistence that the Empire beg them to negotiate. . . .

His hand drew back. *No. I am responsible for our own dignity.*

Decision came. Let Plan Two be set in train. Leave the calculated strength here to invest Avalon. Comparatively little would be required. The sole real purpose was to keep this world's considerable resources from flowing to Ythri and these bases from menacing Cajal's lines back to the Empire. Siege would tie up more men and vessels than occupation would have done, but he could spare them.

The important thing was not to lose momentum. Rather, his freed ships must be off immediately to help in simultaneous assaults on Khrau and Hru. He'd direct the former himself, his second in command the latter. What they had learned here would be quite helpful.

And he was sure of quick victories yonder. Intelligence had failed to learn the extent of Avalonian arming, but not to discover the fact itself; that could not be concealed. By the same token, he knew that no other planet of the Domain had had a Daniel Holm nagging it over the years to build against this storm. He knew that the other Ythrian colonial fleets were small and poorly coordinated, the worlds unarmed.

Quetlan, the home sun, was more formidable. But let him rip spectacularly enough through the spaces between, and he dared hope his enemies would have the wisdom to capitulate before he stabbed them in the heart.

And afterward a few distorted molecules, recording the armistice, will give us Avalon. Very well. Better than fighting. . . . Do they know this? Do they merely want to keep, for a few weeks more, the illusion of freedom? Well, I hope the price they'll be charged for that—levies, restrictions, revisions of their whole society, that might otherwise have been deemed unnecessary—I hope they won't find the price unendurably steep—because endure it they must.

Before sunrise, Ferune departed Mistwood.

That day his home country bore its name well. Fog blew cold, wet, and blinding off the sea. Smokiness prowled the glooms around thick boles of hammerbranch, soaring trunks of lightningrod; moisture dripped from boughs onto fallen leaves, and where it struck a pool which had formed among the ringed stems of a sword-of-sorrow, it made a tiny glass chiming. But deeper inland, where Old Avalon remained, a boomer tree frightened beasts that might have grazed on it, and this noise rolled beneath the house of Ferune and echoed off the hanging shields of his ancestors.

Wings gathered. A trumpet sounded through night. Forth came his sons to meet their chothmates. They carried the body on a litter between them. His uhoths fluttered about, puzzled at his quietness. His widow led the way. Flanking were his daughters, their husbands and grown children, who bore lit torches.

Wings beat. The flight cut upward. When it rose past the fog, this was turned to blue-shadowed white under an ice-pale eastern lightening. Westward over sea, the last stars glimmered in royal purple.

Still the folk mounted, until they were near the top of what unaided flesh could reach. Here the airs whittered thin and chill; but on the rim of a twilit world, the snowpeaks of the Weathermother were kindled by a yet hidden sun.

All this while the flight beat north. Daniel Holm and his family, following in heavy garments and breathing masks, saw wings glow across heaven in one tremendous spearhead. They could barely make out the torchflames which streamed at its point, as sparks like the waning stars. More clearly came the throb from under those pinions. Apart from that, silence was total.

They reached wilderness, a land of crags, boulders, and swift-running streams. There the sons of Ferune stopped. Wings outspread, they hovered on the first faint warmth of morning, their mother before them. Around circled their near kin; and in a wheel, the choth surrounded these. And the sun broke over the mountains.

To Ferune came the new Wyvan of Mistwood. Once more he blew the horn, and thrice he called the name of the dead. Wharr swept by, to kiss farewell. Then the Wyvan spoke the words of the New Faith, which was two thousand years old.

"High flew your spirit on many winds; but downward upon you at last came winging God the Hunter. You met Him in pride, you fought Him well, from you He has honor. Go hence now, that which the talons left, be water and leaves, arise in the wind; and spirit, be always remembered."

His sons tilted the litter. The body fell, and after it the torches.

Wharr slanted off in the beginning measures of the sky dance. A hundred followed her.

Hanging afar, between emptiness and immensity, Daniel Holm said to Christopher: "And that Terran thought we'd surrender."

XI

Liaw of The Tarns spoke. "We are met in the Great Khruath of Avalon, that free folk may choose their way. Our enemy has taken elsewhere most of the might which he brought against us. This is no victory, since those vessels will make war upon the rest of the Domain. Meanwhile he has left sufficient ships to hold us cut off. They are unlikely to attack our world. But they will seek to find and root out our bases among the sister planets and the few warcraft of ours that are left in space. Save for what harassment our brethren aboard can contrive, we have no means of taking the offensive. Our defenses we can maintain indefinitely. Yet no pledge can be given that great harm will not be wrought on Avalon, should the foe launch a determined effort. He has declared that in the end we are sure to be subjugated. This is possibly true. He has then declared that we can expect better treatment if we yield now than if we fight on, though at best we will come under Imperial law and custom. This is certainly true.

"They who speak for you rejected the demand, as was their duty until you could be summoned to decide. I remind you of the hazards of continued war and the threat of a harsh peace should we lose. I remind you furthermore that if we do resist, the free folk of Avalon must give up many of their rights and submit to the dictation of military leaders for as long as the strife may last.

"What say the choths?"

He and his colleagues stood on the olden site, First

Island in the Hesperian Sea. At their backs rose the house
of David Falkayn; before them greensward slanted toward
beach and surf. But no booths or tents had been raised,
no ships lay at anchor, no swarms of delegates flew down
to form ranks beneath the trees. Time was lacking for
ceremonious assemblies. Those elected at regional meetings, and those individuals who signified a wish to speak,
were present electronically.

A computer-equipped staff worked hard inside the
house. However taciturn the average Ythrian was, however unwilling to make a fool of himself by declaiming
the obvious, still, when some two million enfranchised
adults were hooked into a matter of as great moment as
this, the questions and comments that arrived must be
filtered. Those chosen to be heard must wait their turns.

Arinnian knew he would be called. He sat by Eyath before an outsize screen. They were alone on the front,
hence lowest bench. At their backs the tiers rose, the
household of Lythran and Blawsa crowded thereon, to
the seat of the master and his lady. Liaw's slow words
only deepened the quiet in that broad, dark, weapon-
hung chamber; and so did the rustle of feathers, the
scrape of claws or alatans, when someone shifted a little. The air was filled with the woodsmoke odor of Ythrian
bodies. A breeze, gusting in from a window open on
rain, added smells of damp earth and stirred the banners
that hung from high rafters.

"—report on facts concerning—"

The image in the screen became that of a rancher.
Behind him could be seen the North Coronan prairie, a
distant herd, a string of quadrupedal burden-bearing zirraukhs led by a flapping youth, a more up-to-date truck
which passed overhead. He stated, "Food production
throughout the Plains of Long Reach has been satisfactory this year. The forecasts for next season are optimis-
tic. We have achieved 75 percent storage of preserved
meat in bunkers proofed against radioactive contamina-
tion, and expect to complete this task by midwinter.
Details are filed in Library Central. Finished." The scan
returned to the High Wyvans, who promptly called on another area representative.

Eyath caught Arinnian's arm. He felt the pulse in her
fingers, and the claws on the two encircling thumbs bit

him. He looked at her. The bronze-brown crest was
stiffly raised, the amber eyes like lanterns. Fangs gleamed
between her lips. "Must they drone on till eternity molders?" she breathed.

"They need truth before they decide," he whispered
back, and felt the disapproving stares between his shoulderblades.

"What's to decide—when Vodan's in space?"

"You help him best by patience." He wondered who he
was to give counsel. Well, Eyath was young (*me too,
but this day I feel old*) and it was cruel that she could
hope for no word of her betrothed until, probably, war's
end. No mothership could venture in beaming range of
beleaguered Avalon.

At least it was known that Vodan's had been among
those which escaped. Too many orbited in wreck. More
Terrans had been destroyed, of course, thanks to the trap
that Ferune and Holm sprang. But one Ythrian slain was
too many, Arinnian thought, and a million Terrans were
too few.

"—call on the chief of the West Coronan guard."

He scrambled to his feet, realized that was unnecessary,
and opined that he'd better remain standing than compound his gaucherie by sitting down again before he had
spoken. "Uh, Arinnian of Stormgate. We're in good shape,
equipping, training, and assigning recruits as fast as they
come in. But we want more. Uh, since nobody has mentioned it, I'd like to remind people that except for ranking officers, home-guard service is part-time and the volunteer's schedule can be set to minimize interference with
his ordinary work. Our section's cooperation with the North
Oronesians is now being extended through the entire archipelago, and we aim to do likewise in southerly and
easterly directions till, uh, we've an integrated command
for the Brendan's, Fiery, and Shielding Islands as well,
to protect the whole perimeter of Corona.

"Uh, on behalf of my father, the First Marchwarden,
I want to point out a considerable hole in Avalon's defense, namely the absence of a guard for Equatoria, nothing there except some projector and missile launching
sites. True, the continent's uninhabited, but the Terrans
know that, and if they consider an invasion, they aren't
likely to care about preserving a piece of native ecology

intact. I, uh, will receive suggestions about this and pass them along the proper channels." His tongue was dry. "Finished."

He lowered himself. Eyath took his hand, gentler this time. Thank fortune, no one wanted to question him. He could be crisp in discussing strictly technical problems with a few knowledgeable persons, but two million were a bit much for a man without political instincts.

The talk seemed interminable. And yet, at the end, when the vote was called, when Liaw made his matter-of-fact announcement that the data bank recorded 83 percent in favor of continued resistance, scarcely six hours had passed. Humans couldn't have done it.

"Well," Arinnian said into the noise of cramped wings being stretched, "no surprises."

Eyath tugged at him. "Come," she said. "Get your belt. I want to use my muscles before dinner."

Rain beat through dusk, cold and tasting of sky. When they came above the clouds, he and she turned east to get away from their chothmates who also sought exercise. Snowpeaks and glaciers thrust out of whiteness, into a blue-black where gleamed the early stars and a few moving sparks which were orbital fortresses.

They fared awhile in silence, until she said: "I'd like to join the guard."

"Hm? Ah. Yes; welcome."

"But not fly patrol. That's essential, I know, and pleasant if the weather's halfway good; but I don't want a lot of pleasure. Look, see Camelot rising yonder. Vodan may be huddled inside a dead moon of it, waiting and waiting for a chance to hazard his life."

"What would you prefer?" he asked.

Her wings beat more steadily than her voice. "You must be caught in a hurricane of work, which is bound to stiffen. Surely your staff's too small, else why would you be so tired? Can't I help?"

"M-m . . . well—"

"Your assistant, your fetch-and-carry lass, even your personal secretary? I can take an electro-cram in the knowledge and skills, and be ready to start inside a few days."

"No. That's rough."

"I'll survive. Try me. Fire me if I can't grip the task,

and we'll stay friends. I believe I can, though. Maybe better than someone who hasn't known you all these years, and who can be given another job. I'm bright and energetic. Am I not? And . . . Arinnian, I so much need to be with you, till this cripplewing time is outlived."

She reached toward him. He caught her hand. "Very well, galemate." In the wan light she flew as beautiful as ever beneath sun or moon.

"Yes, I'll call for a vote tomorrow," Matthew Vickery said.

"How d'you expect it'll go?" Daniel Holm asked.

The President sighed. "How do you think? Oh, the war faction won't bring in quite the majority of Parliament that it did of the Khruath. A few members will vote their convictions rather than their mail. But I've seen the analysis of that mail, and of the phone calls and— Yes, you'll get your damned resolution to carry on. You'll get your emergency powers, the virtual suspension of civilian government you've been demanding. I do wish you'd read some of those letters or watch some of those tapes. The fanaticism might frighten you as it does me. I never imagined we had that much latent insanity in our midst."

"It's insane to fight for your home?"

Vickery bit his lip. "Yes, when nothing can be gained."

"I'd say we gain quite a chunk. We kicked a sizable hole in the Terran armada. We're tying up a still bigger part, that was originally supposed to be off to Ythri."

"Do you actually believe the Domain can beat the Empire? Holm, the Empire can't *afford* to compromise. Take its viewpoint for a minute if you can. The solitary keeper of the peace among thousands of wildly diverse peoples; the solitary guardian of the borders against the barbarian and the civilized predatory alien, who carry nuclear weapons. The Empire has to be more than almighty. It must maintain credibility, universal belief that it's irresistible, or hell's kettle boils over."

"My nose bleeds for the Empire," Holm said, "but His Majesty will have to solve his problems at somebody else's expense. He gets no free rides from us. Besides, you'll note the Terrans didn't keep throwing themselves at Avalon."

"They had no need to," Vickery replied. "If the need

does arise, they'll be back in force. Meanwhile we're contained." He filled his lungs. "I admit your gamble paid off extraordinarily—"

"Please. 'Investment.' And not mine. Ours."

"But don't you see, now there's nothing further we can use it for except a bargaining counter? We can get excellent terms, and I've dealt with Governor Saracoglu, I know he'll see to it that agreements are honored. Rationally considered, what's so dreadful about coming under the Empire?"

"Well, we'd begin by breaking our oath to Ythri. Sorry, chum. Deathpride doesn't allow."

"You sit here mouthing obsolete words, but I tell you, the winds of change are blowing."

"I understand that's a mighty old phrase too," Holm said. "Ferune had one still older that he liked to quote. How'd it go? '—their finest hour—' "

Tabitha Falkayn shoved off from the dock and hauled on two lines in quick succession. Jib and mainsail crackled, caught the breeze, and bellied taut. The light, open boat heeled till foam hissed along the starboard rail, and accelerated outward. Once past the breakwater, on open sea, she began to ride waves.

"We're planing!" Philippe Rochefort cried.

"Of course," Tabitha answered. "This is a hydrofoil. 'Ware boom." She put the helm down. The yard swung, the hull skipped onto the other tack.

"No keel? What do you do for lateral resistance?"

She gestured at the oddly curved boards which lifted above either rail, pivoting in response to vanes upon them. "Those. The design's Ythrian. They know more about the ways of wind than men and men's computers can imagine."

Rochefort settled down to admire the view. It was superb. Billows marched as far as he could see, blue streaked with violet and green, strewn with sun-glitter, intricately white-foamed. They rumbled and whooshed. Fine spindrift blew off them, salty on the lips, spurring the blood where it struck bare skin. The air was cool, not cold, and singingly alive. Aft, the emerald heights of St. Li dwindled at an astonishing speed.

He had to admit the best part was the big, tawny girl

who stood, pipe in teeth, hawklike pet on shoulder, bleached locks flying, at the tiller. She wore nothing but a kilt, which the wind molded to her loins, and—to be sure—her knife and blaster.

"How far did you say?" he asked.

"'Bout thirty-five kilometers. A couple of hours at this rate. We needn't start back till sundown, plenty of starlight to steer by, so you'll have time for poking around."

"You're too kind, Donna," he said carefully.

She laughed. "No, I'm grateful for an excuse to take an outing. Especially since those patches of atlantis weed fascinate me. Entire ecologies, in areas that may get bigger'n the average island. And the fisher scout told me he'd seen a kraken grazing the fringes of this one. Hope we find him. They're a rare sight. Peaceful, though we dare not come too near something that huge."

"I meant more than this excursion," Rochefort said. "You receive me, a prisoner of war, as your house guest."

Tabitha shrugged. "Why not? We don't bother stockading what few people we've taken. They aren't going anywhere." Her eyes rested candidly on him. "Besides, I want to know you."

He wondered, with an inward thump, how well.

Somberness crossed her. "And," she said, "I hope to . . . make up for what happened. You've got to see that Draun didn't wantonly murder your friend. He's, well, impetuous; and a gun was being pulled; and it *is* wartime."

He ventured a smile. "Won't always be, Donna."

"Tabitha's the name, Philippe; or Hrill when I talk Planha. You don't, of course. . . . That's right. When you go home, I'd like you to realize we Ythrians aren't monsters."

"Ythrians? You?" He raised his brows.

"What else? Avalon belongs to the Domain."

"It won't for much longer," Rochefort said. In haste: "Against that day, I'll do what I can to show you we Terrans aren't monsters either."

He could not understand how she was able to grin so lightheartedly. "If it amuses you to think that, you're welcome. I'm afraid you'll find amusement in rather short supply here. Swimming, fishing, boating, hiking . . . and, yes, reading; I'm addicted to mystery stories and have a hefty stack, some straight from Terra. But that's just about the list. I'm the sole human permanently resident on St. Li, and between them, my business and my duties as a home-guard officer will keep me away a lot."

"I'll manage," he said.

"Sure, for a while," she replied. "The true Ythrians aren't hostile to you. They mostly look on war as an impersonal thing, like a famine where you might have to kill somebody to feed him to your young but don't hate him on that account. They don't go in for chitchat, but if you play chess you'll find several opponents."

Tabitha shortened the mainsheet and left it in a snap cleat. "Still," she said, "Avalonians of either kind don't mass-produce entertainment, the way I hear people do in the Empire. You won't find much on the screens except news, sleepifyingly earnest educational programs, and classic dramas which probably won't mean a thing to you. So . . . when you get bored, tell me and I'll arrange for your quartering in a town like Gray or Centauri."

"I don't expect to be," he said, and added in measured softness, "Tabitha." Nonetheless he spoke honestly when he shook his head, stared over the waters, and continued: "No, I feel guilty at not grieving more, at being as conscious as I am of my fantastic good luck."

"Ha!" she chuckled. "Someday I'll count up the different ways you were lucky. That was an unconverted island you were on, lad, pure Old Avalonian, including a fair sample of the nastier species."

"Need an armed man, who stays alert, fear any animals here?"

"Well, no doubt you could shoot a spathodont dead before it fanged you, though reptiloids don't kill easy. I wouldn't give odds on you against a pack of lycosauroids, however; and if a kakkelak swarm started running up your trousers—" Tabitha grimaced. "But those're tropical mainland beasties. You'd have had your troubles from the plants, which're wider distributed. Suppose a gust stirred the limbs of a surgeon tree as you walked by. Or . . . right across the ridge from where you were, I noticed a hollow full of hell shrub. You're no Ythrian, to breathe those vapors and live."

"Brrr!" he said. "What incurable romantic named this planet?"

"David Falkayn's granddaughter, when he'd decided this

was the place to go," she answered, grave again. "And they were right, both of them. If anything, the problem was to give native life its chance. Like the centaurs, who're a main reason for declaring Equatoria off limits, because they use bits of stone and bone in tool fashion and maybe in a million years they could become intelligent. And by the way, their protection was something Ythri insisted on, hunter Ythri, not the human pioneers."

She gestured. "Look around you," she said. "This is our world. It's going to stay ours."

No, he thought, and the day was dulled for him, *you're wrong, Tabitha-Hrill. My admiral is going to hammer your Ythrians until they have no choice but to hand you over to my Emperor.*

XII

Week after fire-filled week, the Terran armada advanced.

Cajal realized that despite its inauspicious start, his campaign would become a textbook classic. In fact, his decision about Avalon typified it. Any fool could smash through with power like his. As predicted, no other colonial system possessed armament remotely comparable to what he had encountered around Laura. What existed was handled with acceptable skill, but simply had no possibility of winning.

So any butcher could have spent lives and ships, and milled his opposition to dust in the course of months. Intelligence data and Cajal's own estimate had shown that this was the approach his enemies expected him to take. They in their turn would fight delaying actions, send raiders into the Empire, seek to stir up third parties such as Merseia, and in general make the war sufficiently costly for Terra that a negotiated peace would become preferable.

Cajal doubted this would work, even under the most favorable circumstances. He knew the men who sat on the Policy Board. Nevertheless he felt his duty was to avoid victory by attrition—his duty to both realms. Thus he had planned, not a cautious advance where every gain was consolidated before the next was made, but a swordstroke.

Khrau and Hru fell within days of the Terrans' crossing their outermost planetary orbits. Cajal left a few ships in either system and a few occupation troops, mostly technicians, on the habitable worlds.

These forces looked ludicrously small. Marchwarden Rusa collected a superior one and sought to recapture Khrau. The Terrans sent word and hung on. A detachment of the main fleet came back, bewilderingly soon, and annihilated Rusa's command.

On Hru III the choths rose in revolt. They massacred part of the garrison. Then the missiles struck from space. Not many were needed before the siege of the Imperials was called off. The Wyvans were rounded up and shot. This was done with proper respect for their dignity. Some of them, in final statements, urged their people to cooperate with relief teams being rushed from Esperance to the smitten areas.

Meanwhile the invaders advanced on Quetlan. From their main body, tentacles reached out to grab system after system in passing. Most of these Cajal did not bother to occupy. He was content to shatter their navies and go on. After six weeks, the sun of Ythri was englobed by lost positions.

Now the armada was deep into the Domain, more than 50 light-years from the nearest old-established Imperial base. The ornithoids would never have a better chance of cutting it off. If they gathered everything they had for a decisive combat—not a standup slugging match, of course; a running fight that might last weeks—they would still be somewhat outmatched in numbers. But they would have a continuing supply of munitions, which the Imperials would not.

Cajal gave them every opportunity. They obliged.

The Battle of Yarro Cluster took eight standard days, from the first engagement to the escape of the last lonely Ythrian survivors. But the first two of these days were preliminary and the final three were scarcely more than a

mopping up. Details are for the texts. In essence, Cajal
made use of two basic advantages. The first was surprise; he had taken pains to keep secret the large number
of ammunition carriers with him. The second was organization; he could play his fleet like an instrument, lur-
ing and jockeying the ill-coordinated enemy units into
death after death.

Perhaps he also possessed a third advantage, genius.
When that thought crossed his mind, he set himself a pen-
ance.

The remnants of Domain power reeled back toward
Quetlan. Cajal followed leisurely.

Ythri was somewhat smaller than Avalon, somewhat
drier, the cloud cover more thin and hence the land
masses showing more clearly from space, tawny and rusty
in hue, under the light of a sun more cool and yellow
than Laura. Yet it was very lovely, floating among the
stars. Cajal left that viewscreen on and from time to time
glanced thither, away from the face in his comboard.

The High Wyvan Trauvay said, "You are bold to enter our home." His Anglic was fluent, and he employed
a vocalizer for total clarity of pronunciation.

Cajal met the unblinking yellow eyes and answered,
"You agreed to a parley. I trust your honor." *I put faith
in my Supernova and her escort, too. Better remind him.*
"This war is a sorrow to me. I would hate to blacken
any part of your world or take any further lives of your
gallant folk."

"That might not be simple to do, Admiral," Trauvay
said slowly. "We have defenses."

"Observed. Wyvan, may I employ blunt speech?"

"Yes. Particularly since this is, you understand, not a
binding discussion."

No, but half a billion Ythrians are tuned in, Cajal
thought. *I wish they weren't. It's as if I could feel them.*

*What kind of government is this? Not exactly democrat-
ic—you can't hang any Terran label on it, not even "government," really. Might we humans have something to
learn here? Everything we try seems to break down at
last, and the only answer to that which we ever seem
to find is the brute simplicity of Caesar.*

Stop, Juan! You're an officer of the Imperium.

"I thank the Wyvan," Cajal said, "and request him and his people to believe we will not attack them further unless forced or ordered to do so. At present we have no reason for it. Our objectives have been achieved. We can now make good our rightful claims along the border. Any resistance must be sporadic and, if you will pardon the word, pathetic. A comparatively minor force can blockade Quetlan. Yes, naturally individual ships can steal past now and then. But to all intents and purposes, you will be isolated from your extrasystemic possessions, allies, and associates. Please consider how long the Domain can survive as a political entity under such conditions.

"Please consider, likewise, how your holding out will be an endless expense, an endless irritation to the Imperium. Sooner or later, it will decide to eliminate the nuisance. I do not say this is just, I say merely it is true. I myself would appeal an order to open fire. Were it too draconian, I would resign. But His Majesty has many admirals."

Stillness murmured around crucified Christ. Finally Trauvay asked, "Do you call for our surrender?"

"For an armistice," Cajal said.

"On what conditions?"

"A mutual cease-fire, of course . . . by definition! Captured ships and other military facilities will be retained by Terra, but prisoners will be repatriated on both sides. We will remain in occupation of systems we have entered, and will occupy those worlds claimed by the Imperium which have not already been taken. Local authorities and populaces will submit to the military officers stationed among them. For our part, we pledge respect for law and custom, rights of nonseditious free speech and petition, interim economic assistance, resumption of normal trade as soon as possible, and the freedom of any individual who so desires to sell his property on the open market and leave. Certain units of this fleet will stay near Quetlan and frequently pass through the system on surveillance; but they will not land unless invited, nor interfere with commerce, except that they reserve the right of inspection to verify that no troops or munitions are being sent."

Waves passed over the feathers. Cajal wished he knew

how to read them. The tone stayed flat: "You do demand surrender."

The man shook his head. "No, sir, I do not, and in fact that would exceed my orders. The eventual terms of peace are a matter for diplomacy."

"What hope have we if defeat be admitted beforehand?"

"Much." Cajal made ready his lungs. "I respectfully suggest you consult your students of human sociodynamics. To put it crudely, you have two influences to exert, one negative, one positive. The negative one is your potentiality of renewing the fight. Recall that most of your industry remains intact in your hands, that you have ships left which are bravely and ably manned, and that your home star is heavily defended and would cost us dearly to reduce.

"Wyvan, people of Ythri, I give you my most solemn assurance the Empire does not want to overrun you. Why should we take on the burden? Worse than the direct expense and danger would be the loss of a high civilization. We desire, we need your friendship. If anything, this war has been fought to remove certain causes of friction. Now let us go on together.

"True, I cannot predict the form of the eventual peace treaty. But I call your attention to numerous public statements by the Imperium. They are quite explicit. And they are quite sincere, for it is obviously to the best interest of the Imperium that its word be kept credible.

"The Domain must yield various territories. But compensations can be agreed on. And, after all, everywhere that your borders do not march with ours, there is waiting for you a whole universe."

Cajal prayed he was reciting well. His speeches had been composed by specialists, and he had spent hours in rehearsal. But if the experts had misjudged or he had bungled—

O God, let the slaughter end . . . and forgive me that the back of my mind is fascinated by the technical problem of capturing that planet.

Trauvay sat moveless for minutes before he said, "This shall be considered. Please hold yourself in the vicinity for consultations." Elsewhere in the ship, a xenologist who had made Ythrians his lifetime work leaped out of his

chair, laughing and weeping, to shout, "The war's over!
The war's over!"

Bells rang through Fleurville, from the cathedral a great
bronze striding, from lesser steeples a frolic. Rockets
cataracted upward to explode softly against the stars of
summer. Crowds roiled in the streets, drunk more on happiness than on any liquor; they blew horns, they shouted,
and every woman was kissed by a hundred strange men
who suddenly loved her. In daylight, Imperial marines
paraded to trumpets and squadrons of aircraft or small
spacecraft roared recklessly low. But to the capital of
Esperance and Sector Pacis, joy had come by night.

High on a hill, in the conservatory of the gubernatorial
palace, Ekrem Saracoglu looked out over the galaxy of
the city. He knew why it surged so mightily—the noise
reached him as a distant wavebeat—and shone so brilliantly. The pacifist heritage of the colonists was a partial cause; now they could stop hating those brothers who
wore the Emperor's uniform. *Although*, his mind murmured, *I suspect plain animal relief speaks louder. The
smell of fear has been on this planet since the first border
incidents, thick since war officially began. An Ythrian raid,
breaking through our surprised cordons—a sky momentarily incandescent—*

"Peace," Luisa said. "I have trouble believing."

Saracoglu glanced at the petite shape beside him. Luisa
Carmen Cajal y Gomez had not dressed gaily after accepting his invitation to dinner. Her gown was correct as
to length and pattern, but plain gray velvyl. Apart from
a tiny gold cross between the breasts, her jewelry was a
few synthetic diamonds in her hair. They glistened among
high-piled black tresses like the night suns shining through
the transparency overhead, or like the tears that stood on
her lashes.

The governor, who had covered his portliness with
lace, ruffles, tiger-patterned arcton waistcoat, green iridon
culottes, snowy shimmerlyn stockings, and gems wherever he could find a place, ventured to pat her hand.
"You are afraid the fighting may resume? No. Impossible.
The Ythrians are not insane. By taking our armistice
terms, they acknowledged defeat to themselves even
more than to us. Your father should be home soon. His

work is done." He sighed, trusting it wasn't too theatrically. "Mine, of course, will get rougher."

"Because of the negotiations?" she asked.

"Yes. Not that I'll have plenipotentiary status. However, I will be a ranking Terran representative, and the Imperium will rely heavily on the advice of my staff and myself. After all, this sector will continue to border on the Domain, and will incorporate the new worlds."

Her look was disconcertingly weighing from eyes that young. "You'll become quite an important man, won't you, Your Excellency?" Her tone was, if not chilly, cool.

Saracoglu got busy pinching withered petals off a fuchsia. Beside it a cinnamon bush—Ythrian plant—filled the air with fragrance. "Well, yes," he said. "I would not be false to you, Donna, including false modesty."

"The sector expanded and reorganized. You probably getting an elevation in the peerage, maybe a knighthood. At last, pretty likely, called Home and offered a Lord Advisorship."

"One is permitted to daydream."

"You promoted this war, Governor."

Saracoglu ran a palm over his bare scalp. *All right,* he decided. *If she can't see or doesn't care that it was on her account I sent Helga and Georgette packing (surely, by now, the gossip about that has reached her, though she's said no word, given no sign), well, I can probably get them back; or if they won't, there's no dearth of others. No doubt this particular daydream of mine is simply man's eternal silly refusal to admit he's growing old and fat. I've learned what the best condiments are when one must eat disappointment.*

But how vivid she is among the flowers.

"I promoted action to end a bad state of affairs before it got worse," he told her. "The Ythrians are no martyred saints. They advanced their interests every bit as ruthlessly as their resources allowed. Human beings were killed. Donna, my oath is to Terra."

Still her eyes dwelt on him. "Nevertheless you must have known what this would do for your career," she said, still quiet.

He nodded. "Certainly. Will you believe that that did not simplify, it vastly complicated things for me? I *thought* I thought this border rectification would be for the best.

And, yes, I think I can do a better than average job, first in rebuilding out here, not least in building a reconciliation with Ythri; later, if I'm lucky, on the Policy Board, where I can instigate a number of reforms. Ought I to lay down this work in order that my conscience may feel smug? Am I wicked to enjoy the work?"

Saracoglu reached in a pocket for his cigaret case. "Perhaps the answer to those questions is yes," he finished. "How can a mortal man be sure?"

Luisa took a pair of steps in his direction. Amidst the skips of his heart he remembered to maintain his rueful half-smile. "Oh, Ekrem—" She stopped. "I'm sorry, Your Excellency."

"No, I am honored, Donna," he said.

She didn't invite him to use her given name, but she did say, smiling through tears, "I'm sorry, too, for what I hinted. I didn't mean it. I'd never have come tonight if I hadn't gotten to know you for a . . . a decent man."

"I hardly dared hope you would accept," he told her, reasonably truthfully. "You could be celebrating with people your age."

The diamonds threw scintillations when she shook her head. "No, not for something like this. Have you heard I was engaged to be married once? He was killed in action two years ago. Preventive action, it was called—putting down some tribes that had refused to follow the 'advice' of an Imperial resident— Well." She drew breath. "Tonight I couldn't find words to thank God. Peace was too big a gift for words."

"You're the Admiral's daughter," he said. "You know peace is never a free gift."

"Do wars come undeserved?"

A discreet cough interrupted. Saracoglu turned. He was expecting his butler to announce cocktails, and the sight of a naval uniform annoyed him. "Yes?" he snapped.

"If you please, sir," the officer said nervously.

"Pray excuse me, Donna." Saracoglu bowed over Luisa's wonderfully slim hand and followed the man out into the hall.

"Well?" he demanded.

"Courier from our forces at Laura, sir." The officer shivered and was pale. "You know, that border planet Avalon."

"I do know." Saracoglu braced himself.

"Well, sir, they got word of the armistice all right. Only they reject it. They insist they'll keep on fighting."

XIII

The bony, bearded face in the screen said, on a note close to desperation, "Sirs, you are . . . are behaving as if you were mad."

"We've got company," Daniel Holm replied.

"Do you then propose to secede from the Domain?" Admiral Cajal exclaimed.

"No. The idea is to stay in it. We're happy there. No Imperial bureaucrats need apply."

"But the armistice agreement—"

"Sure, let's keep the present cease-fire. Avalon doesn't want to hurt anybody."

Cajal's mouth stiffened. "You cannot pick and choose among clauses. Your government has declared the Empire may occupy this system pending the final peace settlement."

Liaw of The Tarns thrust his frosty head toward the scanner that sent his image to Holm's office and Cajal's orbiting warcraft. "Ythrian practice is not Terran," he said. "The worlds of the Domain are tied to each other principally by vows of mutual fidelity. That our fellows are no longer able to help us does not give them the right to order that we cease defending ourselves. If anything, deathpride requires that we continue the fight for what help it may afford them."

Cajal lifted a fist into view. "Sirs," he rasped, "you seem to think this is the era of the Troubles and your opponents are barbarians who'll lose purpose and organization and go away if they're stalled for a while. The truth is, you're up against Imperial Terra, which thinks in terms of centuries and reigns over thousands of planets. Not that any such time or power must be spent on you. Practically the entire force that broke the Domain can now be brought to bear on your single globe. And it will be, sirs. If you compel the outcome, it will be."

His gaze smoldered upon them. "You have strong defenses," he said, "but you must understand how they can be swamped. Resistance will buy you nothing except the devastation of your homes, the death of thousands or millions. Have *they* been consulted?"

"Yes," Liaw replied. "Between the news of Ythri's capitulation and your own arrival, Khruath and Parliament voted again. A majority favors holding on."

"How big a majority this time?" Cajal asked shrewdly. He saw feathers stir and facial muscles twitch, and nodded. "I do not like the idea of making war on potentially valuable subjects of His Majesty," he said, "most especially not on women and children."

Holm swallowed. "Uh, Admiral. How about . . . evacuating everybody that shouldn't stay or doesn't want to . . . before we start fighting again?"

Cajal sat motionless. His features congealed. When he spoke, it was as if his throat pained him. "No. I may not help an enemy rid himself of his liabilities."

"Are you bound to wage war?" Liaw inquired. "Cannot the cease-fire continue until a peace treaty has been signed?"

"If that treaty gives Avalon to the Empire, will you obey?" Cajal retorted.

"Perhaps."

"Unacceptable. Best to end this affair at once." Cajal hesitated. "Of course, it will take time to set things in order everywhere else and marshal the armada here. The *de jure* cease-fire ends when my ship has returned to the agreed-on distance. But obviously the war will remain *in statu quo*, including the *de facto* cease-fire with respect to Avalon and Morgana, for a short period. I shall confer with Governor Saracoglu. I beseech you and all Avalonians to confer likewise with each other and use this respite to reach the only wise decision. Should you have any word for us, you need but broadcast a request for a parley. The sooner we hear, the milder—the more honorable—treatment you can expect."

"Observed," Liaw said. There followed ritual courtesies, and the screen blanked which had shown Cajal.

Holm and Liaw traded a look across the kilometers between them. At the rear of the man's office, Arinnian stirred uneasily.

"He means it," Holm said.

"How correct is his assessment of relative capabilities?" the Wyvan asked.

"Fairly good. We couldn't block a full-out move to wreck us. Given as many ships as he can whistle up, bombarding, ample stuff would be sure to get past our interception. We depend on the Empire's reluctance to ruin a lot of first-class real estate . . . and, yes, on that man's personal distaste for megadeaths."

"You told me earlier that you had a scheme."

"My son and I are working on it. If it shows any promise, you and the other appropriate people will hear. Meanwhile, I imagine you're as busy as me. Fair winds, Liaw."

"Fly high, Daniel Holm." And that screen blanked.

The Marchwarden kindled a cigar and sat scowling, until he rose and went to the window. Outside was a clear winter's day. Gray did not get the snowfall of the mountains or the northern territories, and the susin stayed green on its hills the year around. But wind whooped, cold and exultant, whitecaps danced on a gunmetal bay, cloaks streamed and fluttered about walking humans, Ythrians overhead swooped through changeable torrents of air.

Arinnian joined him, but had to wet his lips before he could speak. "Dad, do we have a chance?"

"Well, we don't have a choice," Holm said.

"We do. We can swallow our damned pride and tell the people the war's lost."

"They'd replace us, Chris. You know that. Ythri could surrender because Ythri isn't being given away. The other colonies can accept occupation because it's unmistakable to everybody that they couldn't now lick a sick kitten. We're different on both counts." Holm squinted at his son through rank blue clouds of smoke. "You're not scared, are you?"

"Not for myself, I hope. For Avalon— All that rhetoric you hear about staying free. How free are corpses in a charred desert?"

"We're not preparing for destruction," Holm said. "We're preparing to risk destruction, which is something else again. The idea is to make ourselves too expensive an acquisition."

"If Avalon went to the Empire, and we didn't like the conditions, we could emigrate to the Domain."

The Marchwarden's finger traced an arc before the window. "Where would we find a mate to that? And what'd be left of this special society we, our ancestors and us, we built?"

He puffed for a minute before musing aloud: "I read a book once, on the history of colonization. The author made an interesting point. He said you've got to leave most of the surface under plant cover, rooted vegetation and phytoplankton and whatever else there may be. You need it to maintain the atmosphere. And these plants are part of an ecology, so you have to keep many animals too, and soil bacteria and so forth. Well, as long as you must have a biosphere, it's cheaper—easier, more productive—to make it supply most of your food and such, than to synthesize. That's why colonists on terrestroid worlds are nearly always farmers, ranchers, foresters, et cetera, as well as miners and manufacturers."

"So?" his son asked.

"So you grow into your world, generation by generation. It's not walls and machinery, it's a live nature, it's this tree you climbed when you were little and that field your grandfather cleared and yonder hilltop where you kissed your first girl. Your poets have sung it, your artists have drawn it, your history has happened on it, your forebears returned their bones to its earth and you will too, you will too. It is you and you are it. You can no more give it away, freely, than you could cut the heart out of your breast."

Again Holm regarded his son. "I should think you'd feel this stronger than me, Arinnian," he said. "What's got into you?"

"That man," the other mumbled. "He didn't threaten terrible things, he warned, he pleaded. That brought them home to me. I saw . . . Mother, the kids, you, my choth-mates—"

Eyath. Hrill. Hrill who is Tabitha. In these weeks we have worked together, she and Eyath and I. . . . Three days ago I flew between them, off to inspect that sub-marine missile base. Shining bronze wings, blowing fair hair; eyes golden, eyes green; austere jut of keelbone, heavy curve of breasts. . . . She is pure. I know she is. I make too many excuses to see her, be with her. But that damned glib Terran she keeps in her house, his tinsel cosmopolitan glamour, he hears her husky-voiced merriment oftener than I do.

"Grant them their deathpride," Holm said.

Eyath will die before she yields. Arinnian straightened his shoulders. "Yes. Of course, Dad."

Holm smiled the least bit. "After all," he pointed out, "you got the first germ of this ver-r-ry intriguing notion we have to discuss."

"Actually, it . . . wasn't entirely original with me. I got talking to, uh, Tabitha Falkayn, you know her? She dropped the remark, half joking. Thinking about it later, I wondered if—well, anyhow."

"Hm. Quite a girl, seems. Especially if she can stay cheerful these days." Holm appeared to have noticed the intensity of his stare, because he turned his head quickly and said, "Let's get to work. We'll project a map first, hm?"

His thoughts could be guessed. The lift in his tone, the crinkles around his eyes betrayed them. *Well, well. Chris has finally met a woman who's not just a sex machine or a she-Ythrian to him. Dare I tell Ro, yet?— I do dare tell her that our son and I are back together.*

Around St. Li, winter meant rains. They rushed, they shouted, they washed and caressed, it was good to be out in them unclad, and when for a while they sparkled away, they left rainbows behind them.

Still, one did spend a lot of time indoors, talking or sharing music. A clear evening was not to be wasted.

Tabitha and Rochefort walked along the beach. Their fingers were linked. The air being soft, he wore simply the kilt and dagger she had given him, which matched hers.

A full Morgana lifted from eastward waters. Its almost unblemished shield dazzled the vision with whiteness, so that what stars could be seen shone small and tender. That light ran in a quaking glade from horizon to outermost breakers, whose heads it turned into wan fire; the dunes glowed beneath it, the tops of the trees which made a shadow-wall to left became hoar. There was no wind and the surf boomed steadily and inwardly, like a heartbeat. Odors of leaf and soil overlay a breath of sea. The sands gave back the day's warmth and gritted a little as they molded themselves sensuously to the bare foot.

Rochefort said in anguish, "This to be destroyed? Burned, poisoned, ripped to flinders? And you!"

"We suppose it won't happen," Tabitha replied.

"I tell you, I *know* what's to come."

"Is the enemy certain to bombard?"

"Not willingly. But if you Avalonians, in your insane arrogance, leave no alternative—" Rochefort broke off. "Forgive me. I shouldn't have said that. It's just that the news cuts too close."

Her hand tightened on his. "I understand, Phil. You're not the enemy."

"What's bad about joining the Empire?" He waved at the sky. "Look. Sun after sun after sun. They could be yours."

She sighed. "I wish—"

She had listened in utter bewitchment to his tales of those myriad worlds.

Abruptly she smiled, a flash in the moonglow that clad her. "No, I won't wish," she said; "I'll hold you to your promise to show me Terra, Ansa, Hopewell, Cynthia, Woden, Diomedes, Vixen, every last marvel you've been regaling me with, once peace has come."

"If we're still able."

"We will be. This night's too lovely for believing anything else."

"I'm afraid I can't share your Ythrian attitude," he said slowly. "And that hurts also."

"Can't you? I mean, you're brave, I know you are, and I know you can enjoy life as it happens." Her voice and her lashes dropped. "How much you can."

He halted his stride, swung about, and caught her other hand. They stood wordlessly looking.

"I'll try," he said, "because of you. Will you help me?"

"I'll help you with anything, Phil," she answered.

They had kissed before, at first playfully as they came

to feel at ease beside each other, of late more intensely. Tonight she did not stop his hands, nor her own.

"Phil and Hrill," she whispered at last, against him. "Phil and Hrill. Darling, I know a headland, a couple of kilometers further on. The trees shelter it, but you can see moon and water between them and the grass is thick and soft, the Terran grass—"

He followed her lead, hardly able to comprehend his fortune.

She laughed, a catch deep in her breast. "Yes, I planned this," she sang. "I've watched my chance for days. Mind being seduced? We may have little time in fact."

"A lifetime with you is too little," he faltered.

"Now you'll have to help me, my love, my love," she told him. "You're my first. I was always waiting for you."

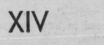

XIV

From the ground, Arinnian hailed Eyath. "Hoy-ah! Come on down and get inside." He grinned as he added in Anglic, "We Important Executives can't stall around."

She wheeled once more. Sunlight from behind turned her wings to a bronze fringed by golden haze. *She could be the sun itself*, he thought, *or the wind, or everything wild and beautiful above this ferroconcrete desert*. Then she darted at the flitter, braked in a brawl of air, and stood before him.

Her gaze fell troubled on the torpedo shape looming at his back. "Must we travel in that?" she asked.

"When we have to bounce around half a planet, yes," he replied. "You'll find it isn't bad. Especially since the hops don't take long. Less than an hour to St. Li." *To Tabby.* "Here, give me your hand."

She did. The fingers, whose talons could flay him, were slim and warm, resting trustfully between his. He led her up the gangway. She had flown in vehicles often before, of course, but always "eyeball" cars, frail and slow for the sake of allowing the cabins to be vitryl bubbles.

"This is a problem the choths like Stormgate, members mostly hunters, are going to have to overcome," he said. "Claustrophobia. You limit your travel capabilities too much when you insist on being surrounded by transparency."

Her head lifted. "If Vodan can suffer worse, I am ashamed I hung back, Arinnian."

"Actually, I hope you'll come to see what Vodan sees. He loves it in space, doesn't he?"

"Y-yes. He's told me that. Not to make a career of, but we do want to visit other planets after the war."

"Let's try today to convince you the journey as well as the goal is something special. . . . M-m-m, do you know, Eyath, two congenial couples traveling together— Well. Here we are."

He assisted her into harness in the copilot's seat, though she was his passenger. "Ordinarily this wouldn't be needful," he explained. "The flitter's spaceable—you could reach Morgana easily, the nearer planets if necessary—so it has counter-acceleration fields available, besides interior weight under free fall. But we'll be flying high, in the fringes of atmosphere, not to create a sonic boom. And while nothing much seems to be going on right now in the war, and we'll have a canopy of fortress orbits above us, nevertheless—"

She brushed her crest across his shoulder. "Of course, Arinnian," she murmured.

He secured himself, checked instruments, received clearance, and lifted. The initial stages were under remote control, to get him past that dance of negagrav projections which guarded the spaceport. Beyond, he climbed as fast as the law allowed, till in the upper stratosphere he fed his boat the power calculated to minimize his passage time.

"O-o-o-oh," Eyath breathed.

They were running quietly. The viewscreens gave outlooks in several directions. Below, Avalon was silver ocean. Around were purple twilight, sun, moon, a few stars: immensity, cold and serene.

"You must've seen pictures," Arinnian said.

"Yes. They're not the same." Eyath gripped his arm. "Thank you, dear galemate."

And I'm bound for Tabby, to tell of a battle plan that may well work, that'll require we work together. How dare I be this happy?

They flew on in the Ythrian silence which could be so much more companionable than human chatter.

There was an overcast at their destination; but when they had pierced its fog they found the sky pearl-gray, the waters white-laced indigo, the island soft green. The landing field was small, carved on the mountainside a few kilometers from the compound where Tabitha dwelt. When Chris called ahead she had promised to meet him.

He unharnessed with fingers that shook a little. Not stopping to help Eyath, he hastened to the airlock. It had opened and the gangway had extruded. A breeze ruffled his hair, warm, damp, perfumed by the janie planted around the field. Tabitha stood near, waving at him.

That was her left hand. Her right clasped the Terran's.

After half a minute she called, "Do you figure to stand there all day, Chris?"

He came down. They two released each other and extended their hands, human fashion. Meanwhile her foot caressed Rochefort's. She was wearing nothing but a few designs in body paint. They included the joyous banality of a heart pierced by an arrow.

Arinnian bowed. "We have an urgent matter to discuss," he said in Planha. "Best we flit straight to Draun's house."

As a matter of fact, Tabitha's partner and superior officer was waiting in her home. "Too many youngsters and retainers at mine," he grunted. "Secrecy must be important, or you'd simply have phoned—though we do see a rattlewing lot of you."

"These are always my welcome guests," the woman said stiffly.

Arinnian wondered if the tension he felt was in the atmosphere or his solitary mind. Draun, lean, scarred, had not erected feathers; but he sat back on tail and alatans in a manner suggesting surliness, and kept stroking a dirk he wore. Tabitha's look seemed to dwell upon

Rochefort less meltingly than it had done at the field, more in appeal.

Glancing around, Arinnian found the living room little changed. Hitherto it had pleased him. She had designed the house herself. The ceiling, a fluoropanel, was low by Ythrian standards, to make the overall proportions harmonious. A few susin mats lay on a floor of polished oak, between large-windowed copperwood walls, beneath several loungers, end tables, a stone urn full of blossoms. While everything was clean-scrubbed, her usual homely clutter was strewn about, here a pipe rack and tobacco jar, there a book, yonder a ship model she was building.

Today, however, he saw texts to inform a stranger about Avalon, and a guitar which must have been lately ordered since she didn't play that instrument. The curtain had not been drawn across the doorway to her sleeping room; Arinnian glimpsed a new wood-and-leather-frame bed, double width.

Eyath's wing touched him. She didn't like Draun. He felt the warmth that radiated from her.

"Yes," he said. "We do have to keep the matter below ground." His gaze clanged on Rochefort's. "I understand you've been studying Planha. How far along are you?"

The Terran's smile was oddly shy for an offplanet enemy who had bedazzled a girl sometimes named Hrill. "Not very," he admitted. "I'd try a few words except you'd find my accent too atrocious."

"He's doing damn well," Tabitha said, and snuggled.

His arm about her waist, Rochefort declared: "I've no chance of passing your plans on to my side, if that's what's worrying you, Citizen—uh, I mean Christopher Holm. But I'd better make my position clear. The Empire *is* my side. When I accepted my commission, I took an oath, and right now I've no way to resign that commission."

"Well said," Eyath told him. "So would my betrothed avow."

"What's honor to a Terran?" Draun snorted. Tabitha gave him a furious look. Before she could reply, Rochefort, who had evidently not followed the Planha, was proceeding:

"As you can see, I . . . expect I'll settle on Avalon after the war. Whichever way the war goes. But I do

believe it can only go one way. Christopher Holm, besides falling in love with this lady, I have with her planet.
Could I possibly make you consider accepting the inevitable before the horror comes down on Tabby and Avalon?"

"No," Arinnian answered.

"I thought not." Rochefort sighed. "Okay, I'll take a
walk. Will an hour be long enough?"

"Oh, yes," Eyath said in Anglic.

Rochefort smiled. "I love your whole people."

Eyath nudged Arinnian. "Do you need me?" she asked.
"You're going to explain the general idea. I've heard that."
She made a whistling noise found solely in the Avalonian
dialect of Planha—a giggle. "You know how wives flee
from their husbands' jokes."

"Hm?" he said. "What'll you do?"

"Wander about with Ph . . . Phee-leep Hroash For.
He has been where Vodan is."

You too? Arinnian thought.

"And he is the mate of Hrill, our friend," Eyath added.

"Go if you wish," Arinnian said.

"An hour, then." Claws ticked, feathers rustled as Eyath
crossed the floor to the Terran. She reached up and took
his arm. "Come; we have much to trade," she said in her
lilting Anglic.

He smiled again, brushed his lips across Tabitha's, and
escorted the Ythrian away. Silence lingered behind them,
save for a soughing in the trees outside. Arinnian stood
where he was. Draun fleered. Tabitha sought her pipes,
chose one and began stuffing it. Her eyes held very closely on that task.

"Blame not me," Draun said. "I'd have halved him like
his bald-skin fellow, if Hrill hadn't objected. Do you know
she wouldn't let me make a goblet from the skull?"

Tabitha stiffened.

"Well, tell me when you tire of his bouncing you,"
Draun continued. "I'll open his belly on Illarian's altar."

She swung to confront him. The scar on her cheek
stood bonelike over the skin. "Are you asking me to end
our partnership?" tore from her. "Or to challenge you?"

"Tabitha Falkayn may regulate her own life, Draun,"
Arinnian said.

"Ar-r-rkh, could be I uttered what I shouldn't," the

other male growled. His plumage ruffled, his teeth flashed forth. "Yet how long must we sit in this cage of Terran ships?"

"As long as need be," Tabitha snapped, still pale and shivering. "Do you want to charge out and die for naught, witless as any saga hero? Or invite the warheads that kindle firestorms across a whole continent?"

"Why not? All dies at last." Draun grinned. "What glorious pyrotechnics to go out in! Better to throw Terra onto hell-wind, alight; but since we can't do that, unfortunately—"

"I'd sooner lose the war than kill a planet, any planet," Tabitha said. "As many times sooner as it has living creatures. And I'd sooner lose this planet than see it killed." She leveled her voice and looked straight at the Ythrian. "Your trouble is, the Old Faith reinforces every wish to kill that war has roused in you—and you've no way to do it."

Draun's expression said, *Maybe. At least I don't rut with the enemy.* He kept mute, though, and Tabitha chose not to watch him. Instead she turned to Arinnian. "Can you change that situation?" she asked. Her smile was almost timid.

He did not return it. "Yes," he answered. "Let me explain what we have in mind."

Since the ornithoids did not care to walk any considerable distance, and extended conversation was impossible in flight, Eyath first led Rochefort to the stables. After repeated visits in recent weeks she knew her way about. A few zirraukhs were kept there, and a horse for Tabitha. The former were smaller than the latter and resembled it only in being warm-blooded quadrupeds—they weren't mammals, strictly speaking—but served an identical purpose. "Can you outfit your beast?" she inquired.

"Yes, now I've lived here awhile. Before, I don't remember ever even seeing a horse outside of a zoo." His chuckle was perfunctory. "Uh, shouldn't we have asked permission?"

"Why? Chothfolk are supposed to observe the customs of their guests, and in Stormgate you don't ask to borrow when you're among friends."

"How I wish we really were."

She braced a hand against a stall in order to reach out a wing and gently stroke the pinions down his cheek.

They saddled up and rode side by side along a trail through the groves. Leaves rustled to the sea breeze, silvery-hued in that clear shadowless light. Hoofs plopped, but the damp air kept dust from rising.

"You're kind, Eyath," Rochefort said at last, awkwardly. "Most of the people have been. More, I'm afraid, than a nonhuman prisoner of war would meet on a human planet."

Eyath sought words. She was using Anglic, for the practice as much as the courtesy. But her problem here was to find concepts. The single phrase which came to her seemed a mere tautology: "One need not hate to fight."

"It helps. If you're human, anyway," he said wryly. "And that Draun—"

"Oh, he doesn't hate you. He's always thus. I feel . . . pity? . . . for his wife. No, not pity. That would mean I think her inferior, would it not? And she endures."

"Why does she stay with him?"

"The children, of course. And perhaps she is not unhappy. Draun must have his good points, since he keeps Hrill in partnership. Still, I will be much luckier in my marriage."

"Hrill—" Rochefort shook his head. "I fear I've earned the hate of your, uh, brother Christopher Holm."

Eyath trilled. "Clear to see, you're where he especially wanted to go. He bleeds so you can hear the splashes."

"You don't mind? Considering how close you two are."

"Well, I do not watch his pain gladly. But he will master it. Besides, I wondered if she might not bind him too closely." *Sheer off from there, lass.* Eyath regarded the man. "We gabble of what does not concern us. I would ask you about the stars you have been at, the spaces you have crossed, and what it is like to be a warrior yonder."

"I don't know," Tabitha said. "Sounds damned iffy."

"Show me the stratagem that never was," Arinnian replied. "Thing is, whether or not it succeeds, we'll have changed the terms of the fight. The Imperials will have no reason to bombard, good reason not to, and Avalon is spared." He glanced at Draun.

The fisher laughed. "Whether I wish that or not, akh?"

he said. "Well, I think any scheme's a fine one which lets us kill Terrans personally."

"Are you sure they'll land where they're supposed to?" Tabitha wondered.

"No, of course we're not sure," Arinnian barked. "We'll do whatever we can to make that area their logical choice. Among other moves, we're arranging a few defections. The Terrans oughtn't to suspect they're due to us, because in fact it is not hard to get off this planet. Its defenses aren't set against objects traveling outward."

"Hm." Tabitha stroked her chin . . . big well-formed hand over square jaw, beneath heavy mouth. . . . "If *I* were a Terran intelligence officer and someone who claimed to have fled from Avalon brought me such a story, I'd put him under—what do they call that obscene gadget?—a hypnoprobe."

"No doubt." Arinnian's nod was jerky. "But these will be genuine defectors. My father has assigned shrewd men to take care of that. I don't know the details, but I can guess. We do have people who're panicked, or who want us to surrender because they're convinced we'll lose regardless. And we have more who feel that way in lesser degree, whom the first kind will trust. Suppose—well, suppose, for instance, we get President Vickery to call a potential traitor in for a secret discussion. Vickery explains that he himself wants to quit, it's political suicide for him to act openly, but he can help by arranging for certain persons to carry certain suggestions to the Terrans. Do you see? I'm not saying that's how it will be done—I really don't know how far we can trust Vickery —but we can leave the specifics to my father's men."

"And likewise the military dispositions which will make the yarn look plausible. Fine, fine," Draun gloated.

"That's what I came about," Arinnian said. "My mission's to brief the various home-guard leaders and get their efforts coordinated."

Rising from his chair, he started pacing, back and forth in front of Tabitha and never looking at her. "An extra item in your case," he went on, staccato. "It'd help tremendously if one of their own brought them the same general information."

Breath hissed between her teeth. Draun rocked forward, off his alatans, onto his toes.

"Yes," Arinnian said. "Your dear Philippe Rochefort. You tell him I'm here because I'm worried about Equatoria." He gave details. "Then I find some business in the neighbor islands and belt-flit with Eyath. Our boat stays behind, carelessly unguarded. You let him stroll freely around, don't you? His action is obvious."

Tabitha's pipestem broke in her grasp. She didn't notice the bowl fall, scattering ash and coals. "No," she said.

Arinnian found he needn't force himself to stop and glare at her as he did. "He's more to you than your world?"

"God stoop on me if ever I make use of him," she said.

"Well, if his noble spirit wouldn't dream of abusing your trust, what have you to fear?"

"I will not make my honor unworthy of his," said Hrill.

"That dungheart?" Draun gibed.

Her eyes went to him, her hand to a table beside her whereon lay a knife.

He took a backward step. "Enough," he muttered.

It was a relief when the following stillness was broken. Someone banged on the door. Arinnian, being nearest, opened it. Rochefort stood there. Behind him were a horse and a zirraukh. He breathed unevenly and blood had retreated from under his dark skin.

"You were not to come back yet," Arinnian told him.

"Eyath—" Rochefort began.

"What?" Arinnian grabbed him by the shoulders. "Where is she?"

"I don't know. I . . . we were riding, talking. . . . Suddenly she screamed. Christ, I can't get that shriek out of my head. And she took off, her wings stormed, she disappeared past the treetops before I could call to her. I . . . I waited, till—"

Tabitha joined them. She started to push Arinnian aside, noticed his stance and how his fingers dug into Rochefort's flesh, and refrained. "Phil," she said low. "Darling, think. She must've heard something terrible. What was it?"

"I can't imagine." The Terran winced under Arinnian's grip but stayed where he was. "She'd asked me to, well, describe the space war. My experiences. I was telling her

of the last fight before we crash-landed. You remember.
I've told you the same."

"An item I didn't ask about?"

"Well, I, I did happen to mention noticing the insigne
on the Avalonian boat, and she asked how it looked."

"And?"

"I told her. Shouldn't I have?"

"What was it?"

"Three gilt stars placed along a hyperbolic curve."

Arinnian let go of Rochefort. His fist smashed into the
man's face. Rochefort lurched backward and fell to the
ground. Arinnian drew his knife, started to pursue, curbed
himself. Rochefort sat up, bewildered, bleeding at the
mouth.

Tabitha knelt beside him. "You couldn't know, my
dear," she said. Her own control was close to breaking.
"What you told her was that her lover is dead."

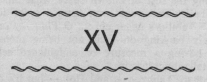

XV

Night brought rising wind. The clouds broke apart into
ragged masses, their blue-black tinged by the humpbacked
Morgana which fled among them. A few stars blinked
hazily in and out of sight. Surf threshed in darkness beyond the beach and trees roared in darkness ashore. The
chill made humans go fully clothed.

Rochefort and Tabitha paced along the dunes. "Where
is she?" His voice was raw.

"Alone," she answered.

"In this weather? When it's likely to worsen? Look, if
Holm can go out searching, at least we—"

"They can both take care of themselves." Tabitha drew
her cloak tight. "I don't think Chris really expects to find
her, unless she wants to be found, and that's doubtful.
He simply must do something. And he has to be away

from us for a while. Her grief grieves him. It's typical
Ythrian to do your first mourning by yourself."

"Saints! I've bugged things good, haven't I?"

He was a tall shadow at her side. She reached through
an arm-slit, groped for and found the reality of his hand.
"I tell you again, you couldn't know," she said. "Anyhow,
best she learn like this, instead of dragging out more
weeks or months, then never being sure he didn't die in
some ghastly fashion. Now she knows he went out cleanly,
too fast to feel, right after he'd won over a brave foe."
She hesitated. "Besides, you didn't kill him. Our own attack did. You might say the war did, like an avalanche
or a lightning stroke."

"The filthy war," he grated. "Haven't we had a gutful
yet?"

Rage flared. She released him. "Your precious Empire
can end it any time, you know."

"It has ended, except for Avalon. What's the sense of
hanging on? You'll force them to bombard you into sub-
mission."

"Showing the rest of known space what kind of thing
the Empire is. That could cost them a great deal in the
long run." Tabitha's anger ebbed. *O Phil, my only!* "You
know we're banking on their not being monsters, and
on their having a measure of enlightened self-interest.
Let's not talk about it more."

"I've got to. Tabby, you and Holm—but it's old Holm,
of course, and a few other old men and Ythrians, who
don't care how many young die as long as they're spared
confessing their own stupid, senile willfulness—"

"Stop. Please."

"I can't. You're mounting some crazy new plan you
think'll let your one little colony hold off all those stars.
I say to the extent it works, it'll be a disaster. Because
it may prolong the fight, sharpen it— No, I can't stand
idly by and let you do that to yourself."

She halted. He did likewise. They peered at each other
through the unrestful wan light. "Don't worry," she said.
"We know what we're about."

"Do you? What is your plan?"

"I mustn't tell you that, darling."

"No," he said bitterly, "but you can let me lie awake
nights, you can poison my days, with fear for you. Listen,

I know a fair amount about war. And about the psychology of the Imperial high command. I could give you a pretty good guess at how they'd react to whatever you tried."

Tabitha shook her head. She hoped he didn't see her teeth catching her lip.

"Tell me," he insisted. "What harm can I do? And my advice— Or maybe you don't propose anything too reckless. If I could be sure of that—"

She could barely pronounce it: "Please. Please."

He laid hands on her shoulders. Moonlight fell into his eyes, making them blank pools. "If you love me, you will," he said.

She stood in the middle of the wind. *I can't lie to him. Can I? But I can't break my oath either. Can I?*

What Arinnian wanted me to tell him—

But I'm not testing you, Phil, Phil. I'm . . . choosing the lesser evil . . . because you wouldn't want your woman to break her oath, would you? I'm giving you what short-lived happiness I can, by an untruth that won't make any difference to your behavior. Afterward, when you learn, I'll kneel to ask your forgiveness.

She was appalled to hear from her throat: "Do we have your parole?"

"Not to use the information against you?" His voice checked for a fractional second. Waves hissed at his back. "Yes."

"Oh, no!" She reached for him. "I never meant—"

"Well, you have my word, sweetheart mine."

In that case—she thought. *But no, I couldn't tell him the truth before I'd consulted Arinnian, who'd be sure to say no, and anyhow Phil would be miserable, in terror for me and, yes, for his friends in their navy, whom honor would not let him try to warn.*

She clenched her fists, beneath the flapping cloak, and said hurriedly: "Well, in fact it's nothing fundamental. You know about Equatoria; the uninhabited continent. Nothing's there except a few thinly scattered emplacements and a skeleton guard. They mostly sit in barracks, because that few trying to patrol that much territory is pointless. Chris has been worried."

"Hm, yes, I've overheard him mention it to you."

"He's gotten his father to agree the defenses are inadequate. In particular, making a close study, they found the Scorpeluna tableland's wide open. Surrounding mountains, air turbulence, and so forth isolate it. An enemy who concentrated on breaking through the orbital fortresses and coming down fast—as soon as he was below fifty kilometers, he'd be shielded from what few rays we can project, and he could doubtless handle what few missiles and aircraft we could send in time. Once on the ground, dug in—you savvy? Bridgehead. We want to strengthen the area. That's all."

She stopped. Dizziness grabbed her. *Did I talk on a single breath?*

"I see," he responded after a while. "Thank you, dearest."

She came to him and kissed him, tenderly because of his hurt mouth.

Later that night the wind dropped, the clouds regathered, and rain fell, slow as tears. By dawn it was used up. Laura rose blindingly out of great waters, into utter blue, and every leaf and blade on the island was jeweled.

Eyath left the crag whereon she had perched the last few hours, after she could breast the weather no more. She was cold, wet, stiff at first. But the air blew keen into nostrils and antlibranchs, blood awoke, soon muscles were athrob.

Rising, rising, she thought, and lifted herself in huge upward spirals. The sea laughed but the island dreamed, and her only sound was the rush which quivered her pinions.

At your death, Vodan, you too were a sun.

Despair was gone, burned out by the straining of her wings, buffeted out by winds and washed out by rain, as he would have demanded of her. She knew the pain would be less quickly healed; but it was nothing she could not master. Already beneath it she felt the sorrow, like a hearthfire at which to warm her hands. Let a trace remain while she lived; let Vodan dwell on in her after she had come to care for another and give that later love his high-heartedness.

She tilted about. From this height she saw more than one island, strewn across the mercury curve of the world. *I don't want to return yet. Arinnian can await me till*

. . . *dusk?* Hunger boiled in her. She had consumed a great deal of tissue. *Bless the pangs, bless this need to hunt—bless the chance, ha!*

Far below, specks, a flock of pteropleuron left their reef and scattered in search of piscoids near the water surface. Eyath chose her prey, aimed and launched herself. When she drew the membranes across her eyes to ward them, the world blurred and dimmed somewhat; but she grew the more aware of a cloven sky streaming and whistling around her; claws which gripped the bend of either wing came alive to every shift of angle, speed, and power.

Her body knew when to fold those wings and fall—when to open them again, brake in thunder, whip on upward—when and how her hands must strike. Her dagger was not needed. The reptiloid's neck snapped at the sheer violence of that meeting.

Vodan, you'd have joyed!

Her burden was handicapping; not heavy, it had nonetheless required wide foils to upbear it. She settled on an offshore rock, butchered the meat and ate. Raw, it had a mild, almost humble flavor. Surf shouted and spouted around her.

Afterward she flew inland, slowly now. She would seek the upper plantations and rest among trees and flowers, in sun-speckled shade; later she would go back aloft; and all the time she would remember Vodan. Since they had not been wedded, she could not lead his funeral dance; so today she would give him her own, their own.

She skimmed low above an orchard. Water, steaming off leaves and ground, made small white mists across the green, beneath the sun. Upwelling currents stroked her. She drank the strong odors of living earth through antlibranchs as well as lungs, until they made her light-headed and started a singing in her blood. *Vodan,* she dreamed, *were you here beside me, we would flit off, none save us. We would find a place for you to hood me in your wings.*

It was as if he were. The beating that closed in from behind and above, the air suddenly full of maleness. Her mind spun. *Am I about to faint? I'd better set down.* She sloped unevenly and landed hard.

Orange trees stood around, not tall nor closely spaced,

but golden lanterns glowed mysteriously in the deeps of their leafage. The soil was newly weeded and cultivated, bare to the sky. Its brown softness embraced her feet, damp, warmed by the sun that dazzled her. Light torrented down, musk and sweetness up, and roared.

Pinions blotted out Laura for a moment. The other descended. She knew Draun.

His crest stood stiff. Every quill around the grinning mouth said: *I hoped I might find you like this, after what's happened.*

"No," she whimpered, and spread her wings to fly.

Draun advanced stiffly over the ground, arms held wide and crook-fingered. "Beautiful, beautiful," he hawked. "Khr-r-r-r."

Her wings slapped. The inrush of air brought strength, but not her own strength. It was a different force that shook her as she might shake a prey.

"Vodan!" she yelled, and somehow flapped off the whirling earth. The lift was slow and clumsy. Draun reached up, hooked foot-claws around an alatan of hers; they tumbled together.

She scratched at his face and groped for her knife. He captured both wrists and hauled her against him. "You don't really want that, you she," his breath gusted in her ear. "Do you now?" He brought her arms around his neck and he himself hugged her. Spread, his wings again shut out the sun, before their plumes came over her eyes.

Her clasp held him close, her wings wrapped below his. She pressed her lids together so hard that dark was full of dancing formless lights. *Vodan,* passed somewhere amidst the noise, *I'll pretend he's you.*

But Vodan would not have gone away afterward, leaving her clawed, bitten, and battered for Arinnian to find.

Tabby was still asleep, Holm still looking for his poor friend, Draun lately departed with a remark about seeing if he couldn't help, the retainers and fishers off on their various businesses. The compound lay quiet under the morning.

Rochefort stole back into the bedroom. She was among the few women he'd known who looked good at this hour. The tall body, the brown skin were too firm to sag or puff; the short fair locks tangled in a way that begged his fingers to play games. She breathed deeply, steadily, no snoring though the lips were a little parted over the whiteness beneath. When he bent above her, through bars of light and shade cast by the blind, she had no smell of sourness, just of girl. He saw a trace of dried tears.

His mouth twisted. The broken lip twinged less than his heart. She'd cried on *his* account, after they came home. "Of course you can't tonight, darling," she'd whispered, leaning over him on an elbow and running the other hand down cheek and breast and flank. "With this trouble, and you pulled ninety different ways, and everything. You'd be damned callous if you could, how 'bout that? Don't you cry. You don't know how, you make it too rough on yourself. Wait till tomorrow or the next night, Phil, beloved. We've got a lifetime."

A large subdivision of my hell was that I couldn't tell you why I was taking it so hard, he thought.

If I kiss you . . . but you might wake and— O all you saints, St. Joan who burned for her people, help me!

The knowledge came that if he dithered too long, she would indeed wake. He gave himself a slow count of one hundred before he slipped back out.

The roofs of the buildings, the peak beyond them, stood in impossible clarity against a sky which a pair of distant wings shared with the sun. The softest greens and umbers shone no less than the most brilliant red. The air was drenched in fragrances of growth and of the sea which tumbled beyond the breakwater. *No. This much beauty is unendurable.* Rochefort walked fast from the area, onto a trail among the orchards. Soon it would join the main road to the landing field.

I can't succeed. Someone'll be on guard; or I'll be unable to get in; or something'll happen and I'll simply have been out for a stroll. No harm in looking, is there?

Merely looking and returning for breakfast. No harm in that, except for letting her Avalonians be killed, maybe by millions, maybe including her—and, yes, my shipmates dying too—uselessly, for no reason whatsoever except pride—when maybe they can be saved. When maybe she'll see that I did what I did to end the war quickly that she might live.

The country lay hushed. Nobody had work on the plantations this time of year.

The landing field was deserted. For as scanty traffic as St. Li got, automated ground control sufficed.

The space flitter stood closed. Rochefort strangled on relief till he remembered: *Could be against no more than weather. They have no worries about thieves here.*

How about curious children?

If somebody comes along and sees me, I can explain I got worried about that. Tabby will believe me.

He wheeled a portable ramp, used for unloading cargo carriers, to the sleek hull. Mounting, his boots went knock . . . knock . . . knock. The entrance was similar to kinds he had known and he found immediately a plate which must cover an exterior manual control. It was not secured, it slid easily aside, and behind was nothing keyed to any individual or signal, only a button. He pressed it. The outer valve purred open and a gangway came forth like a licking tongue.

Father, show me Your will. Rochefort stepped across and inside.

The Ythrian vessel was quite similar to her Terran counterparts. No surprise, when you considered that the flying race learned spaceflight from man, and that on Avalon their craft must often carry humans. In the pilot room, seats and controls were adjustable for either species. The legends were in Planha, but Rochefort puzzled them out. After five minutes he knew he could lift and navigate this boat.

He smote palm into fist, once. Then he buckled down to work.

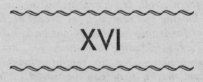

XVI

Arinnian carried Eyath back to the compound on foot. His gravbelt wouldn't safely raise them both and he left it behind. Twice she told him she could fly, or walk at any rate, but in such a weak whisper that he said, "No." Otherwise they did not speak, after the few words she had coughed against his breast while he knelt to hold her.

He couldn't carry that mass long in his arms. Instead, she clung to him, keelbone alongside his back, foot-claws curved over his shoulders, hugging his waist, like a small Ythrian child except that he must help her against the heaviness of the planet by his clasp on her alatans. He had cut his shirt into rags to sponge her hurts with rainwater off the leaves, and into bandages to stop further bleeding. The injuries weren't clinically serious, but it gave him something to use his knife on. Thus the warmth (the heat) and silk featheriness of her lay upon his skin; and the smell of her lovetime, like heavy perfume, was around him and in him.

That's the worst, he kept thinking. *The condition'll last for days—a couple of weeks, given reinforcement. If she encounters him again—*

Is she remorseful? How can she be, for a thing she couldn't halt? She's stunned, of course, harmed, dazed; but does she feel mortally befouled? Ought she to?

Suddenly I don't understand my galemate.

He trudged on. There had been scant rest for him during his search. He ached, his mouth was dry, his brain seemed full of sand. The world was a path he had to walk, so-and-so many kilometers long, except that the kilometers kept stretching. This naturally thinned the path still more, until the world had no room left for anything but a row of betrayals. He tried to shut out consciousness of them by reciting a childish chant in his head for the benefit of his feet. "You *pick* 'em *up* an' *lay* 'em *down.* You *pick* 'em *up*—" But this made him too aware of feet, how they hurt, knees, how they shivered, arms, how they burned, and perforce he went back to the betrayals. Terra-Ythri. Ythri-Avalon. Tabitha-Rochefort. Eyath-Draun, no, Draun-Eyath . . . Vodan-whatsername, that horrible creature in Centauri, yes, Quenna . . . Eyath-anybody, because right now she was anybody's . . . no, a person had self-control, forethought, a person could stay chaste if not preserve that wind-virginity which had been hers. . . . Those hands clasped on his belly, which had lain in his, had lately strained to pull Draun closer; that voice which had sung to him, and was now stilled, had moaned like the voice of any slut— *Stop that! Stop, I say!*

Sight of the compound jarred him back to a sort of reality. No one seemed about. Luck. He'd get Eyath safely put away. Ythrian chemists had developed an aerosol which effectively nullified the pheromones, and doubtless some could be borrowed from a neighbor. It'd keep the local males from strutting and gawking outside her room, till she'd rested enough to fly with him to the boat and thence home to Stormgate.

Tabitha's house stood open. She must have heard his footsteps and breath, for she came to the door. "Hullo," she called. "You found her? . . . Hoy!" She ran. He supposed once he would have appreciated the sight. "She okay?"

"No." He plodded inside. The coolness and shade belonged to a different planet.

Tabitha padded after. "This way," she suggested. "My bed."

"No!" Arinnian stopped. He would have shrugged if he weren't burdened. "Why not?"

Eyath lay down, one wing folded under her, the other spread wide so the pinions trailed onto the floor. The nictitating membranes made her appear blind. "Thank you." She could barely be heard.

"What happened?" Tabitha bent to see. The odor that a male Ythrian could catch across kilometers reached her. "Oh." She straightened. Her jaw set. "Yeh."

Arinnian sought the bathroom, drank glass after glass of cold water, showered beneath the iciest of the needle-spray settings. That and a stimpill brought him back to alertness. Meanwhile Tabitha went in and out, fetching supplies for Eyath's care.

When they were both finished, they met in the living room. She put her lips close to his ear—he felt the tiny puffs of her words—to say very low: "I gave her a sedative. She'll be asleep in a few minutes."

"Good," he answered out of his hatred. "Where's Draun?"

Tabitha stepped back. The green gaze widened. "Why?"

"Can't you guess? Where is he?"

"Why do you want Draun?"

"To kill him."

"You won't!" she cried. "Chris, if it was him, they couldn't help themselves. Neither could you. You know that. Shock and grief brought on premature ovulation, and then he chanced by—"

"He didn't chance by, that slime," Arinnian said. "Or if he did, he could've veered off from the first faint whiff he got, like any decent male. He most certainly didn't have to brutalize her. Where is he?"

Tabitha moved sidewise, in front of the phone. She had gone paler than when Draun mocked her. He shoved her out of his way. She resisted a moment, but while she was strong, she couldn't match him. "At home, you've guessed," Arinnian said. "A bunch of friends to hand, armed."

"To keep you from trying anything reckless, surely, surely," Tabitha pleaded. "Chris, we've a war. He's too important in the guard. We— If Phil were here you'd never— Must I go after a gun?"

He sat down. "Your stud couldn't prevent me calling from a different place," he snapped. She recoiled. "Nor could your silly gun. Be quiet."

He knew the number and stabbed it out. The screen came to life: Draun and, yes, a couple more in the background, blasters at their sides. The Ythrian spoke at once: "I expected this. Will you hear me? Done's done, and no harm in it. Choth law says not, in cases like this, save that a gild may be asked for wounded pride and any child must be provided for. There'll hardly be a brat, from this early in her season, and as for pride, she enjoyed herself." He grinned and stared past the man. "Didn't you, pretty-tail?"

Arinnian craned his neck around. Eyath staggered from the bedroom. Her eyes were fully open but glazed by the drug which had her already half unconscious. Her arms reached toward the image in the screen. "Yes. Come," she croaked. "No. Help me, Arinnian. Help."

He couldn't move. It was Tabitha who went to her and led her back out of sight.

"You see?" Draun said. "No harm. Why, you humans can force your females, and often do, I've heard. I'm not built for that. Anyhow, what's one bit of other folk's sport to you, alongside your hundred or more each year?"

Arinnian had kept down his vomit. It left a burning in

his gullet. His words fell dull and, in his ears, remote, though every remaining sense had become preternaturally sharp. "I saw her condition."

"Well, maybe I did get a bit excited. Your fault, really, you humans. We Ythrians watch your ways and begin to wonder. You grip my meaning? All right, I'll offer gild for any injuries, as certified by a medic. I'll even discuss a possible pride-payment, with her parents, that is. Are you satisfied?"

"No."

Draun bristled his crest a little. "You'd better be. By law and custom, you've no further rights in the matter."

"I'm going to kill you," Arinnian said.

"What? Wait a wingbeat! Murder—"

"Duel. We've witnesses here. I challenge you."

"You've no cause, I say!"

Arinnian could shrug, this time. "Then you challenge me."

"What for?"

The man sighed. "Need we plod through the formalities? Let me see, what deadly insults would fit? The vulgarism about what I can do when flying above you? No, too much a cliché. I'm practically compelled to present a simple factual description of your character, Draun. Thereto I will add that Highsky Choth is a clot of dung, since it contains such a maggot."

"Enough," the Ythrian said, just as quietly though his feathers stood up and his wings shuddered. "You are challenged. Before my gods, your gods, the memory of all our forebears and the hope of all our descent, I, Draun of Highsky, put you, Christopher Holm, called Arinnian of Stormgate, upon your deathpride to meet me in combat from which no more than one shall go alive. In the presence and honor of these witnesses whom I name—"

Tabitha came from behind. By force and surprise, she hauled Arinnian off his chair. He fell to the floor, bounced erect, and found her between him and the screen. Her left hand fended him off, her right was held as if likewise to keep away his enemy, her partner.

"Are you both insane?" she nearly screamed.

"The words have been uttered." Draun peeled his fangs. "Unless he beg grace of me."

"I would not accept a plea for grace from him," Arinnian said.

She stood panting, swinging her head from each to each. The tears poured down her face; she didn't appear to notice. After some seconds her arms dropped, her neck drooped.

"Will you hear me, then?" she asked hoarsely. They held still. Arinnian had begun to tremble under a skin turning cold. Tabitha's fists closed where they hung. "It's not to your honor that you let th-th-those persons your choths ... Avalon ... needs ... be killed or, or crippled. Wait till war's end. I challenge you to do that."

"Well, aye, if I needn't meet nor talk to the Walker," Draun agreed reluctantly.

"If you mean we must cooperate as before," Arinnian said to Tabitha, "you'll have to be our go-between."

"How can she?" Draun jeered. "After the way you bespoke her choth."

"I think I can, somehow," Hrill sighed.

She stood back. The formula was completed. The screen blanked.

Strength poured from Arinnian. He turned to the girl and said, contrite, "I didn't mean that last. Of you I beg grace, to you I offer gild."

She didn't look his way, but sought the door and stared outward. *Toward her lover,* he thought vaguely. *I'll find a tree to rest beneath till Eyath rouses and I can transport her to the flitter.*

A crash rolled down the mountainside and rattled the windows. Tabitha grew rigid. The noise toned away, more and more faint as the thunderbolt fled upward. She ran into the court. "Phil!" she shouted. *Ah,* Arinnian thought. *Indeed. The next betrayal.*

"At ease, Lieutenant. Sit down."

The dark, good-looking young man stayed tense in the chair. Juan Cajal dropped gaze back to desk and rattled the papers in his hands. Silence brimmed his office cabin. *Valenderay* swung in orbit around Pax at a distance which made that sun no more than the brightest of the stars, whose glare curtained Esperance where Luisa waited.

"I have read this report on you, including the transcription of your statements, with care, Lieutenant Rochefort,"

Cajal said finally, "long though it be. That's why I had you sent here by speedster."

"What can I add, sir?" The newcomer's voice was stiff as his body. However, when Cajal raised his look to meet those eyes again, he remembered a gentle beast he had once seen on Nuevo México, in the Sierra de los Bosques Secos, caught at the end of a canyon and waiting for the hunters.

"First," the admiral said, "I want to tender my personal apology for the hypnoprobing to which you were subjected when you rejoined our fleet. It was no way to treat a loyal officer."

"I understand, sir," Rochefort said. "I wasn't surprised, and the interrogators were courteous. You had to be sure I wasn't lying." Briefly, something flickered behind the mask. "To you."

"M-m, yes, the hypnoprobe evokes every last detail, doesn't it? The story will go no further, son. You saw a higher duty and followed."

"Why fetch me in person, sir? What little I had to tell must be in that report."

Cajal leaned back. He constructed a friendly smile. "You'll find out. First I need a bit of extra information. What do you drink?"

Rochefort started. "Sir?"

"Scotch, bourbon, rye, gin, tequila, vodka, akvavit, et cetera, including miscellaneous extraterrestrial bottles. What mixes and chasers? I believe we've a reasonably well-stocked cabinet aboard." When Rochefort sat dumb, Cajal finished: "I like a martini before dinner myself. We're dining together, you realize."

"I am? The, the admiral is most kind. Yes. A martini. Thanks."

Cajal called in the order. Actually he took a small sherry, on the rare occasions when he chose anything; and he suspected Rochefort likewise had a different preference. But it was important to get the boy relaxed.

"Smoke?" he invited. "I don't, but I don't mind either, and the governor gave me those cigars. He's a noted gourmet."

"Uh . . . thank you . . . not till after eating, sir."

"Evidently you're another." Cajal guided the chitchat till

the cocktails arrived. They were large and cold. He lifted his. *"A vuestra salud, mi amigo."*

"Your health—" The embryo of a smile lived half a second in Rochefort's countenance. *"Bonne santé, Monsieur l'Amiral."*

They sipped. "Go ahead, enjoy," Cajal urged. "A man of your proven courage isn't afraid of his supreme boss. Your immediate captain, yes, conceivably; but not me. Besides, I'm issuing you no orders. Rather, I asked for what help and advice you care to give."

Rochefort had gotten over being surprised. "I can't imagine what, sir." Cajal set him an example by taking a fresh sip. Cajal's, in a glass that bore his crest, had been watered.

Not that he wanted Rochefort drunk. He did want him loosened and hopeful.

"I suppose you know you're the single prisoner to escape," the admiral said. "Understandable. They probably hold no more than a dozen or two, from boats disabled like yours, and you were fabulously lucky. Still, you may not know that we've been getting other people from Avalon."

"Defectors, sir? I heard about discontent."

Cajal nodded. "And fear, and greed, and also more praiseworthy motives, a desire to make the best of a hopeless situation and avoid further havoc. They've been slipping off to us, one by one, a few score total. Naturally, all were quizzed, even more thoroughly than you. Your psychoprofile was on record; Intelligence need merely establish it hadn't been tampered with.'"

"They wouldn't do that, sir," Rochefort said. Color returned to his speech. "About the worst immorality you can commit on Avalon is stripping someone else of his basic honor. That costs you yours." He sank back and took a quick swallow. "Sorry, sir."

"Don't apologize. You spoke in precisely the vein I wish. Let me go on, though. The first fugitives hadn't much of interest to tell. Of late— Well, no need for lectures. One typical case will serve. A city merchant, grown rich on trade with nearby Imperial worlds. *He* won't mind us taking over his planet, as long as the war doesn't ruin his property and the aftermath cost him extra taxes. Despicable, or realistic? No matter. The point is, he possessed certain information, and had certain other information given him to pass on, by quite highly placed officials who're secretly of the peace group."

Rochefort watched Cajal over the rim of his glass. "You fear a trap, sir?"

Cajal spread his palms. "The fugitives' sincerity is beyond doubt. But were they fed false data before they left? Your story is an important confirmation of theirs."

"About the Equatorian continent?" Rochefort said. "No use insulting the admiral's intelligence. I probably would not have tried to get away if I didn't believe what I'd heard might be critical. However, I know very little."

Cajal tugged his beard. "You know more than you think, son. For instance, our analysis of enemy fire patterns, as recorded at the first battle of Avalon, does indicate Equatoria is a weak spot. Now you were on the scene for months. You heard them talk. You watched their faces, faces of people you'd come to know. How concerned would you say they really were?"

"Um-m-m. . . ." Rochefort drank anew. Cajal unobtrusively pressed a button which signaled the demand for a refill for him. "Well, sir, the, the lady I was with, Equatoria was out of her department." He hastened onward: "Christopher Holm, oldest son of their top commander, yes, I'd say he worried about it a lot."

"What's the place like? Especially this, ah, Scorpeluna region. We're collecting what information we can, but with so many worlds around, who that doesn't live on them cares about their desert areas?"

Rochefort recommended a couple of books. Cajal didn't remind him that Intelligence's computers must have retrieved these from the libraries days or weeks ago. "Nothing too specific," the lieutenant went on. "I've gathered it's a large, arid plateau, surrounded by mountains they call high on Avalon, near the middle of the continent, which the admiral knows isn't big. Some wild game, perhaps, but no real hope of living off the country." He stopped for emphasis. "Counterattackers couldn't either."

"And they, who have oceans to cross, would actually be further from home than our people from our ships," Cajal murmured.

"A dangerous way down, sir."

"Not after we'd knocked out the local emplacements. And those lovely, sheltering mountains—"

"I thought along the same lines, sir. From what I know of, uh, available production and transportation facilities, and the generally sloppy Ythrian organization, they can't put strong reinforcements there fast. Whether or not my escape alarms them."

Cajal leaned over his desk. "Suppose we did it," he said. "Suppose we established a base for aircraft and ground-to-ground missiles. What do you think the Avalonians would do?"

"They'd have to surrender, sir," Rochefort answered promptly. "They . . . I don't pretend to understand the Ythrians, but the human majority—well, my impression is that they'll steer closer to a *Götterdämmerung* than we would, but they aren't crazy. If we're there, on land, if we can shoot at everything they have, not in an indiscriminate ruin of their beloved planet—that prospect is what keeps them at fighting pitch—but if we can do it selectively, laying our own bodies on the line—" He shook his head. "My apologies. That got tangled. Besides, I could be wrong."

"Your impressions bear out every xenological study I've seen," Cajal told him. "Furthermore, yours come from a unique experience." The new drink arrived. Rochefort demurred. Cajal said: "Please do take it. I want your free-wheeling memories, your total awareness of that society and environment. This is no easy decision. What you can tell me certainly won't make up my mind by itself. However, any fragment of fact I can get, I must."

Rochefort regarded him closely. "You want to invade, don't you, sir?" he asked.

"Of course. I'm not a murder machine. Neither are my superiors."

"I want us to. Body of Christ"— Rochefort signed himself before the crucifix—"how I want it!" He let his glass stand while he added: "One request, sir. I'll pass on everything I can. But if you do elect this operation, may I be in the first assault group? You'll need some Meteors."

"That's the most dangerous, Lieutenant," Cajal warned. "We won't be sure they have no hidden reserves. Therefore we can't commit much at the start. You've earned better."

Rochefort took the glass, and had it been literally that instead of vitryl, his clasp would have broken it. "I request precisely what I've earned, sir."

XVII

The Imperial armada englobed Avalon and the onslaught commenced.

Once more ships and missiles hurtled, energy arrows flew, fireballs raged and died, across multiple thousands of kilometers. This time watchers on the ground saw those sparks brighten, hour by hour, until at last they hurt the eyes, turned the world momentarily livid and cast stark shadows. The fight was moving inward.

* * * * * *

Nonetheless it went at a measured pace. Cajal had hastened his decision and brought in his power as fast as militarily possible—within days—lest the enemy get time to strengthen that vulnerable country of theirs. But now that he was here, he took no needless risks. Few were called for. This situation was altogether different from the last. He had well-nigh thrice his former might at hand, and no worries about what relics of the Avalonian navy might still skulk through the dark reaches of the Lauran System. Patrols reported instrumental indications that these were gathering at distances of one or two astronomical units. Since they showed no obvious intention of casting themselves into the furnace, he saw no reason to send weapons after them.

He did not even order the final demolition of Ferune's flagship, when the robots within knew their foe and opened fire. She was floating too distantly, she had too little ammunition or range left her, to be worth the trouble. It was easier to bypass the poor old hulk and the bones which manned her.

Instead he concentrated on methodically reducing the

planetary defense. Its outer shell was the fortresses, some great, most small, on sentry-go in hundreds of orbits canted at as many angles to the ecliptic. They had their advantages *vis-à-vis* spaceships. They could be continually resupplied from below. Nearly all of them wholly automated, they were less versatile but likewise less fragile than flesh and nerve. A number of the least had gone undetected until their chance came to lash out at a passing Terran.

That, though, had been at the first battle. Subsequently the besieging sub-fleet had charted each, destroyed no few and forestalled attempts at replacement. Nor could the launching of salvos from the ground be again a surprise. And ships in space had their own advantages, e.g., mobility.

Cajal's general technique was to send squadrons by at high velocity and acceleration. As they entered range of a target they unleashed what they had and immediately applied unpredictable vectors to escape return fire. If the first pass failed, a second quickly followed, a third, a fourth . . . until defense was saturated and the station exploded in vapor and shards. Having no cause now to protect his rear or his supply lines, Cajal could be lavish with munitions, and was.

Spacecraft in that kind of motion were virtually hopeless goals for missiles which must rise through atmosphere, against surface gravity, from zero initial speed. The Avalonians soon realized as much and desisted for the time being.

Cajal's plan did not require the preliminary destruction of every orbital unit. That would have been so expensive that he would have had to hang back and wait for more stocks from the Empire; and he was in a hurry. He did decide it was necessary to neutralize the moon, and for a while Morgana was surrounded and struck by such furies that mountains crumbled and valleys ran molten.

Otherwise, on the whole, the Imperials went after those fortresses which, in their ever-changing configurations, would menace his first landing force on the date set by his tactical scheme. In thus limiting his objective, he was enabled to focus his full energies sharply. Those incandescent hours, running into a pair of Avalonian days, were the swiftest penetration ever made of defenses that strong.

Inevitably, he took losses. The rate grew when his ships started passing so close above the atmosphere that ground-based projectors and missile sites became effective. The next step was to nullify certain of these, together with certain other installations.

* * * * * *

Captain Ion Munteanu, commanding fire control aboard H.M.S. *Phobos,* briefed his officers while the ship rushed forward.

"Ours is a special mission, as you must have guessed from this class of vessel being sent. We aren't just going to plaster a spot that's been annoying the boys. We're after a city. I see a hand. Question, Ensign Ozumi?"

"Yes, sir. Two. How and why? We can loose enough torps and decoys, sophisticated enough, that if we keep it up long enough, a few are bound to duck in and around the negafields and burst where they'll do some good. That's against a military target. But surely they've given their cities better protection than that."

"I remind you about eggs and grandmothers, Ensign. Of course they have. Powerful, complicated set-ups, plus rings of exterior surface-to-space launchers. We'll be firing our biggest and best, programmed for detonation at high substratospheric altitude. The pattern I'm about to diagram should allow one, at least, to reach that level before it's intercepted. If not, we start over."

"Sir! You don't mean a continent buster!"

"No, no. Calm down. Remember this ship couldn't accommodate any. We have no orders to damage His Majesty's real estate beyond repair. Ours will be heavy brutes, true, but clean, and shaped to discharge their output straight ahead, mainly in the form of radiation. Blast wouldn't help much against the negafields. We'll whiff the central part of town, and Intelligence tells me the fringes are quite flammable."

"Sir, I don't want to annoy you, but why do we do it?"

"Not wantonly, Ozumi. A landing is to be made. Planetside warfare may go on for a while. This particular town, Centauri they call it, is their chief seaport and industrial capital. We are not going to leave it to send stuff against our friends."

Sweat stood on Ozumi's brow. "Women and children——"

"If the enemy has any sense, he evacuated nonessential persons long ago," Munteanu snapped. "Frankly, I don't give a curse. I lost a brother here, last time around. If you're through sniveling, let's get to work."

Quenna flapped slowly above the Livewell Street canal. Night had fallen, a clear night unlike most in the Delta's muggy winters. Because of that and the blackout, she could see stars. They frightened her. Too many of the cold, nasty little things. And they weren't only that, she was told. They were suns. War came from them, war that screwed up the world.

Fine at first, lots of Ythrians passing through, jingle in their purses, moments when she forgot all except the beauty of the male and her love for him; in between, she could afford booze and dope to keep her happy, especially at parties. Parties were a human idea, she'd heard. (Who was it had told her? She tried to remember the face, the body. She would be able to, if they didn't blur off into the voices and music and happy-making smoke.) A good idea. Like war had seemed. Love, love, love, laugh, laugh, laugh, sleep, sleep, sleep, and if you wake with your tongue tasting bad and needles in your head, a few pills will soon put you right.

Except it went sour. No more navy folk. The Nest empty, a cave, night after night after night, till a lass was ready to scream except that the taped music did that for her. Most humans moving out, too, and those who stayed—she'd even have welcomed human company— keeping underground. The black, quiet nights, the buzzing aloneness by day, the money bleeding off till she could barely buy food, let alone a bottle or a pill to hold off the bad dreams.

Flap, flap. Somebody must be in town and lonesome, now the fighting had started again. "I'm lonesome too," she called. "Whoever you are, I love you." Her voice sounded too loud in this unmoving warm air, above these oily waters and dead pavements, between those shadowy walls and beneath those terrible little stars.

"Vodan?" she called more softly. She remembered him best of the navy folk, almost as well as the first few who had used her, more years back than she cared to count.

He'd been gentle and bothered about his lass at home, as
if that dragglewing deserved him. But she was being silly,
Quenna was. No doubt the stars had eaten Vodan.

She raised her crest. She had her deathpride. She would
not be frightened in the midnight streets. Soon dawn
would break and she could dare sleep.

The sun came very fast.

She had an instant when it filled the sky. Night caught
her then, as her eyeballs melted. She did not know this,
because her plumage was on fire. Her scream drowned
out the following boom, when superfast molecules of air
slipped by the negafields, and she did not notice how it
ruptured eardrums and smashed capillaries. In her delirium of pain, there was nothing except the canal. She
threw herself toward it, missed, and fell into a house which
stood in one blaze. That made no difference, since the canal
waters were boiling.

Apart from factors of morale and war potential, the
strike at Centauri must commit a large amount of Avalonian resources to rescue and relief. It had been well
timed. A mere three hours later, the slot which had been
prepared in the defenses completed itself and the first wave
of invasion passed through.

Rochefort was in the van. He and his hastily assembled
crew had had small chance to practice, but they were
capable men and the Meteor carried out her assignment
with an *élan* he wished he could feel. They ran interference
for the lumbering gunships till these were below the dangerous altitude. En route, they stopped a pair of enemy
missiles. Though no spacecraft was really good in atmosphere, a torpedo boat combined acceptable maneuverability, ample firepower, and more than ample wits aboard.
Machines guided by simple robots were no match.

Having seen his charges close to ground, Rochefort took
his vessel, as per assignment, against the source of the missiles. It lay beyond the mountains, in the intensely green
gorge of a river. The Terran boats roared one after the
next, launched beams and torpedoes against negafields
and bunkers, stood on their tails and sprang to the stratosphere, swept about and returned for the second pass. No
third was needed. A set of craters gaped between cliffs
which sonic booms had brought down in rubble. Roche-

fort wished he could forget how fair that canyon had been.

Returning to Scorpeluna, he found the whole convoy landed. Marines and engineers were swarming from personnel transports, machines from the freighters. Overhead, patrol craft darkened heaven. They were a frantic few days that followed. Hysteria was never far below the skin of purposeful activity. Who knew for certain what the enemy had?

Nothing came. The screen generators were assembled and started. Defensive projectors and missiles were positioned. Sheds were put together for equipment, afterward for men. And no counterattack was made.

Airborne scouts and spaceborne instruments reported considerable enemy activity on the other continents and across the islands. Doubtless something was being readied. But it didn't appear to pose any immediate threat.

The second slot opened. The second wave flowed down, entirely unopposed. Scorpeluna Base spread like an inkblot.

His intention now being obvious, Cajal had various other orbital fortresses destroyed, in order that slots come more frequently. Thereafter he pulled his main fleet back a ways. From it he poured men and equipment groundward.

The last Avalonian ships edged nearer, fled from sorties, returned to slink about, wolves too starveling to be a menace. No serious effort was wasted on them. The essential was to exploit this tacit cease-fire while it lasted. On that account, the Imperials everywhere refrained from offensive action. They worked at digging in where they were and at building up their conquest until it could not merely defend itself, it could lift an irresistible fist above all Avalon.

Because he was known to have the favor of the grand admiral, Lieutenant Philippe Rochefort (newly senior grade) got his application for continued planetside duty approved. Since there was no further call for a space torpedo craft, he found himself flying aerial patrol in a two-man skimmer, a glorified gravsled.

His assigned partner was a marine corporal, Ahmed Nasution, nineteen standard years old, fresh off New Djawa and into the corps. "You know, sir, everybody told me this planet was a delight," he said, exaggerating his ruefulness to make sure his superior got the point. "Join the navy and see the universe, eh?"

"This area isn't typical," Rochefort answered shortly.

"What is," he added, "on an entire world?"

The skimmer flew low above the Scorpelunan plateau. The canopy was shut against broiling air. A Hilsch tube arrangement and self-darkening vitryl did their inadequate best to combat that heat, brazen sky, bloated and glaring sun. The only noises were hum of engine, whirr of passage. Around the horizon stood mountain peaks, dim blue and unreal. Between reached emptiness. Bushes, the same low, reddish-leaved, medicinal-smelling species wherever you looked, grew widely apart on hard red earth. The land was not really flat. It raised itself in gnarly mesas and buttes, it opened in great dry gashes. At a distance could be seen a few six-legged beasts, grazing in the shade of their parasol membranes. Otherwise nothing stirred save heat shimmers and dust devils.

"Any idea when we'll push out of here?" Nasution asked, reaching for a water bottle.

"When we're ready," Rochefort told him. "Easy on the drink. We've several hours to go, you and I."

"Why doesn't the enemy give in, sir? A bunch of us in my tent caught a 'cast of theirs—no orders not to, are there?—a 'cast in Anglic. I couldn't understand it too well, their funny accent and, uh, phrases like 'the Imperials have no more than a footgrip,' you have to stop and figure them out and meanwhile the talking goes on. But Gehenna, sir, we don't *want* to hurt them. Can't they be reasonable and—"

"Sh!" Rochefort lifted an arm. His monitoring radio identified a call. He switched to that band.

"Help! O God, help!— Engineer Group Three . . . wild animals . . . estimate thirty-four kilometers north-northwest of camp— *Help!"*

Rochefort slewed the skimmer about.

He arrived in minutes. The detail, ten men in a ground-car, had been running geological survey to determine the feasibility of blasting and fuse-lining a large missile silo. They were armed, but had looked for no troubles except discomfort. The pack of dog-sized hexapodal lopers found them several hundred meters from their vehicle.

Two men were down and being devoured. Three had scattered in terror, seeking to reach the car, and been individually surrounded. Rochefort and Nasution saw one overwhelmed. The rest stood firm, back to back, and maintained steady fire. Yet those scaly-bristly shapes seemed almost impossible to kill. Mutilated, they dragged their jaws onward.

Rochefort yelled into his transmitter for assistance, swooped, and cut loose. Nasution wept but did good work at his gun. Nevertheless, two more humans were lost before the lycosauroids had been slain.

After that, every group leaving camp got an aerial escort, which slowed operations elsewhere.

"No, Doctor, I've stopped believing it's psychogenic." The major glanced out of the dispensary shack window, to an unnaturally swift sunset which a dust storm made the color of clotted blood. Night would bring relief from the horrible heat . . . in the form of inward-gnawing chill. "I was ready to believe that at first. Your psychodrugs aren't helping any longer, though. And more and more men are developing the symptoms, as you must know better than I. Bellyache, diarrhea, muscle pains, more thirst than this damned dryness will account for. Above all, tremors and fuzzy-headedness. I hate to tell you how necessary a job I botched today."

"I'm having my own troubles thinking." The medical officer passed a hand across his temple. It left a streak of grime, despite the furnace air sucking away sweat before that could form drops. "Frequent blurred vision too? Yes."

"Have you considered a poison in the environment?"

"Certainly. You weren't in the first wave, Major. I was. Intelligence, as well as history, assured us Avalon is acceptably safe. Still, take my word, we'd scarcely established camp when the scientific team was checking."

"How about quizzing Avalonian prisoners?"

"I'm assured this was done. In fact, there've been subsequent commando operations just to collect more for that purpose. But how likely are any except a few specialists to know details about the most forbidding part of a whole continent that nobody inhabits?"

"And of course the Avalonians would have all those experts safely tucked out of reach." The major gusted a weary breath. "So what did your team find?"

The medical officer groped for a stimpill out of the open box on his desk. "There is a, ah, high concentration of heavy metals in local soil. But nothing to worry about. You could breathe the dust for years before you'd require treatment. The shrubs around use those elements in their metabolism, as you'd expect, and we've warned against chewing or burning any part of them. No organic compounds test out as allergens. Look, human and Ythrian biochemistries are so similar the races can eat most of each other's food. If this area held something spectacularly deadly, don't you imagine the average colonist would have heard of it, at least? I'm from Terra—middle west coast of North America—oh, Lord—" For a while his gaze was gone from Scorpeluna. He shook himself. "We lived among oleanders. We cultivated them for their flowers. Oleanders are poisonous. You just need to be sensible about them."

"This has got to have some cause," the major insisted.

"We're investigating," the medic said. "If anyone had foreseen this planet would amount to anything militarily —it'd have been studied before ever we let a war happen, so thoroughly— Too late."

Occasional small boats from the Avalonian remnants slipped among the Terran blockaders at high velocity and maximum variable acceleration. About half were destroyed; the rest got through and returned spaceward. It was known that they exchanged messages with the ground. Given suitable encoding and laser beams, a huge amount of information can be passed in a second or two.

"Obviously they're discussing a move," Cajal snarled at his staff. "Equally obviously, if we try to hunt them, they'll scatter and vanish in sheer distance, sheer numbers of asteroids and moons, same's they did before. And they'll have contingency plans. I do not propose to be diverted, gentlemen. We shall keep our full strength here."

For a growing body of observations indicated that, on

land and sea, under sea and in their skies, the colonists were at last making ready to strike back.

Rochefort heard the shrieking for the better part of a minute before it registered on him. *Dear Jesus,* dragged through his dullness, *what ails me?* His muscles protested bringing the skimmer around. His fingers were sausages on the control board. Beside him, Nasution slumped mute, as the boy had been these past days (weeks? years?). The soft cheeks had collapsed and were untidily covered by black down.

Still, Rochefort's craft arrived to help those which had been floating above a ground patrol. The trouble was, it could then do no more than they. Energy weapons incinerated at a flash hundreds of the cockroach-like things, twenty centimeters long, whose throngs blackened the ground between shrubs. They could not save the men whom these bugs had already reached and were feasting on. Rochefort carefully refrained from noting which skimmer pilots gave, from above, a *coup de grace*. He himself hovered low and hauled survivors aboard. After what he had seen, in his present physical shape, Nasution was too sick to be of use.

Having evidently gotten wind of meat in this hungry land, the kakkelaks swarmed toward the main base. They couldn't fly, but they clattered along astonishingly fast. Every effort must go to flaming a cordon against them.

Meanwhile the Avalonians landed throughout Equatoria. They deployed so quickly and widely—being very lightly equipped—that bombardment would have been futile. All who entered Scorpeluna were Ythrian.

The chief officers of medicine and planetology confronted their commandant. Outside, an equinoctial gale bellowed and rang through starless night; dust scoured over shuddering metal walls. The heat seemed to come in enormous dry blasts.

"Yes, sir," the medical chief said. Being regular navy rather than marine, he held rear admiral's rank. "We've proven it beyond reasonable doubt." He sighed, a sound lost in the noise. "If we'd had better equipment, more staff— Well, I'll save that for the board of inquiry, or the court-martial. The fact is, poor information got us sucked into a death trap."

"Too many worlds." The civilian planetologist shook his gaunt head. "Each too big. Who can know?"

"While you gabble," the commandant said, "men lie in delirium and convulsions. More every day. Talk." His voice was rough with anger and incomplete weeping.

"We suspected heavy-metal poisoning, of course," the medical officer said. "We made repeated tests. The concentration always seemed within allowable limits. Then overnight—"

"Never mind that," the planetologist interrupted. "Here are the results. These bushes growing everywhere around . . . we knew they take up elements like arsenic and mercury. And the literature has described the hell shrub, with pictures, as giving off dangerous vapors. What we did not know is that here *is* a species of hell shrub. It looks entirely unlike its relatives. Think of roses and apples. Besides, we'd no idea how the toxin of the reported kind works, let alone these. That must have been determined after the original descriptions were published, when a purely organic compound was assumed. The volume of information in every science, swamping—" His words limped to a halt.

The commandant waited.

The medical officer took the tale: "The vapors carry the metals in loose combination with a . . . a set of molecules, unheard of by any authority I've read. Their action is, well, they block certain enzymes. In effect, the body's protections are canceled. No metal atoms whatsoever are excreted. Every microgram goes to the vital organs. Meanwhile the patient is additionally weakened by the fact that parts of his protein chemistry aren't working right. The effects are synergistic and exponential. Suddenly one crosses a threshold."

"I . . . see . . ." the commandant said.

"We top officers aren't in too bad a condition yet," the planetologist told him. "Nor are our staffs. We spend most of our time indoors. The men, though—" He rubbed his eyes. "Not that I'd call myself a well man," he mumbled.

"What do you recommend?" the commandant asked.

"Evacuation," the medical chief said. "And I don't recommend it, I tell you we have no alternative. Our people must get immediate proper care."

The commandant nodded. Himself sick, monstrously tired, he had expected some such answer days ago and started his quiet preparations.

"We can't lift off tomorrow," he said in his dragging tones. "We haven't the bottom; most's gone back to space. Besides, a panicky flight would make us a shooting gallery for the Avalonians. But we'll organize to raise the worst cases, while we recall everybody to the main camp. We'll have more ships brought down, in orderly fashion." He could not control the twitch in his upper lip.

As the Imperials retreated, their enemies struck.

They fired no ground-to-ground missiles. Rather, their human contingents went about the construction of bases which had this capability, at chosen spots throughout the Equatorian continent. It was not difficult. They were only interested in short-range weapons, which needed little more than launch racks, and in aircraft, which needed little more than maintenance shacks for themselves and their crews. The largest undertaking was the assembly of massive energy projectors in the peaks overlooking Scorpeluna.

Meanwhile the Ythrians waged guerrilla warfare on the plateau. They, far less vulnerable to the toxicant peculiar to it, were in full health and unburdened by the space-suits, respirators, handkerchiefs which men frantically donned. Already winged, they need not sit in machines which radar, gravar, magnetoscopes could spot across kilometers. Instead they could dart from what cover the ground afforded, spray a trudging column with fire and metal, toss grenades at a vehicle, sleet bullets through any skimmers, and be gone before effective reaction was possible.

Inevitably, they had their losses.

"Hya-a-a-ah!" yelled Draun of Highsky, and swooped from a crag down across the sun-blaze. At the bottom of a dry ravine, a Terran column stumbled toward camp from a half-finished emplacement. Dust turned every man more anonymous than what was left of his uniform. A few armored groundcars trundled among them, a few aircraft above. A gravsled bore rapidly mummifying corpses, stacked.

"Cast them onto hell-wind!" The slugthrower stuttered in Draun's grasp. Recoil kept trying to hurl him off balance, amidst these wild thermals. He gloried that his wings were too strong and deft for that.

The Ythrians swept low, shooting, and onward. Draun saw men fall like emptied sacks. Wheeling beyond range, he saw their comrades form a square, anchored by its cars and artillery, helmeted by its flyers. *They're still brave,* he thought, and wondered if they hadn't best be left alone. But the idea had been to push them into close formation, then on the second pass drop a tordenite bomb among them. "Follow me!"

The rush, the bullets and energy bolts, the appallingly known wail at his back. Draun braked, came about, saw Nyesslan, his oldest son, the hope of his house, spiral to ground on a wing and a half. The Ythrian squadron rushed by. *"I'm coming, lad!"* Draun glided down beside him. Nyesslan lay unconscious. His blood purpled the dust. The second attack failed, broke up in confusion before it won near to the square. True to doctrine, that they should hoard their numbers, the Ythrians beat back out of sight. A platoon trotted toward Draun. He stood above Nyesslan and fired as long as he was able.

"Take out everything they have remaining in orbit," Cajal said. "We need freedom to move our transports continuously."

His chief of staff cleared throat. "Hr-r-rm, the admiral knows about the hostile ships?"

"Yes. They're accelerating inward. It's fairly clear that all which can make planetfall hope to do so; the rest are running interference."

"Shouldn't we organize an interception?"

"We can't spare the strength. Clearing away those forts will empty most of our magazines. Our prime duty is to pull our men out of that mess we . . . I . . . sent them into." Cajal stiffened himself. "If any units can reasonably be spared from the orbital work, yes, let them collect what Avalonians they can, provided they conserve munitions to the utmost and rely mainly on energy weapons. I doubt they'll get many. The rest we'll have to let go their ways, perhaps to our sorrow." His chuckle clanked. "As old Professor Wu-Tai was forever saying at the Academy —remember, Jim?— 'The best foundation that a decision is ever allowed is our fallible assessment of the probabilities.' "

The tropical storms of Avalon were more furious than one who came from a planet of less irradiation and slower spin could well have imagined. For a day and a night, the embarkation of the sickest men was postponed. Besides the chance of losing a carrier, there was a certainty that those flensing rains would kill some of the patients as they were borne from shacks to gangways.

The more or less hale, recently landed, battled to erect levees. Reports, dim and crackling through radio static, were of flash floods leaping down every arroyo.

Neither of these situations concerned Rochefort. He was in an intermediate class, too ill for work, too well for immediate removal. He huddled on a chair among a hundred of his fellows, in a stinking, steaming bunker, tried to control the chills and nausea that went ebb-and-flow through him, and sometimes thought blurrily of Tabitha Falkayn and sometimes of Ahmed Nasution, who had died three days before.

What Avalonian spacecraft ran the gantlet descended to Equatoria, where home-guard officers assigned them their places.

The storm raged to its end. The first Imperial vessels lifted from the wrecked base. They were warships, probing a way for the crammed, improvised hospital hulls which were to follow. Sister fighters moved in from orbit to join them.

Avalon's ground and air defenses opened crossfire. Her space force entered battle.

Daniel Holm sat before a scanner. It gave his words and his skull visage to the planet's most powerful linked transmitters, a broadcast which could not fail to be heard:

"—we're interdicting their escape route. You can't blast us in time to save what we estimate as a quarter million men. Even if we didn't resist, maybe half of them would never last till you brought them to adequate care. And I hate to think about the rest—organ, nerve, brain damage beyond the power of regenerative techniques to heal.

"*We* can save them. We of Avalon. We have the facilities prepared, clear around our planet. Beds, nursing staffs, diagnostic equipment, chelating drugs, supportive treatments. We'd welcome your inspection teams and medical personnel. Our wish is not to play political games with living people. The minute you agree to renew the cease-fire and to draw your fleet far enough back that we can count on early warning, that same minute our rescue groups will take flight for Scorpeluna."

XVIII

The ward was clean and well-run, but forty men must be crowded into it and there was no screen—not that local programs would have interested most of them. Hence they had no entertainment except reading and bitching. A majority preferred the latter. Before long, Rochefort asked for earcups in order that he might be able to use the books lent him. He wore them pretty much around the clock.

Thus he did not hear the lickerish chorus. His first knowledge came from a touch on his shoulder. *Huh?* he thought. *Lunch already?* He raised his eyes from *The Gaiila Folk* and saw Tabitha.

The heart sprang in him and raced. His hands shook so he could barely remove the cups.

She stood athwart the noisy, antiseptic-smelling room as if her only frame were a window behind, open to the blue and blossoms of springtime. A plain coverall disguised the curves and straightness of her. He saw in the countenance that she had lost weight. Bones stood forth still more strongly than erstwhile, under a skin more darkened and hair more whitened by a stronger sun than shone over Gray.

"Tabby," he whispered, and reached.

She took his hands, not pressing them nor smiling much. "Hullo, Phil," said the remembered throaty voice. "You're looking better'n I expected, when they told me you'd three tubes in you."

"You should have seen me at the beginning." He heard his words waver. "How've you been? How's everybody?"

"I'm all right. Most of those you knew are. Draun and Nyesslan bought it."

"I'm sorry," he lied.

Tabitha released him. "I'd have come sooner," she said, "but had to wait for furlough, and then it took time to get a data scan on those long lists of patients and time to get transportation here. We've a lot of shortages and disorganization yet." Her regard was green and grave. "I did feel sure you'd be on Avalon, dead or alive. Good to learn it was alive."

"How could I stay away . . . from you?"

She dropped her lids. "What is your health situation? The staff's too busy to give details."

"Well, when I'm stronger they want to ship me to a regular Imperial navy hospital, take out my liver and grow me a new one. I may need a year, Terran, to recover completely. They promise me I will."

"Splendid." Her tone was dutiful. "You being well treated here?"

"As well as possible, considering. But, uh, my roommates aren't exactly my type and the medics and helpers, both Imperial and Avalonian, can't stop their work for conversation. It's been damned lonesome, Tabby, till you came."

"I'll try to visit you again. You realize I'm on active duty, and most of what leave I'm granted has to be spent at St. Li, keeping the business in shape."

Weakness washed through him. He leaned back into the pillows and let his arms fall on the blanket. "Tabby . . . would you consider waiting . . . that year?"

She shook her head, slowly, and again met his stare. "Maybe I ought to pretend till you're more healed, Phil. But I'm no good at pretending, and besides, you rate better."

"After what I did—"

"And what I did." She leaned down and felt past the

tubes to lay palms on his shoulders. "No, we've never hated on that account, have we, either of us?"

"Then can't we both forgive?"

"I believe we've already done it. Don't you see, though? When the hurting had died down to where I could think, I saw there wasn't anything left. Oh, friendship, respect, memories to cherish. And that's all."

"It isn't enough . . . to rebuild on?"

"No, Phil. I understand myself better than I did before. If we tried, I know what sooner or later I'd be doing to you. And I won't. What we had, I want to keep clean."

She kissed him gently and raised herself.

They talked awhile longer, embarrassed, until he could dismiss her on the plea, not entirely untruthful, that he needed rest. When she was gone he did close his eyes, after donning the earcups which shut out the Terran voices.

She's right, probably, he thought. *And my life isn't blighted. I'll get over this one too, I suppose.* He recalled a girl in Fleurville and hoped he would be transferred to an Esperancian hospital, when or if the cease-fire became a peace.

Outside, Tabitha stopped to put on the gravbelt she had retrieved from the checkroom. The building had been hastily erected on the outskirts of Gray. (She remembered the protests when Marchwarden Holm diverted industrial capacity from war production to medical facilities, at a time when renewed combat seemed imminent. Commentators pointed out that what he had ordered was too little for the casualties of extensive bombardment, too much for those of any plausible lesser-scale affray. He had growled, "We do what we can" and rammed the project through. It helped that the principal home-guard officers urged obedience to him. They knew what he really had in mind—these men whose pain kept the weapons uneasily silent.) Where she stood, a hillside sloped downward, decked with smaragdine susin, starred with chasuble bush and Buddha's cup, to the strewn and begardened city, the huge curve of uprising shoreline, the glitter on Falkayn Bay. Small cottony clouds sauntered before the wind, which murmured and smelled of livewell.

She inhaled that coolness. After Equatoria, it was intoxicating. Or it ought to be. She felt curiously empty.

Wings boomed. An Ythrian landed before her. "Good flight to you, Hrill," the female greeted.

Tabitha blinked. Who—? Recognition came. "Eyath! To you, good landing." *How dull her tone, how sheenless her plumes. I haven't seen her since that day on the island. . . .* Tabitha caught a taloned hand in both of hers. "This is wonderful, dear. Have you been well?"

Eyath's stance and feathers and membranes drawn over her eyes gave answer. Tabitha hunkered down and embraced her.

"I sought you," Eyath mumbled. "I spent the battle at home; afterward too, herding, because I needed aloneness and they told me the planet needs meat." Her head lay in Tabitha's bosom. "Lately I've been freed of that and came to seek—"

Tabitha stroked her back, over and over.

"I learned where you were posted and that you'd mentioned you would stop in Gray on your furlough," Eyath went on. "I waited. I asked of the hotels. Today one said you had arrived and gone out soon after. I thought you might have come here, and trying was better than more waiting."

"What little I can do for you, galemate, tell me."

"It is hard." Eyath clutched Tabitha's arms, painfully, without raising her head. "Arinnian is here too. He has been for some while, working on his father's staff. I sought him and—" A strangled sound, though Ythrians do not weep.

Tabitha foresaw: "He avoids you."

"Yes. He tries to be kind. That is the worst, that he must try."

"After what happened—"

"Ka-a-a-ah. I am no more the same to him." Eyath gathered her will. "Nor to myself. But I hoped Arinnian would understand better than I do."

"Is he the solitary one who can help? What of your parents, siblings, chothmates?"

"They have not changed toward me. Why should they? In Stormgate a, a misfortune like mine is reckoned as that, a misfortune, no disgrace, no impairment. They cannot grasp what I feel."

"And you feel it because of Arinnian. I see." Tabitha looked across the outrageously lovely day. "What can I do?"

"I don't know. Maybe nothing. Yet if you could speak to him—explain—beg grace of him for me—"

Anger lifted. *"Beg* him? Where is he?"

"At work, I, I suppose. His home—"

"I know the address." Tabitha released her and stood up. "Come, lass. No more talk. We're off for a good hard flight in this magnificent weather, and I'll take advantage of being machine-powered to wear you out, and at day's end we'll go to wherever you're staying and I'll see you asleep."

—Twilight fell, saffron hues over silver waters, elsewhere deep blue and the earliest stars. Tabitha landed before Arinnian's door. His windows glowed. She didn't touch the chime plate, she slammed a panel with her fist.

He opened. She saw he had also grown thin, mahogany hair tangled above tired features and disheveled clothes. "Hrill!" he exclaimed. "Why . . . I never— Come in, come in."

She brushed past him and whirled about. The chamber was in disarray, obviously used only for sleeping and bolted meals. He moved uncertainly toward her. Their contacts had been brief, correct, and by phone until the fighting began. Afterward they verified each other's survival, and that was that.

"I'm, I'm glad to see you, Hrill," he stammered.

"I don't know as I feel the same," she rapped. "Sit down. I've got things to rub your nose in, you sanctimonious mudbrain."

He stood a moment, then obeyed. She saw the strickenness upon him and abruptly had no words. They looked, silent, for minutes.

Daniel Holm sat before the screens which held Liaw of The Tarns, Matthew Vickery of the Parliament, and Juan Cajal of the Empire. A fourth had just darkened. It had carried a taped plea from Trauvay, High Wyvan of Ythri, that Avalon yield before worse should befall and a harsher peace be dictated to the whole Domain.

"You have heard, sirs?" Cajal asked.

"We have heard," Liaw answered.

Holm felt the pulse in his breast and temples, not much quickened but a hard, steady slugging. He longed for a cigar—unavailable—or a drink—unadvisable—or a year of sleep—unbroken. *At that,* crossed his mind, *we're in better shape than the admiral. If ever I saw a death's head, it rides his shoulderboards.*

"What say you?" Cajal went on like an old man.

"We have no wish for combat," Liaw declared, "or to deepen the suffering of our brethren. Yet we cannot give away what our folk so dearly bought for us."

"Marchwarden Holm?"

"You won't renew the attack while we've got your people here," the human said roughly. "Not that we'll hold them forever. I told you before, we don't make bargaining counters out of thinking beings. Still, the time and circumstances of their release have to be negotiated."

Cajal's glance shifted to the next screen. "President Vickery?"

A politician's smile accompanied the response: "Events have compelled me to change my opinion as regards the strategic picture, Admiral. I remain firm in my opposition to absolutist attitudes. My esteemed colleague, Governor Saracoglu, has always impressed me as being similarly reasonable. You have lately returned from a prolonged conference with him. Doubtless many intelligent, well-informed persons took part. Did no possibility of compromise emerge?"

Cajal sagged. "I could argue and dicker for days," he said. "What's the use? I'll exercise my discretionary powers and lay before you at once the maximum I'm authorized to offer."

Holm gripped the arms of his chair.

"The governor pointed out that Avalon can be considered as having already met most terms of the armistice," crawled from Cajal. "Its orbital fortifications no longer exist. Its fleet is a fragment whose sequestration, as required, would make no real difference to you. Most important, Imperial units *are* now on your planet.

"Nothing is left save a few technicalities. Our wounded and our medics must be given the acknowledged name of occupation forces. A command must be established over your military facilities; one or two men per station will satisfy that requirement while posing no threat of takeover should the truce come apart. Et cetera. You see the general idea."

"The saving of face," Holm grunted. "Uh-huh. Why not? But how about afterward?"

"The peace treaty remains to be formulated," said the drained voice. "I can tell you in strict confidence, Governor Saracoglu has sent to the Imperium his strongest recommendation that Avalon not be annexed."

Vickery started babbling. Liaw held stiff. Holm gusted a breath and sat back.

They'd done it. They really had.

The talk would go on, of course. And on and on and on, along with infinite petty particulars and endless niggling. No matter. Avalon would stay Ythrian—stay free.

I ought to whoop, he thought. *Maybe later. Too tired now.*

His immediate happiness, quiet and deep, was at knowing that tonight he could go home to Rowena.

XIX

There were no instant insights, no dramatic revelations and reconciliations. But Arinnian was to remember a certain hour.

His work for his father had stopped being very demanding. He realized he should use the free time he had regained to phase back into his studies. Then he decided that nothing was more impractical than misplaced practicality. Tabitha agreed. She got herself put on inactive duty. Eventually, however, she must return to her island and set her affairs in order, if only for the sake of her partner's family. Meanwhile he was still confined to Gray.

He phoned Eyath at her rented room: "Uh, would you, uh, care to go for a sail?"

Yes, she said with every quill.

Conditions were less than perfect. As the boat left the

bay, rain came walking. The hull skipped over choppy olive-dark waves, tackle athrum; water slanted from hidden heaven, long spears which broke on the skin and ran down in cool splinters, rushing where they entered the sea.

"Shall we keep on?" he asked.

"I would like to." Her gaze sought land, a shadow aft. No other vessels were abroad, nor any flyers. "It's restful to be this alone."

He nodded. He had stripped, and the cleanness dwelt in his hair and sluiced over his flesh.

She regarded him from her perch on the cabin top, across the cockpit which separated them. "You had something to tell me," she said with two words and her body.

"Yes." The tiller thrilled between his fingers. "Last night, before she left—" In Planha he need speak no further.

"Galemate, galemate," she breathed. "I rejoice." She half extended her wings toward him, winced, and withdrew them.

"For always," he said in awe.

"I could have wished none better than Hrill, for you," Eyath replied. Scanning him closer: "You remain in fret."

He bit his lip.

Eyath waited.

"Tell me," he forced forth, staring at the deck. "You see us from outside. Am I able to be what she deserves?"

She did not answer at once. Startled not to receive the immediate yea he had expected, Arinnian lifted his eyes to her silence. He dared not interrupt her thought. Waves boomed, rain laughed.

Finally she said, "I believe she is able to make you able."

He nursed the wound. Eyath began to apologize, summoned resolution and did not. "I have long felt," she told him, "that you needed someone like Hrill to show you that—show you how—what is wrong for my folk is right, is the end and meaning of life, for yours."

He mustered his own courage to say, "I knew the second part of that in theory. Now she comes as the glorious fact. Oh, I was jealous before. I still am, maybe I will be till I die, unable to help myself. She, though, she's worth anything it costs. What I am learning, Eyath, my sister, is that she is not you and you are not her, and it is good that you both are what you are."

"She has given you wisdom." The Ythrian hunched up against the rain.

Arinnian saw her grief and exclaimed, "Let me pass the gift on. What befell you—"

She raised her head to look wildly upon him.

"Was that worse than what befell her?" he challenged. "I don't ask for pity"—human word—"because of past foolishness, but I do think my lot was more hard than either of yours, the years I wasted imagining bodily love can ever be bad, imagining it has any real difference from the kind of love I bear to you, Eyath. Now we'll have to right each other. I want you to share my hopes."

She sprang down from the cabin, stumbled to him and folded him in her wings. Her head she laid murmuring against his shoulder. Raindrops glistened within the crest like jewels of a crown.

The treaty was signed at Fleurville on a day of late winter. Little ceremony was involved and the Ythrian delegates left almost at once. "Not in very deep anger," Ekrem Saracoglu explained to Luisa Cajal, who had declined his invitation to attend. "By and large, they take their loss philosophically. But we couldn't well ask them to sit through our rituals." He drew on his cigaret. "Frankly, I too was glad to get off that particular hook."

He had, in fact, simply made a televised statement and avoided the solemnities afterward. A society like Esperance's was bound to mark the formal end of hostilities by slow marches and slower thanksgiving services.

That was yesterday. The weather continued mild on this following afternoon, and Luisa agreed to come to dinner. She said her father felt unwell, which, regardless of his liking and respect for the man, did not totally displease Saracoglu.

They walked in the garden, she and he, as often before. Around paths which had been cleared, snow decked the beds, the bushes and boughs, the top of the wall, still white although it was melting, here and there making thin chimes and gurgles as the water ran. No flowers were left outdoors, the air held only dampness, and the sky was an even dove-gray. Stillness lay beneath it, so that footfalls scrunched loud on gravel.

"Besides," he added, "it was a relief to see the spokesman for Avalon and his cohorts board their ship. The secret-service men I'd assigned to guard them were downright ecstatic."

"Really?" She glanced up, which gave him a chance to dwell on luminous eyes, tip-tilted nose, lips always parted as if in a child's eagerness. But she spoke earnestly—too earnestly, too much of the time, damn it. "I knew there had been some idiot anonymous death threats against them. Were you that worried?"

He nodded. "I've come to know my dear Esperancians. When Avalon dashed their original jubilation—well, you've seen and heard the stuff about 'intransigent militarists.'" He wondered if his fur cap hid his baldness or reminded her of it. Maybe he should break down and get a scalp job.

Troubled, she asked, "Will they ever forget . . . both sides?"

"No," he said. "I do expect grudges will fade. We've too many mutual interests, Terra and Ythri, to make a family fight into a blood feud. I hope."

"We *were* more generous than we had to be. Weren't we? Like letting them keep Avalon. Won't that count?"

"It should." Saracoglu grinned on the left side of his mouth, took a final acrid puff and tossed his cigaret away. "Though everybody sees the practical politics involved. Avalon proved itself indigestible. Annexation would have spelled endless trouble, whereas Avalon as a mere enclave poses no obvious difficulties such as the war was fought to terminate. Furthermore, by this concession, the Empire won some valuable points with respect to trade that might otherwise not have been feasible to insist on."

"I know," she said, a bit impatiently.

He chuckled. "You also know I like to hear myself talk." She grew wistful. "I'd love to visit Avalon."

"Me too. Especially for the sociological interest. I wonder if that planet doesn't foreshadow the distant future."

"How?"

He kept his slow pace and did not forget her arm resting on his; but he squinted before him and said out of his most serious thought, "The biracial culture they're creat-

ing. Or that's creating itself; you can't plan or direct a
new current in history. I wonder if that wasn't the source
of their resistance—like an alloy or a two-phase material,
many times stronger than either part that went into it.
We've a galaxy, a cosmos to fill—"

My, what a mixed bag of metaphors, including this one,
gibed his mind. He laughed inwardly, shrugged outwardly,
and finished: "Well, I don't expect to be around for that.
I don't even suppose I'll have to meet the knottier consequences of leaving Avalon with Ythri."

"What could those be?" Luisa wondered. "You just
said it was the only thing to do."

"Indeed. I may be expressing no more than the natural
pessimism of a man whose lunch at Government House
was less than satisfactory. Still, one can imagine. The
Avalonians, both races, are going to feel themselves more
Ythrian than the Ythrians. I anticipate future generations
of theirs will supply the Domain with an abnormal share,
possibly most of its admirals. Let us hope they do not in
addition supply it with revanchism. And under pacific
conditions, Avalon, a unique world uniquely situated, is
sure to draw more than its share of trade—more important, brains, which follow opportunity. The effects of that
are beyond foreseeing."

Her clasp tightened on his sleeve. "You make me glad
I'm not a statesman."

"Not half as glad as I am that you're not a statesman,"
he said, emphasizing the last syllable. "Come, let's drop
these dismal important matters. Let's discuss—for example, your tour of Avalon. I'm sure it can be arranged, a
few months hence."

She turned her face from him. When the muteness had
lasted a minute, he stopped, as did she. "What's the matter?" he asked, frightened.

"I'm leaving, Ekrem," she said. "Soon. Permanently."

"What?" He restrained himself from seizing her.

"Father. He sent in his resignation today."

"I know he . . . has been plagued by malicious accusations. You recall I wrote to Admiralty Center."

"Yes. That was nice of you." She met his eyes again.

"No more than my duty, Luisa." The fear would not
leave him, but he was pleased to note that he spoke firmly
and maintained his second-best smile. "The Empire needs

good men. No one could have predicted the Scorpeluna disaster, nor done more after the thing happened than Juan Cajal did. Blaming him, calling for court-martial, is wizened spite, and I assure you nothing will come of it."

"But he blames himself," she cried low.

I have no answer to that, he thought.

"We're going back to Nuevo México," she said.

"I realize," he attempted, "these scenes may be unduly painful to him. Need you leave, however?"

"Who else has he?"

"Me. I, ah, will presumably get an eventual summons to Terra—"

"I'm sorry, Ekrem." Her lashes dropped over the delicate cheekbones. "Terra would be no good either. I won't let him gnaw away his heart alone. At home, among his own kind, it will be better." She smiled, not quite steadily, and tossed her head. *"Our* kind. I admit a little homesickness myself. Come visit us sometime." She chose her words: "No doubt I'll be getting married. I think, if you don't mind, I think I'd like to name a boy for you."

"Why, I would be honored beyond anything the Emperor could hang on this downward-slipping chest of mine," he said automatically. "Shall we go inside? The hour's a trifle early for drinks, perhaps; on the other hand, this is a special occasion."

Ah, well, he thought above the pain, *the daydream was a pleasant guest, but now I am freed from the obligations of a host. I can relax and enjoy the games of governor, knight, elevated noble, Lord Advisor, retired statesman dictating interminable and mendacious memoirs.*

Tomorrow I must investigate the local possibilities with respect to bouncy and obliging ladies. After all, we are only middle-aged once.

Summer dwelt in Gray when word reached Avalon. There had been some tension—who could really trust the Empire?—and thus joy amid the human population exploded in festival.

Bird, Christopher Holm and Tabitha Falkayn soon left the merriment. Announcements, ceremonies, feasts could wait; they had decided that the night of final peace would be their wedding night.

Nonetheless they felt no need of haste. That was not

the way of the choths. Rather, two sought to become one with their world, their destiny, and their dead—whether in waiting for lovetime or in love itself—until all trouble had been mastered and they could freely become one with each other.

Beyond the northern headland, the hills were as yet uninhabited, though plants whose ancestral seeds arrived with the pioneers had here long ceased to be foreign. Chris and Tabby landed in a sunset whose red and gold ran berserk above a quiet sea. They pitched camp, ate, drank a small glass of wine and a long kiss; afterward, hand in hand, they walked a trail which followed the ridge.

On their left, as daylight smoldered away, grasses wherein clustered trefoil and sword-of-sorrow fell steeply down to the waters. These glimmered immense, out to a horizon which lost itself in a sky deepening from violet to crystalline black. The evening star stood as a candle among the awakening constellations. On their right was forest, darkling, still sweet from odors of pine. A warm small breeze made harp vines ring and brightness twinkle among the jewelleafs.

"Eyath?" she asked once.

"Homebound," he answered.

That, and his tone and the passage of his mouth across her dimly seen hair, said: *In showing me I must heal her, and how, you healed me, my darling.*

Her fingertips, touching his cheek, said: *To my own gladness, which grew and grew.*

Nevertheless he sensed a question in her. He thought he knew what it was. It had often risen in him; but he, the reader, philosopher, poet, could inquire of the centuries better than she, whose gift was to understand the now.

He did not press her to voice it. Enough for this hour, that she was here and his.

Morgana rose, full, murky-spotted and less bright than formerly. So much had it been scarred. Tabby halted.

"Was it worth it?" she said. He heard the lingering anguish.

"The war, you mean?" he prompted.

"Yes." Her free arm rose. "Look there. Look everywhere—around this globe, out to those suns—death, maiming, agony, mourning, ruin—losses like that yonder, things we've cheated our children of—to make a political point!"

"I've wondered too," he confessed. "Remember, though, we did keep something for the children that they'd otherwise have lost. We kept their right to be themselves."

"You mean to be what we are. Suppose we'd been defeated. We nearly were. The next generation would have grown up as reasonably contented Imperial subjects. Wouldn't they have? So had we the right in the first place to do what we did?"

"I've decided yes," he said. "Not that any simple principle exists, and not that I couldn't be wrong. But it seems to me—well, that which we are, our society or culture or what you want to name it, has a life and a right of its own."

He drew breath. "Best beloved," he said, "if communities didn't resist encroachments, they'd soon be swallowed by the biggest and greediest. Wouldn't they? In the end, dead sameness. No challenges, no inspirations from somebody else's way. What service is it to life if we let that happen?

"And, you know, enmities needn't be eternal. I daresay, oh, for instance, Governor Saracoglu and Admiral Cajal had ancestors on opposite sides at Lepanto." He saw that she didn't grasp his reference. No matter, she followed his drift. "The point is, both strove, both resisted, both survived to give something to the race, something special that none else could have given. Can't you believe that here on Avalon we've saved part of the future?"

"Bloodstained," she said.

"That wasn't needful," he agreed. "And yet, we sophonts being what we are, it was unavoidable. Maybe someday there'll be something better. Maybe, even, this thing of ours, winged and wingless together, will help. We have to keep trying, of course."

"And we do have peace for a while," she whispered.

"Can't we be happy in that?" he asked.

Then she smiled through moonlit tears and said, "Yes, Arinnian, Chris, dearest of all," and sought him.

Eyath left Gray before dawn.

At that hour, after the night's revel, she had the sky to herself. Rising, she captured a wind and rode it further aloft. It flowed, it sang. The last stars, the sinking moon turned sea and land into mystery; ahead, sharp across whiteness, lifted the mountains of home.

It was cold, but that sent the blood storming within her.

She thought: *He who cared for me and he who got me share the same honor. Enough.*

Muscles danced, wings beat, alive to the outermost pinion. The planet spun toward morning. *My brother, my sister have found their joy. Let me go seek my own.*

Snowpeaks flamed. The sun stood up in a shout of light. *High is heaven and holy.*

The Day of
Their Return

To
Marion Zimmer Bradley,
my lady of Darkover

Now a thing was secretly brought to me, and mine ear received a little thereof. In thoughts from the visions of the night, when deep sleep falleth on men, fear came upon me, and trembling, which made all my bones to shake. Then a spirit passed before my face; the hair of my flesh stood up: it stood still, but I could not discern the form thereof: an image was before mine eyes, there was silence, and I heard a voice. . . .

—JOB, iv, 12–16

I

On the third day he arose, and ascended again to the light.

Dawn gleamed across a sea which had once been an ocean. To north, cliffs lifted blue from the steel gray of its horizon; and down them went a streak which was the falls, whose thunder beat dim through a windless cold. The sky stood violet in the west, purple overhead, white in the east where the sun came climbing. But still the morning star shone there, the planet of the First Chosen.

I am the first of the Second Chosen, Jaan knew: *and the voice of those who choose. To be man is to be radiance.*

His nostrils drank air, his muscles exulted. Never had he been this aware. From the brightness of his face to the grit below his feet, he was real.

—O glory upon glory, said that which within him was Caruith.

—It overwhelms this poor body, said Jaan. I am new to resurrection. Do you not feel yourself a stranger in chains?

—Six million years have blown by in the night, said Caruith. I remember waves besparkled and a shout of surf, where now stones lie gaunt beneath us; I remember pride in walls and columns, where ruin huddles above the mouth of the tomb whence we have come; I remember how clouds walked clad in rainbows. Before all, I seek to remember—and fail, because the flesh I am cannot bear the fire I was—I seek to remember the fullness of existence.

Jaan lifted hands to the crown engirdling his brows. —For you, this is a heavy burden, he said.

—No, sang Caruith. I share the opening that it has

3

made for you and your race. I will grow with you, and you with me, and they with us, until mankind is not only worthy to be received into Oneness, it will bring thereunto what is wholly its own. And at last sentience will create God. Now come, let us proclaim it to the people.

He/they went up the mountain toward the Arena. Above them paled Dido, the morning star.

II

East of Windhome the country rolled low for a while, then lifted in the Hesperian Hills. Early summer had gentled their starkness with leaves. Blue-green, gray-green, here and there the intense green-green of oak or cedar, purple of rasmin, spread in single trees, bushes, widely spaced groves, across an onyx tinged red and yellow which was the land's living mantle, fire trava.

A draught blew from sunset. Ivar Frederiksen shivered. Even his gunstock felt cold beneath his hand. The sward he lay on had started to curl up for the night, turning into a springy mat. Its daytime odor of flint and sparks was almost gone. A delphi overarched him: gnarled low trunk, grotto of branches and foliage. Multitudinous rustlings went through it, like whispers in an unknown tongue. His vision ranged over a slope bestrewn with shrubs and boulders, to a valley full of shadow. The riverside road was lost in that dusk, the water a wan gleam. His heart knocked, louder than the sound of the Wildfoss flowing.

Nobody. Will they never come?

A flash caught his eye and breath. An aircraft out of the west?

No. The leaves in their restlessness had confused him. What rose above Hornbeck Ridge was just Creusa. Laughter snapped forth, a sign of how taut were his nerves. As if to seek companionship, he followed the moon. It glimmered ever more bright, waxing while it climbed eastward. A pair of wings likewise caught rays from the hidden sun and shone gold against indigo heaven.

Easy! he tried to scold himself. *You're nigh on disminded. What if this will be your first battle? No excuse. You're ringleader, aren't you?*

Though born to the thin dry air of Aeneas, he felt his nasal passages hurt, his tongue leather. He reached for a canteen. Filled at yonder stream, it gave him a taste of iron.

"Aah—" he began. And then the Imperials were come.

They appeared like that, sudden as a blow. A part of him knew how. Later than awaited, they had been concealed by twilight and a coppice in his line of sight, until their progress brought them into unmistakable view. But had none of his followers seen them earlier? The guerrillas covered three kilometers on both sides of the gorge. This didn't speak well for their readiness.

Otherwise Ivar was caught in a torrent. He didn't know what roared through him, fear, anger, insanity, nor had he time to wonder. He did observe, in a flicker of amazement, no heroic joy or stern determination. His body obeyed plans while something wailed, *How did I get into this? How do I get out?*

He was on his feet. He gave the hunting cry of a spider wolf, and heard it echoed and passed on. He pulled the hood of his jacket over his head, the nightmask over his face. He snatched his rifle off the ground and sprang from the shelter of the delphi.

Every sense was fever-brilliant. He saw each coiled blade of the fire trava whereon he ran, felt how it gave beneath his boots and rebounded, caught a last warmth radiated from a giant rock, drank in the sweetness of a cedar, brushed the roughness of an oak, could have counted the petals a rasmin spread above him or measured the speed at which a stand of plume trava folded against the gathering cold—but that was all on the edge of awareness, as was the play inside of muscles, nerves, blood, lungs, pulse—his being was aimed at his enemies.

They were human, a platoon of marines, afoot save for the driver of a field gun. It hummed along on a gravsled, two meters off the road. Though helmeted, the men were in loose order and walked rather than marched, expecting no trouble on a routine patrol. Most had connected the powerpacks on their shoulders to the heating threads in their baggy green coveralls.

The infrascope on Ivar's rifle told him that. His eyes told of comrades who rose from bush and leaped down the hillsides, masked and armed like him. His ears caught raw young voices, war-calls and wordless yells. Shots crackled. The Aeneans had double the number of their prey, advantage of surprise, will to be free.

They lacked energy weapons; but a sleet of bullets converged on the artillery piece. Ivar saw its driver cast from his seat, a red rag. *We've got them!* He sent a burst himself, then continued his charge, low and zigzag. The plan, the need was to break the platoon and carry their equipment into the wilderness.

The cannon descended. Ivar knew, too late: *Some kind of dead-man switch.* The marines, who had thrown their bodies flat, got up and sought it. A few lay wounded or slain; the rest reached its shelter. Blaster bolts flared and boomed, slugthrowers raved. The Aenean closest to Ivar trembled, rolled over and over, came to a halt and screamed. Screamed. Screamed. His blood on the turf was outrageously bright, spread impossibly wide.

A new Imperial took the big gun's controls. Lightning flew across the river, which threw its blue-whiteness back like molten metal. Thunder hammered. Where that beam passed were no more trees or shrubs or warriors. Smoke roiled above ash.

Blind and deaf, Ivar fell. He clawed at the soil, because he thought the planet was trying to whirl him off.

After a fraction of eternity, the delirium passed. His head still tolled, tatters of light drifted before his vision, but he could hear, see, almost think.

A daggerbush partly screened him. He had ripped his right sleeve and arm on it, but was otherwise unhurt. Nearby sprawled a corpse. Entrails spilled forth. The mask hid which friend this had been. How wrong, how obscene to expose the guts without the face.

Ivar strained through gloom. The enemy had not turned their fieldpiece on this bank of the river. Instead, they used small arms as precision tools. Against their skill and discipline, the guerrillas were glass tossed at armor plate.

Guerrillas? We children? And I led us. Ivar fought not to vomit, not to weep.

He must sneak off. Idiot luck, nothing else, had kept him alive and unnoticed. But the marines were taking prisoners. He saw them bring in several who were lightly injured. Several more, outgunned, raised their hands.

Nobody keeps a secret from a hypnoprobe.

Virgil slipped beneath an unseen horizon. Night burst forth.

Aeneas rotates in twenty hours, nineteen minutes, and a few seconds. Dawn was not far when Ivar Frederiksen reached Windhome.

Gray granite walled the ancestral seat of the Firstman of Ilion. It stood near the edge of an ancient cape. In tiers and scarps, crags and cliffs, thinly brush-grown or naked rock, the continental shelf dropped down three kilometers to the Antonine Seabed. So did the river, a flash by the castle, a clangor of cataracts.

The portal stood closed, a statement that the occupation troops were considered bandits. Ivar stumbled to press the scanner plate. Chimes echoed emptily.

Weariness was an ache which rose in his marrow and seeped through bones and flesh till blood ran thick with it. His knees shook, his jaws clattered. The dried sweat that he could taste and smell on himself stung the cracks in his lips. Afraid to use roads, he had fled a long and rough way.

He leaned on the high steel door and sucked air through a mummy mouth. A breeze sheathed him in iciness. Yet somehow he had never been as aware of the beauty of this land, now when it was lost to him.

The sky soared crystalline black, wild with stars. Through the thin air they shone steadily, in diamond hues; and the Milky Way was a white torrent, and a kindred cloud in the Ula was our sister galaxy spied across a million and a half light-years. Creusa had set; but slower Lavinia rode aloft in her second quarter. Light fell argent on hoarfrost.

Eastward reached fields, meadows, woodlots, bulks that were sleeping farmsteads, and at last the hills. Ivar's gaze fared west. There the rich bottomlands ran in orchards, plantations, canals night-frozen into mirrors, the burnished shield of a salt marsh, to the world's rim. He thought he saw lights move. Were folk abroad already? No, he couldn't make out lamps over such a distance ... lanterns on ghost ships, sailing an ocean that vanished three million years ago. ...

The portal swung wide. Sergeant Astaff stood behind. In defiance of Imperial decree, his stocky frame bore Ilian uniform. He had left off hood and mask, though. In the unreal luminance, his head was not grizzled, it was as white as the words which puffed from him.

"Firstlin' Ivar! Where you been? What's gone on? Your

mother's gnawed fear for you this whole past five-day."

The heir to the house lurched by him. Beyond the gate-way, the courtyard was crisscrossed with moon-shadows from towers, battlements, main keep and lesser building. A hound, of the lean heavy-jawed Hesperian breed, was the only other life in sight. Its claws clicked on flagstones, unnaturally loud.

Astaff pushed a button to close the door. For a time he squinted until he said slowly, "Better give me that rifle, Firstlin'. I know places where Terrans won't poke."

"Me too," sighed from Ivar.

"Didn't do you a lot o' good, stashed away till you were ready for—whatever you've done—hey?" Astaff held out his hand.

"Trouble I'm in, it makes no difference if they catch me with this." Ivar took hold of the firearm. "Except I'd make them pay for me."

Something kindled in the old man. He, like his fathers before him, had served the Firstmen of Ilion for a life-time. Nevertheless, or else for that same reason, pain was in his tone. "Why'd you not ask me for help?"

"You'd have talked me out of it," Ivar said. "You'd have been right," he added.

"What did you try?"

"Ambushin' local patrol. To start stockpilin' weapons. I don't know how many of us escaped. Probably most didn't."

Astaff regarded him.

Ivar Frederiksen was tall, 185 centimeters, slender save for wide shoulders and the Aenean depth of chest. Ex-haustion weighted down his normal agility and hoarsened the tenor voice. Snub-nosed, square-jawed, freckled, his face looked still younger than it was; no noticeable beard had grown during the past hours. His hair, cut short at nape and ears in the nord manner, was yellow, seldom free of a cowlick or a stray lock across the forehead. Beneath dark brows, his eyes were large and green. Under his jacket he wore the high-collared shirt, pouched belt, heavy-bladed sheath knife, thick trousers tucked into half-boots, of ordinary outdoor dress. There was, in truth, little to mark him off from any other upper-class lad of his planet.

That little was enough.

"What caveheads you were," the sergeant said at last.

A twitch of anger: "We should sit clay-soft for Terrans to mold, fire, and use however they see fit?"

"Well," Astaff replied, "I would've planned my strike better, and drilled longer beforetime."

He took Ivar by the elbow. "You're spent like a cartridge," he said. "Go to my quarters. You remember where I bunk, no? Thank Lord, my wife's off visitin' our daughter's family. Grab shower, food, sleep. I've sentry-go till oh-five-hundred. Can't call substitute without drawin' questions; but nobody'll snuff at you."

Ivar blinked. "What do you mean? My own rooms—"

"Yah!" Astaff snorted. "Go on. Rouse your mother, your kid sister. Get 'em involved. Sure. They'll be interrogated, you know, soon's Impies've found you were in that broil. They'll be narcoquizzed, or even 'probed, if any reason develops to think they got clue to your whereabouts. That what you want? Okay. Go bid 'em fond farewell."

Ivar took a backward step, lifted his hands in appeal. "No. I, I, I never thought—"

"Right."

"Of course I'll— What do you have in mind?" Ivar asked humbly.

"Get you off before Impies arrive. Good thing your dad's been whole while in Nova Roma; clear-cut innocent, and got influence to protect family *if* Terrans find no sign you were ever here after fight. Hey? You'll leave soon. Wear servant's livery I'll filch for you, snoutmask like you're sneezewort allergic, weapon under cloak. Walk like you got hurry-up errand. This is big household; nobody ought to notice you especially. I'll've found some yeoman who'll take you in, Sam Hedin, Frank Vance, whoever, loyal and livin' offside. You go there."

"And then?"

Astaff, shrugged. "Who knows? When zoosny's died down, I'll slip your folks word you're alive and loose. Maybe later your dad can wangle pardon for you. But if Terrans catch you while their dead are fresh—son, they'll make example. I know Empire. Traveled through it more than once with Admiral McCormac." As he spoke the name, he saluted. The average Imperial agent who saw would have arrested him on the spot.

Ivar swallowed and stammered, "I . . . I can't thank—"

"You're next Firstman of Ilion," the sergeant snapped. "Maybe last hope we got, this side of Elders returnin'. Now, before somebody comes, haul your butt out of here—and don't forget the rest of you!"

III

Chunderban Desai's previous assignment had been to the delegation which negotiated an end of the Jihannath crisis. That wasn't the change of pace in his career which it seemed. His Majesty's administrators must forever be dickering, compromising, feeling their way, balancing conflicts of individuals, organizations, societies, races, sentient species. The need for skill—quickly to grasp facts, comprehend a situation, brazen out a bluff when in spite of everything the unknown erupted into one's calculations—was greatest at the intermediate level of bureaucracy which he had reached. A resident might deal with a single culture, and have no more to do than keep an eye on affairs. A sector governor oversaw such vastness that to him it became a set of abstractions. But the various ranks of commissioner were expected to handle personally large and difficult territories.

Desai had worked in regions that faced Betelgeuse and, across an unclaimed and ill-explored buffer zone, the Roidhunate of Merseia. Thus he was a natural choice for the special diplomatic team. In his quiet style, he backstopped the head of it, Lord Advisor Chardon, so well that afterward he received a raise in grade, and was appointed High Commissioner of the Virgilian System, at the opposite end of the Empire.

But this was due to an equally natural association of ideas. The mutiny in Sector Alpha Crucis had been possible because most of the Navy was tied up around Jihannath, where full-scale war looked far too likely. After Terra nevertheless, brilliantly, put the rebels down, Merseia announced that its wish all along had been to avoid a major clash and it was prepared to bargain.

When presently the Policy Board looked about for able people to reconstruct Sector Alpha Crucis, Lord Chardon recommended Desai with an enthusiasm that got him put in charge of Virgil, whose human-colonized planet Aeneas had been the spearhead of the revolt.

Perhaps that was why Desai often harked back to the Merseians, however remote from him they seemed these days.

In a rare moment of idleness, while he waited in his Nova Roma office for the next visitor, he remembered his final conversation with Uldwyr.

They had played corresponding roles on behalf of their respective sovereigns, and in a wry way had become friends. When the protocol had, at weary last, been drawn, the two of them supplemented the dull official celebration with a dinner of their own.

Desai recalled their private room in a restaurant. The wall animations were poor; but a place which catered to a variety of sophonts couldn't be expected to understand everybody's art, and the meal was an inspired combination of human and Merseian dishes.

"Have a refill," Uldwyr invited, and raised a crock of his people's pungent ale.

"No, thank you," Desai said. "I prefer tea. That dessert filled me to the scuppers."

"The what? —Never mind, I seize the idea, if not the idiom." Though each was fluent in the other's principal language, and their vocal organs were not very different, it was easiest for Desai to speak Anglic and Uldwyr Eriau. "You've tucked in plenty of food, for certain."

"My particular vice, I fear," Desai smiled. "Besides, more alcohol would muddle me. I haven't your mass to assimilate it."

"What matter if you get drunk? I plan to. Our job is done." And then Uldwyr added: "For now."

Shocked, Desai stared across the table.

Uldwyr gave him back a quizzical glance. The Merseian's face was almost human, if one overlooked thick bones and countless details of the flesh. But his finely scaled green skin had no hair whatsoever, he lacked earflaps, a low serration ran from the top of his skull, down his back to the end of the crocodilian tail which counterbalanced his big, forward-leaning body. Arms and hands were, again, nearly manlike; legs and clawed splay feet could have belonged to a biped dinosaur. He wore black, silver-trimmed military tunic and trousers, colorful emblems of rank and of the Vach Hallen into which he was born. A blaster hung on his hip.

"What's the matter?" he asked.

"Oh ... nothing." In Desai's mind went: *He didn't mean it hostilely—hostilely to me as a person—his remark. He, his whole civilization, minces words less small than we do. Struggle against Terra is just a fact. The Roidhunate will compromise disputes when expediency dictates, but never the principle that eventually the Empire must be destroyed. Because we—old, sated, desirous only of maintaining a peace which lets us pursue our pleasures—we stand in the way of their ambitions for the Race. Lest the balance of power be upset, we block them, we thwart them, wherever we can; and they seek to undermine us, grind us down, wear us out. But this is nothing personal. I am Uldwyr's honorable enemy, therefore his friend. By giving him opposition, I give meaning to his life.*

The other divined his thoughts and uttered the harsh Merseian chuckle. "If you want to pretend tonight that matters have been settled for aye, do. I'd really rather we both got drunk and traded war songs."

"I am not a man of war," Desai said.

Beneath a shelf of brow ridge, Uldwyr's eyelids expressed skepticism while his mouth grinned. "You mean you don't like physical violence. It was quite an effective war you waged at the conference table."

He swigged from his tankard. Desai saw that he was already a little tipsy. "I imagine the next phase will also be quiet," he went on. "Ungloved force hasn't worked too well lately. Starkad, Jihannath—no, I'd look for us to try something more crafty and long-range. Which ought to suit your Empire, *khraich?* You've made a good thing for your Naval Intelligence out of the joint commission on Talwin." Desai, who knew that, kept silence. "Maybe our turn is coming."

Hating his duty, Desai asked in his most casual voice, "Where?"

"Who knows?" Uldwyr gestured the equivalent of a shrug. "I have no doubt, and neither do you, we've a swarm of agents in Sector Alpha Crucis, for instance. Besides the recent insurrection, it's close to the Domain of

Ythri, which has enjoyed better relations with us than with you—" His hand chopped the air. "No, I'm distressing you, am I not? And with what can only be guesswork. Apologies. See here, if you don't care for more ale, why not arthberry brandy? I guarantee a first-class drunk and— You may suppose you're a peaceful fellow, Chunderban, but I know an atom or two about your people, your specific people, I mean. What's that old, old book I've heard you mention and quote from? Rixway?"

"Rig-Veda," Desai told him.

"You said it includes war chants. Do you know any well enough to put into Anglic? There's a computer terminal." He pointed to a corner. "You can patch right into our main translator, now that official business is over. I'd like to hear a bit of your special tradition, Chunderban. So many traditions, works, mysteries—so tiny a lifespan to taste them—"

It became a memorable evening.

Restless, Desai stirred in his chair.

He was a short man with a dark-brown moon face and a paunch. At fifty-five standard years of age, his hair remained black but had receded from the top of his head. The full lips were usually curved slightly upward, which joined the liquid eyes to give him a wistful look. As was his custom, today he wore plain, loosely fitted white shirt and trousers, on his feet slippers a size large for comfort.

Save for the communication and data-retrieval consoles that occupied one wall, his office was similarly unpretentious. It did have a spectacular holograph, a view of Mount Gandhi on his home planet, Ramanujan. But otherwise the pictures were of his wife, their seven children, the families of those four who were grown and settled on as many different globes. A bookshelf held codices as well as reels; some were much-used reference works, the rest for refreshment, poetry, history, essays, most of their authors centuries dust. His desk was less neat than his person.

I shouldn't go taking vacations in the past, he thought. *God knows the present needs more of me than I have to give.*

Or does it? Spare me the ultimate madness of ever considering myself indispensable.

Well, but somebody must man this post. He happens to be me.

*Must somebody? How much really occurs because of
me, how much in spite of or regardless of? How much,
and what, should occur? God! I dared accept the job of
ruling, remaking an entire world—when I knew nothing
more about it than its name, and that simply because it
was the planet of Hugh McCormac, the man who would
be Emperor. After two years, what else have I learned?*

Ordinarily he could sit quiet, but the Hesperian episode
had been too shocking, less in itself than in its implica-
tions. Whatever they were. How could he plan against the
effect on these people, once the news got out, when he,
the foreigner, had no intuition of what that effect might
be?

He put a cigarette into a long, elaborately carved holder
of landwhale ivory. (He thought it was in atrocious taste,
but it had been given him for a birthday present by a ten-
year-old daughter who died soon afterward.) The tobacco
was an expensive self-indulgence, grown on Esperance,
the closest thing to Terran he could obtain hereabouts
while shipping remained sparse.

The smoke-bite didn't soothe him. He jumped up and
prowled. He hadn't yet adapted so fully to the low gravity
of Aeneas, 63 percent standard, that he didn't consciously
enjoy movement. The drawback was the dismal exercises
he must go through each morning, if he didn't want to
turn completely into lard. Unfair, that the Aeneans tended
to be such excellent physical specimens without effort. No,
not really unfair. On this niggard sphere, few could afford
a large panoply of machines; even today, more travel was
on foot or animal back than in vehicles, more work done
by hand than by automatons or cybernets. Also, in earlier
periods—the initial colonization, the Troubles, the slow
climb back from chaos—death had winnowed the unfit out
of their bloodlines.

Desai halted at the north wall, activated its transparency, and gazed forth across Nova Roma.

Though itself two hundred Terran years old, Imperial
House jutted awkwardly from the middle of a city founded seven centuries ago. Most buildings in this district
were at least half that age, and architecture had varied little through time. In a climate where it seldom rained and
never snowed; where the enemies were drought, cold, hurricane winds, drifting dust, scouring sand; where water for
bricks and concrete, forests for timber, organics for syn-

thesis were rare and precious, one quarried the stone which Aeneas did have in abundance, and used its colors and textures.

The typical structure was a block, two or three stories tall, topped by a flat deck which was half garden—the view from above made a charming motley—and half solar-energy collector. Narrow windows carried shutters ornamented with brass or iron arabesques; the heavy doors were of similar appearance. In most cases, the gray ashlars bore a veneer of carefully chosen and integrated slabs, marble, agate, chalcedony, jasper, nephrite, materials more exotic than that; and often there were carvings besides, friezes, armorial bearings, grotesques; and erosion had mellowed it all, to make the old part of town one subtle harmony. The wealthier homes, shops, and offices surrounded cloister courts, vitryl-roofed to conserve heat and water, where statues and plants stood among fishponds and fountains.

The streets were cramped and twisted, riddled with alleys, continually opening on small irrational plazas. Traffic was thin, mainly pedestrian, otherwise groundcars, trucks, and countryfolk on soft-gaited Aenean horses or six-legged green stathas (likewise foreign, though Desai couldn't offhand remember where they had originated). A capital city—population here a third of a million, much the largest—would inevitably hurt more and recover slower from a war than its hinterland.

He lifted his eyes to look onward. Being to south, the University wasn't visible through this wall. What he saw was the broad bright sweep of the River Flone, and ancient high-arched bridges across it; beyond, the Julian Canal, its tributaries, verdant parks along them, barges and pleasure boats upon their surfaces; farther still, the intricacy of many lesser but newer canals, the upthrust of modern buildings in garish colors, a tinge of industrial haze—the Web.

However petty by Terran standards, he thought, that youngest section was the seedbed of his hopes: in the manufacturing, mercantile, and managerial classes which had arisen during the past few generations, whose interests lay less with the scholars and squirearchs than with the Imperium and its Pax.

Or can I call on them? he wondered. *I've been doing it; but how reliable are they?*

A single planet is too big for single me to understand.

Right and left he spied the edge of wilderness. Life lay emerald on either side of the Flone, where it ran majestically down from the north polar cap. He could see hamlets, manors, water traffic; he knew that the banks were croplands and pasture. But the belt was only a few kilometers wide.

Elsewhere reared worn yellow cliffs, black basalt ridges, ocherous dunes, on and on beneath a sky almost purple. Shadows were sharper-edged than on Terra or Ramanujan, for the sun was half again as far away, its disc shrunken. He knew that now, in summer at a middle latitude, the air was chill; he observed on the tossing tendrils of a rahab tree in a roof garden how strongly the wind blew. Come sunset, temperatures would plunge below freezing. And yet Virgil was brighter than Sol, an F7; one could not look near it without heavy eye protection, and Desai marveled that light-skinned humans had ever settled in lands this cruelly irradiated.

Well, planets where unarmored men could live at all were none too common; and there had been the lure of Dido. In the beginning, this was a scientific base, nothing else. No, the second beginning, ages after the unknown builders of what stood in unknowable ruins. . . .

A world, a history like that; and I am supposed to tame them?

His receptionist said through the intercom, "Aycharaych," pronouncing the lilting diphthongs and guttural *ch*'s well. It was programmed to mimic languages the instant it heard them. That gratified visitors, especially nonhumans.

"What?" Desai blinked. The tickler on his desk screened a notation of the appointment. "Oh. Oh, yes." He popped out of his reverie. *That being who arrived on the Llynathawr packet day before yesterday. Wants a permit to conduct studies.* "Send him in, please." (By extending verbal courtesy even to a subunit of a computer, the High Commissioner helped maintain an amicable atmosphere. Perhaps.) The screen noted that the newcomer was male, or at any rate referred to himself as such. Planet of origin was listed as Jean-Baptiste, wherever that might be: doubtless a name bestowed by humans because the autochthons had too many different ones of their own.

The door retracted while Aycharaych stepped through. Desai caught his breath. He had not expected someone this impressive.

Or was that the word? Was "disturbing" more accurate? Xenosophonts who resembled humans occasionally had that effect on the latter; and Aycharaych was more anthropoid than Uldwyr.

One might indeed call him beautiful. He stood tall and thin in a gray robe, broad-chested but wasp-waisted, a frame that ought to have moved gawkily but instead flowed. The bare feet each had four long claws, and spurs on the ankles. The hands were six-fingered, tapered, their nails suggestive of talons. The head arched high and narrow, bearing pointed ears, great rust-red eyes, curved blade of nose, delicate mouth, pointed chin and sharply angled jaws; Desai thought of a Byzantine saint. A crest of blue feathers rose above, and tiny plumes formed eyebrows. Otherwise his skin was wholly smooth across the prominent bones, a glowing golden color.

After an instant's hesitation, Desai said, "Ah ... welcome, Honorable. I hope I can be of service." They shook hands. Aycharaych's was warmer than his. The palm had a hardness that wasn't calluses. *Avian*, the man guessed. *Descended from an analog of flightless birds.*

The other's Anglic was flawless; the musical overtone which his low voice gave sounded not like a mispronunciation but a perfection. "Thank you, Commissioner. You are kind to see me this promptly. I realize how busy you must be."

"Won't you be seated?" The chair in front of the desk didn't have to adjust itself much. Desai resumed his own. "Do you mind if I smoke? Would you care for one?" Aycharaych shook his head to both questions, and smiled; again Desai thought of antique images, archaic Grecian sculpture. "I'm very interested to meet you," he said. "I confess your people are new in my experience."

"We are few who travel off our world," Aycharaych replied. "Our sun is in Sector Aldebaran."

Desai nodded. "M-hm." His business had never involved any society in that region. No surprise. The vaguely bounded, roughly spherical volume over which Terra claimed suzerainty had a diameter of some 400 light-years; it held an estimated four million stars, whereof half were believed to have been visited at least once; approximately 100,000 planets had formalized relations with the Imperium, but for most of them it amounted to no more than acknowledgment of subordination and modest taxes, or merely the obligation to make labor and resources available should the Empire ever have need. In return they got the Pax; and they had a right to join in spatial commerce, though the majority lacked the capital, or the industrial base, or the appropriate kind of culture for that— *Too big, too big. If a single planet overwhelms the intellect, what then of our entire microscopic chip of the galaxy, away off toward the edge of a spiral arm, which we imagine we have begun to be a little acquainted with?*

"You are pensive, Commissioner," Aycharaych remarked.

"Did you notice?" Desai laughed. "You've known quite a few humans, then."

"Your race is ubiquitous," Aycharaych answered politely. "And fascinating. That is my heart reason for coming here."

"Ah . . . pardon me, I've not had a chance to give your documents a proper review. I know only that you wish to travel about on Aeneas for scientific purposes."

"Consider me an anthropologist, if you will. My people have hitherto had scant outside contact, but they anticipate more. My mission for a number of years has been to go to and fro in the Empire, learning the ways of your species, the most numerous and widespread within those borders, so that we may deal wisely with you. I have observed a wonderful variety of life-manners, yes, of thinking, feeling, and perceiving. Your versatility approaches miracle."

"Thank you," said Desai, not altogether comfortably. "I don't believe, myself, we are unique. It merely happened we were the first into space—in our immediate volume and point in history—and our dominant civilization of the time happened to be dynamically expansive. So we spread into many different environments, often isolated, and underwent cultural radiation . . . or fragmentation." He streamed smoke from his nose and peered through it. "Can you, alone, hope to discover much about us?"

"I am not the sole wanderer," Aycharaych said. "Besides, a measure of telepathic ability is helpful."

"Eh?" Desai noticed himself switch over to thinking in Hindi. But what was he afraid of? Sensitivity to neural emissions, talent at interpreting them, was fairly well understood, had been for centuries. Some species were better at it than others; man was among those that brought forth few good cases, none of them first-class. Nevertheless, human scientists had studied the phenomenon as they had studied the wavelengths wherein they were blind. . . .

"You will see the fact mentioned in the data reel concerning me," Aycharaych said. "The staff of Sector Governor Muratori takes precautions against espionage. When I first approached them about my mission, as a matter of routine I was exposed to a telepathic agent, a Ryellian, who could sense that my brain pattern had similarities to hers."

Desai nodded. Ryellians were expert. Of course, this one could scarcely have read Aycharaych's mind on such superficial contact, nor mapped the scope of his capacities; patterns varied too greatly between species, languages, societies, individuals. "What can you do of this nature, if I may ask?"

Aycharaych made a denigrating gesture. "Less than I desire. For example, you need not have changed the verbal form of your interior dream. I felt you do it, but only because the pulses changed. I could never read your mind; that is impossible unless I have known a person long and well, and then I can merely translate surface thoughts, clearly formulated. I cannot project." He smiled. "Shall we say I have a minor gift of empathy?"

"Don't underrate that. I wish I had it in the degree you seem to." Inwardly: *I mustn't let myself fall under his spell. He's captivating, but my duty is to be cold and cautious.*

Desai leaned forward, elbows on desk. "Forgive me if I'm blunt, Honorable," he said. "You've come to a planet which two years ago was in armed rebellion against His Majesty, which hoped to put one of its own sons on the throne by force and violence or, failing that, lead a breakaway of this whole sector from the Empire. Mutinous spirit is still high. I'll tell you, because the fact can't be suppressed for any length of time, we lately had an actual attack on a body of occupation troops, for the purpose of stealing their weapons. Riots elsewhere are already matters of public knowledge.

"Law and order are very fragile here, Honorable. I hope to proceed firmly but humanely with the reintegration of the Virgilian system into Imperial life. At present, practically anything could touch off a further explosion. Were it a major one, the consequences would be disastrous for the Aeneans, evil for the Empire. We're not far from the border, from the Domain of Ythri and, worse, independent war lords, buccaneers, and weird fanatics who have space fleets. Aeneas bulwarked this flank of ours. We can ill afford to lose it.

"A number of hostile or criminal elements took advantage of unsettled conditions to debark. I doubt if my police have yet gotten rid of them all. I certainly don't propose to let in more. That's why ships and detector satellites are in orbit, and none but specific vessels may land—at this port, nowhere else—and persons from them must be registered and must stay inside Nova Roma unless they get specific permission to travel."

He realized how harsh he sounded, and began to beg pardon. Aycharaych broke smoothly through his embarrassment. "Please do not think you give offense, Commissioner. I quite sympathize with your position. Besides, I sense your basic good will toward me. You fear I might, inadvertently, rouse emotions which would ignite mobs or outright revolutionaries."

"I must consider the possibility, Honorable. Even within a single species, the ghastliest blunders are all too easy to make. For instance, my own ancestors on Terra, before spaceflight, once rose against foreign rulers. The conflict took many thousand lives. Its proximate cause was a new type of cartridge which offended the religious sensibilities of native troops."

"A better example might be the Taiping Rebellion."

"What?"

"It happened in China, in the same century as the Indian Mutiny. A revolt against a dynasty of outlanders, though one which had governed for considerable time, became a civil war that lasted for a generation and killed people in the millions. The leaders were inspired by a militant form of Christianity—scarcely what Jesus had in mind, no?"

Desai stared at Aycharaych. "You *have* studied us."

"A little, oh, a hauntingly little. Much of it in your esthetic works, Aeschylus, Li Po, Shakespeare, Goethe, Stur-

geon, Mikhailov . . . the music of a Bach or Richard
Strauss, the visual art of a Rembrandt or Hiroshige ...
Enough. I would love to discuss these matters for months,
Commissioner, but you have not the time. I do hope to
convince you I will not enter as a clumsy ignoramus."

"Why Aeneas?" Desai wondered.

"Precisely because of the circumstances in which it finds
itself, Commissioner. How do humans of an especially
proud, self-reliant type behave in defeat? We need that insight too on Jean-Baptiste, if we are not to risk aggrieving
you in some future day of trouble. Furthermore, I understand Aeneas contains several cultures besides the dominant one. To make comparisons and observe interactions
would teach me much."

"Well—"

Aycharaych waved a hand. "The results of my work will
not be hoarded. Frequently an outsider perceives elements
which those who live by them never do. Or they may take
him into their confidence, or at least be less reserved in his
presence than in that of a human who could possibly be an
Imperial secret agent. Indeed, Commissioner, by his very
conspicuousness, an alien like me might serve as an efficient
gatherer of intelligence for you."

Desai started. *Krishna! Does this uncanny being suspect—? No, how could he?*

Gently, almost apologetically, Aycharaych said, "I persuaded the Governor's staff, and at last had a talk with
His Excellency. If you wish to examine my documents,
you will find I already have permission to carry out my
studies here. But of course I would never undertake anything you disapprove."

"Excuse me." Desai felt bewildered, rushed, boxed in.
Why should he? Aycharaych was totally courteous, eager
to please. "I ought to have checked through the data beforehand. I would have, but that wretched attempt at
guerrilla action— Do you mind waiting a few minutes
while I scan?"

"Not in the slightest," the other said, "especially if you
will let me glance at those books I see over there." He
smiled wider than before. His teeth were wholly nonhuman.

"Yes, by all means," Desai mumbled, and slapped fingers across the information-retriever panel.

Its screen lit up. An identifying holograph was followed

by relevant correspondence and notations. (Fakery was out of the question. Besides carrying tagged molecules, the reel had been deposited aboard ship by an official courier, borne here in the captain's safe, and personally brought by him to the memory bank underneath Imperial House.) The check on Aycharaych's bona fides had been routine, since they were overworked on Llynathawr too, but competently executed.

He arrived on the sector capital planet by regular passenger liner, went straight to a hotel in Catawrayannis which possessed facilities for xenosophonts, registered with the police as required, and made no effort to evade the scanners which occupation authorities had planted throughout the city. He traveled nowhere, met nobody, and did nothing suspicious. In perfectly straightforward fashion, he applied for the permit he wanted, and submitted to every interview and examination demanded of him.

No one had heard of the planet Jean-Baptiste there, either, but it was in the files and matched Aycharaych's description. The information was meager; but who would keep full data in the libraries of a distant province about a backward world which had never given trouble?

The request of its representative was reasonable, seemed unlikely to cause damage, and might yield helpful results. Sector Governor Muratori got interested, saw the being himself, and granted him an okay.

Desai frowned. His superior was both able and conscientious: had to be, if the harm done by the rapacious and conscienceless predecessor who provoked McCormac's rebellion was to be mended. However, in a top position one is soon isolated from the day-to-day details which make up a body of politics. Muratori was too new in his office to appreciate its limitations. And he was, besides, a stern man, who in Desai's opinion interpreted too literally the axiom that government is legitimatized coercion. It was because of directives from above that, after the University riots, the Commissioner of Virgil reluctantly ordered the razing of the Memorial and the total disarmament of the great Landfolk houses—two actions which he felt had brought on more woes, including the lunacy in Hesperia.

Well, then, why am I worried if Muratori begins to show a trifle more flexibility than hitherto?

"I'm finished," Desai said. "Won't you sit down again?"

Aycharaych returned from the bookshelf, holding an Anglic volume of Tagore. "Have you reached a decision, Commissioner?" he asked.

"You know I haven't." Desai forced a smile. "The decision was made for me. I am to let you do your research and give you what help is feasible."

"I doubt if I need bother you much, Commissioner. I am evolved for a thin atmosphere, and accustomed to rough travel. My biochemistry is similar enough to yours that food will be no problem. I have ample funds; and surely the Aenean economy could use some more Imperial credits."

Aycharaych ruffled his crest, a particularly expressive motion. "But please don't suppose I wish to thrust myself on you, waving a gubernatorial license like a battle flag," he continued. "You are the one who knows most and who, besides, must strike on the consequences of any error of mine. That would be a poor way for Jean-Baptiste to enter the larger community, would it not? I intend to be guided by your advice, yes, your preferences. For example, before my first venture, I will be grateful if your staff could plan my route and behavior."

A thawing passed through Desai. "You make me happy, Honorable. I'm sure we can work well together. See here, if you'd care to join me in an early lunch—and later I can have a few appointments shuffled around—"

It became a memorable afternoon.

But toward evening, alone, Desai once more felt troubled.

He should go home, to a wife and children who saw him far too little. He should stop chain-smoking; his palate was chemically burnt. Why carry a world on his shoulders, twenty long Aenean hours a day? He couldn't do it, really, for a single minute. No mortal could.

Yet when he had taken oath of office a mortal must try, or know himself a perjurer.

The Frederiksen affair plagued him like a newly made wound. Suddenly he leaned across his desk and punched the retriever. This room made and stored holographs of everything that happened within it.

A screen kindled, throwing light into dusky corners; for Desai had left off the fluoros, and sundown was upon the city. He didn't enlarge the figures of Peter Jowett and himself, but he did amplify the audio. Voices boomed. He leaned back to listen.

Jowett, richly dressed, sporting a curled brown beard, was of the Web, a merchant and cosmopolite. However, he was no jackal. He had sincerely, if quietly, opposed the revolt; and now he collaborated with the occupation because he saw the good of his people in their return to the Empire.

He said: "—glad to offer you what ideas and information I'm able, Commissioner. Cut me off if I start tellin' you what you've heard *ad nauseam*."

"I hardly think you can," Desai responded. "I've been on Aeneas for two years; your ancestors, seven hundred."

"Yes, men ranged far in the early days, didn't they? Spread themselves terribly thin, grew terribly vulnerable— Well. You wanted to consult me about Ivar Frederiksen, right?"

"And anything related." Desai put a fresh cigarette in his holder.

Jowett lit a cheroot. "I'm not sure what I have to give you. Remember, I belong to class which Landfolk regard with suspicion at best, contempt or hatred at worst. I've never been intimate of his family."

"You're in Parliament. A pretty important member, too. And Edward Frederiksen is Firstman of Ilion. You must have a fair amount to do with him, including socially; most political work goes on outside of formal conferences or debates. I know you knew Hugh McCormac well—Edward's brother-in-law, Ivar's uncle."

Jowett frowned at the red tip of his cigar before he answered slowly: "Matters are rather worse tangled than that, Commissioner. May I recapitulate elementary facts? I want to set things in perspective, for myself as much as you."

"Please."

"As I see it, there are three key facts about Aeneas. One, it began as scientific colony, mainly for purpose of studyin' natives of Dido—which isn't suitable environment for human children, you know. That's origin of University: community of scientists, scholars, and support personnel, around which mystique clusters to this very day. The most ignorant and stupid Aenean stands in some awe of those who are learned. And, of course, University under Empire has become quite distinguished, drawin' students both human and nonhuman from far around. Aeneans are proud of it. Furthermore, it's wealthy as well as respected, thus powerful.

"Fact two. To maintain humans, let alone research establishment, on planet as skimpy as this, you need huge land areas efficiently managed. Hence rise of Landfolk: squires, yeomen, tenants. When League broke down and Troubles came, Aeneas was cut off. It had to fight hard, sometimes right on its own soil, to survive. Landfolk bore brunt. They became quasi-feudal class. Even University caught somethin' of their spirit, givin' military trainin' as regular part of curriculum. You'll recall how Aeneas resisted—a bit bloodily—annexation by Empire, in *its* earlier days. But later we furnished undue share of its officers.

"Fact three. Meanwhile assorted immigrants were tricklin' in, lookin' for refuge or new start or whatever. They were ethnically different. Haughty nords used their labor but made no effort to integrate them. Piecewise, they found niches for themselves, and so drifted away from dominant civilization. Hence tinerans, Riverfolk, Orcans, highlanders, et cetera. I suspect they're more influential, sociologically, than city dwellers or rural gentry care to believe."

Jowett halted and poured himself a cup of the tea which Desai had ordered brought in. He looked as if he would have preferred whiskey.

"Your account does interest me, as making clear how an intelligent Aenean analyzes the history of his world," Desai said. "But what has it to do with my immediate problem?"

"A number of things, Commissioner, if I'm not mistaken," Jowett answered. "To begin, it emphasizes how essentially cut off persons like me are from ... well, if not mainstream, then several mainstreams of this planet's life.

"Oh, yes, we have our representatives in tricameral legislature. But we—I mean our new, Imperium-oriented class of businessmen and their employees—we're minor part of Townfolk. Rest belong to age-old guilds and similar corporate bodies, which most times feel closer to Landfolk and University than to us. Subcultures might perhaps ally with us, but aren't represented; property qualification for franchise, you know. And ... prior to this occupation, Firstman of Ilion was, automatically, Speaker of all three Houses. In effect, global President. His second

was, and is, Chancellor of University, his third elected by
Townfolk delegates. Since you have—wisely, I think—not
dissolved Parliament, merely declared yourself supreme
authority—this same configuration works on.

"I? I'm nothin' but delegate from Townfolk, from one
single faction among them at that. I am not privy to coun-
cils of Frederiksens and their friends."

"Just the same, you can inform me, correct me where
I'm wrong," Desai insisted. "Now let me recite the obvious
for a while. My impressions may turn out to be false.

"The Firstman of Ilion is *primus inter pares* because
Ilion is the most important region and Hesperia its richest
area. True?"

"Originally," Jowett said. "Production and population
have shifted. However, Aeneans are traditionalists."

"What horrible bad luck in the inheritance of that
title—for everybody," Desai said. And, seated alone, he
remembered his thoughts.

*Hugh McCormac was a career Navy officer, who had
risen to Fleet Admiral when his elder brother died
childless in an accident and thus made him Firstman. That
wouldn't have mattered, except for His Majesty (one dare
not speculate why, aloud) appointing that creature Snelund the Governor of Sector Alpha Crucis; and Snelund's
excesses finally striking McCormac so hard that he raised
a rebel banner and planet after planet hailed him Emperor.*

*Well, Snelund is dead, McCormac is fled, and we are
trying to reclaim the ruin they left. But the seeds they
sowed still sprout strange growths.*

*McCormac's wife was (is?) the sister of Edward Fred-
eriksen, who for lack of closer kin has thereby succeeded
to the Firstmanship of Ilion. Edward himself is a mild,
professorial type. I could bless his presence—except for
the damned traditions. His own wife is a cousin of
McCormac. (Curse the way those high families inter-
marry! It may make for better stock, a thousand years
hence; but what about us who must cope meanwhile?)
The Frederiksens themselves are old-established University
leaders. Why, the single human settlement on Dido is
named after their main ancestor.*

*Everybody on this resentful globe discounts Edward
Frederiksen: but not what he symbolizes. Soon everybody
will know what Ivar Frederiksen has done.*

*Potentially, he is their exiled prince, their liberator,
their Anointed. Siva, have mercy.*

"As I understand it," the image of Jowett said, "the boy
raised gang of hotheads without his parents' knowledge.
He's only eleven and a half, after all—uh, that's twenty
years Terran, right? Their idea was to take to wilderness
and be guerrillas until . . . what? Terra gave up? Ythri in-
tervened, and took Aeneas under its wing like Avalon? It
strikes me as pathetically romantic."

"Sometimes romantics do overcome realists," Desai
said. "The consequences are always disastrous."

"Well, in this case, attempt failed. His associates who
got caught identified their leader under hypnoprobe. Don't
bother denyin'; of course your interrogators used hypno-
probes. Ivar's disappeared, but shouldn't be impossible to
track down. What do you need my advice about?"

"The wisdom of chasing him in the first place," Desai
said wearily.

"Oh. Positive. You dare not let him run loose. I do
know him slightly. He has chance of becomin' kind of
prophet, to people who're waitin' for exactly that."

"My impression too. But how should we go after him?
How make the arrest? What kind of trial and penalty?
How publicize? We can't create a martyr. Neither can
we let a rebel, responsible for the deaths and injuries of
Imperial personnel—and Aeneans, remember, Aeneans—
we can't let him go scot-free. I don't know what to do,"
Desai nearly groaned. "Help me, Jowett. You don't want
your planet ripped apart, do you?"

—He snapped off the playback. He had gotten nothing
from it. Nor would he from the rest, which consisted of
what-ifs and maybes. The only absolute was that Ivar
Frederiksen must be hunted down fast.

*Should I refer the problem of what to do after we catch
him to Llynathawr, or directly to Terra? I have the right.*

The legal right. No more. What do they know there?

Night had fallen. The room was altogether black, save
for its glowboards and a shifty patch of moonlight which
hurried Creusa cast through the still-active transparency.
Desai got up, felt his way there, looked outward.

Beneath stars, moons, Milky Way, three sister planets,
Nova Roma had gone elven. The houses were radiance
and shadow, the streets dappled darkness, the river and
canals mercury. Afar in the desert, a dust storm went like

a ghost. Wind keened; Desai, in his warmed cubicle, shivered to think how its chill must cut.

His vision sought the brilliances overhead. Too many suns, too many.

He'd be sending a report Home by the next courier boat. (Home! He had visited Terra just once. When he stole a few hours from work to walk among relics, they proved curiously disappointing. Multisense tapes didn't include crowded airbuses, arrogant guides, tourist shops, or aching feet.) Such vessels traveled at close to the top hyperspeed: a pair of weeks between here and Sol. (But that was 200 light-years, a radius which swept over four million suns.) He could include a request for policy guidelines.

But half a month could stretch out, when he faced possible turmoil or, worse, terrorism. And then his petition must be processed, discussed, annotated, supplemented, passed from committee to committee, referred through layers of executive officialdom for decision; and the return message would take its own days to arrive, and probably need to be disputed on many points when it did— No, those occasional directives from Llynathawr were bad enough.

He, Chunderban Desai, stood alone to act.

Of course, he was required to report everything significant: which certainly included the Frederiksen affair. If nothing else, Terra was *the* data bank, as complete as flesh and atomistics could achieve.

In which case . . . why not insert a query about that Aycharaych?

Well, why?

I don't know, I don't know. He seems thoroughly legitimate; and he borrowed my Tagore . . . No, I will ask for a complete information scan at Terra. Though I'll have to invent a plausible reason for it, when Muratori's approved his proposal. We bureaucrats aren't supposed to have hunches. Especially not when, in fact, I like Aycharaych as much as any nonhuman I've ever met. Far more than many of my fellow men.

Dangerously more?

IV

The Hedin freehold lay well east of Windhome, though close enough to the edge of Ilion that westerlies brought moisture off the canals, marshes, and salt lakes of the Antonine Seabed—actual rain two or three times a year. While not passing through the property, the Wildfoss helped maintain a water table that supplied a few wells. Thus the family carried on agriculture, besides ranching a larger area.

Generation by generation, their staff had become more like kinfolk than hirelings: kinfolk who looked to them for leadership but spoke their own minds and often saw a child married to a son or daughter of the house. In short, they stood in a relationship to their employers quite similar to that in which the Hedins, and other Hesperian yeomen, stood to Windhome.

The steading was considerable. A dozen cottages flanked the manse. Behind, barns, sheds, and workshops surrounded three sides of a paved courtyard. Except for size, at first glance the buildings seemed much alike, whitewashed rammed earth, their blockiness softened by erosion. Then one looked closer at the stone or glass mosaics which decorated them. Trees made a windbreak about the settlement: native delphi and rahab, Terran oak and acacia, Llynathawrian rasmin, Ythrian hammerbranch. Flowerbeds held only exotic species, painstakingly cultivated, eked out with rocks and gravel. True blossoms had never evolved on Aeneas, though a few kinds of leaf or stalk had bright hues.

It generally bustled here, overseers, housekeepers, smiths, masons, mechanics, hands come in from fields or range, children, dogs, horses, stathas, hawks, farm machinery, ground and air vehicles, talk, shouting, laughter, anger, tears, song, a clatter of feet and a whiff of beasts or smoke. Ivar ached to join in. His wait in the storeloft became an entombment.

Through a crack in the shutters he could look down at the daytime surging. His first night coincided with a birthday party for the oldest tenant. Not only the main house was full of glow, but floodlights illuminated the yard for the leaping, stamping dances of Ilion, to music whooped forth by a sonor, while flagons went from mouth to mouth. The next night had been moonlight and a pair of young sweethearts. Ivar did not watch them after he realized what they were; he had been taught to consider privacy among the rights no decent person would violate. Instead, he threshed about in his sleeping bag, desert-thirsty with memories of Tatiana Thane and—still more, he discovered in shame—certain others.

On the third night, as erstwhile, he roused to the cautious unlocking of the door. Sam Hedin brought him his food and water when nobody else was awake. He sat up. A pad protected him from the floor, but as his torso emerged from the sack, chill smote through his garments. He hardly noticed. The body of an Aenean perforce learned how to make efficient use of the shivering reflex. The dark oppressed him, however, and the smell of dust.

A flashbeam picked forth glimpses of seldom-used gear, boxes and loaded shelves. "Hs-s-s," went a whisper. "Get ready to travel. Fast."

"What?"

"Fast, I said. I'll explain when we're a-road."

Ivar scrambled to his feet, out of his nightsuit and into the clothes he wore when he arrived. The latter were begrimed and blood-spotted, but the parched air had sucked away stinks as it did for the slop jar. The other garment he tucked into a bedroll he slung on his back, together with his rifle. Hedin gave him a packet of sandwiches to stuff in his pouchbelt, a filled canteen to hang opposite his knife—well insulated against freezing—and guidance downstairs.

Though the man's manner was grim, eagerness leaped in Ivar. Regardless of the cause, his imprisonment was at an end.

Outside lay windless quiet, so deep that it was if he could hear the planet creak from the cold. Both moons were up to whiten stone and sand, make treetops into glaciers above caverns, strike sparkles from rime. Larger but remoter Lavinia, rising over eastern hills, showed about half her ever-familiar face. Creusa, hurtling toward her, seemed bigger because of being near the full, and glittered as her spin threw light off crystal raggedness. The Milky Way was a frozen cascade from horizon to horizon. Of fellow planets, Anchises remained aloft, lambent yellow. Among the uncountable stars, Alpha and Beta Crucis burned bright enough to join the moons in casting shadows.

A pair of stathas stood tethered, long necks and snouted heads silhouetted athwart the house. *We must have some ways to go,* Ivar thought, *sacrificin' horse-speed in pinch for endurance over long dry stretch. But then why not car?* He mounted. Despite the frigidity, he caught a scent of his beast, not unlike new-mown hay, before he adjusted hood and nightmask.

Sam Hedin led him onto the inland road, shortly afterward to a dirt track which angled off southerly through broken ground where starkwood bush and sword trava grew sparse. Dust puffed from the *plop-plop* of triple pads. Six legs gave a lulling rhythm. Before long the steading was lost to sight, the men rode by themselves under heaven. Afar, a catavale yowled.

Ivar cleared his throat. "Ah-um! Where're we bound, Yeoman Hedin?"

Vapor smoked from breath slot. "Best hidin' place for you I could think of quick, Firstlin'. Maybe none too good."

Fear jabbed. "What's happened?"

"Vid word went around this day, garth to garth," Hedin said. He was a stout man in his later middle years. "Impies out everywhere in Hesperia, ransackin' after you. Reward offered; and anybody who looks as if he or she might know somethin' gets quick narcoquiz. At rate they're workin', they'll reach my place before noon." He paused. "That's why I kept you tucked away, so nobody except me *would* know you were there. But not much use against biodetectors. I invented business which'll keep me from home several days, rode off with remount—plausible, considerin' power shortage—and slipped back after dark to fetch you." Another pause. "They have aircars aprowl, too. Motor vehicle could easily get spotted and overtaken.

That's reason why we use stathas, and no heatin' units for our clothes."

Ivar glanced aloft, as if to see a metal teardrop pounce. An ula flapped by. Pride struggled with panic: "They want me mighty badly, huh?"

"Well, you're Firstlin' of Ilion."

Honesty awoke. Ivar bit his lip. "I ... I'm no serious menace. I bungled my leadership. No doubt I was idiot to try."

"I don't know enough to gauge," Hedin replied judiciously. "Just that Feo Astaff asked if I could coalsack you from Terrans, because you and friends had had fight with marines. Since, you and I've gotten no proper chance to talk. I could just sneak you your rations at night, not dare linger. Nor have newscasts said more than there was unsuccessful assault on patrol. Never mentioned your name, though I suppose after this search they'll have to."

The mask muffled his features, but not the eyes he turned to his companion. "Want to tell me now?" he asked.

"W-well, I—"

"No secrets, mind. I'm pretty sure I've covered our spoor and won't be suspected, interrogated. Still, what can we rely on altogether?"

Ivar slumped. "I've nothin' important to hide, except foolishness. Yes, I'd like to tell you, Yeoman."

The story stumbled forth, for Hedin to join to what he already knew about his companion.

Edward Frederiksen had long been engaged in zoological research on Dido when he married Lisbet Borglund. She was of old University stock like him; they met when he came back to deliver a series of lectures. She followed him to the neighbor world. But even in Port Frederiksen, the heat and wetness of the thick air were too much for her.

She recovered when they returned to Aeneas, and bore her husband Ivar and Gerda. They lived in a modest home outside Nova Roma; both taught, and he found adequate if unspectacular subjects for original study. His son often came along on field trips. The boy's ambitions presently focused on planetology. Belike the austere comeliness of desert, steppe, hills, and dry ocean floors brought that about—besides the hope of exploring among those stars which glittered through their nights.

Hugh McCormac being their uncle by his second marriage, the children spent frequent vacations at Windhome. When the Fleet Admiral was on hand, it became like visiting a hero of the early days, an affable one, say Brian McCormac who cast out the nonhuman invaders and whose statue stood ever afterward on a high pillar near the main campus of the University.

Aeneas had circled Virgil eight times since Ivar's birth, when Aaron Snelund became Governor of Sector Alpha Crucis. It circled twice more—three and a half Terran years—before the eruption. At first the developed worlds felt nothing worse than heightened taxes, for which they got semi-plausible explanations. (Given the size of the Empire, its ministers must necessarily have broad powers.) Then they got the venal appointees. Then they began to hear what had been going on among societies less able to resist and complain. Then they realized that their own petitions were being shunted aside. Then the arrests and confiscations for "treason" started. Then the secret police were everywhere, while mercenaries and officials freely committed outrages upon individuals. Then it became plain that Snelund was not an ordinary corrupt administrator, skimming off some cream for himself, but a favorite of the Emperor, laying grandiose political foundations.

All this came piecemeal, and folk were slow to believe. For most of them, life proceeded about as usual. If times were a bit hard, well, they would outlast it, and meanwhile they had work to do, households and communities to maintain, interests to pursue, pleasures to seek, love to make, errands to run, friends to invite, unfriends to snub, plans to consider, details, details, details like sand in an hourglass. Ivar did not enroll at the University, since it educated its hereditary members from infancy, but he began to specialize in his studies and to have off-planet classmates. Intellectual excitement outshouted indignation.

Then Kathryn McCormac, his father's sister, was taken away to Snelund's palace; and her husband was arrested, was rescued, and led the mutiny.

Ivar caught fire, like most Aenean youth. His military training, hitherto incidental, became nearly the whole. But he never got off the planet, and his drills ended when Imperial warcraft hove into the skies.

The insurrection was over. Hugh McCormac and his family had led the remnants of his fleet into the deeps outside of known space. Because the Jihannath crisis was resolved, the Navy available to guard the whole Empire, the rebels would not return unless they wanted immolation.

Sector Alpha Crucis in general, Aeneas in particular, was to be occupied and reconstructed.

Chaos, despair, shortages which in several areas approached famine, had grown throughout the latter half of the conflict. The University was closed. Ivar and Gerda went to live with their parents in poverty-stricken grandeur at Windhome, since Edward Frederiksen was now Firstman of Ilion. The boy spent most of the time improving his desertcraft. And he gained identification with the Landfolk. *He* would be their next leader.

After a while conditions improved, the University reopened—under close observation—and he returned to Nova Roma. He was soon involved in underground activity. At first this amounted to no more than clandestine bitching sessions. However, he felt he should not embarrass his family or himself by staying at the suburban house, and moved into a cheap room in the least desirable part of the Web. That also led to formative experiences. Aeneas had never had a significant criminal class, but a petty one burgeoned during the war and its aftermath. Suddenly he met men who did not hold the laws sacred.

(When McCormac rebelled, he did it in the name of rights and statutes violated. When Commissioner Desai arrived, he promised to restore the torn fabric.)

Given a conciliatory rule, complaints soon became demands. The favorite place for speeches, rallies, and demonstrations was beneath the memorial to Brian McCormac. The authorities conceded numerous points, reasonable in themselves—for example, resumption of regular mail service to and from the rest of the Empire. This led to further demands—for example, *no* government examination of mail, and a citizens' committee to assure this—which were refused. Riots broke out. Some property went up in smoke, some persons down in death.

The decrees came: No more assemblies. The monument to be razed. The Landfolk, who since the Troubles had

served as police and military cadre, to disband all units
and surrender all firearms, from a squire's ancestral can-
non-equipped skyrover to a child's target pistol given last
Founder's Day.

"We decided, our bunch, we'd better act before 'twas
too late," Ivar said. "We'd smuggle out what weapons we
could, ahead of seizure date, and use them to grab off
heavier stuff. I had as much knowledge of back country as
any, more than most; and, of course, I am Firstlin'. So
they picked me to command our beginnin' operation,
which'd be in this area. I joined my mother and sister at
Windhome, pretendin' I needed break from study. Others
had different cover stories, like charterin' an airbus to
leave them in Avernus Canyon for several days' campout.
We rendezvoused at Helmet Butte and laid our ambush
accordin' to what I knew about regular Impy patrol
routes."

"What'd you have done next, if you'd succeeded?"
Hedin asked.

"Oh, we had that planned. I know couple of oases off in
Ironland that could support us, with trees, caves, ravines
to hide us from air search. There aren't that many occupation troops to cover this entire world."

"You'd spend your lives as outlaws? I should think
you'd soon become bandits."

"No, no. We'd carry on more raids, get more recruits
and popular support, gather strength enemy must reckon
with. Meanwhile we'd hope for sympathy elsewhere in
Empire bringin' pressure on our behalf, or maybe fear of
Ythri movin' in."

"Maybe," Hedin grunted. After a moment: "I've heard
rumors. Great bein' with gold-bronze wings, a-flit in these
parts. Ythrian agent? They don't necessarily want what we
do, Firstlin'."

Ivar's shoulders slumped. "No matter. We failed anyhow. I did."

Hedin reached across to clap him on the back. "Don't
take that attitude. First, military leaders are bound to lose
men and suffer occasional disasters. Second, you never
were one, really. You just happened to get thrown to top
of cards that God was shufflin'." Softly: "For game of sol-
itaire? I won't believe it." His tone briskened. "Firstlin',
you've got no *right* to go off on conscience spin. You and

your fellows together made bad mistake. Leave it at that, and carry on. Aeneas does need you."

"Me?" Ivar exclaimed. His self-importance had crumbled while he talked, until he could not admit he had ever seen himself as a Maccabee. "What in cosmos can I—"

Hedin lifted a gauntleted hand to quiet him. "Hoy. Follow me."

They brought their stathas off the trail, and did not rejoin it for ten kilometers. What they avoided was a herd belonging to Hedin: Terran-descended cattle, gene-modified and then adapted through centuries—like most introduced organisms—until they were a genus of their own. Watchfires glimmered around their mass. Hedin didn't doubt his men were loyal to him; but what they hadn't noticed, they couldn't reveal.

On the way, the riders passed a fragment of wall. Glass-black, seamless, it sheened above moonlight brush and sand. Near the top of what remained, four meters up, holes made an intricate pattern, its original purpose hard to guess. Now stars gleamed through.

Hedin reined in, drew a cross, and muttered before he went on.

Ivar had seen the ruin in the past, and rangehands paying it their respects. He had never thought he would see the yeoman—well-educated, well-traveled, hard-headed master and councilor—do likewise.

After a cold and silent while, Hedin said half defensively, "Kind of symbol back yonder."

"Well . . . yes," Ivar responded.

"Somebody was here before us, millions of years ago. And not extinct natives, either. Where did they come from? Why did they leave? Traces have been found on other planets too, remember. Unreasonable to suppose they died off, no? Lot of people wonder if they didn't go onward instead—out there."

Hedin waved at the stars. Of that knife-bright horde, some belonged to the Empire but most did not. For those the bare eye could see were mainly giants, shining across the light-years which engulfed vision of a Virgil or a Sol. Between Ivar and red Betelgeuse reached all the dominion of Terra, and more. Further on, Rigel flashed and the Pleiades veiled themselves in regions to which the Roidhunate of Merseia gave its name for a blink of time. Beyond these were Polaris, once man's lodestar, and the Orion

Nebula, where new suns and worlds were being born even as he watched, and in billions of years life would look forth and wonder. . . .

Hedin's mask swung toward Ivar again. His voice was low but eerily intense. "That's why we need you, Firstlin'. You may be rash boy, yes, but four hundred years of man on Aeneas stand behind you. We'll need every root we've got when Elders return."

Startled, Ivar said, "You don't believe that, do you? I've heard talk; but you?"

"Well, I don't know." Hedin's words came dwindled through the darkness. "I don't know. Before war, I never thought about it. I'd go to church, and that was that.

"But since— Can so many people be entirely wrong? They are many, I'll tell you. Off in town, at school, you probably haven't any idea how wide hope is spreadin' that Elders will come back soon, bearin' Word of God. It's not crank, Ivar. Nigh everybody admits this is hope, no proof. But could Admiral McCormac have headed their way? And surely we hear rumors about new prophet in barrens—

"I don't know. I do think, and I tell you I'm not alone in it, all this grief here and all those stars there can't be for nothin'. If God is makin' ready His next revelation, why not through chosen race, more wise and good than we can now imagine? And if that's true, shouldn't prophet come first, who prepares us to be saved?"

He shook himself, as if the freeze had pierced his unheated garb. "You're our Firstlin'," he said. "We must keep you free. Four hundred years can't be for nothin' either."

Quite matter-of-factly, he continued: "Tinerans are passin' through, reported near Arroyo. I figure you can hide among them."

V

Each nomad Train, a clan as well as a caravan, wandered a huge but strictly defined territory. Windhome belonged in that of the Brotherband. Ivar had occasionally seen its camps, witnessed raffish performances, and noticed odd jobs being done for local folk before it moved on, afterward heard the usual half-amused, half-indignant accusations of minor thefts and clever swindles, gossip about seductions, whispers about occult talents exercised. When he dipped into the literature, he found mostly anecdotes, picturesque descriptions, romantic fiction, nothing in depth. The Aenean intellectual community took little serious interest in the undercultures on its own planet. Despite the centuries, Dido still posed too many enigmas which were more fascinating and professionally rewarding.

Ivar did know that Trains varied in their laws and customs. Hedin led him across a frontier which had no guards nor any existence in the registries at Nova Roma, identified solely by landmarks. Thereafter they were in Waybreak country, and he was still less sure of what to expect than he would have been at home. The yeoman took a room in the single inn which Arroyo boasted. "I'll stay till you're gone, in case of trouble," he said. "But mainly, you're on your own from here." Roughly: "I wish 'twere otherwise. Fare always well, lad."

Ivar walked through the village to the camp. Its people were packing for departure. Fifty or so brilliantly painted carriages, and gaudy garb on the owners, made their bustle and clamor into a kind of rainbowed storm in an otherwise drab landscape. Arroyo stood on the eastern slope of the hills, where scrub grew sparse on dusty ground to feed some livestock. The soil became more dry and bare for every kilometer that it hunched on downward, until at the horizon began the Ironland desert.

Scuttling about in what looked like utter confusion, men, women, and children alike threw him glances and shouted remarks in their own language that he guessed were derisive. He felt awkward and wholly alone among them—this medium-sized, whip-slim race of the red-brown skins and straight blue-black hair. Their very vehicles hemmed him in alienness. Some were battered old trucks of city make; but fantastic designs swirled across them, pennons blew, amulets dangled, wind chimes rang. Most were wagons, drawn by four to eight stathas, and these were the living quarters. Stovepipes projected from their arched roofs and grimy curtains hung in their windows. Beneath paint, banners, and other accessories, their panels were elaborately carved; demon shapes leered, hex signs radiated, animals real and imaginary cavorted, male and female figures danced, hunted, worked, gambled, engendered, and performed acts more esoteric.

A man came by, carrying a bundle of knives and swords wrapped in a cloak. He bounded up into the stairless doorway of one wagon, gave his load to a person inside, sprang down again to confront Ivar. "Hey-ah, varsiteer," he said amicably enough. "What'd you like? The show's over."

"I . . . I'm lookin' for berth," Ivar faltered. He wet his lips, which felt caked with dust. It was a hot day, 25 degrees Celsius or so. Virgil glared in a sky which seemed to lack its usual depth, and instead was burnished.

"No dung? What can a townsitter do worth his keep? We're bound east, straight across the Dreary. Not exactly a Romeburg patio. We'd have to sweep you up after you crumbled." The other rubbed his pointed chin. "Of course," he added thoughtfully, "you might make pretty good nose powder for some girl."

Yet his mockery was not unkind. Ivar gave him closer regard. He was young, probably little older than the Firstling. Caught by a beaded fillet, his hair fell to his shoulders in the common style, brass earrings showing through. Like most tineran men, he kept shaved off what would have been a puny growth of beard. Bones and luminous gray eyes stood forth in a narrow face. He was nearly always grinning, and whether or not he stood still, there was a sense of quivering mobility about him. His clothes—

fringed and varicolored shirt, scarlet sash, skin-tight leather trousers and buskins—were worn-out finery demoted to working dress. A golden torque encircled his neck, tawdry-jeweled rings his fingers, a spiral of herpetoid skin the left arm. A knife sat on either hip, one a tool, one a weapon, both delicate-looking compared to those miniature machetes the Landfolk carried.

"I'm not—well, yes, I am from Nova Roma, University family," Ivar admitted. "But, uh, how'd you know before I spoke?"

"O-ah, your walk, your whole way. Being geared like a granger, not a cityman, won't cover that." The Anglic was rapid-fire, a language coequal in the Trains with Haisun and its argots. But this was a special dialect, archaic from the nord viewpoint, one which, for instance, made excessive use of articles while harshly clipping the syllables. "That's a rifle to envy, yours, and relieve you of if you're uncareful. A ten-millimeter Valdemar convertible, right?"

"And I can use it," Ivar said in a rush. "I've spent plenty of time in outlands. You'll find me good pot hunter, if nothin' else. But I'm handy with apparatus too, especially electric. And strong, when you need plain muscle."

"Well-ah, let's go see King Samlo. By the way, I'm Mikkal of Redtop." The tineran nodded at his wagon, whose roof justified its name. A woman of about his age, doubtless his wife, poised in the doorway. She was as exotically pretty as girls of her type were supposed to be in the folklore of the sedentary people. A red-and-yellow-zig-zagged gown clung to a sumptuous figure, though Ivar thought it a shame how she had loaded herself with junk ornaments. Catching his eye, she smiled, winked, and swung a hip at him. Her man didn't mind; it was a standard sort of greeting.

"You'll take me?" Ivar blurted.

Mikkal shrugged. Infinitely more expressive than a nord's, the gesture used his entire body. Sunlight went iridescent over the scales coiled around his left arm. "Sure-ah. An excuse not to work." To the woman: "You, Dulcy, go fetch the rest of my gear." She made a moue at him before she scampered off into the turmoil.

"Thanks ever so much," Ivar said. "I—I'm Rolf Mariner." He had given the alias considerable thought, and was proud of the result. It fitted the ethnic background he could not hope to disguise, while free of silly giveaways like his proper initials.

"If that's who you want to be, fine," Mikkal gibed, and led the way.

The racket grew as animals were brought in from pasture, stathas, mules, goats, neomoas. The dogs which herded them, efficiently at work in response to whistles and signals from children, kept silence. They were tall, ebon, and skeletally built except for the huge rib cages and water-storing humps on the shoulders.

Goldwheels was the largest wagon, the single motorized one. A small companion stood alongside, black save for a few symbols in red and silver, windowless. Above its roof, a purple banner bore two crescents. Mikkal sensed Ivar's curiosity and explained, "That's the shrine."

"Oh . . . yes." Ivar remembered what he had read. The king of a band was also its high priest, who besides presiding over public religious ceremonies, conducted secret rites with a few fellow initiates. He was required to be of a certain family (evidently Goldwheels in the Waybreak Train) but need not be an eldest son. Most of a king's women were chosen with a view to breeding desired traits, and the likeliest boy became heir apparent, to serve apprenticeship in another Train. Thus the wanderers forged alliances between their often quarrelsome groups, more potent than the marriages among individuals which grew out of the periodic assemblies known as Fairs.

The men who were hitching white mules to the shrine seemed no more awed than Mikkal. They hailed him loudly. He gave them an answer which made laughter erupt. Youngsters milling nearby shrilled. A couple of girls tittered, and one made a statement which was doubtless bawdy. *At my expense,* Ivar knew.

It didn't matter. He smiled back, waved at her, saw her preen waist-long tresses and flutter her eyelids. *After all, to them—if I prove I'm no dumb clod, and I will, I will—to them I'm excitin' outsider.* He harked back to his half-desperate mood of minutes ago, and marveled. A buoyant confidence swelled in him, and actual merriment bubbled beneath. The whole carefree atmosphere had entered him, as it seemed to enter everybody who visited an encampment.

King Samlo returned from overseeing a job. Folk lifted hands in casual salute. When he cared to exercise it, his

power was divine and total; but mostly he ruled by con-
sensus.

He was a contrast to his people, large, blocky-boned,
hooknosed. His mahogany features carried a fully developed beard and mustache. He limped. His garb was
white, more clean than one would have thought possible
here. Save for tooled-leather boots, crimson-plumed tur-
ban, and necklace of antique coins, it had little decoration.

His pale gaze fell on Ivar and remained as he lowered
himself into an ornate armchair outside his wagon. "Hey-
ah, stranger," he said. "What's your lay?"

Ivar bowed, not knowing what else to do. Mikkal took
the word: "He tags himself Rolf Mariner, claims he's a
hunter and jack-o'-hands as well as a varsiteer, and wants
to come along."

The king didn't smile. His gravity marked him off yet
more than did his appearance. Nonetheless, Ivar felt un-
afraid. Whether dreamy runaways, failed adults, or fugitives from justice, occasionally nords asked to join a
Train. If they made a plausible case for themselves, or if a
whim blew in their favor, they were accepted. They remained aliens, and probably none had lasted as much as a
year before being dismissed. The usual reason given was
that they lacked the ability to pull their freight in a hard
and tricky life.

Surely that was true. Ivar expected that a journey with
these people would stretch him to his limits. He did not
expect he would snap. Who could await that, in this blithe
tumult?

There passed through him: *In spite of everything they
suffered, I've heard, I've read a little, about how those
guests always hated to leave, always afterward mourned
for lost high days—how those who'd lasted longest would
try to get into different troop, or kill themselves*— But let
him not fret when all his blood sang.

"Um-m-m-hm," Samlo said. "Why do you ask this?"

"I've tired of these parts, and have no readier way to
leave them," Ivar replied.

Mikkal barked laughter. "He knows the formula, anyhow! Invoke the upper-class privacy fetish, plus a hint that
if we don't know why he's running, we can't be blamed if
the tentacles find him amongst us."

"Impie agents aren't city police or gentry housecarls,"
the king said. "They got special tricks. And . . . a few

days back, a clutch of seethe-heads affrayed a marine patrol on the Wildfoss, remember? Several escaped. If you're on the flit, Mariner, why should we risk trouble to help you across Ironland?"

"I didn't say I was, sir," Ivar responded. "I told Mikkal, here, I can be useful to you. But supposin' I am in sabota with Terrans, is that bad? I heard tinerans cheer Emperor Hugh's men as they left for battle."

"Tinerans'll cheer anybody who's on hand with spending money," Mikkal said. "However, I'll 'fess most of us don't like the notion of the stars beswarmed by townsitters. It makes us feel like the universe is closing in." He turned to Samlo. "King, why not give this felly-oh a toss?"

"Will you be his keeper?" the seated man asked. Aside to Ivar: "We don't abandon people in the desert, no matter what. Your keeper has got to see you through."

"Sure-ah," Mikkal said. "He has a look of new songs and jokes in him."

"Your keeper won't have much to spare," Samlo warned. "If you use up supplies and give no return—well, maybe after we're back in the green and you dismissed, he'll track you down."

"He won't want to, sir . . . King," Ivar promised.

"Better make sure of that," Samlo said. "Mikkal, the shooting gallery's still assembled. Go see how many light-sweeps he can hit with that rifle of his. Find some broken-down equipment for him to repair; the gods know we have enough. Run him, and if he's breathing hard after half a dozen clicks, trade him back, because he'd never get across the Dreary alive." He rose, while telling Ivar: "If you pass, you'll have to leave that slugthrower with me. Only hunting parties carry firearms in a Train, and just one to a party. We'd lose too many people otherwise. Now I have to go see the animal acts get properly bedded down. You be off too."

VI

In a long irregular line, herd strung out behind, the caravan departed. A few persons rode in the saddle, a few more in or on the vehicles; most walked. The long Aenean stride readily matched wagons bumping and groaning over roadless wrinkled hills. However, the going was stiff, and nobody talked without need. Perched on rooftops, musicians gave them plangent marches out of primitive instruments, drums, horns, gongs, bagpipes, many-stringed guitars. A number of these players were handicapped, Ivar saw: crippled, blind, deformed. He would have been shocked by so much curable or preventable woe had they not seemed as exhilarated as he was.

Near sundown, Waybreak was out on the undulant plain of Ironland. Coarse red soil reached between clumps of gray-green starkwood or sword trava, dried too hard for there to be a great deal of dust. Samlo cried halt by an eroded lava flow from which thrust a fluted volcanic plug. "The Devil's Tallywhacker," Mikkal told his protégé. "Traditional first-night stopping place out of Arroyo, said to be protection against hostile gods. *I* think the practice goes back to the Troubles, when wild gangs went around, starveling humans or stranded remnants of invader forces, and you might need a defensible site. Of course, nowadays we just laager the wagons in case a zoosny wind should blow up or something like that. But it's as well to maintain cautionary customs. The rebellion proved the Troubles can come again, and no doubt will . . . as if that'd ever needed proof."

"Uh, excuse me," Ivar said, "but you sound, uh, surprisin'ly sophisticated—" His voice trailed off.

Mikkal chuckled. "For an illiterate semi-savage? Well,

matter o' fact, I'm not. Not illiterate, anyhow. A part of us have to read and write if we're to handle the outside world, let alone operate swittles like the Treasure Map. Besides, I like reading, when I can beg or steal a book."

"I can't understand why you—I mean, you're cut off from things like library banks, not to mention medical and genetic services, everything you could have—"

"At what price?" Mikkal made a spitting noise, though he did not waste the water. "We'd either have to take steady work to gain the jingle, or become welfare clients, which'd mean settling down as even meeker law-lickers. The end of the Trains, therefore the end of us. Didn't you know? A tineran can't quit. Stuff him into a town or nail him down on a farm, it's a mercy when death sets his corpse free to rot."

"I'd heard that," Ivar said slowly.

"But thought the tale must be an extravaganza, hey? No, it's true. It's happened. Tinerans jailed for any length of time sicken and die, if they don't suicide first. Even if for some reason like exile from the Train, they have to turn sitter, 'free workers' "—the tone spoke the quotation marks—"they can't breed and they don't live long. . . . That's why we have no death penalty. Twice I've seen the king order a really bad offender cast out, and word sent to the rest of the Trains so none would take him in. Both times, the felly begged for a hundred and one lashes instead." Mikkal shook himself. "C'mon, we've work to do. You unhitch the team, hobble them, and bring them to where the rest of the critters are. Dulcy'll answer your questions. Since I've got you for extra hands, I'll get my tools resharpened early, this trek." He performed as juggler and caster of edged weapons and, he added blandly, card sharp and dice artist.

Men erected a collapsible trough, filled it from a water truck, added the vitamin solutions necessary to supplement grazing upon purely native vegetation. Boys would spend the night watching over the small, communally owned herd and the draught animals. Besides spider wolves or a possible catavale, hazards included crevices, sand hells, a storm howling down with the suddenness and ferocity common anywhere on Aeneas. If the weather stayed mild, night chill would not be dangerous until the route entered the true barrens. These creatures were the product of long breeding, the quadrupeds and hexapods heavily haired, the big neomoas similarly well feathered.

Of course, all Ironland was not that bleak, or it would have been uncrossable. The Train would touch at oases where the tanks could be refilled with brackish water and the bins with forage.

Inside the wagon circle, women and girls prepared the evening meal. In this nearly fuelless land they cooked on glowers. Capacitors had lately been recharged at a power station. To have this done, and earn the wherewithal to pay, was a major reason why the migrations passed through civilized parts.

Virgil went down. Night came almost immediately after. A few lamps glowed on wagonsides, but mainly the troop saw by stars, moons, auroral flickers to northward. A gelid breeze flowed off the desert. As if to shelter each other, folk crowded around the kettles. Voices racketed, chatter, laughter, snatches of song.

Except for being ferociously spiced, the fare was simple, a thick stew scooped up on rounds of bread, a tarry-tasting tea for drink. Tinerans rarely used alcohol, never carried it along. Ivar supposed that was because of its dehydrating effect.

Who needed it, anyway? He had not been this happy in the most joyous beer hall of Nova Roma, and his mind stayed clear into the bargain.

He got his first helping and hunkered down, less easily than they, beside Mikkal and Dulcy. At once others joined them, more and more till he was in a ring of noise, faces, unwashed but crisp-smelling bodies. Questions, remarks, japes roiled over him. "Hey-ah, townboy, why've you gone walkabout? . . . Hoping for girls? Well, I hope you won't be too tired to oblige 'em, after a day's hike . . . Give us a song, a story, a chunk o' gossip, how 'bout that? . . . Ay-uh, Banji, don't ride him hard, not yet. Be welcome, lad . . . You got coin on you? Listen, come aside and I'll explain how you can double your money. . . . Here, don't move, I'll fetch you your seconds. . . ."

Ivar responded as best he dared, in view of his incognito. He would be among these people for quite a while, and had better make himself popular. Besides, he liked them.

At length King Samlo boomed through the shadows: "Cleanup and curfew!" His followers bounced to obey the first part of the command. Ivar decided that the chaos earlier in the day, and now, was only apparent. Everyone knew his or her job. They simply didn't bother about military snap and polish.

Musicians gathered around the throne. "I thought we were ordered to bed," Ivar let fall.

"Not right away," Dulcy told him. "Whenever we can, we have a little fun first, songfest or dance or—" She squeezed his hand. "You think what you can do, like tell us news from your home. He'll call on you. Tonight, though, he wants— Yes. Fraina. Fraina of Jubilee. Mikkal's sister . . . half-sister, you'd say; their father can afford two wives. She's good. Watch."

The wanderers formed a ring before their wagons. Ivar had found he could neither sit indefinitely on his hams like them, nor crosslegged on the ground; after dark, his bottom would soon have been frozen. There was no energy to lavish on heated garments. He stood leaned against Redtop, hidden in darkness.

The center of the camp was bright silver, for Lavinia was high and Creusa hurrying toward the full. A young woman trod forth, genuflected to the king, stood erect and drew off her cloak. Beneath, she wore a pectoral, a broad brass girdle upholding filmy strips fore and aft, and incidental jewelry.

Ivar recognized her. Those delicate features and big gray eyes had caught his attention several times during the day. Virtually unclad, her figure seemed boy-slim save in the bosom. No, he decided, that wasn't right; her femaleness was just more subtle and supple than he had known among his own heavy folk.

The music wailed. She stamped her bare feet, once, twice, thrice, and broke into dance.

The wind gusted from Ivar. He had seen tineran girls perform before, and some were a wild equal of any ballerina—but none like this. *They save the best for their own,* he guessed; then thought vanished in the swirl of her.

She leaped, human muscles against Aenean gravity, rose flying, returned swimming. She flowed across ground, fountained upward again, landed to pirouette on a toe, a top that gyrated on and on and on, while it swung in ever wider precessions until she was a wheel, which abruptly became an arrow and at once the catavale which dodged the shaft and rent the hunter. She snapped her

cloak, made wings of it, made a lover of it, danced with it
and her floating hair and the plume of her breath. She
banished cold; moonlight sheened on sweat, and she made
the radiance ripple across her. She was the moonlight herself, the wind, the sound of pipes and drums and the
rhythmic handclaps of the whole Train and of Ivar; and
when she soared away into the night and the music ended,
men roared.

Inside, Mikkal's wagon was well laid out but had scant
room because of the things that crowded it. At the forward
end stood a potbellied stove, for use when fuel was available. Two double-width bunks, one above the other, occupied the left wall, a locker beneath and extensible table
between. The right wall was shelves, cupboard, racks, to
hold an unholy number of items: the stores and equipment
of everyday life, the costumes and paraphernalia of shows,
a kaleidoscope of odd souvenirs and junk. From the ceiling dangled an oil lantern, several amulets, and bunches of
dry food, sausages, onions, dragon apples, maufry, and
more, which turned the air pungent.

Attached to the door was a cage. An animal within sat
up on its hind legs as Mikkal, Dulcy, and Ivar entered.
The Firstling wondered why anybody would keep so un-
prepossessing a creature. It was about 15 centimeters in
length, quadrupedal though the forepaws came near re-
sembling skinny hands. Coarse gray fur covered it
beneath a leathery flap of skin which sprang from the
shoulders and reached the hindquarters, a kind of natural
mantle. The head was wedge-shaped, ears pointed and
curved like horns, mouth needle-fanged. That it could not
be a native Aenean organism was proved by the glittery
little red eyes, three of them in a triangle.

"What's that?" Ivar asked.

"Why, our luck," Dulcy said. "Name of Larzo." She
reached into the cage, which had no provision for closing.
"C'mon out and say hey-ah, Larzo, sweet."

"Your, uh, mascot?"

"Our what?" Mikkal responded. "Oh, I grab you. A ju,
like those?" He jerked his thumb at the hanging grotesques. "No. It's true, lucks're believed to help us, but
mainly they're pets. I never heard of a wagon, not in any
Train, that didn't keep one."

A vague memory of it came to Ivar from his reading.

No author had done more than mention in passing a custom which was of no obvious attractiveness or significance.

Dulcy had brought the animal forth. She cuddled it on her lap when the three humans settled side by side onto the lower bunk, crooned and offered it bits of cheese. It accepted that, but gave no return of her affection.

"Where're they from originally?" Ivar inquired.

Mikkal spread his hands. "Who knows? Some immigrant brought a pair or two along, I s'pose, 'way back in the early days. They never went off on their own, but tinerans got in the habit of keeping them and—" He yawned. "Let's doss. The trouble with morning is, it comes too damn early in the day."

Dulcy returned the luck to its cage. She leaned across Ivar's lap to do so. When her hand was free, she stroked him there, while her other fingers rumpled his hair. Mikkal blinked, then smiled. "Why not?" he said. "You'll be our companyo a spell, Rolf, and I think we'll both like you. Might as well start right off."

Unsure of himself, though immensely aware of the woman snuggled against him, the newcomer stammered, "Wh-what? I, I don't follow—"

"You take her first tonight," Mikkal invited.

"*Huh*? But, but, but—"

"You left your motor running," Mikkal said, while Dulcy giggled. After a pause: "Shy? You nords aften are, till you get drunk. No need among friends."

Ivar's face felt ablaze.

"Aw, now," Dulcy said. "Poor boy, he's too unready." She kissed him lightly on the lips. "Never mind. We've time. Later, if you want. Only if you want."

"Sure, don't be afraid of us," Mikkal added. "I don't bite, and she doesn't very hard. Go on to your rest if you'd rather."

Their casualness was like a benediction. Ivar hadn't imagined himself getting over such an embarrassment, immediately at that. "No offense meant," he said. "I'm, well, engaged to be married, at home."

"If you change your mind, let me know," Dulcy murmured. "But if you don't, I'll not doubt you're a man. Different tribes have different ways, that's all." She kissed him again, more vigorously. "Goodnight, dear."

He scrambled into the upper bunk, where he undressed

and crawled into his sleeping bag that she had laid out for
him. Mikkal snuffed the lantern, and soon he heard the
sounds and felt the quiverings below him, and thereafter
were darkness, stillness, and the wind.

He was long about getting to sleep. The invitation given
him had been too arousing. Or was it that simple? He'd
known three or four sleazy women, on leaves from his
military station. His friends had known them too. For a
while he swaggered. Then he met star-clean Tatiana and
was ashamed.

I'm no prig, he insisted to himself. Let them make what
they would of their lives on distant, corrupted Terra, or in
a near and not necessarily corrupted tineran wagon. A
child of Firstmen and scholars had another destiny to follow. Man on Aeneas had survived because the leaders
were dedicated to that survival: disciplined, constant men
and women who ever demanded more of themselves than
they did of their underlings. And self-command began
in the inmost privacies of the soul.

A person stumbled, of course. He didn't think he had
fallen too hard, upon those camp followers, in the weird
atmosphere of wartime. But a ... an orgy was something
else again. Especially when he had no flimsiest excuse.
Then why did he lie there, trying not to toss and turn, and
regret so *very* greatly that he should stay faithful to his
Tanya? Why, when he summoned her image to help him,
did Fraina come instead?

VII

Covering a hill in the middle of Nova Roma, the University of Virgil was a town within the city, and most of it older than most of the latter. The massive, crenelated wall around it still bore scars from the Troubles. *Older in truth than the Empire*, Desai thought. His glance passed over man-hewn red and gray stones to an incorporated section of glassy iridescence. A chill touched his spine. *That part is older than humanity.*

Beyond the main gateway, he entered a maze of courts, lanes, stairs, unexpected little gardens or trees, memorial plaques or statues, between the buildings. Architecture was different here from elsewhere. Even the newer structures—long, porticoed, ogive-windowed, until they rose in towers—preserved a tradition going back to the earliest settlers. *Or do they?* wondered Desai. *If these designs are from ancient Terra, they are crossbreeds that mutated. Gothic arches but Russko spires, except that in low gravity those vaultings soar while those domes bulge . . . and yet it isn't mismatched, it's strong and graceful in its own way, it belongs on Aeneas as . . . I do not.*

Chimes toned from a belfry which stood stark athwart darkling blue and a rusty streak of high-borne dustcloud. No doubt the melody was often heard. But it didn't sound academic to him; it rang almost martial.

Campus had not regained the crowded liveliness he had seen in holos taken before the revolt. In particular, there were few nonhumans, and perhaps still fewer humans from other colonies. But he passed among hundreds of Aeneans. Hardly a one failed to wear identification: the hooded, color-coded cloaks of teaching faculty, which might or might not overlay the smock of researcher; stu-

dent jackets bearing emblems of their colleges and, if they
were Landfolk, their Firstmen. (Beneath were the tunics,
trousers, and half-boots worn by both sexes—among
nords, anyhow—except on full-dress occasions when
women revived antique skirts.) Desai noticed, as well, the
shoulder patches on many, remembrance of military or
naval units now dissolved. *Should I make those illegal? ...
And what if my decree was generally disobeyd?*

He felt anger about him like a physical force. Oh, here
a couple of young fellows laughed at a joke, there several
were flying huge kites, yonder came a boy and girl hand in
hand, near two older persons learnedly conversing; but the
smiles were too few, the feet on flagstones rang too loud.

He had visited the area officially, first taking pains to
learn about it. That hadn't thawed his hosts, but today it
saved his asking for directions and thus risking recognition. Not that he feared violence; and he trusted he had
the maturity to tolerate insult; however— His way took
him past Rybnikov Laboratories, behind Pickens Library,
across Adzel Square to Borglund Hall, which was residen-
tial.

The south tower, she had said. Desai paused to see
where Virgil stood. After two years—more than one,
Aenean—he had not developed an automatic sense of how
he faced. The compass on a planet was always defined to
make its sun rise in the east; and a 25-degree axial tilt
wasn't excessive, shouldn't be confusing; and he ought to
be used to alien constellations by now. *Getting old. Not
very adaptable any longer.* Nor had he developed a reflex
to keep him from ever looking straight at that small, savage disc. Blind for a minute, he worried about retinal
burn. Probably none. Blue-eyed Aeneans kept their sight,
didn't they? *Let's get on with business. Too much else is
waiting back at the office as is, and more piling up every
second.*

The circular stairway in the tower was gloomy enough
to make him stumble, steep enough to make him pant and
his heart flutter. Low gravity didn't really compensate for
thin air, at his age. He rested for a time on the fourth-
floor landing before he approached an oaken door and
used a knocker which centuries of hands had worn shapeless.

Tatiana Thane let him in. "Good day," she said tone-
lessly.

Desai bowed. "Good day, my lady. You are kind to give me this interview."

"Do I have choice?"

"Certainly."

"I didn't when your Intelligence Corps hauled me in for questionin'." Her speech remained flat. A note of bitterness would at least have expressed some human relationship.

"That is why I wished to see you in your own apartment, Prosser Thane. To emphasize the voluntariness. Not that I believe you were arrested, were you? The officers merely assumed you would cooperate, as a law-abiding—citizen." Desai had barely checked himself from saying "subject of His Majesty."

"Well, I won't assault you, Commissioner. Have you truly come here unescorted as you claimed you would?"

"Oh, yes. Who'd pay attention to a chubby chocolate-colored man in a particularly thick mantle? Apropos which, where may I leave it?"

Tatiana indicated a peg in the entry. This layout was incredibly archaic. No doubt the original colonists hadn't had the economic surplus to automate residences, and there'd been sufficient pinch ever afterward to keep alive a scorn of "effete gadgetry." The place was chilly, too, though the young woman was rather lightly if plainly clad.

Desai's glance recorded her appearance for later study. She was tall and slim. The oval face bore a curved nose, arched brows above brown eyes, broad full mouth, ivory complexion, between shoulder-length wings of straight dark hair. *Old University family*, he recalled, *steeped in its lore, early destined for a scholarly career. Somewhat shy and bookish, but no indoor plant; she takes long walks or longer animalback rides, spends time in the desert, not to mention the jungles of Dido. Brilliant linguist, already responsible for advances in understanding certain languages on that planet. Her enthusiasm for the Terran classics doubtless kindled Ivar Frederiksen's interest in them and in history ... though in his case, perhaps one might better say the vision of former freedom fighters inflamed him. She appears to have more sense than that: a serious girl, short on humor, but on the whole, as good a fiancée as any man could hope for.*

That was the approximate extent of the report on her. There were too many more conspicuous Aeneans to inves-

tigate. The Frederiksen boy hadn't seemed like anyone to
worry about either, until he ran amok.

Tatiana led Desai into the main room of her small suite.
Its stone was relieved by faded tapestries and scuffed rug,
where bookshelves, a fine eidophonic player, and assorted
apparatus for logico-semantic analysis did not occupy the
walls. Furniture was equally shabby-comfortable, leather
and battered wood. Upon a desk stood pictures he supposed were of her kin, and Ivar's defiant in the middle of
them. Above hung two excellent views, one of a Didonian,
one of Aeneas seen from space, tawny-red, green- and
blue-mottled, north polar cap as white as the streamers of
ice-cloud. Her work, her home.

A trill sounded. She walked to a perch whereon, tiny
and fluffy, a native tadmouse sat. "Oh," she said. "I forgot
it's his lunchtime." She gave the animal seeds and a caress.
A sweet song responded.

"What is his name, if I may ask?" Desai inquired.

She was obviously surprised. "Why ... Frumious Bandersnatch."

Desai sketched another bow. "Pardon me, my lady. I
was given a wrong impression of you."

"What?"

"No matter. When I was a boy on Ramanujan, I had a
local pet I called Mock Turtle ... Tell me, please, would
a tadmouse be suitable for a household which includes
young children?"

"Well, that depends on them. They mustn't get rough."

"They wouldn't. Our cat's tail went unpulled until,
lately, the poor beast died. It couldn't adjust to this
planet."

She stiffened. "Aeneas doesn't make every newcomer
welcome, Commissioner. Sit down and describe what you
want of me."

The chair he found was too high for his comfort. She
lowered herself opposite him, easily because she topped
him by centimeters. He wished he could smoke, but to ask
if he might would be foolish.

"As for Ivar Frederiksen," Tatiana said, "I tell you
what I told your Corpsmen: I was not involved in his al-
leged action and I've no idea where he may be."

"I have seen the record of that interview, Prosser
Thane." Desai chose his words with care. "I believe you.

The agents did too. None recommended a narcoquiz, let alone a hypnoprobing."

"No Aenean constable has right to so much as propose that."

"But Aeneas rebelled and is under occupation," Desai said in his mildest voice. "Let it re-establish its loyalty, and it will get back what autonomy it had before." Seeing how resentment congealed her eyes, he added low: "The loyalty I speak of does not involve more than a few outward tokens of respect for the throne, as mere essential symbols. It is loyalty to the Empire—above all, to its Pax, in an age when spacefleets can incinerate whole worlds and when the mutiny in fact took thousands of lives—it is that I mean, my lady. It is that I am here about, not Ivar Frederiksen."

Startled, she swallowed before retorting, "What do you imagine I can do?"

"Probably nothing, I fear. Yet the chance of a hint, a clue, any spark of enlightenment no matter how faint, led me to call you and request a confidential talk. I emphasize 'request.' You cannot help unless you do so freely."

"What do you want?" she whispered. "I repeat, I'm not in any revolutionary group—never was, unless you count me clerkin' in militia durin' independence fight—and I don't know zero about what may be goin' on." Pride returned. "If I did, I'd kill myself rather than betray him. Or his cause."

"Do you mind talking about them, though? Him and his cause."

"How—?" Her answer faded out.

"My lady," Desai said, and wondered how honest his plea sounded to her, "I am a stranger to your people. I have met hundreds by now, myself, while my subordinates have met thousands. It has been of little use in gaining empathy. Your history, literature, arts are a bit more helpful, but the time I can devote to them is very limited, and summaries prepared by underlings assigned to the task are nearly valueless. One basic obstacle to understanding you is your pride, your ideal of disciplined self-reliance, your sense of privacy which makes you reluctant to bare the souls of even fictional characters. I know you have normal human emotions; but how, on Aeneas, do they normally work? How does it *feel* to be you?

"The only persons here with whom I can reach some

approximation of common ground are certain upper-class
Townfolk, entrepreneurs, executives, innovators—cosmo-
polites who have had a good deal to do with the most developed parts of the Empire."

"Squatters in Web," she sneered. "Yes, they're easy to
fathom. Anything for profit."

"Now you are the one whose imagination fails," Desai
reproved her. "True, no doubt a number of them are
despicable opportunists. Are there absolutely none among
Landfolk and University? Can you not conceive that an
industrialist or financier may honestly believe cooperation
with the Imperium is the best hope of his world? Can you
not entertain the hypothesis that he may be right?"

He sighed. "At least recognize that the better we Impies
understand you, the more to your advantage it is. In fact,
our empathy could be vital. Had— Well, to be frank, had
I known for sure what I dimly suspected, the significance
in your culture of the McCormac Memorial and the armed
households, I might have been able to persuade the sector
government to rescind its orders for dismantling them.
Then we might not have provoked the kind of thing which
has made your betrothed an outlaw."

Pain crossed her face. "Maybe," she said.

"My duty here," he told her, "is first to keep the Pax,
including civil law and order; in the longer run, to assure
that these will stay kept, when the Terran troops finally go
home. But what must be done? How? Should we, for example, should we revise the basic structure altogether?
Take power from the landed gentry especially, whose mili-
tarism may have been the root cause of the rebellion, and
establish a parliament based on strict manhood suffrage?"
Desai observed her expressions; she was becoming more
open to him. "You are shocked? Indignant? Denying to
yourself that so drastic a change is permanently possible?"

He leaned forward. "My lady," he said, "among the
horrors with which I live is this knowledge, based on all
the history I have studied and all the direct experience I
have had. It is terrifyingly easy to swing a defeated and
occupied nation in *any* direction. It has occurred over and
over. Sometimes, two victors with different ideologies divided such a loser among them, for purposes of 'reform.'
Afterward the loser stayed divided, its halves perhaps
more fanatical than either original conqueror."

Dizziness assailed him. He must breathe deeply before

he could go on: "Of course, an occupation may end too soon, or it may not carry out its reconstruction thoroughly enough. Then a version of the former society will revive, though probably a distorted version. Now how soon is too soon, how thoroughly is enough? And to what end?

"My lady, there are those in power who claim Sector Alpha Crucis will never be safe until Aeneas has been utterly transformed: into an imitation Terra, say most. I feel that that is not only wrong—you have something unique here, something basically good—but it is mortally dangerous. In spite of the pretensions of the psychodynamicists, I don't believe the consequences of radical surgery, on a proud and energetic people, are foreseeable.

"I want to make minimal, not maximal changes. They may amount to nothing more than strengthening trade relations with the heart stars of the Empire, to give you a larger stake in the Pax. Or whatever seems necessary. At present, however, I don't know. I flounder about in a sea of reports and statistics, and as I go down for the third time, I remember the old old saying, 'Let me write a nation's songs, and I care not who may write its laws.'

"Won't you help me understand your songs?"

Silence fell and lasted, save for a wind whittering outside, until the tadmouse offered a timid arpeggio. That seemed to draw Tatiana from her brown study. She shook herself and said, "What you're askin' for is closer acquaintance, Commissioner. Friendship."

His laugh was nervous. "I'll settle for an agreement to disagree. Of course, I haven't time for anywhere near as much frank discussion as I'd like—as I really need. But if, oh, if you young Aeneans would fraternize with the young marines, technicians, spacehands—you'd find them quite decent, you might actually take a little pity on their loneliness, and they do have experiences to relate from worlds you've never heard of—"

"I don't know if it's possible," Tatiana said. "Certainly not on my sole recommendation. Not that I'd give any, when your dogs are after my man."

"I thought that was another thing we might discuss," Desai said. "Not where he may be or what his plans are, no, no. But how to get him out of the trap he's closed on himself. Nothing would make me happier than to give him a free pardon. Can we figure out a method?"

She cast him an astonished look before saying slowly, "I do believe you mean that."

"Beyond question I do. I'll tell you why. We Impies have our agents and informers, after all, not to mention assorted spy devices. We are not totally blind and deaf to events and to the currents beneath them. The fact could not be kept secret from the people that Ivar Frederiksen, the heir to the Firstmanship of Ilion, has led the first open, calculated renewal of insurgency. His confederates who were killed, hurt, imprisoned are being looked on as martyrs. He, at large, is being whispered of as the rightful champion of freedom—the rightful king, if you will—who shall return." Desai's smile would have been grim were his plump features capable of it. "You note the absence of public statements by his relatives, aside from nominal expressions of regret at an 'unfortunate incident.' We authorities have been careful not to lean on them. Oh, but we have been careful!"

The tenuous atmosphere was like a perpetual muffler on his unaccustomed ears. He could barely hear her: "What might you do . . . for him?"

"If he, unmistakably of his own free will, should announce he's changed his mind—not toadying to the Imperium, no, merely admitting that through most of its history Aeneas didn't fare badly under it and this could be made true again—why, I think he could not only be pardoned, along with his associates, but the occupation government could yield on a number of points."

Wariness brought Tatiana upright. "If you intend this offer to lure him out of hidin'—"

"No!" Desai said, a touch impatiently. "It's not the kind of message that can be broadcast. Arrangements would have to be made beforehand in secret, or it would indeed look like a sellout. Anyhow, I repeat that I don't think you know how to find him, or that he'll try contacting you in the near future."

He sighed. "But perhaps— Well, as I told you, what I mainly want to learn, in my clumsy and tentative fashion, is what drives him. What drives all of you? What are the possibilities for compromise? How can Aeneas and the Imperium best struggle out of this mess they have created for each other?"

She regarded him for a second period of quiet, until she asked, "Would you care to have lunch?"

The sandwiches and coffee had been good; and seated in her kitchenette bay, which was vitryl supported on the backs of stone dragons, one had an unparalleled view across quads, halls, towers, battlements, down and on to Nova Roma, the River Flone and its belt of green, the ocherous wilderness beyond.

Desai inhaled fragrance from his cup, in lieu of the cigarette he had not yet ventured to mention. "Then Ivar is paradoxical," he remarked. "By your account, he is a skeptic on his way to becoming the charismatic lord of a deeply religious people."

"What?" He'd lost count of how often today he had taken the girl aback. "Oh, no. We've never been such. We began as scientific base, remember, and in no age of piety." She ran fingers through her hair and said after a moment, "Well, true, there always were some believers, especially among Landfolk. . . . m-m, I suppose tendency does go back beyond Snelund administration, maybe several lifetimes . . . reaction to general decadence of Empire?—but our woes in last several years have certainly accelerated it—more and more, people are turnin' to churches." She frowned. "They're not findin' what they seek, though. That's Ivar's problem. He underwent conversion in early adolescence, he tells me, then later found creed unbelievable in light of science—unless, he says, they dilute it to cluck of soothin' noises, which is not what he wants."

"Since I came here for information, I have no business telling you what you are," Desai said. "Nevertheless, I do have a rather varied background and— Well, how would this interpretation strike you? Aenean society has always had a strong *faith*. A faith in the value of knowledge, to plant this colony in the first place; a faith in, oh, in the sheer right and duty of survival, to carry it through the particularly severe impact of the Troubles which it suffered; a faith in service, honor, tradition, demonstrated by the fact that what is essentially paternalism continued to be viable in easier times. Now hard times have come back. Some Aeneans, like Ivar, react by making a still greater emotional commitment to the social system. Others look to the supernatural. But however he does it, the average Aenean must serve something which is greater than himself."

Tatiana frowned in thought. "That may be. That may

be. Still, I don't think 'supernatural' is right word, except
in highly special sense. 'Transcendental' might be better.
For instance, I'd call Cosmenosis philosophy rather than
religion." She smiled a trifle. "I ought to know, bein' Cos-
menosist myself."

"I seem to recall— Isn't that an increasingly popular
movement in the University community?"

"Which is large and ramified, don't forget. Yes, Commissioner, you're right. And I don't believe it's mere fad."

"What are the tenets?"

"Nothing exact, really. It doesn't claim to be revealed
truth, simply way of gropin' toward . . . insight, oneness.
Work with Didonians inspired it, orignally. You can guess
why, can't you?"

Desai nodded. Through his mind passed the picture he
had seen, and many more: in a red-brown rain forest,
beneath an eternally clouded sky, stood a being which was
triune. Upon the platformlike shoulders of a large mono-
ceroid quadruped rested a feathered flyer and a furry
brachiator with well-developed hands. Their faces ran out
in tubes, which connected to the big animal to tap its
bloodstream. It ate for all of them.

Yet they were not permanently linked. They belonged
to their distinct genera, reproduced their separate kinds
and carried out many functions independently.

That included a measure of thinking. But the Didonian
was not truly intelligent until its—no, heesh's—three members were joined. Then not only did veins link; nervous
systems did. The three brains together became more than
the sum of the three apart.

How much more was not known, perhaps not definable
in any language comprehensible to man. The next world
sunward from Aeneas remained as wrapped in mystery as
in mist. That Didonian societies were technologically primitive proved nothing; human ones were, until a geologi-
cally infinitesimal moment ago, and Terra was an easier
globe on which to find lawfulness in nature. That communication with Didonians was extraordinarily difficult, limited after seven hundred years to a set of pidgin dialects,
proved nothing either, beyond the truism that their minds
were alien beyond ready imagining.

What is a mind, when it is the temporary creation of
three beings, each with its own individuality and memories,
each able to have any number of different partners? What

is personality—the soul, even—when these shifting link-
ages perpetuate those recollections, in a ghostly diminu-
endo that lasts for generations after the experiencing
bodies have died? How many varieties of race and culture
and self are possible, throughout the ages of an entire infi-
nite-faceted world? What may we learn from them, or
they from us?

Without Dido for lure, probably men would never have
possessed Aeneas. It was so far from Terra, so poor and
harsh—more habitable for them than its sister, but by no
great margin. By the time that humans who lacked such
incentive had filled more promising planets, no doubt the
Ythrians would have occupied this one. It would have
suited them far better than it did *Homo sapiens.*

How well had it suited the Builders, uncertain
megayears in the past, when there were no Didonians and
Aeneas had oceans—?

"Excuse me." Desai realized he had gone off into a reverie. "My mind wandered. Yes, I've meditated on the—
the Neighbors, don't you call them?—quite a bit, in what
odd moments fall to my lot. They must have influenced
your society enormously, not just as an inexhaustible research objective, but by their, well, example."

"Especially of late, when we think we may be reachin'
true communication in some few cases," Tatiana replied.
Ardor touched her tone. "Think: such way of existence,
on hand for us to witness and . . . and meditate on, you
said. Maybe you're right, we do need transhumanness in
our lives, here on this planet. But maybe, Commissioner,
we're right in feelin' that need." She swept her hand in an
arc at the sky. "What are we? Sparks, cast up from a
burnin' universe whose creation was meanin'less accident?
Or children of God? Or parts, masks of God? Or seed
from which God will at last grow?" Quieter: "Most of us
Cosmenosists think—yes, Didonians have inspired it, their
strange unity, such little as we've learned of their beliefs,
dedications, poetry, dreams—we think reality is always
growin' toward what is greater than itself, and first duty
of those that stand highest is to help raise those lower—"

Her gaze went out the window, to the fragment of what
had been . . . something, ages ago . . . and, in these latter
centuries, had never really been lost in the wall which
used it. "Like Builders," she finished. "Or Elders, as Land-

folk call them, or—oh, they've many names. Those who came before us."

Desai stirred. "I don't want to be irreverent," he said uncomfortably, "but, well, while apparently a starfaring civilization did exist in the distant past, leaving relics on a number of planets, I can't quite, um-m, swallow this notion I've heard on Aeneas, that it went onto a more exalted plane—rather than simply dying out."

"What would destroy it?" she challenged. "Don't you suppose we, puny mankind, are already too widespread for extinction, this side of cosmos itself endin'—or, if we perish on some worlds, we won't leave tools, carvin's, synthetics, fossilized bones, traces enough to identify us for millions of years to come? Why not Builders, then?"

"Well," he argued, "a brief period of expansion, perhaps scientific bases only, no true colonies, evacuated because of adverse developments at home—"

"You're guessin'," Tatiana said. "In fact, you're whistlin' past graveyard that isn't there. I think, and I'm far from alone, Builders never needed to do more than they did. They were already beyond material gigantism, by time they reached here. I think they outgrew these last vestiges we see, and left them. And Didonian many-in-one gives us clue to what they became; yes, they may have started that very line of evolution themselves. And on their chosen day they will return, for all our sakes."

"I have heard talk about these ideas, Prosser Thane, but—"

Her look burned at him. "You assume it's crankery. Then consider this. Right on Aeneas are completest set of Builder ruins known: in Orcan region, on Mount Cronos. We've never investigated them as we should, at first because of other concerns, later because they'd become inhabited. But now... oh, rumors yet, nothin' but the kind of rumors that're forever driftin' in on desert wind . . . still, they whisper of a forerunner—"

She saw she might have spoken too freely, broke off and snapped self-possession into place. "Please don't label me fanatic," she said. "Call it hope, daydream, what you will. I agree we have no proof, let alone divine revelation." He could not be sure how much or how little malice dwelt in her smile. "Still, Commissioner, what if bein's five or ten million years ahead of us *should* decide Terran Empire is in need of reconstruction?"

Desai returned to his office so near the end of the post-ed working day that he planned to shove everything aside till tomorrow and get home early. It would be the first time in a couple of weeks he had seen his children before they were asleep.

But of course his phone told him he had an emergency call. Being a machine, it refrained from implying he ought to have left a number where he could be reached. The message had come from his chief of Intelligence.

Maybe it isn't crucial, went his tired thought. *Feinstein's a good man, but he's never quite learned how to delegate.*

He made the connection. The captain responded directly. After ritual salutations and apologies:

"—that Aycharaych of Jean-Baptiste, do you remember him? Well, sir, he's disappeared, under extremely suspicious circumstances.

" . . . No, as you yourself, and His Excellency, decided, we had no reasonable cause to doubt him. He actually arranged to travel with a patrol of ours, for his first look at the countryside.

" . . . As nearly as I can make out from bewildered reports, somehow he obtained the password. You know what precautions we've instituted since the Hesperian incident? The key guards don't know the passwords themselves, consciously. Those're implanted for posthypnotic recognition and quick re-forgetting. To prevent accidents, they're nonsense syllables, or phrases taken from obscure languages used at the far side of the Empire. If Aycharaych could read them in the minds of the men—remembering also his nonhuman brain structure—then he's more of a telepath, or knows more tricks, than is supposed to be possible.

"Anyhow, sir, with the passwords he commandeered a flyer, talked it past an aerial picket, and is flat-out gone.

" . . . Yes, sir, naturally I've had the file on him checked, cross-correlated, everything we can do with what we've got on this wretched dustball. No hint of motivation. Could be simple piracy, I imagine, but dare we assume that?"

"My friend," Desai answered, while exhaustion slumped his shoulders, "I cannot conceive of one thing in the universe which we truly dare assume."

VIII

"Hee-ah!" Mikkal lashed his statha into full wavelike gallop. The crag bull veered. Had it gone down the talus slope, the hunters could not have followed. Boots, or feet not evolved for this environment, would have been slashed open by the edges of the rocks. And the many cinnabar-colored needles which jutted along the canyon would have screened off a shot.

As was, the beast swung from the rim and clattered across the mountainside. Then, from behind an outcrop striped in mineral colors, Fraina appeared on her own mount.

The bull should have fled her too, uphill toward Ivar. Instead, it lowered its head and charged. The trident horns sheened like steel. Her statha reared in panic. The bull was almost as big as it, and stronger and faster.

Ivar had the only gun, his rifle; the others bore javelins. "*Ya-lawa!*" he commanded his steed: in Haisun, "Freeze!" He swung stock to cheek and sighted. Bare rock, red dust, scattered gray-green bushes, and a single rahab tree stood sharp in the light of noontide Virgil. Shadows were purple but the sky seemed almost black above raw peaks. The air lay hot, suckingly dry, soundless except for hoof-drum and human cries.

If I don't hit that creature, Fraina may die, went through Ivar. *But no use hittin' him in the hump. And anywhere else is wicked to try for, at this angle and speed, and her in line of fire—* The knowledge flashed by as a part of taking aim. He had no time to be afraid.

The rifle hissed. The bullet trailed a whipcrack. The crag bull leaped, bellowed, and toppled.

"Rolf, Rolf, Rolf!" Fraina caroled. He rode down to

her with glory in him. When they dismounted, she threw arms around him, lips against his.

For all its enthusiasm, it was a chaste kiss; yet it made him a trifle giddy. By the time he recovered, Mikkal had arrived and was examining the catch.

"Good act, Rolf." His smile gleamed white in the thin face. "We'll feast tonight."

"We've earned it." Fraina laughed. "Not that folk always get paid what's owing them, or don't get it swittled from them afterward."

"The trick is to be the swittler," Mikkal said.

Fraina's gaze fell tenderly on Ivar. "Or to be smart enough to keep what you've been strong enough to earn," she murmured.

His heart knocked. She was more beautiful than she ought to be, now in this moment of his victory, and in the trunks and halter which clad her. Mikkal wore simply a loincloth and crossed shoulderbelts to support knives, pouch, canteen. Those coppery skins could stand a fair amount of exposure, and it was joy to feel warmth upon them again. Ivar struck to loose, full desert garb, blouse, trousers, sun-visored burnoose.

That plateau known as the Dreary of Ironland was behind them. There would be no more struggle over stonefields or around crevasses of a country where nothing stirred save them and the wind, nothing lived save them alone; no more thirst when water must be rationed till food went uncooked and utensils were cleaned with sand; no more nights so cold that tents must be erected to keep the animals alive.

As always, the passage had frayed nerves thin. Ivar appreciated the wisdom of the king in sequestering firearms. At that, a couple of knife fights had come near ending fatally. The travelers needed more than easier conditions, they needed something to cheer them. This first successful hunt on the eastern slope of the Ferric Mountains ought to help mightily.

And, though the country here was gaunt, they were over the worst. The Waybreak Train was headed down toward the Flone Valley, to reach at last the river itself, its cool green banks and the merry little towns snuggled along it, south of Nova Roma. If now the hunters laughed overmuch and over-shrilly while they butchered the crag

bull, Ivar thought it was not beneath a Firstling's dignity
to join in.

Moreover, Fraina was with him, they were working together. . . . Their acquaintance was not deep. Time and energy had been lacking for that. Besides, despite her dancing, she behaved shyly for a tineran girl. But for the rest
of his stay in the troop— *I hope I've honor not to seduce
her and leave her cryin' behind, when at last I go. (I begin to understand why, no matter hardships, sharpest pain
may be to leave.) And Tanya, of course, mustn't forget
Tanya.*

*Let me, though, enjoy Fraina's nearness while I can.
She's so vivid. Everything is. I never knew I could feel this
fully and freely, till I joined wanderers.*

He forced his attention to the task on hand. His heavy
sheath knife went through hide, flesh, gristle, even the
thinner bones, much more quickly and easily than did the
slender blades of his comrades. He wondered why they
didn't adopt the nord model, or at least add it to their tool
kit; then, watching how cunningly they worked, he decided
it wouldn't fit their style. *Hm, yes, I begin to see for my
self, cultures are unities, often in subtle ways.*

Finished, meat loaded on stathas, the three of them
went to rest by the spring which had attracted their
quarry. It made a deliciously chilly bowlful in the hollow
of a rock, the shadow of a bluff. Plume trava nodded
white above mossy chromabryon; spearflies darted silver
bright; the stream clinked away over stones till the desert
swallowed it up. The humans drank deep, then leaned lux-
uriously back against the cliff, Fraina between the men.

"Ay-ah," Mikkal sighed. "No need for hurry. I make us
barely ten clicks from the Train, if we set an intercept
course. Let's relax before lunch."

"Good idea," Ivar said. He and Fraina exchanged
smiles.

Mikkal reached across her. In his hand were three
twists of paper enclosing brown shreds. "Smoke?" he invited.

"What?" Ivar said. "I thought you tinerans avoided tobacco. Dries mouth, doesn't it?"

"Oh, this's marwan." At the puzzled look he got, Mikkal
explained: "Never heard of it? Well, I don't suppose your
breed would use the stuff. It's a plant. You dry and smoke
it. Has a similar effect to alcohol. Actually better, I'd say,

though I admit the taste leaves a trifle to be desired along-side a fine whiskey."

"*Narcotic?*" Ivar was shocked.

"Not that fierce, Rolf. Hell-near to a necessity, in fact, when you're away from the Train, like on a hunting or scouting trip." Mikkal grimaced. "These wilds are too in-human. With a lot of friends around, you're screened. But by yourself, you need to take the edge off how alone and mortal you are."

Never before had Ivar heard him confess to a weak-ness. Mikkal was normally cheerful. When his temper, too, flared in the Dreary, he had not gone for his steel but used an equally whetted tongue, as if he felt less pressure than most of his fellows to prove masculinity. Now— *Well, I reckon I can sympathize. It is oppressive, this size and silence. Unendin' memento mori. Never thought so before, out in back country, but I do now. If Fraina weren't here to keep me glad, I might be tempted to try his drug.*

"No, thank you," Ivar said.

Mikkal shrugged. On the way back, his hand paused be-fore the girl. She made a refusing gesture. He arched his brows, whether in surprise or sardonicism, till she gave him a tiny frown and headshake. Then he grinned, tucked away the extra cigarettes, put his between his lips and snapped a lighter to it. Ivar had scarcely noticed the by-play, and gave it no thought except to rejoice that in this, also, Fraina kept her innocence. Mostly he noticed the sweet odors of her, healthy flesh and sun-warmed hair and sweat that stood in beads on her half-covered breasts.

Mikkal drew smoke into his lungs, held it, let it out very slowly and drooped his lids. "Aaah," he said, "and again aaah. I become able to think. Mainly about ways to treat these steaks and chops. The women'll make stew tonight, no doubt. I'll insist the rest of the meat be started in a proper marinade. Take the argument to the king if I must. I'm sure he'll support me. He may be a vinegar beak, our Samlo, but all kings are, and he's a sensible vinegar beak."

"He certainly doesn't behave like average tineran," Ivar said.

"Kings don't. That's why we have them. I can't deny we're a flighty race, indeed I boast of it. However, that means we must have somebody who'll tie us down to cau-tion and foresight."

"I, yes, I do know about special trainin' kings get. Must be real discipline, to last through lifetime in your society."

Fraina giggled. Mikkal, who had taken another drag, kicked heels and whooped. "What'd I say?" Ivar asked.

The girl dropped her glance. He believed he saw her blush, though that was hard to tell on her complexion. "Please, Mikkal, don't be irrev'rent," she said.

"Well, no more'n I have to," her half-brother agreed. "Still, Rolf might's well know. It's not a secret, just a matter we don't talk about. Not to disillusion youngsters too early, et cetera." His eyes sparkled toward Ivar. "Only the lodge that kings belong to is supposed to know what goes on in the shrines, and in the holy caves and booths where Fairs are held. But the royal wives and concubines take part, and girls will pass on details to their friends. You think we common tinerans hold lively parties. We don't know what liveliness is!"

"But it's our religion," Fraina assured Ivar. "Not the godlings and jus and spells of everyday. This is to honor the powers of life."

Mikkal chuckled. "Aye-ah, officially those're fertility rites. Well, I've read some anthropology, talked to a mixed bag of people, even taken thought once in a while when I'd nothing better to do. *I* figure the cult developed because the king has to have all-stops-out orgies fairly often, if he's to stay the kind of sobersides we need for a leader."

Ivar stared before him, half in confusion, half in embarrassment. Wouldn't it make more sense for the tinerans as a whole to be more self-controlled? Why was this extreme emotionalism seemingly built into them? Or was that merely his own prejudices speaking? Hadn't he been becoming more and more like them, and savoring every minute of it?

Fraina laid a hand on his arm. Her breath touched his cheek. "Mikkal has to poke fun," she said. "I believe it's both holy and unholy, what the king does. Holy because we must have young—too many die small, human and animal—and the powers of life are real. Unholy because, oh, he takes on himself the committing of . . . excesses, is that the word? On behalf of the Train, he releases our beast side, that otherwise would tear the Train apart."

I don't understand, quite, Ivar thought. *But,* thrilled

within him, *she's thoughtful, intelligent, grave, as well as sweet and blithe.*

"Yah, I should start Dulcy baby-popping," Mikkal said. "The wet stage isn't too ghastly a nuisance, I'm told." When weaned, children moved into dormitory wagons. "On the other hand," he added, "I've told a few whoppers myself, when I had me a mark with jingle in his pockets—"

A shape blotted out the sun. They bounded to their feet.

That which was descending passed the disc, and light blazed off the gold-bronze pinions of a six-meter wingspan. Air whistled and thundered. Fraina cried out. Mikkal poised his javelin. "Don't!" Ivar shouted. "*Ya-lawa!* He's Ythrian!"

"O-o-oh, ye-e-es," Mikkal said softly. He lowered the spear though he kept it ready. Fraina gripped Ivar's arm and leaned hard against him.

The being landed. Ivar had met Ythrians before, at the University and elsewhere. But his astonishment at this arrival was such that he gaped as if he were seeing one for the first time.

Grounded, the newcomer used those tremendous wings, folded downward, for legs, claws at the bend of them spreading out to serve as feet, the long rear-directed bones lending extra support when at rest. That brought his height to some 135 centimeters, mid-breast on Ivar, farther up on the tinerans; for his mass was a good 25 kilos. Beneath a prowlike keelbone were lean yellow-skinned arms whose hands, evolved from talons, each bore three sharp-clawed fingers flanked by two thumbs, and a dewclaw on the inner wrist. Above were a strong neck and a large head proudly held. The skull bulged backward to contain the brain, for there was scant brow, the face curving down in a ridged muzzle to a mouth whose sensitive lips contrasted curiously with the carnivore fangs behind. A stiff feather-crest rose over head and neck, white edged with black like the fan-shaped tail. Otherwise, apart from feet, arms, and huge eyes which burned gold and never seemed to waver or blink, the body was covered with plumage of lustrous brown.

He wore an apron whose pockets, loops, and straps supported what little equipment he needed. Knife, canteen, and pistol were the only conspicuous items. He could live off the country better than any human.

Mikkal inhaled smoke, relaxed, smiled, lifted and dipped his weapon in salute. "Hay-ah, wayfarer," he said formally, "be welcome among us in the Peace of Water, where none are enemies. We're Mikkal of Redtop and my sister Fraina of Jubilee, from the Waybreak Train; and our companyo is Rolf Mariner, varsiteer."

The Anglic which replied was sufficiently fluent that one couldn't be sure how much of the humming accent and sibilant overtones were due to Ythrian vocal organs, how much simply to this being an offplanet dialect the speaker had learned. "Thanks, greetings, and fair winds wished for you. I hight Erannath, of the Stormgate choth upon Avalon. Let me quench thirst and we can talk if you desire."

As awkward on the ground as he was graceful aloft, he stumped to the pool. When he bent over to drink, Ivar glimpsed the gill-like antlibranchs, three on either side of his body. They were closed now, but in flight the muscles would work them like bellows, forcing extra oxygen into the bloodstream to power the lifting of the great weight. That meant high fuel consumption too, he remembered. No wonder Erannath traveled alone, if he had no vehicle. This land couldn't support two of him inside a practical radius of operations.

"He's gorgeous," Fraina whispered to Ivar. "What did you call him?"

"Ythrian," the Firstling replied. "You mean you don't know?"

"I guess I have heard, vaguely, but I'm an ignorant wanderfoot, Rolf. Will you tell me later?"

Ha! Won't I?

Mikkal settled himself back in the shade where he had been. "Might I ask what brings you, stranger?"

"Circumstances," Erannath replied. His race tended to be curt. A large part of their own communication lay in nuances indicated by the play of marvelously controllable quills.

Mikkal laughed. "In other words, yes, I might ask, but no, I might not get an answer. Wouldn't you like to palaver a while anyhow? Yo, Fraina, Rolf, join the party."

They did. Erannath's gaze lingered on the Firstling. "I have not hitherto observed your breed fare thus," he said.

"I—wanted a change—" Ivar faltered.

"He hasn't told exactly why, and no need for you to, either," Mikkal declared. "But see here, Aeronaut, your re-

mark implies you *have* been observing, and pretty exten-
sively too. Unless you're given to reckless generalization,
which I don't believe your kind is."

Expressions they could not read rippled across the
feathers. "Yes," the Ythrian said after a moment, "I am
interested in this planet. As an Avalonian, I am naturally
familiar with humans, but of a rather special sort. Being
on Aeneas, I am taking the opportunity to become acquainted, however superficially, with a few more."

"U-u-uh-huh." Mikkal lounged crosslegged, smoking, idly
watching the sky, while he drawled. "Somehow I doubt
they've heard of you in Nova Roma. The occupation authorities have planted their heaviest buttocks on space
traffic, in and out. Want to show me your official permit
to flit around? As skittery as the guiders of our Terran des-
tinies are nowadays, would they give a visitor from our
esteemed rival empire the freedom of a key near-the-bor-
der world? I'm only fantasizing, but it goes in the direction of you being stranded here. You came in during the
revolt, let's suppose, when that was easy to do unbeknownst, and you're biding your time till conditions ease
up enough for you to get home."

Ivar's fingers clenched on his gunstock. But Erannath
sat imperturbable. "Fantasize as you wish," he said dryly,
"if you grant me the same right." Again his eyes smote
the Firstling.

"Well, our territory doesn't come near Nova Roma,"
Mikkal continued. "We'd make you welcome, if you care
to roll with us as you've probably done already in two or
three other Trains. Your songs and stories should be
uncommon entertaining. And . . . maybe when we reach
the green and start giving shows, we can work you into an
act."

Fraina gasped. Ivar smiled at her. "Yes," he whispered,
"without that weed in him—unless he was in camp—
Mikkal wouldn't have nerve to proposition those claws
and dignity, would he?" Her hair tickled his face. She
squeezed his hand.

"My thanks," Erannath said. "I will be honored to guest
you, for a few days at least. Thereafter we can discuss
further."

He went high above them, hovering, soaring, wheeling
in splendor, while they rode back across the tilted land.

"What *is* he?" Fraina asked. Hoofbeats clopped beneath her voice. A breeze bore smoky orders of starkwood. They recalled the smell of the Ythrian, as if his forefathers once flew too near their sun.

"A sophont," Mikkal said redundantly. He proceeded: "More bright and tough than most. Maybe more than us. Could be we're stronger, we humans, simply because we outnumber them, and that simply because of having gotten the jump on them in space travel and, hm, needing less room per person to live in."

"A bird?"

"No," Ivar told her. "They're feathered, yes, warm-blooded, two sexes. However, you noticed he doesn't have a beak, and females give live birth. No lactation—no milk, I mean; the lips're for getting the blood out of prey."

"You bespoke an empire, Mikkal," she said, "and, ye-ih, I do remember mentions aforetime. Talk on, will you?"

"Let Rolf do that," the man suggested. "He's schooled. Besides, if he has to keep still much longer, he'll make an awful mess when he explodes."

Ivar's ears burned. *True*, he thought. But Fraina gave him such eager attention that he plunged happily forward.

"Ythri's planet rather like Aeneas, except for havin' cooler sun," he said. "It's about a hundred light-years from here, roughly in direction of Beta Centauri."

"That's the Angel's Eye," Mikkal interpolated.

Don't tinerans use our constellations? Ivar wondered. *Well, we don't use Terra's; our sky is different.* "After humans made contact, Ythrians rapidly acquired modern technology," he went on. "Altogether variant civilization, of course, if you can call it civilization, they never havin' had cities. Noneless, it lent itself to spacefarin', same as Technic culture, and in time Ythrians began to trade and colonize, on smaller scale than humans. When League fell apart and Troubles followed, they suffered too. Men restored order at last by establishin' Terran Empire, Ythrians by their Domain. It isn't really an empire, Mikkal. Loose alliance of worlds.

"Still, it grew. So did Empire, Terra's, that is, till they met and clashed. Couple centuries ago, they fought. Ythri lost war and had to give up good deal of border territory. But it'd fought too stiffly for Imperium to think of annexin' entire Domain.

"Since, relations have been ... variable, let's say. Some

affrays, though never another real war; some treaties and joint undertakin's, though often skulduggery on both sides; plenty of trade, individuals and organizations visitin' back and forth. Terra's not happy about how Domain of Ythri is growin' in opposite direction from us, and in strength. But Merseia's kept Imperium too busy to do much in these parts—except stamp out freedom among its own subjects."

"Nothing like that to make a person objective about his government," Mikkal remarked aside.

"I see," Fraina said. "How clearly you explain. . . . Didn't I hear him tell he was, m-m, from Avalon?"

"Yes," Ivar replied. "Planet in Domain, colonized by humans and Ythrians together. Unique society. It'd be reasonable to send Avalonian to spy out Aeneas. He'd have more rapport with us, more insight, than ordinary Ythrians."

Her eyes widened. "He's a spy?"

"Intelligence agent, if you prefer. Not skulkin' around burglarizin' Navy bases or any such nonsense. Gatherin' what bits of information he can, to become part of their picture of Terran Empire. I really can't think what else he'd be. They must've landed him here while space-traffic control was broken down because of independence war. As Mikkal says, eventually he'll leave—I'd guess when Ythrians again have consulate in Nova Roma, that can arrange to smuggle him out."

"You don't care, Rolf?"

"Why should I? In fact—"

Ivar finished the thought in his head. *We got no Ythrian help in our struggle. I'm sure Hugh McCormac tried, and was refused. They wouldn't risk new war. But . . . if we could get clandestine aid—arms and equipment slipped to us, interstellar transport furnished, communications nets made available—we could build strength of freedom forces till— We failed because we weren't rightly prepared. McCormac raised standard almost on impulse. And he wasn't tryin' to split Empire, he wanted to rule it himself. What would Ythri gain by that? Whereas if our purpose was to break Sector Alpha Crucis loose, make it independent or even bring it under Ythri's easygoin' suzerainty— wouldn't that interest them? Perhaps be worth war, especially if we got Merseian help too—* He looked up at

Erannath and dreamed of wings which stormed hither-
ward in the cause of liberty.

An exclamation drew him back to his body. They had
topped a ridge. On the farther slope, mostly buried by a
rockslide, were the remnants of great walls and of
columns so slim and poised that it was as if they too were
flying. Time had not dimmed their nacreous luster.

"Why ... Builder relic," Ivar said. "Or do you call them
Elders?"

"*La-Sarzen*," Fraina told him, very low. "The High
Ones." Upon her countenance and, yes, Mikkal's, lay awe.

"We're off our usual route," the man breathed. "I'd forgotten that this is where some of them lived."

He and his sister sprang from their saddles, knelt with
uplifted arms, and chanted. Afterward they rose, crossed
themselves, and spat: in this parched country, a deed of
sacrifice. As they rode on, they gave the ruins a wide
berth, and hailed them before dropping behind the next
rise.

Erannath had not descended to watch. Given his vision,
he need not. He cruised through slow circles like a sign in
heaven.

After a kilometer, Ivar dared ask: "Is that ... back
yonder ... part of your religion? I wouldn't want to be
profane."

Mikkal nodded. "I suppose you could call it sacred.
Whatever the High Ones are, they're as near godhood as
makes no difference."

That doesn't follow, Ivar thought, keeping silence. *Why
is it so nearly universal belief?*

"Some of their spirit must be left in what they made,"
Fraina said raptly. "We need its help. And, when they
come back, they'll know we keep faith in them."

"Will they?" Ivar couldn't help the question.

"Yes," Mikkal said. In him, sober quiet was twice powerful. "Quite likely during our own lifetimes, Rolf. Haven't
you heard the tale that's abroad? Far south, where the
dead men dwell, a prophet has arisen to prepare the
way——"

He shivered in the warmth. "I don't know if that's true,
myself," he finished in a matter-of-fact tone. "But we can
hope, can't we? C'mon, tingle up these lazy beasts and let's
get back to the Train."

IX

The mail from Terra was in. Chunderban Desai settled back with a box of cigarettes, a samovar of tea, and resignation to the fact that he would eat lunch and dinner and a midnight snack off his desk. This did not mean he, his staff, or his equipment were inefficient. He would have no need to personally scan two-thirds of what was addressed to his office. But he did bear ultimate responsibility for a globe upon which dwelt 400 million human beings.

Lord Advisor Petroff of the Policy Board was proposing a shakeup of organizational structure throughout the occupied zone, and needed reports and opinions from every commissioner. Lord Advisor Chardon passed on certain complaints from Sector Governor Muratori, about a seeming lack of zeal in the reconstruction of the Virgilian System, and asked for explanations. Naval Intelligence wanted various operations started which would attempt to learn how active Merseian agents were throughout the Alpha Crucis region. BuEc wanted a fresh survey made of mineral resources in the barren planets of each system in the sector, and studies of their exploitability as a method of industrial recovery. BuSci wanted increased support for research on Dido, adding that that should help win over the Aeneans. BuPsy wanted Dido evacuated, fearing that its cloud cover and vast wildernesses made it potentially too useful to guerrillas. The Throne wanted immediate in-depth information on local results should His Majesty make a contemplated tour of the subjugated rebel worlds. . . .

Night filled the wall transparency, and a chill tiny Creusa hurtled above a darkened city, when a thing Desai himself had requested finally crossed the screen. He surged out of sleepiness with a gasp. *I'd better have that selector reprogrammed!* His fingers shook almost too badly for him to insert a fresh cigarette in his holder and inhale it to ignition. He never noticed how tongue, palate, throat, and lungs protested.

"—no planet named, nicknamed, or translated as Jean-Baptiste, assuredly not in any known language or dialect of the Empire, nor in any exterior space for which records are available. Saint John, Hagios Ioannes, and the continent of San Juan on Nuevo México were all named after a co-author of the basic Christian canon, a person distinct from the one who figures as active in events described therein and is termed in Fransai Jean-Baptiste, in Anglic John the Baptist. . . .

"The origin of the individual self-denominated Aycharaych (v. note 3 on transcription of the voice print) has been identified, from measurement upon holographic material supplied (ref. 2), with a probability deemed high albeit nonquantifiable due to paucity of data.

"When no good correlation was obtained with any species filed with the Imperial Xenological Register, application was made to Naval Intelligence. It was reported by this agency that as a result of a scan of special data banks, Aycharaych can be assumed to be from a planet subject to the Roidhun of Merseia. It was added that he should be considered an agent thereof, presumably dispatched on a mission inimical to the best interests of His Majesty.

"Unfortunately, very little is known about the planet in question. A full account is attached, but will be found scarcely more informative than the summary which follows.

"According to a few casual mentions made in the presence of Imperial personnel and duly reported by them, the planet is referred to as Chereion (v. note 3). It is recorded as having been called variously 'cold, creepy,' 'a mummy dwarf,' and 'a silent ancient,' albeit some favorable notice was taken of art and architecture. These remarks were made in conversation by Merseians (or, in one instance, a non-Merseian of the Roidhunate) by whom the planet had been visited briefly in the course of voyages directed elsewhere. From this it may perhaps be inferred that Chereion is terrestroid verging on subterrestroid, of low mean temperature, sufficiently small and/or old that a substantial loss of atmosphere and hydrosphere has been suffered. In short, it may be considered possibly not too dissimilar to Aeneas as the latter is described in the files. Nothing has been scanned which would make it possible for the sun to be located or spectrally classified. It must be emphasized that Chereion is obscure, seldom touched at, and never heard of by the average Merseian.

"Some indications were noted, which owing to lack of planet. Identification of subject Aycharaych as of this Chereion may be more highly regarded than this by the top levels of the Roidhunate hierarchy, and that indeed the dearth of interest in it may have been deliberately instigated rather than straightforwardly caused by primitiveness, poverty, or other more usual factors. If so, presumably its entire populace has, effectively, been induced to cooperate, suggesting that some uniqueness may be found in their psychology.

"The Chereionites are not absolutely confined to their planet. Indentification of subject Aycharaych as of this race was made from pictures taken with microcameras upon two different occasions, one a reception at the Terran Embassy on Merseia, one more recently during negotiations in re Jihannath. In either case, a large and mixed group being present, no more than brief queries were made, eliciting replies such as those listed above. But it should be pointed out that if a Chereionite was present at any affair of such importance (and presumably at others for which no data are on hand) then he must have been considered useful to the Roidhunate.

"As an additional fragment, the following last-minute and essentially anecdotal material is here inserted. Naval Intelligence, upon receipt of the request from this office, was moved to instigate inquiries among such of its own personnel as happened to be readily available. In response, this declaration, here paraphrased, was made by one Cmdr. Dominic Flandry:

"He had been on temporary assignment to Talwin, since he was originally concerned in events leading to the joint Terran-Merseian research effort upon that planet (v. note 27) and his special knowledge might conceivably help in gathering militarily useful data. While there, he cultivated the friendship of a young Merseian officer. The intimation is that he introduced the latter to various debaucheries; whatever the method was, he got him talking fairly freely. Having noticed a member of a species new to him in the

Merseian group, Flandry asked what manner of sophont this might be. The officer, intoxicated at the time, gave the name of the planet, Chereion, then went on to mumble of a race of incredible antiquity, possessing powers his government keeps secret: a race which seemingly had once nurtured a high civilization, and which said officer suspected might now cherish ambitions wherein his own people are a mere means to an end. Flandry thinks the officer might well have said more; but abruptly the ranking Merseians present ended the occasion and left with all their personnel. Flandry would have pursued the matter further, but never saw his informant or the Chereionite again. He filed this story as part of his report, but Regional Data Processing did not evaluate it as more than a rumor, and thus did not forward it to the central banks.

"The foregoing is presented only in the interest of completeness. Sensationalism is to be discouraged. It is recommended that a maximum feasible effort be instigated for the apprehension of the being Aycharaych, while every due allowance is made for other programs which have rightfully been given a higher priority than the possible presence of a lone foreign operative. Should such effort be rewarded with success, the subject is to be detained while HQNI is notified. . . ."

Desai stared into darkness. *But there is mention of Jean-Baptiste in the files on Llynathawr,* he thought. *Easy enough for an employee in Merseia's pay to insert false data . . . probably during the chaos of the civil war. . . . Uldwyr, you green devil, what have you or yours in mind for my planet?*

The Flone Valley is for the most part a gentler land than the edge of Ilion. Rolling on roads toward the great stream, Waybreak had no further need for the discipline of the desert. Exuberance kindled as spent energies returned.

On a mild night, the Train camped in a pasture belonging to a yeoman family with which it had made an agreement generations ago. There was no curfew; wood for a bonfire was plentiful; celebration lasted late. But early on, when Fraina had danced for them, she went to where Ivar sat and murmured, "Want to take a walk? I'll be back soon's I've swapped clothes"—before she skipped off to Jubilee.

His blood roared. It drowned the talk to which he had been listening while he watched a succession of performances. When he could hear again, the words felt dwindled and purposeless, like the hum of a midgeling swarm.

"Yes, I was briefly with two other nomad groups," Erannath was saying, "the Dark Stars north of Nova Roma, near the Julia River, and the Gurdy Men in the Fort Lunacy area. The differences in custom are interesting but, I judge, mere eddies in a single wind."

King Samlo, seated on his chair, the only one put out, tugged his beard. "You ought to visit the Magic Fathers, then, who I was apprenticed to," he said. "And the Glorious make women the heads of their wagons. But they're over in Tiberia, across the Antonine Seabed, so I don't know them myself."

"Perhaps I will go see," Erannath answered, "though I feel certain of finding the same basic pattern."

"Funny," said the yeoman. "You, xeno—no offense meant; I had some damn fine nonhuman shipmates durin' war of independence—you get around more on our planet than I ever have, or these professional travelers here."

He had come with his grown sons to join the fun. Minors and womenfolk stayed behind. Not only was the party sure to become licentious; brawls might explode. Fascinated by Erannath, he joined the king, Padro of Roadlord, the widow Mara of Tramper, and a few more in conversation on the fringes of the circle. They were older folk, their bodies dimmed; the feverish atmosphere touched them less.

What am I doin' here? Ivar wondered. Exultation: *Waitin' for Fraina, that's what. . . . Earlier, I thought I'd better not get too involved in things. Well, chaos take caution!*

The bonfire flared and rumbled at the center of the wagons. Whenever a stick went *crack*, sparks geysered out of yellow and red flames. The light flew across those who were seated on the ground, snatched eyes, teeth, earrings, bracelets, bits of gaudy cloth out of shadow, cast them back and brought forth instead a dice game, a boy and girl embraced, a playful wrestling match, a boy and girl already stealing off into the farther meadow. Around the blaze, couples had begun a stamping ring-dance, to the music of a lame guitarist, a hunchbacked drummer, and a blind man who sang in plangent Haisun. It smelled of smoke and humanity.

The flicker sheened off Erannath's plumage, turned his eyes to molten gold and his crest to a crown. In its skyey accent his speech did not sound pedantic: "Outsiders often do explore more widely than dwellers, Yeoman Vasiliev, and see more, too. People tend to take themselves for granted."

"I dunno," Samlo argued. "To you, don't the big differences shadow out the little ones that matter to us? You have wings, we don't; we have proper legs, you don't. Doesn't that make us seem pretty much alike to you? How can you say the Trains are all the same?"

"I did not say that, King," Erannath replied. "I said I have observed deep-going common factors. Perhaps you are blinkered by what you call the little differences that matter. Perhaps they matter more to you than they should."

Ivar laughed and tossed in: "Question is, whether we can't see forest for trees, or can't see trees for forest."

Then Fraina was back, and he sprang up. She had changed to a shimmerlyn gown, ragged from years but cut so as to be hardly less revealing than her dancer's costume. Upon her shoulder, alongside a blueblack cataract of hair, sat the luck of Jubilee, muffled in its mantle apart from the imp head.

"Coming?" she chirruped.

"N-n-n-need you ask?" Ivar gave the king a nord-style bow. "Will you excuse me, sir?"

Samlo nodded. A saturnine smile crossed his mouth.

As he straightened, Ivar grew aware of the intentness of Erannath. One did not have to be Ythrian to read hatred in erected quills and hunched stance. His gaze followed that of the golden orbs, and met the red triplet of the luck's. The animal crouched, bristled, and chittered.

"What's wrong, sweet?" Fraina reached to soothe her pet.

Ivar recalled how Erannath had declined the hospitality of any wagon and spent his whole time outdoors, even the bitterest nights, when he must slowly pump his wings while he slept to keep his metabolism high enough that he wouldn't freeze to death. In sudden realization, the Firstling asked him, "Don't you like lucks?"

"No," said the Ythrian.

After a moment: "I have encountered them elsewhere. In Planha we call them *liayalre*. Slinkers."

Fraina pouted. "Oh, foof! I took poor Tais along for a gulp of fresh air. C'mon, Rolf."

She tucked her arm beneath Ivar's. He forgot that he had never cared for lucks either.

Erannath stared after him till he was gone from sight.

Beyond the ring of vehicles, the meadow rolled wide, its dawn trava turf springy and sweet underfoot, silver-gray beneath heaven. Trees stood roundabout, intricacies of pine, massivenesses of hammerbranch, cupolas of delphi. Both moons tinged their boughs white; and of the shadows, those cast by Creusa stirred as the half-disc sped eastward. Stars crowded velvet blackness. The Milky Way was an icefall.

Music faded behind him and her, until they were alone with a tadmouse's trill. He was speechless, content to marvel at the fact that she existed.

She said at last, quietly, looking before her: "Rolf, there's got to be High Ones. This much joy can't just've happened."

"High Ones? Or God? Well—" *Non sequitur, my dear. To us this is beautiful because certain apes were adapted to same kind of weather, long ago on Terra. Though we may feel subtle enchantment in deserts, can we feel it as wholly as Erannath must? . . . But doesn't that mean that Creator made every kind of beauty? It's bleak, believin' in nothin' except accident.*

"Never mind philosophy," he said. Recklessly: "Waste of time I could spend by your side."

She slipped an arm around his waist. He felt it like fire. *I'm in love*, he knew through the thunders. *Never before like this. Tanya—*

She sighed. "Aye-ah. How much've we left?"

"Forever?"

"No. You can't stay in the Train. It's never happened."

"Why can't it?"

"Because you sitters—wait, Rolf, I'm sorry, you're too good for that word, you're a strider—you people who have rooted homes, you're—not weak—but you haven't got our kind of toughness."

Which centuries of deaths have bred.

"I'm afraid for you," Fraina whispered.

"What? Me?" His pride surged in a wave of anger that

he knew, far off at the back of his mind, was foolish.
"Hoy, listen, I survived Dreary crossin' as well as next
man, didn't I? I'm bigger and stronger than anybody else;
maybe no so wiry, not so quick, but by chaos, if we struck
dryout, starveout, gritstorm, whatever, I'd stay alive!"

She leaned closer. "And you're smart, too, Rolf, full of
book stories—what's more, full of skills we're always short
on. Yet you'll have to go. Maybe because you're too much
for us. What could we give you, for the rest of your life?"

You, his pulse replied. *And freedom to be myself....
Drop your damned duties, Ivar Frederiksen. You never
asked to be born to them. Stop thinkin' how those lights
overhead are political points, and let them again be stars.*

"I, I, I don't think I could ever get tired of travelin', if
you were along," he blurted. "And, uh, well, I can haul
my load, maybe give Waybreak somethin' really valuable—"

"Until you got swittled, or knifed. Rolf, darling, you're
innocent. You know in your bones that most people are
honest and don't get violent without reason. It's not true.
Not in the Trains, it isn't. How can you change your
skeleton, Rolf?"

"Could you help me?"

"Oh, if I could!" The shifty moonlight caught a glimmer
of tears.

Abruptly Fraina tossed her head and stated, "Well, if
nothing else, I can shield you from the first and worst,
Rolf."

"What do you mean?" By now used to mercurial
changes of mood, he chiefly was conscious of her looks,
touch, and fragrance. They were still walking. The luck
on her shoulder, drawn into its mantle, had virtually
seceded from visibility.

"You've a fair clutch of jingle along, haven't you?"

He nodded. Actually the money was in bills, Imperial
credits as well as Aenean libras, most of it given him in a
wad by Sergeant Astaff before he left Windhome. ("Withdrew my savin's, Firstlin'. No worry. You'll pay me back
if you live, and if you don't live, what futterin' difference'll
my account make?" How remote and unreal it seemed!)
Tinerans had no particular concept of privacy. (*I've
learned to accept that, haven't I? Privacy is in my brain.
What matter if Dulcy casually goes through my pockets, if
she and Mikkal and I casually dress and undress in their*

wagon, if they casually make love in bunk below mine?)
Thus it was general knowledge that Rolf Mariner was
well-heeled. No one stole from a fellow in the Train. The
guilt would have been impossible to hide, and meant exile.
After pickpocket practice, the spoils were returned. He
had declined invitations to gamble, that being considered
a lawful way of picking a companion clean.

"We'll soon reach the river," Fraina said. "We'll move
along it, from town to town, as far as our territory
stretches. Carnival at every stop. Hectic—well, you've
been to tineran pitches, you told me. The thing is, those
times we're on the grab. It's us against—is 'against' the
word?—*zans.* We don't wish harm on the sitters, but we're
after everything we can hook. At a time like that, somebody might forget you're not an ordinary sitter. We even
fall out with our kind, too often."

Why? passed across Ivar. *Granted this society hasn't
same idea as mine of what constitutes property or con-
tract. Still, if anything, shouldn't nomads be more alert
than usual when among aliens, more united and coordinated? But no, I remember from Brotherband visits to
Windhome, excitement always affected them too, till
they'd as likely riot among each other as with Landfolk.*

He lost the question. They had halted near an argent-
roofed delphi. Stars gleamed, moons glowed, and she held
both his hands.

"Let me keep your moneta for you, Rolf," she offered.
"I know how to stash it. Afterward—"

"There will be an afterward!"

"There's got to be," she wept, and came to him.

He let go all holds, save upon her. Soon they went into
the moon-dappled grotto of the delphi. The luck stayed
outside, waiting.

He who had been Jaan the Shoemaker, until Caruith returned after six million swings of the world around the
sun, looked from the snag of a tower across the multitude
which filled the marketplace. From around the Sea of
Orcus, folk had swarmed hither for Radmas. More were
on Mount Cronos this year than ever before in memory or
chronicle. They knew the Deliverer was come and would
preach unto them.

They made a blue-shadowy dimness beneath the wall
whereon he stood: a face, a lancehead, a burnoose, a hel-

met, picked out of the dusk which still welled between surrounding houses and archways. Virgil had barely risen
over the waters, and the Arena blocked off sight of it, so
that a phantom mother-of-pearl was only just beginning to
awaken in the great ruin. Some stars remained yet in the
sky. Breath indrawn felt razor keen. Released, it ghosted.
Endless underneath silence went the noise of the falls.

—Go, Caruith said.

Their body lifted both arms. Amplified, their voice
spoke forth into the hush.

"People, I bring you stern tidings.

"You await rescue, first from the grip of the tyrant,
next and foremost from the grip of mortality—of being
merely, emptily human. You wait for transcendence.

"Look up, then, to yonder stars. Remember what they
are, not numbers in a catalog, not balls of burning gas,
but reality itself, even as you and I are real. We are not
eternal, nor are they; but they are closer to eternity than
we. The light of the farthest that we can see has crossed
an eon to come to us. And the word it bears is that first it
shone upon those have gone before.

"They shall return. I, in whom lives the mind of Caruith, pledge this, if we will make our world worthy to receive them.

"Yet that may not be done soon nor easily. The road
before us is hard, steep, bestrewn with sharp shards.
Blood will mark the footprints we leave, and at our backs
will whiten the skulls of those who fell by the way. Like
one who spoke upon Mother Terra, long after Caruith but
long before Jaan, I bring you not peace but a sword."

X

Boseville was typical of the small towns along the Flone between Nova Roma and the Cimmerian Mountains. A cluster of neatly laid out, blocky but gaily colored buildings upon the right bank, it looked across two kilometers' width of brown stream to a ferry terminal, pastures, and timberlots. At its back, canals threaded westward through croplands. Unlike the gaunt but spacious country along the Ilian Shelf, this was narrow enough, and at the same time rich enough, that many of its farmers could dwell in the community. Besides agriculture, Boseville lived off service industries and minor manufacturing. Most of its trade with the outside world went through the Riverfolk. An inscribed monolith in the plaza commemorated its defenders during the Troubles. Nothing since had greatly disturbed it, including rebellion and an occupation force which it never saw.

Of was that true any longer? More and more, Ivar wondered.

He had accompanied Erannath into town while the tinerans readied their pitches. The chance of his being recognized was negligible, unless the Terrans had issued bulletins on him. He was sure they had not. To judge by what broadcasts he'd seen when King Samlo ordered the Train's single receiver brought forth and tuned in—a fair sample, even though the nomads were not much given to passive watching—the Wildfoss affair had been soft-pedaled almost to the point of suppression. Evidently Commissioner Desai didn't wish to inspire imitations, nor make a hero figure out of the Firstling of Ilion.

Anyhow, whoever might identify him was most unlikely to call the nearest garrison.

Erannath wanted to explore this aspect of nord culture. It would be useful having a member of it for companion, albeit one from a different area. Since he was of scant help in preparing the shows, Ivar offered to come along. The Ythrian seemed worth cultivation, an interesting and, in his taciturn fashion, likable sort. Besides, Ivar discovered with surprise that, after the frenetic caravan, he was a bit homesick for his own people.

Or so he thought. Then, when he walked on pavement between walls, he began to feel stifled. How seldom these folk really laughed aloud! How drably they dressed! And where were the male swagger, the female ardor? He wondered how these sitters had gotten any wish to beget the children he saw. Why, they needed to pour their merriment out of a tankard.

Not that the beer wasn't good. He gulped it down. Erannath sipped.

They sat in a waterfront tavern, wood-paneled, rough-raftered, dark and smoky. Windows opened on a view of the dock. A ship, which had unloaded cargo here and taken on consignments for farther downstream, was girding to depart.

"Don't yonder crew want to stay for our carnival?" Ivar asked.

A burly, bearded man, among the several whom Erannath's exotic presence had attracted to this table, puffed his pipe before answering slow: "No, I don't recall as how Riverfolk ever go to those things. Seems like they, m-m-m, shun tinerans. Maybe not bad idea."

"Why?" Ivar challenged. *Are they nonhuman, not to care for Fraina's dancin' or Mikkal's blade arts or—*

"Always trouble. I notice, son, you said, 'Our carnival.' Have care. It brings grief, tryin' to be what you're not born to be."

"I'll guide my private life, if you please."

The villager shrugged. "Sorry."

"If the nomads are a disturbing force," Erannath inquired, "why do you allow them in your territory?"

"They've always been passin' through," said the oldest man present. "Tradition gives rights. Includin' right to pick up part of their livin'—by entertainments, cheap merchandise, odd jobs, and, yes, teachin' prudence by fleecin' the foolish."

"Besides," added a young fellow, "they do bring color,

excitement, touch of danger now and then. We might not live this quietly if Waybreak didn't overnight twice in year."

The jaws of the bearded man clamped hard on his pipestem before he growled, "We're soon apt to get over-supplied with danger, Jim."

Ivar stiffened. A tingle went through him. "What do you mean . . . may I ask?"

A folk saying answered him: "Either much or little."

But another customer, a trifle drunk, spoke forth. "Rumors only. And yet, somethin's astir up and down river, talk of one far south who's promised Elders will return and deliver us from Empire. Could be wishful thinkin', of course. But damn, it feels right somehow. Aeneas *is* special. I never paid lot of attention to Dido before; however, lately I've begun givin' more and more thought to everything our filosofs have learned there. I've gone out under Mornin' Star and tried to think myself toward Oneness, and you know, it's helped me. Should we let Impies crush us back into subjects, when we may be right at next stage of evolution?"

The bearded man frowned. "That's heathenish talk, Bob. Me, I'll hold my trust in God." To Ivar: "God's will be done. I never thought Empire was too bad, nor do I now. But it has gone morally rotten, and maybe we are God's chosen instruments to give it cleansin' shock." After a pause: "If's true, we'll need powerful outside help. Maybe He's preparin' that for us too." All their looks bent on Erannath. "I'm plain valley dweller and don't know anything," the speaker finished, "except that unrest is waxin', and hope of deliverance."

Hastily, the oldster changed the subject.

Night had toppled upon them when Firstling and Ythrian returned to camp. After they left town, stars gave winter-keen guidance to their feet. Otherwise the air was soft, moist, full of growth odors. Gravel scrunched beneath the tread of those bound the same way. Voices tended to break off when a talker noticed the nonhuman, but manners did not allow butting into a serious conversation. Ahead, lamps on poles glowed above wagons widespread among tents. The skirl of music loudened.

"What I seek to understand," Erannath said, "is this Aenean resentment of the Imperium. My race would resist such overlordship bitterly. But in human terms, it has on the whole been light, little more than a minor addition to taxes and the surrender of sovereignty over outside, not domestic, affairs. In exchange, you get protection, trade, abundant offplanet contacts. Correct?"

"Perhaps once," Ivar answered. The beer buzzed in his head. "But then they set that Snelund creature over us. And since, too many of us are dead in war, while Impies tell us to change ways of our forefathers."

"Was the late governorship really that oppressive, at least where Aeneas was concerned? Besides, can you not interpret the situation as that the Imperium made a mistake, which is being corrected? True, it cost lives and treasure to force the correction. But you people showed such deathpride that the authorities are shy of pushing you very hard. Simple cooperativeness would enable you to keep virtually all your institutions, or have them restored."

"How do you know?"

Erannath ignored the question. "I could comprehend anger at the start of the occupation," he said, "if afterward it damped out when the Imperial viceroy proved himself mild. Instead . . . my impression is that at first you Aeneans accepted your defeat with a measure of resignation—but since, your rebellious emotions have swelled; and lacking hopes of independence in reality, you project them into fantasy. *Why?*"

"I reckon we were stunned, and're startin' to recover. And could be those hopes aren't altogether wild." Ivar stared at the being who trotted along beside him so clumsily, almost painfully. Erannath's crest bobbed to the crutchlike swing of his wings; shadows along the ground dimmed luster of eyes and feathers. "What're you doin', anyway, tellin' me I should become meek Imperial subject? You're Ythrian—from free race of hunters, they claim—from rival power we once robbed of plenty real estate—What're you tryin' to preach at me?"

"Nothing. As I have explained before, I am a xenologist specializing in anthropology, here to gather data on your species. I travel unofficially, *hyai,* illegally, to avoid restrictions. More than this it would be unwise to say, even as you have not seen fit to detail your own circumstances. I ask questions in order to get responses which may help me map Aenean attitudes. Enough."

When an Ythrian finished on that word, he was terminating a discussion. Ivar thought: *Well, why shouldn't he pretend he's harmless? It'll help his case, get him merely deported, if Impies happen to catch him. . . . Yes, probably he is spyin', no more. But if I can convince him, make him tell them at home, how we really would fight year after year for our freedom, if they'd give us some aid— maybe they would!*

The blaze of it in him blent into the larger brilliance of being nearly back in camp, nearly back to Fraina.

And then—

They entered a crowd milling between faded rainbows of tentcloth. Lamps overhead glared out the stars. Above the center pitch, a cylinder of colored panes rotated around the brightest light: red, yellow, green, blue, purple flickered feverish across the bodies and faces below. A hawker chanted of his wares, a barker of games of chance, a cook of the spiceballs whose frying filled every nostril around him. Upon a platform three girls danced, and though their performance was free and small-town nords were supposed to be close with a libra, coins glittered in arcs toward their leaping feet. Beneath, the blind and crippled musicians sawed out a melody which had begun to make visitors jig. No alcohol or other drugs were in sight; yet sober riverside men mingled with tinerans in noisy camaraderie, marveled like children at a strolling magician or juggler, whooped, waved, and jostled. Perched here and there upon wagons, the lucks of Waybreak watched.

It surged in Ivar: *My folk! My joy!*

And Fraina came by, scarcely clad, nestled against a middle-aged local whose own garb bespoke wealth. He looked dazed with desire.

Ivar stopped. Beside him, abruptly, Erannath stood on hands to free his wings.

"What goes?" Ivar cried through the racket. Like a blow to the belly, he knew. More often than not, whenever they could, nomad women did this thing.

But not Fraina! We're in love!

She rippled as she walked. Light sheened off blue-black hair, red skin, tilted wide eyes, teeth between half-parted lips. A musk of femaleness surfed outward from her.

"Let go my girl!" Ivar screamed.

He knocked a man over in his plunge. Others voiced an-

ger as he thrust by. His knife came forth. Driven by
strength and skill, that heavy blade could take off a human
hand at the wrist, or go through a rib to the heart.

The villager saw. A large person, used to command, he
held firm. Though unarmed, he crouched in a stance
remembered from his military training days.

"Get away, clinkerbrain," Fraina ordered Ivar.

"No, you slut!" He struck her aside. She recovered too
fast to fall. Whirling, he knew in bare time that he really
shouldn't kill this yokel, that she'd enticed him and—Ivar's
empty hand made a fist. He smote at the mouth. The riv-
erdweller blocked the blow, a shock of flesh and bone, and
bawled:

"Help! Peacemen!" That was the alarm word. Small
towns kept no regular police; but volunteers drilled and
patrolled together, and heeded each other's summons.

Fraina's fingernails raked blood from Ivar's cheek.
"You starting a riot?" she shrilled. A Haisun call followed.

Rivermen tried to push close. Men of the Train tried to
deflect them, disperse them. Oaths and shouts lifted. Scuf-
fles broke loose.

Mikkal of Redtop slithered through the mob, bounded
toward the fight. His belt was full of daggers. *"Il-krozny
ya?"* he barked.

Fraina pointed at Ivar, who was backing her escort
against a wagon. *"Vakhabo!"* And in loud Anglic: "Kill
me that dog! He hit me—your sister!"

Mikkal's arm moved. A blade glittered past Ivar's ear,
to thunk into a panel and shiver. "Stop where you're at,"
the tineran said. "Drop your slash. Or you're dead."

Ivar turned from an enemy who no longer mattered.
Grief ripped through him. "But you're my friend," he
pleaded.

The villager struck him on the neck, kicked him when
he had tumbled. Fraina warbled glee, leaped to take the
fellow's elbow, crooned of his prowess. Mikkal tossed
knife after knife aloft, made a wheel of them, belled when
he had the crowd's attention: "Peace! Peace! We don't
want this stranger. We cast him out. You care to jail him?
Fine, go ahead. Let's the rest of us get on with our fun."

Ivar sat up. He barely noticed the aches where he had
been hit. Fraina, Waybreak were lost to him. He could no

more understand why than he could have understood it if he had suddenly had a heart attack.

But a wanderer's aliveness remained. He saw booted legs close in, and knew the watch was about to haul him off. It jagged across his awareness that then the Imperials might well see a report on him.

His weapon lay on the ground. He snatched it and sprang erect. A war-whoop tore his throat. "Out of my way!" he yelled after, and started into the ring of men. If need be, he'd cut a road through.

Wings cannonaded, made gusts of air, eclipsed the lamps. Erannath was aloft.

Six meters of span roofed the throng in quills and racket. What light came through shone burnished on those feathers, those talons. Unarmed though he was, humans ducked away from scything claws, lurched from buffeting wingbones. "Hither!" Erannath whistled. "To me, Rolf Mariner! *Raiharo!*"

Ivar sprang through the lane opened for him, out past tents and demon-covered wagons, into night. The aquiline shape glided low above, black athwart the Milky Way. "Head south," hissed in darkness. "Keep near the river-bank." The Ythrian swung by, returned for a second pass. "I will fly elsewhere, in their view, draw off pursuit, soon shake it and join you." On the third swoop: "Later I will go to the ship which has left, and arrange passage for us. Fair winds follow you." He banked and was gone.

Ivar's body settled into a lope over the fields. The rest of him knew only: *Fraina. Waybreak. Forever gone? Then what's to live for?*

Nevertheless he fled.

XI

After a boat, guided by Erannath, brought him aboard the *Jade Gate*, Ivar fell into a bunk and a twisting, nightmare-haunted sleep. He was almost glad when a gong-crash roused him a few hours later.

He was alone in a cabin meant for four, cramped but pleasant. Hardwood deck, white-painted overhead, bulkheads lacquered in red and black, were surgically clean. Light came dimly through a brass-framed window to pick out a dresser and washbowl. Foot-thuds and voices made a cheerful clamor beneath the toning of the bronze. He didn't know that rapid, musical language.

I suppose I ought to go see whatever this is, he thought, somewhere in the sorrow of what he had lost. It took his entire will to put clothes on and step out the door.

Crewfolk were bouncing everywhere around. A young man noticed him, beamed, and said, "Ahoa to you, welcome passenger," in the singsong River dialect of Anglic.

"What's happenin'?" Ivar asked mechanically.

"We say good morning to the sun. Watch, but please to stand quiet where you are."

He obeyed. The pre-dawn chill lashed some alertness into him and he observed his surroundings with a faint growth of interest.

Heaven was still full of stars, but eastward turning wan. The shores, a kilometer from either side of the vessel, were low blue shadows, while the water gleamed as if burnished, except where mist went eddying. High overhead, the wings of a vulch at hover caught the first daylight. As gong and crew fell silent, an utter hush returned, not really broken by the faint pulse of engines.

The craft was more than 50 meters in length and 20 in

the beam, her timber sides high even at the waist, then at the blunt bow rising sharply in two tiers, three at the rounded stern. Two sizable deckhouses bracketed the amidships section, their roofs fancifully curved at the ends. Fore and aft of them, kingposts supported cargo booms, as well as windmills to help charge the capacitors which powered the vessel. Between reared a mast which could be set with three square sails. Ivar glimpsed Erannath on the topmost yard. He must have spent the night there, for lack of the frame which would suit him better than a bunk.

An outsize red-and-gold flag drooped from an after staff. At the prow the gigantic image of a Fortune Guardian scowled at dangers ahead. In his left hand he bore a sword against them, in his right a lotus flower.

There posed an old man in robe and tasseled cap, beside him a woman similarly clad though bareheaded, near them a band who wielded gong, flutes, pipas, and drum. The crew, on their knees save for what small children were held by their mothers, occupied the decks beneath.

As light strengthened, the stillness seemed to deepen yet further, and frost on brightwork glittered like the stars.

Then Virgil stood out of the east. Radiance shivered across waters. The ancient raised his arms and cried a brief chant, the people responded, music rollicked, everybody cheered, the ship's business resumed.

Ivar stretched numbed hands toward the warmth that began to flow out of indigo air. Vapors steamed away and he saw the cultivated lands roll green, a flock of beasts, an early horseman or a roadborne vehicle, turned into toys by distance. Closer were the brood of *Jade Gate*. A stubby tug drew a freight-laden barge, two trawlers spread their nets, and in several kayaks, each accompanied by an osel, herders kept a pod of river pigs moving along.

For those not on watch, the first order of the day was evidently to get cleaned up. Some went below, some peeled off their clothes and dived overboard, to frisk about till they were ready to climb back on a Jacob's ladder. Merriment loudened. It was not like tineran glee. Such japes as he heard in Anglic were gentle rather than stinging, laughter was more a deep clucking than a shrill peal. Whoever passed near Ivar stopped to make a slight bow and bid him welcome aboard.

They're civilized without bein' rigid, strong without bein' cruel, happy without bein' foolish, shrewd without bein' crooked, respectful of learnin' and law, useful in their work, he knew dully; *but they are not wild red wanderers.*

Handsome enough, of course. They averaged a bit taller than tinerans, shorter than nords, the build stocky, skin tawny, hair deep black where age had not bleached it. Heads were round, faces broad and high of cheekbones, eyes brown and slightly oblique, lips full, noses tending to flatness though beaks did occur. Only old men let beards grow, and both sexes banged their hair across the brows and bobbed it off just under the ears. Alike too was working garb, blue tunics and bell-bottomed trousers. Already now, before the frost was off, many went barefoot; and the nudity of the swimmers showed a fondness for elaborate tattoos.

He knew more about them than he had about the nomads. It was still not much. This was his first time aboard a craft of theirs, aside from once when one which plied as far north as Nova Roma held open house. Otherwise his experience was confined to casual reading and a documentary program recorded almost a century ago.

Nevertheless the Kuang Shih had bonds to the ruling culture of Aeneas, in a way that the tinerans did not. They furnished the principal transportation for goods, and for humans who weren't in a hurry, along the entire lower Flone—as well as fish, flesh, and fiber taken from the river, and incidental handicrafts, exchanged for the products and energy recharges of industrial culture.

If they held themselves aloof when ashore, it was not due to hostility. They were amply courteous in business dealings, downright cordial to passengers. It was simply that their way of life satisfied them, and had little in common with that of rooted people. The most conservative Landfolk maintained less far-reaching and deep-going blood ties—every ship and its attendants an extended family, strictly exogamous and, without making a fuss about it, moral—not to speak of faith, tradition, law, custom, arts, skills, hopes, fears altogether different.

I dreamed Waybreak might take me in, and instead it cast me out. Jade Gate—is that her name?—will no doubt treat me kindly till we part, but I'd never imagine bein' taken into her.

No matter. O Fraina!

"Sir—"

The girl who shyly addressed him brought back the dancer, hurtfully, by her very unlikeness. Besides her race, she was younger, he guessed eight or nine, demurely garbed so that he couldn't be sure how much her slight figure had begun to fill out. (Not that he cared.) Her features were more delicate than usual, and she bowed lower to him.

"Your pardon, please, welcome passenger," she said in a thin voice. "Do you care for breakfast?"

She offered him a bowl of cereals, greens, and bits of meat cooked together, a cup of tea, a napkin, and eating utensils such as he was used to. He grew aware that crewfolk were in line at the galley entrance. A signal must have called them without his noticing through the darkness that muffled him. Most found places on deck to hunker and eat in convivial groups.

"Why, why, thank you," Ivar said. He wasn't hungry, but supposed he could get the food down. It smelled spicy.

"We have one dining saloon below, with table and benches, if you wish," the girl told him.

"No!" The idea of being needlessly enclosed, after desert heavens and then nights outdoors in valley summer with Fraina, sickened him.

"Pardon, pardon." She drew back a step. He realized he had yelled.

"I'm sorry," he said. "I'm in bad way. Didn't mean to sound angry. Right here will be fine." She smiled and set her burden down on the planks, near a bulwark against which he could rest, "Uh, my name is Iv—Rolf Mariner."

"This person is Jao, fourth daughter to Captain Riho Mea. She bade me to see to your comfort. Can I help you in any wise, Sir Mariner?" The child dipped her head above bridged fingertips.

"I ... well, I don't know." *Who can help me, ever again?*

"Perhaps if I stay near you one while, show you over our ship later? You may think of something then."

Her cleanliness reminded him of his grime and sour sweat-smell, unkempt hair and stubbly chin. "I, uh, I should have washed before breakfast."

"Eat, and I will lead you to the bath, and bring what else you need to your cabin. You are our only guest this trip." Her glance swept aloft and came aglow. "Ai, the

beautiful flyer from the stars. How could I forget? Can
you summon him while I fetch his food?"

"He eats only meat, you know. Or, no, I reckon you
wouldn't. Anyhow, I'll bet he's already caught piece of
wild game. He sees us, and he'll come down when he
wants to."

"If you say it, sir. May I bring my bowl, or would you
rather be undisturbed?"

"Whatever you want," Ivar grunted. "I'm afraid I'm
poor company this mornin'."

"Perhaps you should sleep further? My mother the captain will not press you. But she said that sometime this
day she must see you and your friend, alone."

Passengers had quarters to themselves if and when a
vessel was operating below capacity in that regard. Crew
did not. Children were raised communally from birth ...
physically speaking. The ties between them and their parents were strong, far stronger than among tinerans, although their ultimate family was the ship as a whole. Married couples were assigned cubicles, sufficient for sleeping
and a few personal possessions. Certain soundproofed cabins were available for study, meditation, or similar purposes. Aside from this, privacy of the body did not exist,
save for chaplain and captain.

The latter had two chambers near the bridge. The
larger was living room, office, and whatever else she
deemed necessary.

Her husband greeted her visitors at the door, then politely excused himself. He was her third, Jao had remarked
to Ivar. Born on the *Celestial Peace*, when quite a young
girl Mea had been wedded by the usual prearrangement to
a man of the *Red Bird Banner*. He drowned when a skiff
capsized; the Flone had many treacheries. She used her inheritance in shrewd trading, garnering wealth until the
second officer of the *Jade Gate* met her at a fleet festival
and persuaded her to move in with him. He was a wid-
ower, considerably older than she; it was a marriage of
convenience. But most were, among the Kuang Shih.
Theirs functioned well for a number of years, efficiently
combining their talents and credit accounts, incidentally
producing Jao's youngest sister. At last an artery in his
brain betrayed him, and rather than linger useless he requested the Gentle Cup. Soon afterward, the captain died

also, and the officers elected Riho Mea his successor.
Lately she had invited Haleku Uan of the *Yellow Dragon*
to marry her. He was about Ivar's age.

Jao must have read distaste on the Firstling's countenance, for she had said quietly: "They are happy together.
He is merely one carpenter, nor can she raise him higher,
nor can he inherit from her except in *lung*—pro-por-tion
to children of hers that are his too; and she is past child-
bearing and he knew it."

He thought at the time that she was defending her
mother, or even her stepfather. As days passed, he came
to believe she had spoken unspectacular truth. The Riverfolk had their own concept of individuality.

To start with, what did riches mean? Those who were
not content to draw their regular wage, but drove personal
bargains with the Ti Shih, the Shorefolk, could obtain no
more than minor luxuries for themselves; a ship had room
for nothing else. Beyond that, they could simply make
contributions to the floating community. That won re-
wards of prestige. But anybody could get the same by out-
standing service or, to a lesser extent, unusual prowess or
talent.

Prestige might bring promotion. However, authority
gave small chance for self-aggrandizement either, in a society which followed the same peaceful round through
century after century.

Why, then, did the people of the land think of Riverfolk
as hustlers, honest but clever, courteous but ambitious?
Ivar decided that these were the personality types who
dealt with the people of the land. The rest kept pretty
much to themselves. And yet, that latter majority had
abundant ways to express itself.

These ideas came to him later. They did have their
genesis the evening he first entered the cabin of Captain
Riho.

Sunbeams struck level, amber-hued, through the starboard windows of the main room. They sheened off a
crystal on a shelf, glowed off a scroll of trees and calligra-
phy above. The chamber was so austerely furnished as to
feel spacious. In one corner, half-hidden by a carved
screen, stood a desk and a minimum of data and communications equipment. In another stood a well-filled book-
case. Near the middle of the reed matting which covered
the deck was a padded, ring-shaped bench, with a low ta-

ble at the center and a couple of detachable back rests for the benefit of visiting Ti Shih.

The skipper came forward, and Ivar began changing his mind about her and her man. She was of medium height, plump yet extraordinarily light on her feet. Years had scarcely touched the snubnosed, dark-ivory face, apart from crinkles around the eyes and scattered white in the hair. Her mouth showed capacity for a huge grin. She wore the common blue tunic and trousers, zori on bare feet, fireburst tattoo on the arm which slid from its sleeve as she offered her hand. The palm was warm and callused.

"Ahoa, welcome passengers." Her voice verged on hoarseness. "Will you not honor me by taking seats and refreshment?" She bowed them toward the bench, and from the inner room fetched a trayful of tea, cakes, and slices of raw ichthyoid flesh. The ship lurched in a crosscurrent off a newly formed sandbar, and she came near dropping her load. She rapped out a phrase. Catching Erannath's alert look, she translated it for him. Ivar was a little shocked. He had thought soldiers knew how to curse.

She kicked off her sandals, placed herself crosslegged opposite her guests, and opened a box of cigars that stood on the table. "You want?" she offered. They both declined. "Mind if I do?" Ivar didn't—*What has creation got that's worth mindin'?*—and Erannath stayed mute though a ripple passed over his plumes. Captain Riho stuck a fat black cylinder between her teeth and got it ignited. Smoke smote the air.

"I hope you are comfortable?" she said. "Sir ... Erannath ... if you will give my husband the specs for your kind of bed—"

"Later, thank you," the flyer snapped. "Shall we get to the point?"

"Fine. Always I was taught, Ythrians do not waste words. Here is my first pleasure to meet your breed. If you will please to pardon seeming rudeness—you *are* aboard curious-wise. I would not pry but must know certain things, like where you are bound."

"We are not sure. How far do you go?"

"Clear to the Linn, this trip. Solstice comes near, our Season of Returnings."

"Fortunate for us, if I happen to have cash enough on

my person to buy that long a passage for two." Erannath touched his pocketed apron.

I have none, Ivar thought. *Fraina swittled me out of everything, surely knowin' I'd have to leave Train. Only, did she have to provoke my leavin' so soon?* He paid no attention to the dickering.

"—well," Erannath finished. "We can come along to the end of the river if we choose. We may debark earlier."

Riho Mea frowned behind an acrid blue veil. "Why might that be?" she demanded. "You understand, sirs, I have one ship to worry about, and these are much too interesting times."

"Did I not explain fully enough, last night when I arrived on board? I am a scientist studying your planet. I happened to join a nomad group shortly after Rolf Mariner did—for reasons about which he has the right not to get specific. As often before, violence lofted at the carnival. It would have led either to his death at nomad hands, or his arrest by the Bosevilleans. I helped him escape."

"Yes, those were almost your exact words."

"I intended no offense in repeating them, Captain. Do humans not prefer verbal redundancy?"

"You miss my course, Sir Erannath," she said a touch coldly. "You have *not* explained enough. We could take you on in emergency, for maybe that did save lives. However, today is not one such hurry. Please to take refreshment, you both, as I will, to show good faith. I accuse you of nothing, but you are intelligent and realize I must be sure we are not harboring criminals. Matters are very skittly, what with the occupation."

She laid her cigar in an ashtray, crunched a cookie, slurped a mouthful of tea. Ivar bestirred himself to follow suit. Erannath laid claws on a strip of meat and ripped it with his fangs. "Good," said the woman. "Will you tell your tale, Sir Mariner?"

Ivar had spent most of the day alone, stretched on his bunk. He didn't care what became of him, and his mind wasn't working especially well. But from a sense of duty, or whatever, he had rehearsed his story like a dog mumbling a bone. It plodded forth:

"I'm not guilty of anything except disgust, Captain, and I don't think that's punishable, unless Impies have made it illegal since I left. You know, besides bannin' free speech, they razed McCormac Memorial in Nova Roma. My parents . . . well, they don't condone Imperium, but they kept talkin' about compromise and how maybe we Aeneans were partly in wrong, till I couldn't stand it. I went off into wilderness to be by myself—common practice ashore, you probably know—and met tineran Train there. Why not join them for while? It'd be change for me, and I had skills they could use. Last night, as my friend told, senseless brawl happened. I think, now, it was helped along by tinerans I'd thought were my . . . friends, so they could keep money and valuable rif—article I'd left with them."

"As a matter of fact," Erannath said, "he is technically guilty of assault upon a Boseville man. He did no harm, though. He merely suffered it. I doubt that any complaint has been filed. These incidents are frequent at those affairs, and everyone knows it." He paused. "They do not know why this is. I do."

Startled from his apathy, Ivar regarded the Ythrian almost as sharply as Riho Mea did. He met their gazes in turn—theirs were the eyes which dropped—and let time go by before he said with no particular inflection: "Perhaps I should keep my discovery for the Intelligence service of the Domain. However, it is of marginal use to us, whereas Aeneans will find it a claw struck into their backs."

The captain chewed her cigar before she answered: "You mean you will tell me if I let you stay aboard." Erannath didn't bother to speak his response. "How do I know—" She caught herself. "Please to pardon this person. I wonder what evidence you have for whatever you will say."

"None," he admitted. "Once given the clue, you humans can confirm the statement."

"Say on."

"If I do, you will convey us, and ask no further questions?"

"I will judge you by your story."

Erannath studied her. At length he said: "Very well, for I hear your deathpride." He was still during a heartbeat. "The breath of tineran life is that creature they call the luck, keeping at least one in every wagon. We call it the slinker."

"Hoy," broke from Ivar, "how would you know—?"

"Ythrians have found the three-eyed beasts on a number of planets." Erannath did not keep the wish to kill out

of his voice; and his feathers began to stand erect. "Not
on our home. God did not lay that particular snare for us.
But on several worlds like it, which naturally we investigated more thoroughly than your race normally does—the
lesser terrestroid globes. Always slinkers are associated
with fragments of an earlier civilization, such as Aeneas
has. We suspect they were spread by that civilization,
whether deliberately, accidentally, or through their own
design. Some of us theorize that they caused its downfall."

"Wait a minute," Ivar protested. "Why have we humans
never heard of them?"

"You have, on this world," Erannath replied. "Probably
elsewhere too, but quite incidentally, notes buried in your
data banks, because you are more interested in larger and
moister planets. And for our part, we have had no special
reason to tell you. We learned what slinkers are early in
our starfaring, when first we had scant contact with Terrans, afterward hostile contact. We developed means to
eradicate them. They long ago ceased to be a problem in
the Domain, and no doubt few Ythrians, even, have heard
of them nowadays."

Too much information, too big a universe, passed
through Ivar.

"Besides," Erannath went on, "it seems humans are
more susceptible than Ythrians. Our two brain-types are
rather differently organized, and the slinkers' resonate better with yours."

"Resonate?" Captain Riho scowled.

"The slinker nervous system is an extraordinarily well-
developed telepathic transceiver," Erannath said. "Not of
thoughts. We really don't know what level of reasoning
ability the little abominations possess. Nor do we care, in
the way that human scientists might. When we had established what they do, our overwhelming desire was merely
to slay them."

"What do they do, then?" Ivar asked around a lump of
nausea.

"They violate the innermost self. In effect, they receive
emotions and feed these back; they act as amplifiers." It
was terrifying to see Erannath where he crouched. His dry
phrases ripped forth. "Perhaps those intelligences you call
the Builders developed them as pets, pleasure sources. The
Builders may have had cooler spirits than you or we do.
Or perhaps they degenerated from the effects, and died.

"I said that the resonance with us Ythrians is weak. Nonetheless we found explorers and colonists showing ugly behavior. It would start as bad dreams, go on to murderously short temper, to year-around ovulation, to— Enough. We tracked down the cause and destroyed it.

"You humans are more vulnerable, it appears. You are lucky that slinkers prefer the deserts. Otherwise all Aeneans might be addicted.

"Yes, addiction. They don't realize it themselves, they think they keep these pets merely because of custom, but the tinerans are a nation of addicts. Every emotion they begin to feel is fed back into them, amplified, radiated, reamplified, to the limit of what the organism can generate. Do you marvel that they act like constitutional psychopaths? That they touch no drugs in their caravans, but require drugs when away, and cannot survive being away very long?

"At that, they must have adapted; there must have been natural selection. Many can think craftily, like the female who reaved your holdings, Rolf Mariner. I wonder if her kind are not born dependent on the poison.

"You should thank her, though, that she got you cast out as early as she did!"

Ivar covered his face. "O God, no."

"I need clean sky and a beast to hunt," Erannath grated. "I will be back tomorrow."

He left. Ivar wept on Riho Mea's breast. She held him close, stroked his hair and murmured.

"You'll get well, poor dear, we'll make you well. The river flows, flows, flows. . . . Here is peace."

Finally she left him on her husband's bunk, exhausted of tears and ready to sleep. The light through the windows was gold-red. She changed into her robe and went onto the foredeck, to join chaplain and crew in wishing the sun goodnight.

XII

South of Cold Landing the country began to grow steep and stony, and the peaks of the Cimmerian range hung ghostlike on its horizon. There the river would flow too swiftly for the herds. But first it broadened to fill a valley with what was practically a lake: the Green Bowl, where ships bound farther south left their animals in care of a few crewfolk, to fatten on water plants and molluscoids.

Approaching that place, Ivar paddled his kayak with an awkwardness which drew amiable laughter from his young companions. They darted spearfly-fast over the surface; or, leaping into the stream, they raced the long-bodied webfooted brown osels which served them for herd dogs, while he wallowed more clumsily than the fat, flippered, snouted chuho—water pigs—which were being herded.

He didn't mind. Nobody is good at everything, and he was improving at a respectable pace.

Wavelets blinked beneath violet heaven, chuckled, swirled, joined livingly with his muscles to drive the kayak onward. This was the reality which held him, not stiff crags and dusty-green brush on yonder hills. A coolness rose from it, to temper windless warmth of air. It smelled damp, rich. Ahead, *Jade Gate* was a gaudily painted castle; farther on moved a sister vessel; trawlers and barges already waited at Cold Landing. Closer at hand, the chuho browsed on wetcress. Now and then an osel heeded the command of a boy or girl and sped to turn back a straggler. Herding on the Flone was an ideal task, he thought. Exertion and alertness kept a person fully alive, while nevertheless letting him enter into that peace, beauty, majesty which was the river.

To be sure, he was a mere spectator, invited along because these youngers liked him. That was all right.

Jao maneuvered her kayak near his. "Goes it well?" she asked. "You do fine, Rolf." She flushed, dropped her glance, and added timidly: "I think not I could do that fine in your wilderness. But sometime I would wish to try."

"Sometime . . . I'd like to take you," he answered.

On this duty in summer, one customarily went nude, so as to be ready at any time for a swim. Ivar was too fair-skinned for that, and wore a light blouse and trousers Erannath had had made for him. He turned his own eyes elsewhere. The girl was far too young for the thoughts she was old enough to arouse—besides being foreign to him—no, never mind that, what mattered was that she was sweet and trusting and—

Oh, damnation, I will not be ashamed of thinkin' she's female. Thinkin' is all it'll ever amount to. And that I do, that I can, measures how far I've gone toward gainin' back my sanity.

The gaiety and the ceremoniousnesses aboard ship; the little towns where they stopped to load and unload, and the long green reaches between; the harsh wisdom of Erannath, serene wisdom of Iang Weii the chaplain, pragmatic wisdom of Riho Mea the captain, counseling him; the friendliness of her husband and other people his age; the, yes, the way this particular daughter of hers followed him everywhere around; always the river, mighty as time, days and nights, days and nights, feeling like a longer stretch than they had been, like a foretaste of eternity: these had healed him.

Fraina danced no more through his dreams. He could summon a memory for inspection, and understand how the reality had never come near being as gorgeous as it seemed, and pity the wanderers and vow to bring them aid when he became able.

When would that be? How? He was an outlaw. As he emerged from his hurt, he saw ever more clearly how passive he had been. Erannath had rescued him and provided him with this berth—why? What reason, other than pleasure, had he to go to the river's end? And if he did, what next?

He drew breath. *Time to start actin' again, instead of bein' acted on. First thing I need is allies.*

Jao's cry brought him back. She pointed to the nigh shore. Her paddle flew. He toiled after. Their companions saw, left one in charge of the herd, and converged on the same spot.

A floating object lay caught in reeds: a sealed wooden box, arch-lidded, about two meters in length. Upon its black enamel he identified golden symbols of Sun, Moons, and River.

"*Ai-ya, ai-ya, ai-ya*," Jao chanted. Suddenly solemn, the rest chimed in. Though ignorant of the Kuang Shih's primary language, Ivar could recognize a hymn. He held himself aside.

The herders freed the box. Swimmers pushed it out into midstream. Osels under sharp command kept chuhos away. It drifted on south. They must have seen aboard *Jade Gate*, because the flag went to half-mast.

"What was that?" Ivar then ventured to ask.

Jao brushed the wet locks off her brow and answered, surprised, "Did you not know? That was one coffin."

"Huh? I— Wait, I beg your pardon, I do seem to remember—"

"All our dead go down the river, down the Yun Kow at last—the Linn—to the Tien Hu, what you call the Sea of Orcus. It is our duty to launch again any we find stranded." In awe: "I have heard about one seer who walks there now, who will call back the Old Shen from the stars. Will our dead then rise from the waters?"

Tatiana Thane had never supposed she could mind being by herself. She had always had a worldful of things to do, read, watch, listen to, think about.

Daytimes still weren't altogether bad. Her present work was inherently solitary: study, meditation, cut-and-try, bit by bit the construction of a semantic model of the language spoken around Mount Hamilcar on Dido, which would enable humans to converse with the natives on a more basic level than pidgin allowed. Her dialogues were with a computer, or occasionally by vid with the man under whom she had studied, who was retired to his estate in Heraclea and too old to care about politics.

Since she became a research fellow, students had treated her respectfully. Thus she took a while—when she missed Ivar so jaggedly, when she was so haunted by fear for him—to realize that this behavior had become an avoidance. Nor was she overtly snubbed at faculty rituals, meetings, dining commons, chance encounters in corridor or quad. These days, people didn't often talk animatedly. Thus likewise she took a while to realize that they never did with her any more, and, except for her parents, had let her drop from their social lives.

Slowly her spirit wore down.

The first real break in her isolation came about 1700 hours on a Marsday. She was thinking of going to bed, however poorly she would sleep. Outside was a darker night than ordinary, for a great dustcloud borne along the tropopause had veiled the stars. Lavinia was a blurred dim crescent above spires and domes. Wind piped. She sprawled in her largest chair and played with Frumious Bandersnatch. The tadmouse ran up and down her body, from shins to shoulders and back, trilling. The comfort was as minute as himself.

The knocker rapped. For a moment she thought she hadn't heard aright. Then her pulse stumbled, and she nearly threw her pet off in her haste to open the door. He clung to her sweater and whistled indignation.

A man stepped through, at once closing the door behind him. Though the outside air that came along was cold as well as ferric-harsh, no one would ordinarily have worn a nightmask. He doffed his and she saw the bony middle-aged features of Gabriel Stewart. They had last been together on Dido. His work was to know the Hamilcar region backwards and forwards, guide scientific parties and see to their well-being.

"Why . . . why . . . hello," she said helplessly.

"Draw your blinds," he ordered. "I'd as soon not be glimpsed from beneath."

She stared. Her backbone pringled. "Are you in trouble, Gabe?"

"Not officially—yet."

"I'd no idea you were on Aeneas. Why didn't you call?"

"Calls can be monitored. Now cover those windows, will you?"

She obeyed. Stewart removed his outer garments. "It's good to see you again," she ventured.

"You may not think that after I've spoken my piece." He unbent a little. "Though maybe you will. I recall you as bold lass, in your quiet way. And I don't suppose First-lin' of Ilion made you his girl for nothin'."

"Do you have news of Ivar?" she cried.

" 'Fraid not. I was hopin' you would. . . . Well, let's talk."

He refused wine but let her brew a pot of tea. Meanwhile he sat, puffed his pipe, exchanged accounts of everything that had happened since the revolution erupted. He had gone outsystem, in McCormac's hastily assembled Intelligence corps, and admitted ruefully that meanwhile the war was lost in his own bailiwick. As far as he could discover, upon being returned after the defeat, some Terran agent had not only managed to rescue the Admiral's wife from Snelund—a priceless bargaining counter, no doubt—but while on Dido had hijacked a patriot vessel whose computer held the latest codes. . . . "I got wonderin' about possibility of organizin' Didonians to help fight on, as guerrillas or even as navy personnel. At last I hitched ride to Aeneas and looked up my friend—m-m, never mind his name; he's of University too, on a secondary campus. Through him, I soon got involved in resistance movement."

"There is one?"

He regarded her somberly. "You ask that, Ivar Frederiksen's bride to be?"

"I was never consulted." She put teapot and cups on a table between them, sank to the edge of a chair opposite his, and stared at the fingers wrestling in her lap. "He— It was crazy impulse, what he did. Wasn't it?"

"Maybe then. Not any longer. Of course, your dear Commissioner Desai would prefer you believe that."

Tatiana braced herself and met his look. "Granted," she said, "I've seen Desai several times. I've passed on his remarks to people I know—not endorsin' them, simply passin' them on. Is that why I'm ostracized? Surely University folk should agree we can't have too much data input."

"I've queried around about you," Stewart replied. "It's curious kind of tension. Outsider like me can maybe identify it better than those who're bein' racked. On one hand, you are Ivar Frederiksen's girl. It could be dangerous gettin' near you, because he may return any day. That makes cowardly types ride clear of you. Then certain others— Well, you do have *mana*. I can't think of better word for it. They sense you're big medicine, because of bein' his chosen, and it makes them vaguely uncomfortable. They aren't used to that sort of thing in their neat, scientifically ordered lives. So they find excuses to themselves for postponin' any resumption of former close relations with you.

"On other hand"—he trailed a slow streamer of smoke—"you are, to speak blunt, lettin' yourself be used by enemy. You may think you're relayin' Desai's words for whatever those're worth as information. But mere fact that you will receive him, will talk civilly with him, means you lack full commitment. And this gets you shunned by those who have it. Cut off, you don't know how many already do. Well, they *are* many. And number grows day by day."

He leaned forward. "When I'd figured how matters stand, I had to come see you, Tatiana. My guess is, Desai's half persuaded you to try wheedlin' Frederiksen into surrender, if and when you two get back in touch. Well, you mustn't. At very least, hold apart from Impies." Starkly: "Freedom movement's at point where we can start makin' examples of collaborators. I know you'd never be one, consciously. Don't let yon Desai bastard snare you."

"But," she stammered in her bewilderment, "but what do you mean to do? What can you hope for? And Ivar—he's nothin' but young man who got carried away—fugitive, completely powerless, if, if, if he's still alive at all—"

"He is," Stewart told her. "I don't know where or how, or what he's doin', but he is. Word runs too widely to have no truth behind it." His voice lifted. "You've heard also. You must have. Signs, tokens, precognitions. . . . Never mind his weaklin' father. Ivar is rightful leader of free Aeneas—when Builders return, which they will, which they will. And you are his bride who will bear his son that Builders will make more than human."

Belief stood incandescent in his eyes.

XIII

South of the Green Bowl, hills climbed ever faster. Yet for a while the stream continued to flow peaceful. Ivar wished his blood could do likewise.

Seeking tranquillity, he climbed to the foredeck for a clear view across night. He stopped short when he spied others on hand than the lookout who added eyes to the radar.

Through a crowd of stars and a torrent of galaxy, Creusa sped past Lavinia. Light lay argent ashore, touching crests and crags, swallowed by shadows farther down. It shivered and sparked on the water, made ghostly the sails which had been set to use a fair wind. That air murmured cold through quietness and a rustle at the bows.

Fore and aft, separated by a few kilometers for safety, glowed the lights of three companion vessels. No few were bound this way, to celebrate the Season of Returnings.

Ivar saw the lookout on his knees under the figurehead, and a sheen off Erannath's plumage, and Riho Mea and Iang Weii in their robes. Captain and chaplain were completing a ritual, it seemed. Mute, now and then lifting hands or bowing heads, they had watched the moons draw near and again apart.

"Ah," Mea gusted. The crewman rose.

"I beg pardon," Erannath said. "Had I known a religious practice was going on, I would not have descended here. I stayed because that was perhaps less distracting than my takeoff would have been."

"No harm done," Mea assured him. "In fact, the sight of you coming down gave one extra glory."

"Besides," Iang said in his mild voice, "though this is something we always do at certain times, it is not strictly

111

religious." He stroked his thin white beard. "Have we Kuang Shih religion, in the same sense as the Christians or Jews of the Ti Shih or the pagans of the tineran society? This is one matter of definition, not so? We preach nothing about gods. To most of us that whole subject is not important. Whether or not gods, or God, exist, is it not merely one scientific question—cosmological?"

"Then what do you hunt after?" the Ythrian asked.

"Allness," the chaplain replied. "Unity, harmony. Through rites and symbols. We know they are only rites and symbols. But they say to the opened mind what words cannot. The River is ongoingness, fate; the Sun is life; Moons and Stars are the transhuman."

"We contemplate these things," Riho Mea added. "We try to merge with them, with everything that is." Her glance fell on Ivar. "Ahoa, Sir Mariner," she called. "Come, join our party."

Iang, who could stay solemn longer than her, continued: "Our race, or yours, has less gift for the whole *ch'an*—understanding—than the many-minded people of the Morning Star. However, when the Old Shen return, mankind will gain the same immortal singleness, and have moreover the strengths we were forced to make in ourselves, in order to endure being alone in our skulls."

"You too?" Erannath snapped. "Is everybody on Aeneas waiting for these mentors and saviors?"

"More and more, we are," Mea said. "Up the Yun Kow drifts word—"

Ivar, who had approached, felt as if touched by lightnings. Her gaze had locked on him. He knew: *These are not just easy-goin', practical sailors. I should've seen it earlier. That coffin—and fact they're bound on dangerous trip to honor both their ancestors and their descendants—and now this—no, they're as profoundly eschatological as any Bible-and-blaster yeoman.*

"Word about liberation?" he exclaimed.

"Aye, though that's the bare beginning," she answered. Iang nodded, while the lookout laid hand on sheath knife.

Abruptly she said, "Would you like to talk about this ... Rolf Mariner? I'm ready for one drink and cigar in my cabin anyway."

His pulses roared. "You also, good friend and wise man," he heard her propose to Iang.

"I bid you goodnight, then," Erannath said.

The chaplain bowed to him. "Forgive us our confidentiality."

"Maybe we should invite you along," Mea said. "Look here, you are not one plain scientist like you claim. You are one Ythrian secret agent, collecting information on the key human planet Aeneas, no?" When he stayed silent, she laughed. "Never mind. Point is, we and you have the same enemy, the Terran Empire. At least, Ythri shouldn't mind if the Empire loses territory."

"Afterward, though," Iang murmured, "I cannot help but wonder how well the carnivore soul may adapt to the enlightenment the Old Shen will bring."

Moonlight turned Erannath's feather to silver, his eyes to mercury. "Do you look on your species as a chosen people?" he said, equally low. At once he must have regretted his impulse, for he went on: "Your intrigues are no concern of mine. Nor do I care if you decide I am something more than an observer. If you are opposed to the occupation authorities, presumably you won't betray me to them. I wish to go on a night hunt. May fortune blow your way."

His wings spread, from rail to rail. The wind of his rising gusted and boomed. For a while he gleamed high aloft, before vision lost him among the stars.

Mea led Iang and Ivar to her quarters. Her husband greeted them, and this time he stayed: a bright and resolute young man, the dream of freedom kindled within him.

When the door had been shut, the captain said: "Ahoa, Ivar Frederiksen, Firstling of Ilion."

"How did you know?" he whispered.

She grinned, and went for the cigar she had bespoken. "How obvious need it be? Surely that Ythrian has suspected. Why else should he care about one human waif? But to him, humans are so foreign—so alike-seeming—and besides, being a spy, he couldn't dare use data services—he must have been holding back, trying to confirm his guess. Me, I remembered some choked-off news accounts. I called up Nova Roma public files, asked for pictures and—O-ah, no fears. I am one merchant myself, I know how to disguise my real intents."

"You, you will . . . help me?" he faltered.

They drew close around him, the young man, the old man, the captain. "You will help *us*," Iang said. "You are the Firstling—our rightful leader that every Aenean can follow—to throw out those mind-stifling Terrans and make ready for the Advent that is promised— What can we do for you, lord?"

Chunderban Desai broke the connection and sat for a while staring before him. His wife, who had been out of the room, came back in and asked what was wrong.

"Peter Jowett is dead," he told her.

"Oh, no." The two families had become friendly in the isolation they shared.

"Murdered."

"What?" The gentleness in her face gave way to horror.

"The separatists," he sighed. "It has to be. No melodramatic message left. He was killed by a rifle bullet as he left his office. But who else hated him?"

She groped for the comfort of his hand. He returned the pressure. "A real underground?" she said. "I didn't know."

"Nor I, until now. Oh, I got reports from planted agents, from surveillance devices, all the usual means. Something was brewing, something being organized. Still, I didn't expect outright terrorism this soon, if ever."

"The futility is nearly the worst part. What chance have they?"

He rose from his chair. Side by side, they went to a window. It gave on the garden of the little house they rented in the suburbs: alien plants spiky beneath alien stars and moons, whose light fell on the frosted helmet of a marine guard.

"I don't know," he said. Despite the low gravity, his back slumped. "They must have some. It isn't the hopeless who rebel, it's those who think they see the end of their particular tunnels, and grow impatient."

"You have given them hope, dear."

"Well ... I came here thinking they'd accept their military defeat and work with me like sensible people, to get their planet reintegrated with the Empire. After all, except for the Snelund episode, Aeneas has benefited from the Imperium, on balance; and we're trying to set up precautions against another Snelund. Peter agreed. Therefore they killed him. Who's next?"

Her fingers tightened on his. "Poor Olga. The poor children. Should I call her tonight or, or what?"

He stayed in the orbit of his own thoughts. "Rumors of a deliverer—not merely a political liberator, but a savior—no, a whole race of saviors—that's what's driving the Aeneans," he said. "And not the dominant culture alone. The others too. In their different ways, they all wait for an apocalypse."

"Who is preaching it?"

He chuckled sadly. "If I knew that, I could order the party arrested. Or, better yet, try to suborn him. Or them. But my agents hear nothing except these vague rumors. Never forget how terribly few we are, and how marked, on an entire world. . . . We did notice what appeared to be a centering of the rumors on the Orcan area. We investigated. We drew blank, at least as far as finding any proof of illegal activities. The society there, and its beliefs, always have been founded on colossal prehuman ruins, and evidently has often brought forth millennialist prophets. Our people had more urgent things to do than struggle with the language and ethos of some poverty-stricken dwellers on a dead sea floor." His tone · strengthened. "Though if I had the personnel for it, I would probe further indeed. This wouldn't be the first time that a voice from the desert drove nations mad."

The phone chimed again. He muttered a swear word before he returned to accept the call. It was on scramble code, which automatically heterodyned the audio output so that Desai's wife could not hear what came to him a couple of meters away. The screen was vacant, too.

She could see the blaze on his face; and she heard him shout after the conversation ended, as he surged from his chair: "Brahma's mercy, yes! We'll catch him and end this thing!"

XIV

Jade Gate had nearly reached the Linn when the Terrans came.

The Cimmerian Mountains form the southern marge of Ilion. The further south the Flone goes through them, until its final incredible plunge off the continental rim, the steeper and deeper is the gorge it has cut for itself. In winter it runs quiet between those walls, under a sheath of ice. But by midsummer, swollen with melt off the polar cap, it is a race, and they must have skillful pilots who would venture along that violence.

At the port rail of the main deck, Ivar and Jao watched. Water brawled, foamed, spouted off rocks, filled air with an ongoing cannonade and made the vessel rock and shudder. Here the stream had narrowed to a bare 300 meters between heaped boulders and talus. Behind, cliffs rose for a pair of kilometers. The rock was gloomy-hued and there was only a strip of sky to see, from which Virgil had already sunk. The brighter stars gleamed in its duskiness. Down under the full weight of shadow, it was cold. Spray dashed into faces and across garments. Forward, the canyon dimmed out in mist. Nevertheless he spied three ships in that direction, and four aft. More than these were rendezvous-bound.

As the deck pitched beneath her, the girl caught his arm. "What was that?" he shouted through the noise, and barely heard her reply:

"Swerve around one obstacle, I'm sure. Nothing here is ever twice the same."

"Have you had any wrecks?"

"Some few per century. Most lives are saved."

"God! You'll take such risk, year after year, for ... ritual?"

"The danger is part of the ritual, Rolf. We are never so one with the world as when— Ai-ah!"

His gaze followed hers aloft, and his heart lurched. Downward came slanting the torpedo shape of a large flyer. Upon its armored flank shone the sunburst of Empire.

"Who is that?" she cried innocently.

"A marine troop. After me. Who else?" He didn't rasp it loud enough for her to hear. When he wrenched free and ran, she stared in hurt amazement.

He pounded up the ladder to the bridge, where he knew Mea stood by the pilot. She came out to meet him. Grimness bestrode her countenance. She had bitten her cigar across. "Let's get you below," she snapped, and shoved at him.

He stumbled before her, among crewfolk who boiled with excitement. The aircraft whined toward the lead end of the line. *"Chao yu li!"* Mea exclaimed. "We've that much luck, at least. They don't know which vessel is ours."

"They might know its name," he replied. "Whoever gave me away—"

"Aye. Here, this way. . . . Hold." Erannath had emerged from his cabin. "You!" She pointed at the next deckhouse. "Into that door!"

The Ythrian halted, lifted his talons. "Move!" the captain bawled. "Or I'll have you shot!"

For an instant his crest stood stiff. Then he obeyed. The three of them entered a narrow, throbbing corridor. Mea bowed to Erannath. "I am sorry, honored passenger," she said. Partly muffled by bulkheads, the air was less thunderous here. "Time lacked for requesting your help courteously. You are most good that you obliged regardless. Please to come."

She trotted on. Ivar and Erannath followed, the Ythrian rocking clumsily along on his wing-feet while he asked, "What has happened?"

"Impies," the young man groaned. "We had to get out of sight from above. If either of us got glimpsed, that'd've ended this game. Not that I see how it can go on much longer."

Erannath's eyes smoldered golden upon him. "What game do you speak of?"

"I'm fugitive from Terrans."

"And worth the captain's protection? A-a-a-ah. . . ."

Mea stopped at an intercom unit, punched a number, spoke rapid-fire for a minute. When she turned back to her companions, she was the barest bit relaxed.

"I raised our radioman in time," she said. "Likely the enemy will call, asking which of us is *Jade Gate*. My man is alerting the others in our own language, which surely the Terrans don't understand. We Riverfolk stick together. Everybody will act stupid, claim they don't know, garble things as if they had one poor command of Anglic." Her grin flashed. "To act stupid is one skill of our people."

"Were I the Terran commander," Erannath said, "I would thereupon beam to each ship individually, requiring its name. And were I the captain of any, I would not court punishment by lying, in a cause which has not been explained to me."

Mea barked laughter. "Right. But I suggested *Portal of Virtue* and *Way to Fortune* both answer they are *Jade Gate*, as well as this one. The real names could reasonably translate to the same as ours. They can safely give the Terrans that stab."

She turned bleak again: "At best, though, we buy short time to smuggle you off, Ivar Frederiksen, and you, Erannath, spy from Ythri. I dare not give you any firearms. That would prove our role, should you get caught." The man felt the knife he had kept on his belt since he left Windhome. The nonhuman wasn't wearing his apron, thus had no weapons. The woman continued: "When the marines flit down to us, we'll admit you were here, but claim we had no idea you were wanted. True enough, for everybody except three of us; and we can behave plenty innocent. We'll say you must have seen the airboat and fled, we know not where."

Ivar thought of the starkness that walled them in and pleaded, "Where, for real?"

Mea led them to a companionway and downward. As she hastened, she said across her shoulder: "Some Orcans always climb the Shelf to trade with us after our ceremonies are done. You may meet them at the site, otherwise on their way to it. Or if not, you can probably reach the Tien

Hu by yourselves, and get help. I feel sure they will help. Theirs is the seer they've told us of."

"Won't Impies think of that?" Ivar protested.

"No doubt. Still, I bet it's one impossible country to ransack." Mea stopped at a point in another corridor, glanced about, and rapped, "Aye, you may be caught. But you *will* be caught if you stay aboard. You may drown crossing to shore, or break your neck off one cliff, or thousand other griefs. Well, are you our Firstling or not?"

She flung open a door and ushered them through. The room beyond was a storage space for kayaks, and also held a small crane for their launching. "Get in," she ordered Ivar. "You should be able to reach the bank. Just work at not capsizing and not hitting anything, and make what shoreward way you can whenever you find one stretch not too rough. Once afoot, send the boat off again. No sense leaving any clue to where you landed. Afterward, rocks and mist should hide you from overhead, if you go carefully.... Erannath, you fly across, right above the surface."

Half terrified and half carried beyond himself, Ivar settled into the frail craft, secured the cover around his waist, gripped the paddle. Riho Mea leaned toward him. He had never before seen tears in her eyes. "All luck sail with you, Firstling," she said unsteadily, "for all our hopes do." Her lips touched his.

She opened a hatch in the hull and stood to the controls of the crane. Its motor whirred, its arm descended to lay hold with clamps to rings fore and aft, it lifted Ivar outward and lowered him alongside.

The river boomed and brawled. The world was a cold wet grayness of spray blown backward from the falls. Phantom cliffs showed through. Ivar and Erannath rested among house-sized boulders.

Despite his shoes, the stones along the bank had been cruel to the human. He ached from bruises where he had tripped and slashes where sharp edges had caught him. Weariness filled every bone like a lead casting. The Ythrian, who could flutter above obstacles, was in better shape, though prolonged land travel was always hard on his race.

By some trick of echo in their shelter, talk was possible at less than the top of a voice. "No doubt a trail goes down the Shelf to the seabed," Erannath said. "We must presume the Terrans are not fools. When they don't find us aboard any ship, they will suppose us bound for Orcus, and call Nova Roma for a stat of the most detailed geodetic survey map available. They will then cruise above that trail. We must take a roundabout way."

"That'll likely be dangerous to me," Ivar said dully.

"I will help you as best I can," Erannath promised. Perhaps the set of his feathers added: *If God the Hunter hurls you to your death, cry defiance as you fall.*

"Why are you interested in me, anyhow?" Ivar demanded.

The Ythrian trilled what corresponded to a chuckle. "You and your fellows have taken for granted I'm a secret agent of the Domain. Let's say, first, that I wondered if you truly were plain Rolf Mariner, and accompanied you to try to find out. Second, I have no desire myself to be taken prisoner. Our interests in escape coincide."

"Do they, now? You need only fly elsewhere."

"But you are the Firstling of Ilion. Alone, you'd perish or be captured. Captain Riho doesn't understand how different this kind of country is from what you are used to. With my help, you have a fair chance."

Ivar was too worn and sore to exult. Yet underneath, a low fire awoke. *He is interested in my success! So interested he'll gamble his whole mission, everything he might have brought home, to see me through. Maybe we really can get help from Ythri, when we break Sector Alpha Crucis free.*

This moment was premature to voice such things aloud. Presently the two of them resumed their crawling journey.

For a short stretch, the river again broadened until a fleet could lie to, heavily anchored and with engineers standing by to supply power on a whistle's notice. The right bank widened also, in a few level hectares which had been cleared of detritus. There stood an altar flanked by stone guardians, eroded almost shapeless. There too lay traces of campfires; but no Orcans had yet arrived. Here the rush of current was lost under the world-shivering steady roar of the Linn, only seven kilometers distant. Its edge was never visible through the spray flung aloft.

Tonight the wind had shifted, driving the perpetual fog south till it hung as a moon-whitened curtain between vast black walls. The water glistened. Darkling upon it rested those vessels which had arrived. Somehow their riding lights and the colored lanterns strung throughout their rigging lacked cheeriness, when the Terran warcraft hung above on its negafield and watched. The air was cold; ice crackled in Ivar's clothes and Erannath's feathers.

Humans have better night vision than Ythrians. Ivar was the first to see. "Hsssh!" He drew his companion back, while sickness caught his throat. Then Erannath identified those shimmers and shadows ahead. Three marines kept watch on the open ground.

No way existed to circle them unnoticed; the bank lay bare and moonlit to the bottom of an unscalable precipice. Ivar shrank behind a rock, thought wildly of swimming and knew that here he couldn't, of weeping and found that now he couldn't.

Unheard through the noise, Erannath lifted. Moon-glow tinged him. But sight was tricky for men who sat high in a hull. Otherwise they need not have placed sentries.

Ivar choked on a breath. He saw the great wings scythe back down. One man tumbled, a second, a third, in as many pulsebeats. Erannath landed among them where they sprawled and beckoned the Firstling.

Ivar ran. Strangely, what broke from him was, "Are they dead?"

"No. Stunned. I hold a Third Echelon in *hyai-lu*. I used its triple blow, both alatan bones and a ... do you say rabbit punch?" Erannath was busy. He stripped the twoways off wrists, grav units off torsos, rifles off shoulders, gave one of each to Ivar and tossed the rest in the Flone. When they awoke, the marines would be unable to radio, rise, or fire signals, and must wait till their regular relief descended.

If they awoke. The bodies looked ghastly limp to Ivar. He thrust that question aside, unsure why it should bother him when they were the enemy and when in joyous fact he and his ally had lucked out, had won a virtually certain means of getting to their goal.

They did not hazard immediate flight. On the further side of the meeting ground the Orcan trail began. Though narrow, twisting, and vague, often told only by cairns, it was better going than the shoreline had been. Anything would be. Ivar limped and Erannath hobbled as if unchained.

When they entered the concealing mists, they dared rise. And that was like becoming a freed spirit. Ivar wondered if the transcendence of humanness which the prophet promised could feel this miraculous. The twin cylinders he wore drove him through roaring wet smoke till he burst forth and beheld the side of a continent.

It toppled enormously, more steep and barren than anywhere in the west, four kilometers of palisades, headlands, ravines, raw slopes of old landslides, down and down to the dead ocean floor. Those were murky heights beneath stars and moons; but over them cascaded the Linn. It fell almost half the distance in a single straight leap, unhidden by spume, agleam like a drawn sword. The querning of it toned through heaven.

Below sheened the Orcan Sea, surrounded by hills which cultivation mottled. Beyond, desert glimmered death-white.

Erannath swept near. "Quick!" he commanded. "To ground before the Terrans come and spot us."

Ivar nodded, took his bearings from the constellations, and aimed southwest, to where Mount Cronos raised its dim bulk. They might as well reduce the way they had left to go.

Air skirled frigid around him. His teeth clattered till he forced them together. This was not like the part of the Antonine Seabed under Windhome. There it was often warm of summer nights, and never too hot by day. But there it was tempered by plenteous green life.

Yonder so-called Sea of Orcus was no more than a huge lake, dense and bitter with salts leached into it. Mists and lesser streams off the Linn gave fresh water to the rim of its bowl. And that was all. Nothing ran far on southward. Winds bending up from the equator sucked every moisture into themselves and scattered it across immensities. That land lay bare because those same winds had long ago blown away the rich bottom soil which elsewhere was the heritage left Aeneas by its oceans.

Here was the sternest country where men dwelt upon this planet. Ivar knew it had shaped their tribe, their souls. He knew little more. No outsider did.

Aliens— He squinted at Erannath. The Ythrian descended as if upon prey, magnificent as the downward-rushing falls. *I thought for a moment you must've been one who betrayed me,* passed through Ivar. *Can't be, I reckon.*

Then: who did?

XV

Dawnlight shivered upon the sea and cast sharp blue shadows across dust. From the Grand Tower, a trumpet greeted the sun. Its voice blew colder than the windless air.

Jaan left his mother's house and walked a street which twisted between shuttered gray blocks of houses, down to the wharf. What few people were abroad crossed arms and bowed to him, some in awe, some in wary respect. In the wall-enclosed narrowness dusk still prevailed, making their robes look ghostly.

The wharf was Ancient work, a sudden dazzling contrast to the drabness and poverty of the human town. Its table thrust iridescent, hard and cool beneath the feet, out of the mountainside. Millions of years had broken a corner off it but not eroded the substance. What they had done was steal the waves which once lapped its lower edge; now brush-grown slopes fell steeply to the water a kilometer beneath.

The town covered the mountain for a similar distance upward, its featureless adobe blocks finally huddling against the very flanks of the Arena which crowned the peak. That was also built by the Ancients, and even ruined stood in glory. It was of the same shining, enduring material as the wharf, elliptical in plan, the major axis almost a kilometer and the walls rearing more than 30 meters before their final upthrust in what had been seven towers and remained three. Those walls were not sheer; they fountained, in pillars, terraces, arches, galleries, setbacks, slim bridges, winglike balconies, so that light and shadow played endlessly and the building was like one eternal cool fire.

Banners rose, gold and scarlet, to the tops of flagstaffs on the parapets. The Companions were changing their guard.

Jaan's gaze turned away, to the northerly horizon where the continent reared above the Sea of Orcus. With Virgil barely over them, the heights appeared black, save for the Linn. Its dim thunder reverberated through air and earth.

—I do not see them flying, he said.

—No, they are not, replied Caruith. For fear of pursuit, they landed near Alsa and induced a villager to convey them in his truck. Look, there it comes.

Jaan was unsure whether his own mind or the Ancient's told his head to swing about, his eyes to focus on the dirt road snaking uphill from the shoreline. Were the two beginning to become one already? It had been promised. To be a part, no, a characteristic, a memory, of Caruith ... oh, wonder above wonders. . . .

He saw the battered vehicle more by the dust it raised than anything else, for it was afar, would not reach the town for a while yet. It was not the only traffic at this early hour. Several groundcars moved along the highway that girdled the sea; a couple of tractors were at work in the hills behind, black dots upon brown and wan green, to coax a crop out of niggard soil; a boat slid across the thick waters, trawling for creatures which men could not eat but whose tissues concentrated minerals that men could use. And above the Arena there poised on its negafield an aircraft the Companions owned. Though unarmed by Imperial decree, it was on guard. These were uneasy times.

"Master."

Jaan turned at the voice and saw Robhar, youngest of his disciples. The boy, a fisherman's son, was nearly lost in his ragged robe. His breath steamed around shoulder-length black elflocks. He made his bow doubly deep. "Master," he asked, "can I serve you in aught?"

—He kept watch for hours till we emerged, and then did not venture to address us before we paused here, Caruith said. His devotion is superb.

—I do not believe the rest care less, Jaan replied out of his knowledge of humankind: which the mightiest nonhuman intellect could never totally sound. They are older, lack endurance to wait sleepless and freezing on the chance that we may want them; they have, moreover, their daily work, and most of them their wives and children.

—The time draws nigh when they must forsake those, and all others, to follow us.

—They know that. I am sure they accept it altogether. But then should they not savor the small joys of being human as much as they may, while still they may?

—You remain too human yourself, Jaan. You must become a lightning bolt.

Meanwhile the prophet said, "Yes, Robhar. This is a day of destiny." As the eyes before him flared: "Nonetheless we have practical measures to take, no time for rejoicing. We remain only men, chained to the world. Two are bound hither, a human and an Ythrian. They could be vital to the liberation. The Terrans are after them, and will surely soon arrive in force to seek them out. Before then, they must be well hidden; and as few townsfolk as may be must know about them, lest the tale be spilled.

"Hurry. Go to the livery stable of Brother Boras and ask him to lend us a statha with a pannier large enough to hide an Ythrian—about your size, though we will also need a blanket to cover his wing-ends that will stick forth. Do not tell Boras why I desire this. He is loyal, but the tyrants have drugs and worse, should they come to suspect anyone knows something. Likewise, give no reasons to Brother Ezzara when you stop at his house to borrow a robe, sandals, and his red cloak with the hood. Order him to remain indoors until further word.

"Swiftly!"

Robhar clapped hands in sign of obedience and sped off, over the cobblestones and into the town.

Jaan waited. The truck would inevitably pass the wharf. Meanwhile, nobody was likely to have business here at this hour. Any who did chance by would see the prophet's lonely figure limned against space, and bow and not venture to linger.

—The driver comes sufficiently near for me to read his mind, whispered Caruith. I do not like what I see.

—What? asked Jaan, startled. Is he not true to us? Why else should he convey two outlaws?

—He is true, in the sense of wishing Aeneas free of the Empire and, indeed, Orcus free of Nova Roma. But he has not fully accepted our teaching, nor made an absolute commitment to our cause. For he is an impulsive and vac-

illating man. Ivar Frederiksen and Erannath of Avalon
woke him up with a story about being scientists marooned
by the failure of their aircraft, in need of transportation to
Mount Cronos where they could get help. He knew the
story must be false, but in his resentment of the Terrans
agreed anyway. Now, more and more, he worries, he re-
grets his action. As soon as he is rid of them, he will
drink to ease his fears, and the drink may well unlock his
tongue.

—Is it not ample precaution that we transfer them out
of his care? What else should we do? ... No! Not murder!

—Many will die for the liberation. Would you hazard
their sacrifice being in vain, for the sake of a single life today?

—Imprisonment, together with the Ythrian you warn
me about—

—The disappearance of a person who has friends and
neighbors is less easy to explain away than his death.
Speak to Brother Velib. Recall that he was among the
few Orcans who went off to serve with McCormac; he
learned a good deal. It is not hard to create a believable
"accident."

—No.

Jaan wrestled; but the mind which shared his brain was
too powerful, too plausible. It is right that one man die
for the people. Were not Jaan and Caruith themselves
prepared to do so? By the time the truck arrived, the
prophet had actually calmed.

By then, too, Robhar had returned with the statha and
the disguise. Everybody knew Ezzara by the red cloak he
affected. Its hood would conceal a nord's head; long
sleeves, and dirt rubbed well into sandaled feet, would conceal fair skin. Folk would observe nothing save the prophet, accompanied by two of his disciples, going up to the
Arena and in through its gates, along with a beast whose
burden might be, say, Ancient books that he had found in
the catacombs.

The truck halted. Jaan accepted the salutation of the
driver, while trying not to think of him as really real. The
man opened the back door, and inside the body of the vehicle were the Ythrian and the Firstling of Ilion.

Jaan, who had never before seen an Ythrian in the
flesh, found he was more taken by that arrogance of
beauty (which must be destroyed, it mourned within him)

than by the ordinary-looking blond youth who had so swiftly become a hinge of fate. He felt as if the blue eyes merely stared, while the golden ones searched.

They saw: a young man, more short and stocky than was common among Orcans, in an immaculate white robe, rope belt, sandals he had made himself. The countenance was broad, curve-nosed, full-lipped, pale-brown, handsome in its fashion; long hair and short beard were mahogany, clean and well-groomed. His own eyes were his most striking feature, wide-set, gray, and enormous. Around his brows went a circlet of metal with a faceted complexity above the face, the sole outward token that he was an Ancient returned to life after six million years.

He said, in his voice that was as usual slow and soft: "Welcome, Ivar Frederiksen, deliverer of your world."

Night laired everywhere around Desai's house. Neighbor lights felt star-distant; and there went no whisper of traffic. It was almost with relief that he blanked the windows.

"Please sit down, Prosser Thane," he said. "What refreshment may I offer you?"

"None," the tall young woman answered. After a moment she added, reluctantly and out of habit: "Thank you."

"Is it that you do not wish to eat the salt of an enemy?" His smile was wistful. "I shouldn't imagine tradition requires you refuse his tea."

"If you like, Commissioner." Tatiana seated herself, stiff-limbed in her plain coverall. Desai spoke to his wife, who fetched a tray with a steaming pot, two cups, and a plate of cookies. She set it down and excused herself. The door closed behind her.

To Desai, that felt like the room closing in on him. It was so comfortless, so ... impoverished, in spite of being physically adequate. His desk and communications board filled one corner, a reference shelf stood nearby, and otherwise the place was walls, faded carpet, furniture not designed for a man of his race or culture: apart from a picture or two, everything rented, none of the dear clutter which makes a home.

Our family moves too much, too often, too far, like a bobbin shuttling to reweave a fabric which tears because it is rotted. I was always taught on Ramanujan that we do best to travel light through life. But what does it do to the children, this flitting from place to place, though always into the same kind of Imperial-civil-servant enclave? He sighed. The thought was old in him.

"I appreciate your coming as I requested," he began. "I hope you, ah, took precautions."

"Yes, I did. I slipped into alley, reversed my cloak, and put on my nightmask."

"That's the reason I didn't visit you. It would be virtually impossible to conceal the fact. And surely the terrorists have you under a degree of surveillance."

Tatiana withheld expression. Desai plodded on: "I hate for you to take even this slight risk. The assassins of a dozen prominent citizens might well not stop at you, did they suspect you of, um, collaboration."

"Unless I'm on their side, and came here to learn whatever I can for them," Tatiana said in a metallic tone.

Desai ventured a smile. "That's the risk *I* take. Not very large, I assume." He lifted the teapot and raised his brows. She gave a faint nod. He poured for her and himself, lifted his cup and sipped. The heat comforted.

"How about gettin' to business?" she demanded.

"Indeed. I thought you would like to hear the latest news of Ivar Frederiksen."

That caught her! She said nothing, but she sat bolt upright and the brown gaze widened.

"This is confidential, of course. From a source I shan't describe, I have learned that he joined a nomad band, later got into trouble with it, and took passage on a southbound ship of Riverfolk together with an Ythrian who may or may not have met him by chance but is almost certainly an Intelligence agent of the Domain. They were nearly at the outfall when I got word and sent a marine squad to bring him in. Thanks to confusion—obviously abetted by the sailors, though I don't plan to press charges—he and his companion escaped."

Red and white ran across her visage. She breathed quickly and shallowly, caught up her cup and gulped deep.

"You know I don't want him punished if it can be avoided," Desai said. "I want a chance to reason with him."

"I know that's what you claim," Tatiana snapped.

"If only people would understand," Desai pleaded. "Yes, the Imperium wronged you. But we are trying to make it good. And others would make tools of you, for prying apart what unity, and safety in unity, this civilization has left."

"What d'you mean? Ythrians? Merseians?" Her voice gibed.

Desai reached a decision. "Merseians. Oh, they are far off. But if they can again preoccupy us on this frontier— They failed last time, because McCormac's revolt caught them, too, by surprise. A more carefully engineered sequel would be different. Terra might even lose this entire sector, while simultaneously Merseia grabbed away at the opposite frontier. The result would be a truncated, shaken, weakened Empire, a strengthened Roidhunate flushed with success . . . and the Long Night brought that much closer."

He said into her unvoiced but unmistakable scorn: "You disbelieve? You consider Merseia a mere bogeyman? Please listen. A special agent of theirs is loose on Aeneas. No common spy or troublemaker. A creature of unique abilities; so important that, for the sake of his mission, a whole nonexistent planet was smuggled into the data files at Catawrayannis; so able—including fantastic telepathic feats—that all by himself he easily, almost teasingly escaped our precautions and disappeared into the wilds. Prosser Thane, Merseia is risking more than this one individual. It's giving away to us the fact that the Roidhunate includes such a species, putting us on our guard against more like him. No competent Intelligence service would allow that for anything less than the highest stakes.

"Do you see what a net your betrothed could get tangled in?"

Have I registered? Her face has gone utterly blank.

After a minute, she said: "I'll have to think on that, Commissioner. Your fears may be exaggerated. Let's stay with practicalities tonight. You were wonderin' about Ivar and this companion of his . . . who suggests Ythri may also be stickin' claws into our pot, right? Before I can suggest anything, you'd better tell me what else you know."

Desai armored himself in dryness. "Presumably they took refuge in the Orcan country," he said. "I've just had a report from a troop dispatched there to search for them. After several days of intensive effort, including depth quizzing of numerous people who might be suspected of knowledge, they have drawn blank. I can't leave them tied down, futile except for fueling hatred of us by their presence: not when sedition, sabotage, and violence are growing so fast across the whole planet. We need them to patrol the streets of, say, Nova Roma."

"Maybe Ivar didn't make for Orcus," Tatiana suggested.

"Maybe. But it would be logical, no?"

She uttered a third "Maybe," and then surprised him: "Did your men quiz that new prophet of theirs?"

"As a matter of fact, yes. No result. He gave off weird quasi-religious ideas that we already know a little about; they're anti-Imperial, but it seems better to let him vent pressure on behalf of his followers than to make a martyr of him. No, he revealed no knowledge of our Firstling. Nor did such as we could find among those persons who've constituted themselves an inner band of apostles."

It was clear that Tatiana stayed impersonal only by an effort. Her whole self must be churning about her sweetheart. "I'm astonished you got away with layin' hands on him or them. You could've touched off full-dress revolt, from all I've heard."

"I did issue instructions to handle cult leaders with micromanipulators. But after the search had gone on for a while, this ... Jaan ... voluntarily offered to undergo narco with his men, to end suspicion and, as he put it, leave the Terrans no further reason to remain. A shrewd move, if what he wanted was to get rid of them. After that big a concession from his side, they could scarcely do less than withdraw."

"Well," she challenged, "has it occurred to you that Ivar may *not* be in yon area?"

"Certainly. Although ... the lead technician of the quiz team reported Jaan showed an encephalogram not quite like any ever recorded before. As if his claim were true, that—what is it?—he is possessed by some kind of spirit. Oh, his body is normal-human. There's no reason to suppose the drug didn't suppress his capacity to lie, as it would for anyone else. But—"

"Mutation, I'd guess, would account for brain waves. They're odd and inbred folk, in environment our species never was evolved for."

"Probably. I'd have liked to borrow a Ryellian telepath from the governor's staff—considered it seriously, but decided that the Merseian agent, with the powers and knowledge he must have, would know how to guard against that, if he were involved. If I had a million skilled investigators, to study every aspect of this planet and its different peoples for a hundred intensive years—"

Desai abandoned his daydream. "We don't escape the possibility that Ivar and the Ythrian are in that region, unbeknownst to the prophet," he said. "A separate group could have smuggled them in. I understand Mount Cronos is riddled with tunnels and vaults, dug by the Elder race and never fully explored by men."

"But 'twould be hopeless quest goin' through them, right?" Tatiana replied.

"Yes. Especially when the hiding place could as well be far out in the desert." Desai paused. "This is why I asked you to come here, Prosser Thane. You know your fiancé. And surely you have more knowledge of the Orcans than our researchers can dig out of books, data banks, and superficial observation. Tell me, if you will, how likely would Ivar and they be to, m-m, get together?"

Tatiana fell silent. Desai loaded his cigarette holder and puffed and puffed. Finally she said, slowly:

"I don't think close cooperation's possible. Differences go too deep. And Ivar, at least, would have sense enough to realize it, and not try."

Desai refrained from comment, merely saying, "I wish you would describe that society for me."

"You must've read reports."

"Many. All from an outside, Terran viewpoint, including summaries my staff made of nord writings. They lack feel. You, however—your people and the Orcans have shared a world for centuries. If nothing else, I'm trying to grope toward an intuition of the relationship: not a bald socio-economic redaction, but a sense of the spirit, the tensions, the subtle and basic influences between cultures."

Tatiana sat for another time, gathering her thoughts. At last she said: "I really can't tell you much, Commissioner. Would you like capsule of history? You must know it already."

"I do not know what you consider important. Please."

"Well . . . those're by far our largest, best-preserved Builder relics, on Mount Cronos. But they were little studied, since Dido commanded most attention. Then Troubles came, raids, invasions, breakdown toward feudalism. Certain non-nords took refuge in Arena for lack of better shelter."

"Arena?" Desai wondered.

"Giant amphitheater on top of mountain, if amphitheater is what it was."

"Ah, that's not what 'arena' means . . . No matter. I realize words change in local dialects. Do go on."

"They lived in that fortresslike structure, under strict discipline. When they went out to farm, fish, herd, armed men guarded them. Gradually these developed into military order, Companions of Arena, who were also magistrates, technical decision-makers—land bein' held in common—and finally became leaders in religious rites, religion naturally comin' to center on those mysterious remains.

"When order was restored, at first Companions resisted planetary government, and had to be beaten down. That made them more of priesthood, though they keep soldierly traditions. Since, they've given Nova Roma no particular trouble; but they hold aloof, and see their highest purpose as findin' out what Builders were, and are, and will be."

"Hm." Desai stroked his chin. "Are their people—these half million or so who inhabit the region—would you call them equally isolated from the rest of Aeneas?"

"Not quite. They trade, especially caravans across Antonine Seabed to its more fertile parts, bringin' minerals and bioproducts in exchange for food, manufactures, and whatnot. Number of their young men take service with nords for several years, to earn stake; they've high talent for water dowsin', which bears out what I said earlier about mutations among them. On whole, though, average continent dweller never sees an Orcan. And they do keep apart, forbid outside marriages on pain of exile, hold themselves to be special breed who will at last play special role related to Builders. Their history's full of prophets who had dreams about that. This Jaan's merely latest one."

Desai frowned. "Still, isn't his claim unique—that he is, at last, the incarnation, and the elder race will return in his lifetime—or whatever it is that he preaches?"

"I don't know." Tatiana drew breath. "One thing, however; and this's what you called me here for, right? In spite of callin' itself objective rather than supernatural, what Orcans have got behaves like religion. Well, Ivar's skeptic; in fact, he's committed unbeliever. I can't imagine him throwin' in with gang of visionaries. They'd soon conflict too much."

Now Desai went quiet to ponder. *The point is well taken. That doesn't mean it's true.*

And yet what can I do but accept it ... unless and until I hear from my spy, whatever has hapened to him? (And that is something I may well never know.)

He shook himself. "So whether or not Ivar received help from an individual Orcan or two, you doubt he's contacted anyone significant, or will have any reason to linger in so forbidding an area. Am I correct, Prosser Thane?"

She nodded.

"Could you give me an idea as to where he might turn, how we might reach him?" Desai pursued.

She did not deign to answer.

"As you will," he said tiredly. "Bear in mind, he's in deadly danger as long as he is on the run: danger of getting shot by a patrol, for instance, or of committing a treasonable act which it would be impossible to pardon him for."

Tatiana bit her lip.

"I will not harass you about this," he promised. "But I beg you—you're a scientist, you should be used to entertaining radical new hypotheses and exploring their consequences—I beg you to consider the proposition that his real interests, and those of Aeneas, may lie with the Empire."

"I'd better go pretty soon," she said.

Later, to Gabriel Stewart, she exulted:

"He's got to be among Orcans. Nothin' else makes sense. He our rightful temporal leader, Jaan our mental one. Word'll go like fire in dry trava under a zoosny wind."

"But if prophet didn't know where he was—" fretted the scout.

Tatiana rapped forth a laugh. "Prophet did know! Do you imagine Builder mind couldn't control human body reactions to miserable dose of narcotic? Why, simple schizophrenia can cause that."

He considered her. "You believe those rumors, girl? Rumors they are, you understand, nothin' more. Our outfit has no liaison with Arena."

"We'd better develop one.... Well, I admit we've no proof Builders are almost ready to return. But it makes sense." She gestured as if at the stars which her blinded window concealed. "Cosmenosis— What'd be truly fantastic is no purpose, no evolution, in all of that yonder." Raptly: "Desai spoke about Merseian agent operatin' on Aeneas. Not Merseian by race, though. Somebody strange enough to maybe, just maybe, be forerunner for Builders."

"Huh?" he exclaimed.

"I'd rather not say more at this point, Gabe. However, Desai also spoke about adoptin' workin' hypothesis. Until further notice, I think this ought to be ours, that there is at least *somethin'* to those stories. We've got to dig deeper, collect hard information. At worst, we'll find we're on our own. At best, who knows?"

"If nothin' else, it'd make good propaganda," he remarked cynically. He had not been back on Aeneas sufficiently long to absorb its atmosphere of expectation. "Uh, how do we keep enemy from reasonin' and investigatin' along same lines?"

"We've no guaranteed way," Tatiana said. "I've been thinkin', though, and— Look, suppose I call Desai tomorrow or next day, claim I've had change of heart, try wheedlin' more out of him concernin' yon agent. But mainly what I'll do is suggest he check on highlanders of Chalce. They're tough, independent-minded clansmen, you probably recall. It's quite plausible they'd rally 'round Ivar if he went to them, and that he'd do so on his own initiative. Well, it's big and rugged country, take many men and lots of time to search over. Meanwhile—"

XVI

The room within the mountain was spacious, and its lining of Ancient material added an illusion of dreamlike depths beyond. Men had installed heated carpeting, fluoropanels, furniture, and other basic necessities, including books and an eidophone to while away the time. Nevertheless, as hours stretched into days he did not see, Ivar grew half wild. Erannath surely suffered worse; from a human viewpoint, all Ythrians are born with a degree of claustrophobia. But he kept self-control grimly in his talons.

Conversation helped them both. Erannath even reminisced:

"—wing-free. As a youth I wandered the whole of Avalon ... hai-ha, storm-dawns over seas and snowpeaks! Hunting a spathodont with spears! Wind across the plains, that smelled of sun and eternity! ... Later I trained to become a tramp spacehand. You do not know what that is? An Ythrian institution. Such a crewman may leave his ship whenever he wishes to stay for a while on some planet, provided a replacement is available; and one usually is." His gaze yearned beyond the shimmering walls. "Khrrr, this is a universe of wonders. Treasure it, Ivar. What is outside our heads is so much more than what can nest inside them."

"Are you still spaceman?" the human asked.

"No. I returned at length to Avalon with Hlirr, whom I had met and wedded on a world where rings flashed rainbow over oceans the color of old silver. That also is good, to ward a home and raise a brood. But they are grown now, and I, in search of a last long-faring before God

136

stoops on me, am here"—he gave a harsh equivalent of a chuckle—"in this cave."

"You're spyin' for Domain, aren't you?"

"I have explained, I am a xenologist, specializing in anthropology. That was the subject I taught throughout the settled years on Avalon, and in which I am presently doing field work."

"Your bein' scientist doesn't forbid your bein' spy. Look, I don't hold it against you. Terran Empire is my enemy same as yours, if not more. We're natural allies. Won't you carry that word back to Ythri for me?"

Ripplings went over Erannath's plumage. "Is every opponent of the Empire your automatic friend? What of Merseia?"

"I've heard propaganda against Merseians till next claim about their bein' racist and territorially aggressive will throw me into anaphylactic shock. Has Terra *never* provoked, yes, menaced them? Besides, they're far off: Terra's problem, not ours. Why should Aeneas supply young men to pull Emperor's fat out of fire? What's he ever done for us? And, God, what hasn't he done to us?"

Erannath inquired slowly, "Do you indeed hope to lead a second, successful revolution?"

"I don't know about leadin'," Ivar said, hot-faced. "I hope to help."

"For what end?"

"Freedom."

"What is freedom? To do as you, an individual, choose? Then how can you be certain that a fragment of the Empire will not make still greater demands on you? I should think it would have to."

"Well, uh, well, I'd be willin' to serve, as long as it was my own people."

"How willing are your people themselves to be served—as individuals—in your fashion? You see no narrowing of your freedom in whatever the requirements may be for a politically independent Alpha Crucis region, any more than you see a narrowing of it in laws against murder or robbery. These imperatives accord with your desires. But others may feel otherwise. What is freedom, except having one's particular cage reach further than one cares to fly?"

Ivar scowled into the yellow eyes. "You talk strange,

for Ythrian. For Avalonian, especially. Your planet sure
resisted bein' swallowed up by Empire."

"That would have wrought a fundamental change in our
lives: for example, by allowing unrestricted immigration,
till we were first crowded and then outvoted. You, however— In what basic way might an Alpha Crucian Repub-
lic, or an Alpha Crucian province of the Domain, differ
from Sector Alpha Crucis of the Empire? You get but one
brief flight through reality, Ivar Frederiksen. Would you
truly rather pass among ideologies than among stars?"

"Uh, I'm afraid you don't understand. Your race
doesn't have our idea of government."

"It's irrelevant to us. My fellow Avalonians who are of
human stock have come to think likewise. I must wonder
why you are so intense, to the point of making it a
deathpride matter, about the precise structure of a political organization. Why do you not, instead, concentrate
your efforts toward arrangements whereby it will generally
leave you and yours alone?"

"Well, if our motivation here is what puzzles you, then
tell them on Ythri—" Ivar drew breath.

Time wore away; and all at once, it was a not a single
man who came in a plain robe, bringing food and remov-
ing discards: it was a figure in uniform that trod through
the door and announced, "The High Commander!"

Ivar scrambled to his feet. The feather-crest stood stiff
upon Erannath's head. For this they had abided.

A squad entered, forming a double line at taut attention. They were typical male Orcans: tall and lean, brown
of skin, black and bushy of hair and closely cropped
beard, their faces mostly oval and somewhat flat, their
nostrils flared and lips full. But these were drilled and
dressed like soldiers. They wore steel helmets which swept
down over the neck and bore self-darkening vitryl visors
now shoved up out of the way; blue tunics with insignia of
rank and, upon the breast of each, an infinity sign; gray
trousers tucked into soft boots. Besides knives and knuck-
ledusters at their belts they carried, in defiance of Imperial
decree, blasters and rifles which must have been kept hidden from confiscation.

Yakow Harolsson, High Commander of the Companions of the Arena, followed. He was clad the same as his
men, except for adding a purple cloak. Though his beard

was white and his features scored, the spare form remained erect. Ivar snapped him a salute.

Yakow returned it and in the nasal Anglic of the region said: "Be greeted, Firstling of Ilion."

"Have ... Terrans gone ... sir?" Ivar asked. His pulse banged, giddiness passed through him, the cool underground air felt thick in his throat.

"Yes. You may come forth." Yakow frowned. "In disguise, naturally, garb, hair and skin dyes, instruction about behavior. We dare not assume the enemy has left no spies or, what is likelier, hidden surveillance devices throughout the town—perhaps in the very Arena." From beneath discipline there blazed: "Yet forth shall you come, to prepare for the Deliverance."

Erannath stirred. "I could ill pass as an Orcan," he said dryly.

Yakow's gaze grew troubled as it sought him. "No. We have provided for you, after taking counsel."

A vague fear made Ivar exclaim, "Remember, sir, he's liaison with Ythri, which may become our ally."

"Indeed," Yakow said without tone. "We could simply keep you here, Sir Erannath, but from what I know of your race, you would find that unendurable. So we have prepared a safe place elsewhere. Be patient for a few more hours. After dark you will be led away."

To peak afar in wilderness, Ivar guessed, happy again, *where he can roam skies, hunt, think his thoughts, till we're ready for him to rejoin us—or we rejoin him—and afterward send him home.*

On impulse he seized the Ythrian's right hand. Talons closed sharp but gentle around his fingers. "Thanks for everything, Erannath," Ivar said. "I'll miss you ... till we meet once more."

"That will be as God courses," answered his friend.

The Arena took its name from the space it enclosed. Through a window in the Commander's lofty sanctum, Ivar looked across tier after tier, sweeping in an austere but subtly eye-compelling pattern of grand ellipses, down toward the central pavement. Those levels were broad enough to be terraces rather than seats, and the walls between them held arched openings which led to the halls and chambers of the interior. Nevertheless, the suggestion of an antique theater was strong.

A band of Companions was drilling; for though it had seldom fought in the last few centuries, the order remained military in character, and was police as well as quasi-priesthood. Distance and size dwindled the men to insects. Their calls and footfalls were lost in hot stillness, as were any noises from town; only the Linn resounded, endlessly grinding. Most life seemed to be in the building itself, its changeful iridescences and the energy of its curves.

"Why did Elders make it like this?" Ivar wondered aloud.

A scientific base, combining residences and workrooms? But the ramps which connected floors twisted so curiously; the floors themselves had their abrupt rises and drops, for no discernible reason; the vaulted corridors passed among apartments no two of which were alike. And what had gone on in the crater middle? Mere gardening, to provide desert-weary eyes with a park? (But these parts were fertile, six million years ago.) Experiments? Games? Rites? Something for which man, and every race known to man, had no concept?

"Jaan says the chief purpose was to provide a gathering place, where minds might conjoin and thus achieve transcendence," Yakow answered. He turned to his escort. "Dismissed," he snapped. They saluted and left, closing behind them the human-installed door.

It had had to be specially shaped, to fit the portal of this suite. The outer office where the two men stood was like the inside of a multi-faceted jewel; colors did not sheen softly, as they did across the exterior of the Arena, but glanced and glinted, fire-fierce, wherever a sunbeam struck. Against such a backdrop, the few articles of furniture and equipment belonging to the present occupancy seemed twice austere: chairs fashioned of gnarly starkwood, a similar table, a row of shelves holding books and a comset, a carpet woven from the mineral-harsh plants that grew in Orcan shallows.

"Be seated, if you will," Yakow said, and folded his lankness down.

Won't he offer me anyhow a cup of tea? flickered in Ivar. Then, recollection from reading: *No, in this country, food or drink shared creates bonds of mutual obligation. Reckon he doesn't feel quite ready for that with me.*

Do I with him? Ivar took a seat confronting the stern old face.

Disconcertingly, Yakow waited for him to start conversation. After a hollow moment, Ivar attempted: "Uh, that Jaan you speak of, sir. Your prophet, right? I'd not demean your faith, please believe me. But may I ask some questions?"

Yakow nodded; the white beard brushed the infinity sign on his breast. "Whatever you wish, Firstling. Truth can only be clarified by questionings." He paused. "Besides— let us be frank from our start—in many minds it is not yet certitude that Jaan has indeed been possessed by Caruith the Ancient. The Companions of the Arena have taken no official position on the mystery."

Ivar started. "But I thought—I mean, religion—"

Yakow lifted a hand. "Pray hearken, Firstling. We serve no religion here."

"What? Sir, you believe, you've believed for, for hundreds of years, in Elders!"

"As we believe in Virgil or the moons." A ghost-smile flickered. "After all, we see them daily. Likewise do we see the Ancient relics."

Yakow grew earnest. "Of your patience, Firstling, let me explain a little. 'Religion' means faith in the supernatural, does it not? Most Orcans, like most Aeneans everywhere, do have that kind of faith. They maintain a God exists, and observe different ceremonies and injunctions on that account. If they have any sophistication, however, they admit their belief is nonscientific. It is not subject to empirical confirmation or disconfirmation. Miracles may have happened through divine intervention; but a miracle, by definition, involves a suspension of natural law, hence cannot be experimentally repeated. Aye, its historical truth or falsity can be indirectly investigated. But the confirmation of an event proves nothing, since it *could* be explained away scientifically. For example, if we could show that there was in fact a Jesus Christ who did in fact rise from his tomb, he may have been in a coma, not dead. Likewise, a disconfirmation proves nothing. For example, if it turns out that a given saint never lived, that merely shows people were naïve, not that the basic creed is wrong."

Ivar stared. *This talk—and before we've even touched*

*on any practicalities—from hierophant of impoverished
isolated desert dwellers?*

He collected his wits. *Well, nobody with access to electronic communications is truly isolated. And I wouldn't be
surprised if Yakow studied at University. I've met a few
Orcans there myself.*

*Just because person lives apart, in special style, it
doesn't mean he's ignorant or stupid. . . . M-m, do Terrans
think this about us?* The question aroused a mind-sharpen-
ing resentment.

"I repeat," Yakow was saying, "in my sense of the
word, we have no shared religion here. We do have a doctrine.

"It is a fact, verifiable by standard stratigraphic and ra-
dioisotopic dating methods, a fact that a mighty civilization kept an outpost on Aeneas, six thousand thousand
years ago. It is a reasonable inference that those beings
did not perish, but rather went elsewhere, putting childish
things away as they reached a new stage of evolution. And
it may conceivably be wishful thinking, but it does seem
more likely than otherwise, that the higher sentiences of
the cosmos take a benign interest in the lower, and seek to
aid them upward.

"This hope, if you wish to call it no more than that, is
what has sustained us."

The words were in themselves dispassionate; and though
the voice strenghtened, the tone was basically calm. Yet
Ivar looked into the countenance and decided to refrain
from responding:

*What proof have we of any further evolution? We've
met many different races by now, and some are wildly different, not just in their bodies but in their ways of thinkin'
and their capabilities. Still, we've found none we could call
godlike. And why should intelligence progress indefinitely?
Nothin' else in nature does. Beyond that point where technology becomes integral to species survival, what selection
pressure is there to increase brains? If anything, we
sophonts already have more than's good for us.*

He realized: *That's orthodox modern attitude, of course.
Maybe reflectin' sour grapes, or weariness of decadent society. No use denyin', what we've explored is one atom off
outer skin of one dustmote galaxy. . . .*

Aloud, he breathed, "Now Jaan claims Elders are about
to return? And mind of theirs is already inside him?"

"Crudely put," Yakow said. "You must talk to him yourself, at length." He paused. "I told you, the Companions do not thus far officially accept his claims. Nor do we reject them. We do acknowledge that, overnight, somehow a humble shoemaker gained certain powers, certain knowledge. 'Remarkable' is an altogether worthless word for whatever has happened."

"Who is he?" Ivar dared ask. "I've heard nothin' more than rumors, hints, guesses."

Yakow spoke now as a pragmatic leader. "When he first arose from obscurity, and ever more people began accepting his preachments: we officers of the Arena saw what explosive potential was here, and sought to hold the story quiet until we could at least evaluate it and its consequences. Jaan himself has been most cooperative with us. We could not altogether prevent word from spreading beyond our land. But thus far, the outside planet knows only vaguely of a new cult in this poor corner."

It may not know *any more than that,* Ivar thought; *however, it's sure ready to* believe *more. Could be I've got news for you, Commander.* "Who is he, really?"

"The scion of a common family, though once well-to-do as prosperity goes in Orcus. His father, Gileb, was a trader who owned several land vehicles and claimed descent from the founder of the Companions. His mother, Nomi, has a genealogy still more venerable, back to the first humans on Aeneas."

"What happened?"

"You may recall, some sixteen years ago this region suffered a period of turmoil. A prolonged sandstorm brought crop failure and the loss of caravans; then quarreling over what was left caused old family feuds to erupt anew. They shook the very Companions. For a time we were ineffective."

Ivar nodded. He had been searching his memory for news stories, and come upon accounts of how this man had won to rule over the order, restored its discipline and morale, and gone on to rescue his entire society from chaos. But that had been the work of years.

"His possessions looted by enemies who sought his blood, Gileb fled with his wife and their infant son," Yakow went on in a level tone. "They trekked across the Antonine, barely surviving, to a small nord settlement in the fertile part of it. There they found poverty-stricken refuge.

"When Gileb died, Nomi returned home with her by then half-dozen children, to this by then pacified country. Jaan had learned the shoemaker's trade, and his mother was—is—a skillful weaver. Between them, they supported the family. There was never enough left over for Jaan to consider marrying.

"Finally he had his revelation ... made his discovery ... whatever it was."

"Can you tell me?" Ivar asked low.

The gaze upon him hardened. "That can be talked of later," said Yakow. "For now, methinks best we consider what part you might play, Firstling, in the liberation of Aeneas from the Empire—maybe of mankind from humanness."

XVII

In headcloth, robe, and sandals, skin stained brown and hair black, Ivar would pass a casual glance. His features, build, and blue eyes were not typical; but though the Orcans had long been endogamous, not every gene of their originally mixed heritage was gone, and occasional throwbacks appeared; to a degree, the prophet himself was one. More serious anomalies included his dialect of Anglic, his ignorance of the native language, his imperfect imitation of manners, gait, a thousand subtleties.

Yet surely no Terran, boredly watching the playback from a spy device, would notice those differences. Many Orcans would likewise fail to do so, or would shrug off what they did see. After all, there were local and individual variations within the region; besides, this young man might well be back from several years' service among nords who had influenced him.

Those who looked closely and carefully were the least likely to mention a word of what they saw. For the stranger walked in company with the shoemaker.

It had happened erenow. Someone would hear Jaan preach, and afterward request a private audience. Customarily, the two of them went off alone upon the mountain.

Several jealous pairs of eyes followed Jaan and Ivar out of town. They spoke little until they were well away from people, into a great and aloof landscape.

Behind and above, rocks, bushes, stretches of bare gray dirt reached sharply blue-shadowed, up toward habitation and the crowning Arena. Overhead, the sky was empty save for the sun and one hovering vulch. Downward, land tumbled to the sullen flatness of the sea. Around were hills

which bore thin green and scattered houses. Traffic
trudged on dust-smoking roads. Ilion reared dark, the
Linn blinding white, to north and northeast; elsewhere the
horizon was rolling nakedness. A warm and pungent wind
stroked faces, fluttered garments, mumbled above the
mill-noise of the falls.

Jaan's staff swung and thumped in time with his feet as
he picked a way steadily along a browser trail. Ivar used
no aid but moved like a hunter. That was automatic; his
entire consciousness was bent toward the slow words:

"We can talk now, Firstling. Ask or declare what you
will. You cannot frighten or anger me, you who have
come as a living destiny."

"I'm no messenger of salvation," Ivar said low. "I'm
just very fallible human bein', who doesn't even believe in
God."

Jaan smiled. "No matter. I don't myself, in conventional
terms. We use 'destiny' in a most special sense. For the
moment, let's put it that you were guided here, or aided to
come here, in subtle ways"—his extraordinary eyes locked
onto the other and he spoke gravely—"because you have
the potential of becoming a savior."

"No, I, not me."

Again Jaan relaxed, clapped him on the shoulder, and
said, "I don't mean that mystically. Think back to your
discussions with High Commander Yakow. What Aeneas
needs is twofold, a uniting faith and a uniting secular
leader. The Firstman of Ilion, for so you will become in
time, has the most legitimate claim, most widely accepted,
to speak for this planet. Furthermore, memory of Hugh
McCormac will cause the entire sector to rally around
him, once he raises the liberation banner afresh.

"What Caruith proclaims will fire many people. But it is
too tremendous, too new, for them to live with day-to-
day. They must have a ... a political structure they understand and accept, to guide them through the upheaval.
You are the nucleus of that, Ivar Frederiksen."

"I, I don't know—I'm no kind of general or politician,
in fact I failed miserably before, and—"

"You will have skilled guidance. But never think we
want you for a figurehead. Remember, the struggle will
take years. As you grow in experience and wisdom, you
will find yourself taking the real lead."

Ivar squinted through desert dazzlement at a far-off dust devil, and said with care:

"I hardly know anything so far ... Jaan ... except what Yakow and couple of his senior officers have told me. They kept insistin' that to explain—religious?—no, transcendental—to explain transcendental aspect of this, only you would do."

"Your present picture is confused and incomplete, then," Jaan said.

Ivar nodded. "What I've learned— Let me try and summarize, may I? Correct me where I'm wrong.

"All Aeneas is primed to explode again. Touchoff spark would be hope, any hope. Given some initial success, more and more peoples elsewhere in Sector Alpha Crucis would join in. But how're we to start? We're broken, disarmed, occupied.

"Well, you preach that superhuman help is at hand. My part would be to furnish political continuity. Aeneans, especially nords, who couldn't go along with return of Elders, might well support Firstman of Ilion in throwin' off Terran yoke. And even true believers would welcome that kind of reinforcement, that human touch: especially since we men must do most of work, and most of dyin', ourselves."

Jaan nodded. "Aye," he said. "Deliverance which is not earned is of little worth in establishing freedom that will endure, of no worth in raising us toward the next level of evolution. The Ancients will *help* us. As we will afterward help them, in their millennial battle. . . . I repeat, we must not expect an instant revolution. To prepare will take years, and after that will follow years more of cruel strife. For a long time to come, your chief part will be simply to stay alive and at large, to be a symbol that keeps the hope of eventual liberation alight."

Ivar nerved himself to ask, "And you, meanwhile, do what?"

"I bear the witness," Jaan said; his tone was nearer humble than proud. "I plant the seeds of faith. As Caruith, I can give you, the Companions, the freedom leaders everywhere, some practical help: for instance, by reading minds under favorable circumstances. But in the ultimate, I am the embodiment of that past which is also the future.

"Surely at last I too must go hide in the wilds from the Terrans, after they realize my significance. Or perhaps they will kill me. No matter. That only destroys this body. And in so doing, it creates the martyr, it fulfills the cycle. For Caruith shall rise again."

The wind seemed to blow cold along Ivar's bones. "Who is Caruith? What is he?"

"The mind of an Ancient," Jaan said serenely.

"Nobody was clear about it, talkin' to me—"

"They felt best I explain to you myself. For one thing, you are not a semi-literate artisan or herdsman. You are well educated; you reject supernaturalism; to you, Caruith must use a different language from my preachings to common Orcans."

Ivar walked on, waiting. A jackrat scuttered from the bleached skull of a statha.

Jaan looked before him. He spoke in a monotone that, somehow, sang.

"I will begin with my return hither, after the exile years. I was merely a shoemaker, a trade I had learned in what spare time I found between the odd jobs which helped keep us alive. Yet I had also the public data screens, to read, watch, study, learn somewhat of this universe; and at night I would often go forth under the stars to think.

"Now we came back to Mount Cronos. I dreamed of enlisting in the Companions, but that could not be; their training must begin at a far earlier age than mine. However, a sergeant among them, counselor and magistrate to our district, took an interest in me. He helped me carry on my studies. And at last he arranged for me to assist, part time and for a small wage, in archaeological work.

"You realize that that is the driving force behind the Companions today. They began as a military band, and continue as civil authorities. Nova Roma could easily reorganize that for us, did we wish. But generations of prophets have convinced us the Ancients cannot be dead, must still dwell lordly in the cosmos. Then what better work is there than to seek what traces and clues are left among us? And who shall better carry it out than the Companions?"

Ivar nodded. This was a major reason why the University had stopped excavation in these parts: to avoid creating resentment among the inhabitants and their leaders. The paucity of reported results, ever since, was as-

sumed to be due to lack of notable finds. Suddenly Ivar
wondered how much had been kept secret.

The hypnotic voice went on: "That work made me feel,
in my depths, how vastly space-time overarches us and yet
how we altogether belong in it. I likewise brooded upon
the idea, an idea I first heard while in exile, that the Didonians have a quality of mind, of being, which is as far
beyond ours as ours is beyond blind instinct. Could the
Ancients have it too—not in the primitive dim unities of
our Neighbors, but in perfection? Might *we* someday have
it?

"So I wondered, and took ever more to wandering by
myself, aye, into the tunnels beneath the mountain when
no one else was there. And my heart would cry out for an
answer that never came.

"Until—

"It was a night near midwinter. The revolution had not
begun, but even here we knew how the oppression waxed,
and the people seethed, and chaos grew. Even we were in
scant supply of certain things, because offworld trade was
becoming irregular, as taxation and confiscation caused
merchantmen to move from this sector, and the spaceport
personnel themselves grew demoralized till there was no
proper traffic control. Yes, a few times out-and-out pirates
from the barbarian stars slipped past a fragmented guard
to raid and run. The woe of Aeneas was heavy on me.

"I looked at the blaze of the Crux twins, and at the
darkness which cleaves the Milky Way where the nebulae
hide from us the core of our galaxy: and walking along
the mountainside, I asked if, in all that majesty, our lives
alone could be senseless accidents, our pain and death for
nothing.

"It was cruelly cold, though. I entered the mouth of a
newly dug-out Ancient corridor, for shelter; or did something call me? I had a flashbeam, and almost like a sleep-
walker found myself bound deeper and deeper down those
halls.

"You must understand, the wonderful work itself had
not collapsed, save at the entrance, after millions of years
of earthquake and landslide. Once we dug past that, we
found a labyrinth akin to others. With our scanty man-
power and equipment, we might take a lifetime to map
the entire complex.

"Drawn by I knew not what, I went where men have

not yet been. With a piece of chalkstone picked from the
rubble, I marked my path; but that was well-nigh the last
glimmer of ordinary human sense in me, as I drew kilometer by kilometer near to my finality.

"I found it in a room where light shone cool from a tall
thing off whose simplicity my eyes glided; I could only see
that it must be an artifact, and think that most of it must
be not matter but energy. Before it lay this which I now
wear on my head. I donned it and—

"—there are no words, no thoughts for what came—

"After three nights and days I ascended; and in me
dwelt Caruith the Ancient."

XVIII

A bony sketch of a man, Colonel Mattu Luuksson had returned Chunderban Desai's greetings with a salute, declined refreshment, and sat on the edge of his lounger as if
he didn't want to submit his uniform to its self-adjusting
embrace. Nevertheless the Companion of the Arena spoke
courteously enough to the High Commissioner of Imperial
Terra.

"—decision was reached yesterday. I appreciate your
receiving me upon such short notice, busy as you must
be."

"I would be remiss in my duty, did I not make welcome
the representative of an entire nation," Desai answered.
He passed smoke through his lungs before he added, "It
does seem like, um, rather quick action, in a matter of this
importance."

"The order to which I have the honor to belong does
not condone hesitancy," Mattu declared. "Besides, you understand, sir, my mission is exploratory. Neither you nor
we will care to make a commitment before we know the
situation and each other more fully."

Desai noticed he was tapping his cigarette holder on the
edge of the ashtaker, and made himself stop. "We could
have discussed this by vid," he pointed out with a mildness
he didn't quite feel.

"No, sir, not very well. More is involved than words.
An electronic image of you and your office and any number of your subordinates would tell us nothing about the
total environment."

"I see. Is that why you brought those several men
along?"

"Yes. They will spend a few days wandering around the

city, gathering experiences and impressions to report to our council, to help us estimate the desirability of more visits."

Desai arched his brows. "Do you fear they may be corrupted?" The thought of fleshpots in Nova Roma struck him as weirdly funny; he choked back a laugh.

Mattu frowned—in anger or in concentration? *How can I read so foreign a face?* "I had best try to explain from the foundations, Commissioner," he said, choosing each word. "Apparently you have the impression that I am here to protest the recent ransacking of our community, and to work out mutually satisfactory guarantees against similar incidents in future. That is only a minor part of it.

"Your office appears to feel the Orcan country is full of rebellious spirits, in spite of the fact that almost no Orcans joined McCormac's forces. The suspicion is not unnatural. We dwell apart; our entire ethos is different from yours."

From Terra's sensate pragmatism, you mean, Desai thought. *Or its decadence, do you imply?* "As a keeper of law and order yourself," he said, "I trust you sympathize with the occasional necessity of investigating every possibility, however remote."

A Terran, in a position similar to Mattu's, would generally have grinned. The colonel stayed humorless: "More contact should reduce distrust. But this would be insufficient reason to change long-standing customs and policies.

"The truth is, the Companions of the Arena and the society they serve are not as rigid, not as xenophobic, as popular belief elsewhere has it. Our isolation was never absolute; consider our trading caravans, or those young men who spend years outside, in work or in study. It is really only circumstance which has kept us on the fringe— and, no doubt, a certain amount of human inertia.

"Well, the times are mutating. If we Orcans are not to become worse off, we must adapt. In the course of adaptation, we can better our lot. Although we are not obsessed with material wealth, and indeed think it disastrous to acquire too much, yet we do not value poverty, Commissioner; nor are we afraid of new ideas. Rather, we feel our own ideas have strength to survive, and actually spread among people who may welcome them."

Desai's cigaret was used up. He threw away the ill-smelling stub and inserted a fresh one. Anticipating, his palate winced. "You are interested in enlarged trade relationships, then," he said.

"Yes," Mattu replied. "We have more to offer than is commonly realized. I think not just of natural resources, but of hands and brains, if more of our youth can get adequate modern educations."

"And, hm-m-m, tourism in your area?"

"Yes," Mattu snapped. Obviously the thought was distasteful to him as an individual. "To develop all this will take time, which we have, and capital, which we have not. The nords were never interested ... albeit I confess the Companions never made any proposal to them. We have now conceived the hope that the Imperium may wish to help."

"Subsidies?"

"They need not be great, nor continue long. In return, the Imperium gains not simply our friendship, but our influence, as Orcans travel further and oftener across Aeneas. You face a nord power structure which, on the whole, opposes you, and which you are unlikely to win over. Might not Orcan influence help transform it?"

"Perhaps. In what direction, though?"

"Scarcely predictable at this stage, is it? For that matter, we could still decide isolation is best. I repeat, my mission is no more than a preliminary exploration—for both our sides, Commissioner."

Chunderban Desai, who had the legions of the Empire at his beck, looked into the eyes of the stranger; and it was Chunderban Desai who felt a tinge of fear.

The young lieutenant from Mount Cronos had openly called Tatiana Thane to ask if he might visit her "in order to make the acquaintance of the person who best knows Ivar Frederiksen. Pray understand, respected lady, we do not lack esteem for him. However, indirectly he has been the cause of considerable trouble for us. It has occurred to me that you may advise us how we can convince the authorities we are not in league with him."

"I doubt it," she answered, half amused at his awkward earnestness. The other half of her twisted in re-aroused pain, and wanted to deny his request. But that would be cowardice.

When he entered her apartment, stiff in his uniform, he offered her a token of appreciation, a hand-carved pendant from his country. To study the design, she must hold it in her palm close to her face; and she read the engraved question, *Are we spied on?*

Her heart sprang. After an instant, she shook her head, and knew the gesture was too violent. No matter. Stewart sent a technician around from time to time, who verified that the Terrans had planted no bugs. Probably the underground itself had done so. . . . The lieutenant extracted an envelope from his tunic and bowed as he handed it to her.

"Read at your leisure," he said, "but my orders are to watch you destroy this afterward."

He seated himself. His look never left her. She, in her own chair, soon stopped noticing. After the third time through Ivar's letter, she mechanically heeded Frumious Bandersnatch's plaintive demand for attention.

Following endearments which were nobody else's business, and a brief account of his travels:

"—prophet, though he denies literal divine inspiration. I wonder what difference? His story is latter-day Apocalypse.

"I don't know whether I can believe it. His quiet certainty carries conviction; but I don't claim any profound knowledge of people. I could be fooled. What *is* undeniable is that under proper conditions he can read my mind, better than any human telepath I ever heard of, better than top-gifted humans are supposed to be able to. Or nonhumans, even? I was always taught telepathy is not universal language; it's not enough to sense your subject's radiations, you have to learn what each pattern means to *him*; and of course patterns vary from individual to individual, still more from culture to culture, tremendously from species to species. And to this day, phenomenon's not too well understood. I'd better just give you Jean's own story, though my few words won't have anything of overwhelming *impression* he makes.

"He says, after finding this Elder artifact I mentioned, he put 'crown' on his head. I suppose that would be natural thing to do. It's adjustable, and ornamental, and maybe he's right, maybe command was being broadcast. Anyhow, something indescribable happened, heaven and hell together, at first mostly hell because of fear and strangeness and uprooting of his whole mind, later mostly heaven—and now, Jaan says, neither word is any good, there are no words for what he experiences, what he is.

"In scientific terms, if they aren't pseudoscientific (where do you draw line, when dealing with unknown?), what he says happened is this. Long ago, Elders, or Ancients as they call them here, had base on Aeneas, same as on many similar planets. It was no mere research base. They were serving huge purpose I'll come to later. Suggestion is right that they actually caused Didonians to evolve, as one experiment among many, all aimed at creating more intelligence, more consciousness, throughout cosmos.

"At last they withdrew, but left one behind whom Jean gives name of Caruith, though he says spoken name is purely for benefit of our limited selves. It wasn't original Caruith who stayed; and original wasn't individual like you or me anyway, but part—aspects?—attribute?—of glorious totality which Didonians only hint at. What Caruith did was let heeshself be scanned, neurone by neurone, so entire personality pattern could be recorded in some incredible fashion.

"Sorry, darling, I just decided pronoun like 'heesh' is okay for Neighbors but too undignified for Ancients. I'll say 'he' because I'm more used to that; could just as well, or just as badly, be 'she,' of course.

"When Jaan put on circlet, apparatus was activated, and stored pattern was imposed on his nervous system.

"You can guess difficulties. What shabby little word, 'difficulties'! Jaan has human brain, human body; and in fact, Elders thought mainly in terms of Didonian finding their treasure. Jaan can't do anything his own organism hasn't got potential for. Original Caruith could maybe solve a thousand simultaneous differential equations in his 'head,' in split second, if he wanted to; but Caruith using Jaan's primitive brain can't. You get idea?

"Noneless, Elders had realized Didonians might not be first in that room. They'd built flexibility into system. Furthermore, all organisms have potentials that aren't ordinarily used. Let me give you clumsy example. You play chess, paint pictures, hand-pilot aircraft, and analyze languages. I know. But suppose you'd been born into world where nobody had invented chess, paint, aircraft, or semantic analysis. You see? Or think how sheer physical and mental training can bring out capabilities in almost anybody.

"So after three days of simply getting adjusted, to point where he could think and act at all, Jaan came back topside. Since then, he's been integrating more and more with this great mind that shares his brain. He says at last they'll become *one*, more Caruith than Jaan, and he rejoices at prospect.

"Well, what does he preach? What do Elders want? Why did they do what they have done?

"Again, it's impossible to put in few words. I'm going to try but I know I will fail. Maybe your imagination can fill in gaps. You've certainly got good mind, sweetheart.

"Ancients, Elders, Builders, High Ones, Old Shen, whatever we call them—and Jaan won't give them separate name, he says that would be worse misleading than 'Caruith' already is—evolved billions of years ago, near galactic center where stars are older and closer together. We're way out on thin fringe of spiral arm, you remember. At that time, there had not been many generations of stars, elements heavier than helium were rare, planets with possibility of life were few. Elders went into space and found it lonelier than we can dream, we who have more inhabited worlds around than anybody has counted. They turned inward, they deliberately forced themselves to keep on evolving mind, lifetime after lifetime, because they had no one else to talk to— How I wish I could send you record of Jaan explaining!

"Something happened. He says he isn't yet quite able to understand what. Split in race, in course of millions of years; not ideological difference as we think of ideology, but two different ways of perceiving, of evaluating reality, two different purposes to impose on universe. We dare not say one branch is good, one evil; we can only say they are irreconcilable. Call them Yang and Yin, but don't try to say which is which.

"In crudest possible language, *our* Elders see goal of life as consciousness, transcendence of everything material, unification of mind not only in this galaxy but throughout cosmos, so its final collapse won't be end but will be beginning. While Others seek—mystic oneness with energy—supreme experience of Acceptance— No, I don't suppose you can fairly call them death-oriented.

"Jaan likes old Terran quotation I know, as describing Elders: 'To strive, to seek, to find, and not to yield.' (Do you know it?) And for Others, what? Not 'Kismet,' really; that at least implies doing God's will, and Others deny God altogether. Nor 'nihilism,' which I reckon implies desire for chaos, maybe as necessary for rebirth. What Others stand for is so alien that— Oh, I'll write, knowing I'm wrong, that they believe rise, fall, and infinite extinction are our sole realities, and sole fulfillment that life can ultimately have is harmony with this curve.

"In contrast, Jaan says life, if it follows Elder star, will at last *create* God, *become* God.

"To that end, Elders have been watching new races arise on new planets, and helping them, guiding them, sometimes even bringing them into being like Didonians. They can't watch always over everything; they haven't over us. For Others have been at work too, and must be opposed.

"It's not war as we understand war; not on that level. On our level, it is.

"Analogy again. You may be trying to arrive at some vital decision that will determine your entire future. You may be reasoning, you may be wrestling with your emotions, but it's all in your mind; nobody else need see a thing.

"Only it's *not* all in your mind. Unhealthy body means unhealthy thinking. Therefore, down on cellular level, your white blood corpuscles and antigens are waging relentless, violent war on invaders. And its outcome will have much to do with what happens in your head—maybe everything. Do you see?

"It's like that. What intelligent life (I mean sophonts as we know them; Elders and Others are trans-intelligent) does is crucial. And one tiny bit of one galaxy, like ours, can be turning point. Effects multiply, you see. Just as it took few starfaring races to start many more on same course, irreversible change, so it could take few new races who go over to wholly new way of evolution for rest to do likewise eventually.

"Will that level be of Elders or of Others? Will we break old walls and reach, however painfully, for what is infinite, or will we find most harmonious, beautiful, noble way to move toward experience of oblivion?

"You see what I was getting at, that words like 'positive' and 'negative,' 'active' and 'passive,' 'evolutionism' and 'nihilism,' 'good' and 'evil' don't mean anything in this context? Beings unimaginably far beyond us have two opposing ways of comprehending reality. Which are we to choose?

"We have no escape from choosing. We can accept authority, limitations, instructions; we can compromise; we can live out our personal lives safely; and it's victory for Others throughout space we know, because right now *Homo sapiens* does happen to be leading species in these parts. Or we can take our risks, strike for our freedom, and if we win it, look for Elders to return and raise us, like children of theirs, toward being more than what we have ever been before.

"That's what Jaan says. Tanya, darling, I just don't know—"

She lifted eyes from the page. It flamed in her: *I do. Already.*

Nomi dwelt with her children in a two-room adobe at the bottom end of Grizzle Alley. Poverty flapped and racketed everywhere around them. It did not stink, for even the poorest Orcans were of cleanly habits and, while there was scant water to spare for washing, the air quickly parched out any malodors. Nor were there beggars; the Companions took in the desperately needy, and assigned them what work they were capable of doing. But ragged shapes crowded this quarter with turmoil: milling and yelling children, women overburdened with jugs and baskets, men plying their trades, day laborer, muledriver, carter, scavenger, artisan, butcher, tanner, priest, minstrel, vendor chanting or chaffering about his pitiful wares. Among battered brown walls, on tangled lanes of rutted iron-hard earth, Ivar felt more isolated than if he had been alone in the Dreary.

The mother of the prophet put him almost at ease. They had met briefly. Today he asked for Jaan, and heard the latter was absent, and was invited to come in and wait over a cup of tea. He felt a trifle guilty, for he had in fact made sure beforehand that Jaan was out, walking and earnestly talking with his disciples, less teaching them than using them for a sounding board while he groped his own way toward comprehension and integration of his double personality.

But I must learn more myself, before I make that terrible commitment he wants. And who can better give me some sense of what he really is, than this woman?

She was alone, the youngsters being at work or in school. The inside of the hut was therefore quiet, once its door had closed off street noise. Sunlight slanted dusty through the glass of narrow windows; few Orcans could afford vitryl. The room was cool, shadowy, crowded but, in its neatness, not cluttered. Nomi's loom filled one corner, a half-finished piece of cloth revealing a subtle pattern of subdued hues. Across from it was a set of primitive kitchen facilities. Shut-beds for her and her oldest son took most of the remaining space. In the middle of the room was a plank table surrounded by benches, whereat she seated her guest. Food on high shelves or hung from the rafters—a little preserved meat, more dried vegetables and hardtack—made the air fragrant. At the rear an open doorway showed a second room, occupied mostly by bunks.

Nomi moved soft-footed across the clay floor, poured from the pot she had made ready, and sat down opposite Ivar in a rustle of skirts. She had been beautiful when young, and was still handsome in a haggard fashion. If anything, her gauntness enhanced a pair of wonderful gray eyes, such as Jaan had in heritage from her. The coarse blue garb, the hood which this patriarchal society laid over the heads of widows, on her were not demeaning; she had too much inner pride to need vanity.

They had made small talk while she prepared the bitter Orcan tea. She knew who he was. Jaan said he kept no secrets from her, because she could keep any he asked from the world. Now Ivar apologized: "I didn't mean to interrupt your work, my lady."

She smiled. "A welcome interruption, Firstling."

"But, uh, you depend on it for your livin'. If you'd rather go on with it—"

She chuckled. "Pray take not away from me this excuse for idleness."

"Oh. I see." He hated to pry, it went against his entire training, and he knew he would not be good at it. But he had to start frank discussion somehow. "It's only, well, it seemed to me you aren't exactly rich. I mean, Jaan hasn't been makin' shoes since—what happened to him."

"No. He has won a higher purpose." She seemed amused by the inadequacy of the phrase.

"Uh, he never asks for contributions, I'm told. Doesn't that make things hard for you?"

She shook her head. "His next two brothers have reached an age where they can work part time. It could

be whole time, save that I will not have it; they must get
what learning they can. And . . . Jaan's followers help us.
Few of them can afford any large donation, but a bit of
food, a task done for us without charge, such gifts mount
up."

Her lightness had vanished. She frowned at her cup and
went on with some difficulty: "It was not quite simple for
me to accept at first. Ever had we made our own way, as
did Gileb's parents and mine ere we were wedded. But
what Jaan does is so vital that— Ay-ah, acceptance is a
tiny sacrifice."

"You do believe in Caruith, then?"

She lifted her gaze to his, and his dropped as she answered, "Shall I not believe my own good son and my husband's?"

"Oh, yes, certainly, my lady," he floundered. "I beg
your pardon if I seemed to— Look, I am outsider here,
I've only known him few days and— Do you see? You
have knowledge of him to guide you in decidin' he's not,
well, victim of delusion. I don't have that knowledge, not
yet, anyway."

Nomi relented, reached across the table and patted his
hand. "Indeed, Firstling. You do right to ask. I am glad-
dened that in you he has found the worthy comrade he
needs."

Has he?

Perhaps she read the struggle on his face, for she continued, low-voiced and looking beyond him:

"Why should I wonder that you wonder? I did likewise.
When he vanished for three dreadful days, and came
home utterly changed— Yes, I thought a blood vessel must
have burst in his brain, and wept for my kind, hard-work-
ing first-born boy, who had gotten so little from life.

"Afterward I came to understand how he had been sin-
gled out as no man ever was before in all of space and
time. But that wasn't a joy, Firstling, as we humans know
joy. His glory is as great and as cruel as the sun. Most
likely he shall have to die. Only the other night, I dreamed
he was Shoemaker Jaan again, married to a girl I used to
think about for him, and they had laid their first baby in
my arms. I woke laughing. . . ." Her fingers closed hard on
the cup. "That cannot be, of course."

Ivar never knew if he would have been able to probe

further. An interruption saved him: Robhar, the youngest disciple, knocking at the door.

"I thought you might be here, sir," the boy said breathlessly. Though the master had identified the newcomer only by a false name, his importance was obvious. "Caruith will come as soon as he can." He thrust forward an envelope. "For you."

"Huh?" Ivar stared.

"The mission to Nova Roma is back, sir," Robhar said, nigh bursting with excitement. "It brought a letter for you. The messenger gave it to Caruith, but he told me to bring it straight to you."

To Heraz Hyronsson stood on the outside. Ivar ripped the envelope open. At the end of several pages came the bold signature *Tanya.* His own account to her had warned her how to address a reply.

"Excuse me," he mumbled, and sat down to gulp it.

Afterward he was very still for a while, his features locked. Then he made an excuse for leaving, promised to get in touch with Jaan soon, and hurried off. He had some tough thinking to do.

XIX

None but a few high-ranking officers among the Companions had been told who Ivar was. They addressed him as Heraz when in earshot of others. He showed himself as seldom as feasible, dining with Yakow in the Commander's suite, sleeping in a room nearby which had been lent him, using rear halls, ramps, and doorways for his excursions. In that vast structure, more than half of it unpopulated, he was never conspicuous. The corps knew their chief was keeping someone special, but were too disciplined to gossip about it.

Thus he and Yakow went almost unseen to the chamber used as a garage. Jaan was already present, in response to word from a runner. A guard saluted as the three men entered an aircar; and no doubt much went on in his head, but he would remain close-mouthed. The main door glided aside. Yakow's old hands walked skillfully across the console. The car lifted, purred forth into the central enclosure, rose a vertical kilometer, and started leisurely southward.

A wind had sprung up as day rolled toward evening. It whined around the hull, which shivered. The Sea of Orcus bore whitecaps on its steel-colored surface and flung waves against its shores; where spray struck and evaporated, salt was promptly hoar. The continental shelf glowed reddish from long rays filtered through a dust-veil which obscured the further desert; the top of that storm broke off in thin clouds and streamed yellow across blue-black heaven.

Yakow put controls on automatic, swiveled his seat around, and regarded the pair who sat aft of him. "Very well, we have the meeting place you wanted, Firstling," he said. "Now will you tell us why?"

Ivar felt as if knives and needles searched him. He flicked his glance toward Jaan's mild countenance, remembered what lay beneath it, and recoiled to stare out the canopy at the waters which they were crossing. *I'm supposed to cope with these two?* he thought despairingly.

Well, there's nobody else for job. Nobody in whole wide universe. Against his loneliness, he hugged to him the thought that they might prove to be in truth his comrades in the cause of liberation.

"I, I'm scared of possible spies, bugs," he said.

"Not in my part of the Arena," Yakow snapped. "You know how often and thoroughly we check."

"But Terrans have resources of, of entire Empire to draw on. They could have stuff we don't suspect. Like telepathy." Ivar forced himself to turn back to Jaan. *"You* scan minds."

"Within limits," the prophet cautioned. "I have explained."

Yes. He took me down into mountain's heart and showed me machine—device—whatever it is that he says held record of Caruith. He wouldn't let me touch anything, though I couldn't really blame him, and inside I was just as glad for excuse not to. And there he sensed my thoughts. I tested him every way I could imagine, and he told me exactly what I was thinkin', as well as some things I hadn't quite known I was thinkin'. Yes.

He probably wouldn't've needed telepathy to see my sense of privacy outraged. He smiled and told me—

"Fear not. I have only my human nervous system, and it isn't among the half-talented ones which occur rarely in our species. By myself, I cannot resonate any better than you, Firstling." Bleakly: "This is terrible for Caruith, like being deaf or blind; but he endures, that awareness may be helped to fill reality. And down here—" Glory: "Here his former vessel acts to amplify, to recode, like a living brain center. Within its range of operation, Caruith-Jaan is part of what he rightfully should be: of what he will be again, when his people return and make for us that body we will have deserved."

I can believe anyway some fraction of what he claimed. Artificial amplification and relayin' of telepathy are beyond Terran science; but I've read of experiments with

*it, in past eras when Terran science was more progressive
than now. Such technology is not too far beyond our
present capabilities: almost matter of engineerin' development rather than pure research.*

*Surely it's negligible advance over what we know, com-
pared to recordin' of entire personality, and reimposition
of pattern on member of utterly foreign species. . . .*

"Well," Ivar said, "if you, usin' artifact not really intended for your kind of organism, if you scan minds within
radius of hundred meters or so—then naturally endowed
bein's ought to do better."

"There are no nonhumans in Orcan territory," Yakow
said.

"Except Erannath," Ivar retorted.

Did the white-bearded features stiffen? Did Jaan wince?
"Ah, yes," the Commander agreed. "A temporary excep-
tion. No xenosophonts are in Arena or town."

"Could be human mutants, maybe genetic-tailored,
who've infiltrated." Ivar shrugged. "Or maybe no telepathy
at all; maybe some gadget your detectors won't register. I
repeat, you probably don't appreciate as well as I do what
variety must exist on thousands of Imperial planets. Nobody can keep track. Imperium could well import surprise
for us from far side of Empire." He sighed. "Or, okay,
call me paranoid. Call this trip unnecessary. You're probably right. Fact is, however, I've got to decide what to
do—question involvin' not simply me, but my whole society—and I feel happier discussin' it away from any imaginable surveillance."

Such as may lair inside Mount Cronos.

*If it does, I don't think it's happened to tap my thoughts
these past several hours. Else my sudden suspicions that
came from Tanya's letter could've gotten me arrested.*

Jaan inquired shrewdly, "Has the return of our Nova
Roma mission triggered you?"

Ivar nodded with needless force.

"The message you received from your betrothed—"

"I destroyed it," Ivar admitted, for the fact could not
be evaded were he asked to show the contents. "Because
of personal elements." They weren't startled; most nords
would have done the same. "However, you can guess
what's true, that she discussed her connection with freedom movement. My letter to her and talks with your

emissary had convinced her our interests and yours are identical in throwin' off Imperial yoke."

"And now you wish more details," Yakow said.

Ivar nodded again. "Sir, wouldn't you? Especially since it looks as if Commissioner Desai will go along with your plan. That'll mean Terrans comin' here, to discuss and implement economic growth of this region. What does that imply for our liberation?"

"I thought I had explained," said Jaan patiently. "The plan is Caruith's. Therefore it is long-range, as it must be; for what hope lies in mere weapons? Let us rise in force before the time is ready, and the Empire will crush us like a thumb crushing a sandmite."

Caruith's plan— The aircar had passed across the sea and the agricultural lands which fringed its southern shore, to go out over the true desert. This country made the Dreary of Ironland seem lush. Worn pinnacles lifted above ashen dunes; dust scudded and whirled; Ivar glimpsed fossil bones of an ocean monster, briefly exposed for wind to scour away, the single token of life. Low in the west, Virgil glowered through a haze that whistled.

"Idea seems . . . chancy, over-subtle. . . . Can any nonhuman fathom our character that well?" he fretted.

"Remember, in me he is half human," Jaan replied; "and he has a multimillion-year history to draw on. Men are no more unique than any other sophonts. Caruith espies likenesses among races to which we are blind."

"I too grow impatient," Yakow sighed. "I yearn to see us free, but can hardly live long enough. Yet Caruith is right. We must prepare all Aeneans, so when the day comes, all will rise together."

"The trade expansion is a means to that end," Jaan assured. "It should cause Orcans to travel across the planet, meeting each sort of other Aenean, leavening with faith and fire. Oh, our agents will not be told to preach; they will not know anything except that they have practical bargains to drive and arrangements to make. But they will inevitably fall into conversations, and this will arouse interest, and nords or Riverfolk or tinerans or whoever will invite friends to come hear what the outlander has to say."

"I've heard that several times," Ivar replied, "and I still have trouble understandin'. Look, sirs. You don't expect mass conversion to Orcan beliefs, do you? I tell you, that's impossible. Our different cultures are too strong in their particular reverences—traditional religions, paganism, Cosmenosis, ancestor service, whatever it may be."

"Of course," Jaan said softly. "But can you not appreciate, Firstling, their very conviction is what counts? Orcans will by precept and example make every Aenean redouble his special fervor. And nothing in my message contradicts any basic tenet of yonder faiths. Rather, the return of the Ancients fulfills all hopes, no matter what form they have taken."

"I know, I know. Sorry, I keep on bein' skeptical. But never mind. I don't suppose it can do any harm; and as you say, it might well keep spirit of resistance alive. What about me, though? What am I supposed to be doin' meanwhile?"

"At a time not far in the future," Yakow said, "you will raise the banner of independence. We need to make preparations first; mustn't risk you being seized at once by the enemy. Most likely, you'll have to spend years offplanet, waging guerrilla warfare on Dido, for example, or visiting foreign courts to negotiate for their support."

Ivar collected his nerve and interrupted: "Like Ythri?"

"Well ... yes." Yakow dismissed his own infinitesimal hesitation. "Yes, we might get help from the Domain, not while yours is a small group of outlaws, but later, when our cause comes to look more promising." He leaned forward. "To begin with, frankly, your role will be a gadfly's. You will distract the Empire from noticing too much the effects of Orcans traveling across Aeneas. You cannot hope to accomplish more, not for the first several years."

"I don't know," Ivar said with what stubbornness he could rally. "We might get clandestine help from Ythri sooner, maybe quite soon. Some hints Erannath let drop—" He straightened in his seat. "Why not go talk to him right away?"

Jaan looked aside. Yakow said, "I fear that isn't practical at the moment, Firstling."

"How come? Where is he?"

Yakow clamped down sternness. "You yourself worry about what the enemy may eavesdrop on. What you don't know, you cannot let slip. I must request your patience in this matter."

It shuddered in Ivar as if the wind outside blew between

his ribs. He wondered how well he faked surrender and relaxation. "Okay."

"We had better start back," Yakow said. "Night draws nigh."

He turned himself around and then the aircraft. A dusk was already in the cabin, for the storm had thickened. Ivar welcomed the concealment of his face. And did outside noise drown the thud-thud-thud of his pulse? He said most slowly, "You know, Jaan, one thing I've never heard bespoken. What does Caruith's race look like?"

"It doesn't matter," was the reply. "They are more mind than body. Indeed, their oneness includes numerous different species. Think of Dido. In the end, all races will belong."

"Uh-huh. However, I can't help bein' curious. Let's put it this way. What did the body look like that actually lay down under scanner?"

"Why . . . well—"

"Come on. Maybe your Orcans are so little used to pictures that they don't insist on description. I assure you, companyo, other Aeneans are different. They'll ask. Why not tell me?"

"*Kah*, hm, *kah*—" Jaan yielded. He seemed a touch confused, as if the consciousness superimposed on his didn't work well at a large distance from the reinforcing radiations of the underground vessel. "Yes. He . . . male, aye, in a bisexual warm-blooded species . . . not mammalian; descended from ornithoids. . . . human-seeming in many ways, but beautiful, far more refined and sculptured than us. Thin features set at sharp angles; a speaking voice like music— No." Jaan broke off. "I will not say further. It has no significance."

You've said plenty, tolled in Ivar.

Talk was sparse for the rest of the journey. As the car moved downward toward an Arena that had become a bulk of blackness studded with a few lights, the Firstling spoke. "Please, I want to go off by myself and think. I'm used to space and solitude when I make important decisions. How about lendin' me this flitter? I'll fly to calm area, settle down, watch moons and stars—return before mornin' and let you know how things appear to me. May I?"

He had well composed and mentally rehearsed his speech. Yakow raised no objection; Jaan gave his shoulder a sympathetic squeeze. "Surely," said the prophet. "Courage and wisdom abide with you, dear friend."

When he had let the others out, Ivar lifted fast, and cut a thunderclap through the air in his haste to be gone. The dread of pursuit bayed at his heels.

Harsh through him went: *They aren't infallible. I took them by surprise. Jaan should've been prepared with any description but true one—one that matches what Tanya relayed to me from Commissioner Desai, about Merseian agent loose on Aeneas.*

Stiffening wind after sunset filled the air around the lower mountainside with fine sand. Lavinia showed a dim half-disc overhead, but cast no real light; and there were no stars. Nor did villages and farmsteads scattered across the hills reveal themselves. Vision ended within meters.

Landing on instruments, Ivar wondered if this was lucky for him. He could descend unseen, where otherwise he would have had to park behind some ridge or grove kilometers away and slink forward afoot. Indeed, he had scant choice. Walking any distance through a desert storm, without special guidance equipment he didn't have along, posed too much danger of losing his way. But coming so near town and Arena, he risked registering on the detectors of a guard post, and somebody dispatching a squad to investigate.

Well, the worst hazard lay in a meek return to his quarters. He found with a certain joy that fear had left him, as had the hunger and thirst of supperlessness, washed away by the excitement now coursing through him. He donned the overgarment everyone took with him on every trip, slid back the door, and jumped to the ground.

The gale hooted and droned. It sheathed him in chill and a scent of iron. Grit stung. He secured his nightmask and groped forward.

For a minute he worried about going astray in spite of planning. Then he stubbed his toe on a rock which had fallen off a heap, spoil from the new excavation. The entrance was dead ahead uphill, to that tunnel down which Jaan had taken him.

He didn't turn on the flashbeam he had borrowed from the car's equipment, till he stood at the mouth. Thereafter he gripped it hard, as his free hand sought for a latch.

Protection from weather, the manmade door needed no

lock against a folk whose piety was founded on relics.
When he had closed it behind him, Ivar stood in abrupt
silence, motionless cold, a dark whose thickness was broken only by the wan ray from the flash. His breath sounded too loud in his ears. Fingers sought comfort from the
heavy sheath knife he had borne from Windhome; but it
was his solitary weapon. To carry anything more, earlier,
would have provoked instant suspicion.

What will I find?

*Probably nothin'. I can take closer look at Caruith ma-
chine, but I haven't tools to open it and analyze. As for
what might be elsewhere ... these corridors twist on and
on, in dozen different sets.*

*Noneless, newest discovery, plausibly barred to public
while exploration proceeds, is most logical place to
hide—whatever is to be hidden. And*—his gaze went to
the dust of megayears, tumbled and tracked like the dust
of Luna when man first fared into space—*I could find
traces which'll lead me further, if any have gone before
me.*

He began to walk. His footfalls clopped hollowly back
off the ageless vaulting.

*Why am I doin' this? Because Merseians may have part
in events? Is it bad if they do? Tanya feels happy about
what she's heard. She thinks Roidhunate might really
come to our aid, and hopes I can somehow contact that
agent.*

*But Ythri might help too. In which case, why won't Or-
can chiefs let me see Erannath? Their excuse rings thin.*

*And if Ancients are workin' through Merseians, as is
imaginable, why have they deceived Jaan? Shouldn't he
know?*

*(Does he? It wouldn't be information to broadcast. Ter-
ran Imperium may well dismiss Jaan's claims as simply another piece of cultism, which it'd cause more trouble to
suppress than it's worth ... but never if Imperium suspected Merseia was behind it! So maybe he is withholdin' full
story. Except that doesn't feel right. He's too sincere, too
rapt, and, yes, too bewildered, to play double game. Isn't
he?)*

*I've got to discover truth, or lose what right I ever had
to lead my people.*

Ivar marched on into blindness.

XX

A kilometer deep within the mountain, he paused outside the chamber of Jaan's apotheosis. His flashbeam barely skimmed the metal enigma before seeking back to the tunnel floor.

Here enough visits had gone on of late years that the dust was scuffed confusion. Ivar proceeded down the passage. The thing in the room cast him a last reflection and was lost to sight. He had but the one bobbing blob of luminance to hollow out a place for himself in the dark. Now that he advanced slowly, carefully, the silence was well-nigh total. *Bad-a-bad,* went his heart, *bad-a-bad, bad-a-bad.*

After several meters, the blurriness ended. He would not have wondered to see individual footprints. Besides Jaan, officers of the Companions whom the prophet brought hither had surely ventured somewhat further. What halted him was sudden orderliness. The floor had been swept smooth.

He stood for minutes while his thoughts grew fangs. When he continued, the knife was in his right fist.

Presently the tunnel branched three ways. That was a logical point for people to stop. Penetrating the maze beyond was a task for properly equipped scientists; and no scientists would be allowed here for a long while to come. Ivar saw that the broom, or whatever it was, had gone down all the mouths. *Quite reasonable,* trickled through him. *Visitors wouldn't likely notice sweepin' had been done, unless they came to place where change in dust layers was obvious. Or unless they half expected it, like me ... expected strange traces would have to be wiped out....*

170

He went into each of the forks, and found that the hand-iwork ended after a short distance in two of them. What reached onward was simply the downdrift of geological ages. The third had been swept for some ways farther, though not since the next-to-last set of prints had been made. Two sets of those were human, one Ythrian; only the humans had returned. Superimposed were other marks, which were therefore more recent.

They were the tracks of a being who walked on birdlike claws.

Again Ivar stood. Cold gnawed him.

Should I turn right around and run?

Where could I run to?

And Erannath— That decided him. What other friend remained to the free Aeneans? If the Ythrian was alive.

He stalked on. A pair of doorways gaped along his path. He flashed light into them, but saw just empty chambers of curious shape.

Then the floor slanted sharply downward, and he rounded a curve, and from an arch ahead of him in the right wall there came a wan yellow glow.

He gave himself no chance to grow daunted, snapped off his beam and glided to the spot. Poised for a leap, he peered around the edge.

Another cell, this one hexagonal and high-domed, reached seven meters into the rock. Shadows hung in it as heavy, chill, and stagnant as the air. They were cast by a ponderous steel table to which were welded a lightglobe, a portable sanitary facility, and a meter-length chain. Free on its top stood a plastic tumbler and water pitcher, free on the floor lay a mattress, the single relief from iridescent hardness.

"Erannath!" Ivar cried.

The Ythrian hunched on the pad. His feathers were dull and draggled, his head gone skull-gaunt. The chain ended in a manacle that circled his left wrist.

Ivar entered. The Ythrian struggled out of dreams and knew him. The crest erected, the yellow eyes came ablaze. *"Hyaa-aa,"* he breathed.

Ivar knelt to embrace him. "What've they done?" the man cried. "Why? My God, those bastards—"

Erannath shook himself. His voice came hoarse, but strength rang into it. "No time for sentiment. What brought you here? Were you followed?"

"I g-g-got suspicious." Ivar hunkered back on his heels, hugged his knees, mastered his shock. The prisoner was all too aware of urgency; that stood forth from every quivering plume. And who could better know what dangers dwelt in this tomb? Never before had Ivar's mind run swifter.

"No," he said, "I don't think they suspect me in turn. I made excuse to flit off alone, came back and landed under cover of dust storm, found nobody around when I entered. What got me wonderin' was letter today from my girl. She'd learned of Merseian secret agent at large on Aeneas, telepath of some powerful kind. His description answers to Jaan's of Caruith. Right away, I thought maybe cruel trick was bein' played. Jaan should've had less respect for my feelin's and examined—I didn't show anybody letter, and kept well away from Arena as much as possible, before returnin' to look for myself."

"You did well." Erannath stroked talons across Ivar's head; and the man knew it for an accolade. "Beware. Aycharaych is near. We must hope he sleeps, and will sleep till you have gone."

"Till we have."

Erannath chuckled. His chain clinked. He did not bother to ask, How do you propose to cut this?

"I'll go fetch tools," Ivar said.

"No. Too chancy. You must escape with the word. At that, if you do get clear, I probably will be released unharmed. Aycharaych is not vindictive. I believe him when he says he sorrows at having to torture me."

Torture? No marks. . . . Of course. Keep sky king chained, buried alive, day after night away from sun, stars, wind. It'd be less cruel to stretch him over slow fire. Ivar gagged on rage.

Erannath saw, and warned: "You cannot afford indignation either. Listen. Aycharaych has talked freely to me. I think he must be lonely, shut away down here with nothing but his machinations and the occasional string he pulls on his puppet prophet. Or is his reason that, in talking, he brings associations into my consciousness, and thus reads more of what I know? This is why I have been kept alive. He wants to drain me of data."

"What is he?" Ivar whispered.

"A native of a planet he calls Chereion, somewhere in the Merseian Roidhunate. Its civilization is old, old—

formerly wide-faring and mighty—yes, he says the Chereionites were the Builders, the Ancients. He will not tell me what made them withdraw. He confesses that now they are few, and what power they wield comes wholly from their brains."

"They're not, uh, uh, super-Didonans, though . . . galaxy-unifyin' intellects . . . as Jaan believes?"

"No. Nor do they wage a philosophical conflict among themselves over the ultimate destiny of creation. Those stories merely fit Aycharaych's purpose." Erannath hunched on the claws of his wings. His head thrust forward against nacre and shadow. "Listen," he said. "We have no more than a sliver of time at best. Don't interrupt, unless I grow unclear. Listen. Remember."

The words blew harshly forth, like an autumn gale: "They preserve remnants of technology on Chereion which they have not shared with their masters the Merseians—if the Merseians are really their masters and not their tools. I wonder about that. Well, we must not stop to speculate. As one would await, the technology relates to the mind. For they are extraordinary telepaths, more gifted than the science we know has imagined is possible.

"There is some ultimate quality of the mind which goes deeper than language. At close range, Aycharaych can read the thoughts of *any* being—any speech, any species, he claims—without needing to know that being's symbolism. I suspect what he does is almost instantly to analyze the pattern, identify universals of logic and conation, go on from there to reconstruct the whole mental configuration—as if his nervous system included not only sensitivity to the radiation of others, but an organic semantic computer fantastically beyond anything that Technic civilization has built.

"No matter! Their abilities naturally led Chereionite scientists to concentrate on psychology and neurology. It's been ossified for millions of years, that science, like their whole civilization: ossified, receding, dying. . . . Perhaps Aycharaych alone is trying to act on reality, trying to stop the extinction of his people. I don't know. I do know that he serves the Roidhunate as an Intelligence officer with a roving commission. This involves brewing trouble for the Terran Empire wherever he can.

"During the Snelund regime, he looked through Sector Alpha Crucis. It wasn't hard, when misgovernment had already produced widespread laxity and confusion. The conflict over Jihannath was building toward a crisis, and Merseia needed difficulties on this frontier of Terra's.

"Aycharaych landed secretly on Aeneas and prowled. He found more than a planet growing rebellious. He found the potential of something that might break the Empire apart. For all the peoples here, in all their different ways, are profoundly religious. Give them a common faith, a missionary cause, and they can turn fanatic."

"No," Ivar couldn't help protesting.

"Aycharaych thinks so. He has spent a great deal of his time and energy on your world, however valuable his gift would make him elsewhere."

"But—one planet, a few millions, against the—"

"The cult would spread. He speaks of militant new religions in your past—Islam, is that the name of one?—religions which brought obscure tribes to world power, and shook older dominions to their roots, in a single generation.

"I *must* hurry. He found the likeliest place for the first spark was here, where the Ancients brood at the center of every awareness. In Jaan the dreamer, whose life and circumstances chanced to be a veritable human archetype, he found the likeliest tinder.

"He cannot by himself project a thought into a brain which is not born to receive it. But he has a machine which can. That is nothing fantastic; human, Ythrian, or Merseian engineers could develop the same device, had they enough incentive. We don't, because for us the utility would be marginal; electronic communications suit our kind of life better.

"Aycharaych, though— Telepathy of several kinds belongs to evolution on his planet. Do you remember the slinkers that the tinerans keep? I inquired, and he admitted they came originally from Chereion. No doubt their effect on men suggested his plan to him.

"He called Jaan down to where he laired in these labyrinths. He drugged him and . . . thought at him . . . in some way he knows, using that machine—until he had imprinted a set of false memories and an idiom to go with them. Then he released his victim."

"Artificial schizophrenia. Split personality. A man who was sane, made to hear 'voices.' " Ivar shuddered.

Erannath was harder-souled; or had he simply lived

with the fact longer, in his prison? He went on: "Aycharaych departed, having other mischief to wreak. What he had done on Aeneas might or might not bear fruit; if not, he had lost nothing except his time.

"He returned lately, and found success indeed. Jaan was winning converts throughout the Orcan country. Rumors of the new message were spreading across a whole globe of natural apostles, always eager for anything that might nourish faith, and now starved for a word of hope.

"Events must be guided with craft and patience, of course, or the movement would most likely come to naught produce not a revolution followed by a crusade, but merely another sect. Aycharaych settled down to watch, to plot, ever oftener to plant in Jaan, through his thought projector, a revelation from Caruith—"

The Ythrian chopped off. He hissed. His free hand raked the air. Ivar whirled on his heel, sprang to stand crouched.

The figure in the doorway, limned against unending night, smiled. He was more than half humanlike, tall and slender in a gray robe; but his bare feet ended in claws. The skin glowed golden, the crest on the otherwise naked head rose blue, the eyes were warm bronze. His face was ax-thin, superbly molded. In one delicate hand he aimed a blaster.

"Greeting," he almost sang.

"You woke and sensed," grated from Erannath.

"No," said Aycharaych. "My dreams always listen. Afterward, however, yes, I waited out your conversation."

"Now what?" asked Ivar from the middle of nightmare.

"Why, that depends on you, Firstling," Aycharaych replied with unchanged gentleness. "May I in complete sincerity bid you welcome?"

"You—workin' for Merseia—"

The energy gun never wavered; yet the words flowed serene: "True. Do you object? Your desire is freedom. The Roidhunate's desire is that you should have it. This is the way."

"T-t-treachery, murder, torture, invadin' and twistin' men's bein's—"

"Existence always begets regrettable necessities. Be not overly proud, Firstling. You are prepared to launch a revolutionary war if you can, wherein millions would perish, millions more be mutilated, starved, hounded, brought to sorrow. Are you not? I do no more than help you. Is that horrible? What happiness has Jaan lost that has not already been repaid him a thousandfold?"

"How about Erannath?"

"Heed him not," croaked Ythrian to human. "Think why Merseia wants the Empire convulsed and shattered. Not for the liberty of Aeneans. No, to devour us piecemeal."

"One would expect Erannath to talk thus." Aycharaych's tone bore the least hint of mirth. "After all, he serves the Empire."

"What?" Ivar lurched where he stood. "Him? No!"

"Who else can logically have betrayed you, up on the river, once he felt certain of who you are?"

"He came along—"

"He had no means of preventing your escape, as it happened. Therefore his duty was to accompany you, in hopes of sending another message later, and meanwhile gather further information about native resistance movements. It was the same basic reason as caused him earlier to help you get away from the village, before he had more than a suspicion of your identity.

"I knew his purpose—I have not perpetually lurked underground, I have moved to and fro in the world—and gave Jaan orders, who passed them on to Yakow." Aycharaych sighed. "It was distasteful to all concerned. But my own duty has been to extract what I can from him."

"Erannath," Ivar begged, "it isn't true!"

The Ythrian lifted his head and said haughtily, "Truth you must find in yourself, Ivar Frederiksen. What do you mean to do: become another creature of Aycharaych's, or strike for the life of your people?"

"Have you a choice?" the Chereionite murmured. "I wish you no ill. Nevertheless, I too am at war and cannot stop to weigh out single lives. You will join us, fully and freely, or you will die."

How can I tell what I want? Through dread and anguish, Ivar felt the roan eyes upon him. Behind them must be focused that intellect, watching, searching, reading. *He'll know what I'm about to do before I know myself.* His knife clattered to the floor. *Why not yield? It may well be right—for Aeneas—no matter what Erannath says. And elsewise—*

Everything exploded. The Ythrian seized the knife. Balanced on one huge wing, he swept the other across Ivar, knocking the human back behind the shelter of it.

Aycharaych must not have been heeding what went on in the hunter's head. Now he shot. The beam flared and seared. Ivar saw blinding blueness, smelled ozone and scorched flesh. He bent away from death.

Erannath surged forward. Behind him remained his chained hand. He had hacked it off at the wrist.

A second blaster bolt tore him asunder. His uncrippled wing smote. Cast back against the wall, Aycharaych sank stunned. The gun fell from him.

Ivar pounced to grab the weapon. Erannath stirred. Blood pumped from among blackened plumes. An eye was gone. Breath whistled and rattled.

Ivar dropped on his knees, to cradle his friend. The eye that remained sought for him. "Thus God ... tracks me down. . . . I would it had been under heaven," Erannath coughed. *"Eyan haa wharr, Hlirr talya—"* The light in the eye went out.

A movement caught Ivar's glance. He snatched after the gun. Aycharaych had recovered, was bound through the doorway.

For a heartbeat Ivar was about to yell, Stop, we're allies! That stayed his hand long enough for Aycharaych to vanish. Then Ivar knew what the Chereionite had seen: that no alliance could ever be.

I've got to get out, or Erannath—everybody—has gone for naught. Ivar leaped to his feet and ran. Blood left a track behind him.

He noticed with vague surprise that at some instant he had recovered his flash. Its beam scythed. *Can't grieve yet. Can't be afraid. Can't do anything but run and think.*

Is Aycharaych ahead of me? He's left prints in both directions. No, I'm sure he's not. He realizes I'll head back aboveground; and I, whose forebears came from heavier world than his, would overhaul him. So he's makin' for his lair. Does it have line to outside? Probably not. And even if it does, would he call? That'd give his whole game away. No, he'll have to follow after me, use his hell-machine to plant "intuition" in Jaan's mind—

The room of revelations appeared. Ivar halted and spent a minute playing flame across the thing within. He couldn't tell if he had disabled it or not, but he dared hope.

Onward. Out the door. Down the mountainside, through the sharp dust, athwart the wind which Erannath had died without feeling. To the aircar. Aloft.

The storm yelled and smote.

He burst above, into splendor. Below him rolled the blown dry clouds, full of silver and living shadow beneath Lavinia and hasty Creusa. Stars blazed uncountable. Ahead reared the heights of Ilion; down them glowed and thundered the Linn.

This world is ours. No stranger will shape its tomorrows.

An image in the radar-sweep screen made him look behind. Two other craft soared into view. Had Aycharaych raised pursuit? Decision crystallized in Ivar, unless it had been there throughout these past hours, or latent throughout his life. He activated the radio.

The Imperials monitored several communication bands. If he identified himself and called for a military escort, he could probably have one within minutes.

Tanya, he thought, *I'm comin' home.*

XXI

Chimes rang from the bell tower of the University. They played the olden peals, but somehow today they sounded at peace.

Or was Chunderban Desai wishfully deceiving himself? He wasn't sure, and wondered if he or any human ever could be.

Certainly the young man and woman who sat side by side and hand in hand looked upon him with wariness that might still mask hostility. Her pet, in her lap, seemed touched by the same air, for it perched quiet and kept its gaze on the visitor. The window behind them framed a spire in an indigo sky. It was open, and the breeze which carried the tones entered, cool, dry, pungent with growth odors.

"I apologize for intruding on you so soon after your reunion," Desai said. He had arrived three minutes ago. "I shan't stay long. You want to take up your private lives again. But I did think a few explanations and reassurances from me would help you."

"No big trouble, half hour in your company, after ten days locked away by myself," Ivar snapped.

"I am sorry about your detention, Firstling. It wasn't uncomfortable, was it? We did have to isolate you for a while. Doubtless you understand our need to be secure about you while your story was investigated. But we also had to provide for your own safety after your release. That took time. Without Prosser Thane's cooperation, it would have taken longer than it did."

"Safety—huh?" Ivar stared from him to Tatiana.

She closed fingers on the tadmouse's back, as if in search of solace. "Yes," she said, barely audibly.

179

"Terrorists of the self-styled freedom movement," Desai stated, his voice crisper than he felt. "They had already assassinated a number of Aeneans who supported the government. Your turning to us, your disclosure of a plot which might indeed have pried this sector loose from the Empire—you, the embodiment of their visions—could have brought them to murder again."

Ivar sat mute for a time. The bells died away. He didn't break the clasp he shared with Tatiana, but his part lost strength. At last he asked her, "What did you do?"

She gripped him harder. "I persuaded them. I never gave names ... Commissioner Desai and his officers never asked me for any ... but I talked to leaders, I was go-between, and— There'll be general amnesty."

"For past acts," the Imperial reminded. "We cannot allow more like them. I am hoping for help in their prevention." He paused. "If Aeneas is to know law again, tranquillity, restoration of what has been lost, you, Firstling, must take the lead."

"Because of what I am, or was?" Ivar said harshly.

Desai nodded. "More people will heed you, speaking of reconciliation, than anyone else. Especially after your story has been made public, or as much of it as is wise."

"Why not all?"

"Naval Intelligence will probably want to keep various details secret, if only to keep our opponents uncertain of what we do and do not know. And, m-m-m, several high-ranking officials would not appreciate the news getting loose, of how they were infiltrated, fooled, and led by the nose to an appalling brink."

"You, for instance?"

Desai smiled. "Between us, I have persons like Sector Governor Muratori in mind. I am scarcely important enough to become a sensation. Now they are not ungrateful in Llynathawr. I can expect quite a free hand in the Virgilian System henceforward. One policy I mean to implement is close consultation with representatives of every Aenean society, and the gradual phasing over of government to them."

"Hm. Includin' Orcans?"

"Yes. Commander Yakow was nearly shattered to learn the truth; and he is tough, and had no deep emotional commitment to the false creed—simply to the welfare of his people. He agrees the Imperium can best help them through their coming agony."

Ivar fell quiet anew. Tatiana regarded him. Tears glimmered on her lashes. She must well know that same kind of pain. Finally he asked, "Jaan?"

"The prophet himself?" Desai responded. "He knows no more than that for some reason you fled—defected, he no doubt thinks—and afterward an Imperial force came for another search of Mount Cronos, deeper-going than before, and the chiefs of the Companions have not opposed this. Perhaps you can advise me how to tell him the truth, before the general announcement is made."

Bleakness: "What about Aycharaych?"

"He has vanished, and his mind-engine. We're hunting for him, of course." Desai grimaced. "I'm afraid we will fail. One way or another, that wily scoundrel will get off the planet and home. But at least he did not destroy us here."

Ivar let go of his girl, as if for this time not she nor anything else could warm him. Beneath a tumbled lock of yellow hair, his gaze lay winter-blue. "Do you actually believe he could have?"

"The millennialism he was engineering, yes, it might have, I think," Desai answered, equally low. "We can't be certain. Very likely Aycharaych knows us better than we can know ourselves. But ... it has happened, over and over, through man's troubled existence: the Holy War, which cannot be stopped and which carries away kingdoms and empires, though the first soldiers of it be few and poor.

"Their numbers grow, you see. Entire populations join them. Man has never really wanted a comfortable God, a reasonable or kindly one; he has wanted a faith, a cause, which promises everything but mainly which requires everything.

"Like moths to the candle flame—

"More and more in my stewardship of Aeneas, I have come to see that here is a world of many different peoples, but all of them believers, all strong and able, all sharing some tradition about mighty forerunners and all unready to admit that those forerunners may have been as tragically limited, ultimately as doomed, as we.

"Aeneas was in the forefront of struggle for a political end. When defeat came, that turned the dwellers and their energies back toward transcendental things. And then Aycharaych invented for them a transcendence which the most devout religionist and the most hardened scientist could alike accept.

"I do not think the tide of Holy War could have been stopped this side of Regulus. The end of it would have been humanity and humanity's friends ripped into two realms. No, more than two, for there *are* contradictions in the faith, which I think must have been deliberately put there. For instance, is God the Creator or the Created? —Yes, heresies, persecutions, rebellions . . . states lamed, chaotic, hating each other worse than any outsider—"

Desai drew breath before finishing: "—such as Merseia. Which would be precisely what Merseia needs, first to play us off against ourselves, afterward to overrun and subject us."

Ivar clenched fists on knees. "Truly?" he demanded.

"Truly," Desai said. "Oh, I know how useful the Merseian threat has often been to politicians, industrialists, military lords, and bureaucrats of the Empire. That does not mean the threat isn't real. I know how propaganda has smeared the Merseians, when they are in fact, according to their own lights and many of ours, a fairly decent folk. That does not mean their leaders won't risk the Long Night to grasp after supremacy.

"Firstling, if you want to be worthy of leading your own world, you must begin by dismissing the pleasant illusions. Don't take my word, either. Study. Inquire. Go see for yourself. Do your personal thinking. But always follow the truth, wherever it goes."

"Like that Ythrian?" Tatiana murmured.

"No, the entire Domain of Ythri," Desai told her. "Erannath was my agent, right. But he was also theirs. They sent him by prearrangement: because in his very foreignness, his conspicuousness and seeming detachment, he could learn what Terrans might not.

"Why should Ythri do this?" he challenged. "Had we not fought a war with them, and robbed them of some of their territory?

"But that's far in the past, you see. The territory is long ago assimilated to us. Irredentism is idiocy. And Terra did not try to take over Ythri itself, or most of its colonies, in the peace settlement. Whatever the Empire's faults, and they are many, it recognizes certain limits to what it may wisely do.

"Merseia does not.

"Naturally, Erannath knew nothing about Aycharaych when he arrived here. But he did know Aeneas is a key planet in this sector, and expected Merseia to be at work somewhere underground. Because Terra and Ythri have an overwhelming common interest—peace, stability, containment of the insatiable aggressor—and because the environment of your world suited him well, he came to give whatever help he could."

Desai cleared his throat. "I'm sorry," he said. "I didn't intend that long a speech. It surprised me too. I'm not an orator, just a glorified bureaucrat. But here's a matter on which billions of lives depend."

"Did you find his body?" Ivar asked without tone.

"Yes," Desai said. "His role is another thing we cannot make public: too revealing, too provocative. In fact, we shall have to play down Merseia's own part, for fear of shaking the uneasy peace.

"However, Erannath went home on an Imperial cruiser; and aboard was an honor guard."

"That's good," Ivar said after a while.

"Have you any plans for poor Jaan?" Tatiana asked.

"We will offer him psychiatric treatment, to rid him of the pseudo-personality," Desai promised. "I am told that's possible."

"Suppose he refuses."

"Then, troublesome though he may prove—because his movement won't die out quickly unless he himself denounces it—we will leave him alone. You may disbelieve this, but I don't approve of using people."

Desai's look returned to Ivar. "Likewise you, Firstling," he said. "You won't be coerced. Nobody will pressure you. Rather, I warn you that working with my administration, for the restoration of Aeneas within the Empire, will be hard and thankless. It will cost you friends, and years of your life that you might well spend more enjoyably, and pain when you must make the difficult decision or the inglorious compromise. I can only hope you will join us."

He rose. "I think that covers the situation for the time being," he said. "You have earned some privacy, you two. Please think this over, and feel free to call on me whenever you wish. Now, good day, Prosser Thane, Firstling

Frederiksen." The High Commissioner of the Terran Empire bowed. "Thank you."

Slowly, Ivar and Tatiana rose. They towered above the little man, before they gave him their hands.

"Probably we will help," Ivar said. "Aeneas ought to outlive Empire."

Tatiana took the sting out of that: "Sir, I suspect we owe you more thanks than anybody will ever admit, least of all you."

As Desai closed the door behind him, he heard the tadmouse begin singing.

Jaan walked forth alone before sunrise.

The streets were canyons of night where he often stumbled. But when he came out upon the wharf that the sea had lapped, heaven enclosed him.

Behind this wide, shimmering deck, the town was a huddle turned magical by moonlight. High above lifted the Arena, its dark strength frosted with radiance. Beneath his feet, the mountain fell gray-white and shadow-dappled to the dim shield of the waters. North and east stood Ilion, cloven by the Linn-gleam.

Mostly he knew sky. Stars thronged a darkness which seemed itself afire, till they melted together in the cataract of the Milky Way. Stateliest among them burned Alpha and Beta Crucis; yet he knew many more, the friends of his life's wanderings, and a part of him called on them to guide him. They only glittered and wheeled. Lavinia was down and Creusa hastening to set. Low above the barrens hung Dido, the morning star.

Save for the distant falls it was altogether still here, and mortally cold. Outward breath smoked like wraiths, inward breath hurt.

—Behold what is real and forever, said Caruith.

—Let me be, Jaan said. You are a phantom. You are a lie.

—You do not believe that. We do not.

—Then why is your chamber now empty, and I alone in my skull?

—The Others have won—not even a battle, if we remain steadfast; a skirmish in the striving of life to become God. You are not alone.

—What should we do?

—Deny their perjuries. Proclaim the truth.

—But you are not there! broke from Jaan. You are a branded part of my own brain, hissing at me; and I can be healed of you.

—Oh, yes, Caruith said in terrible scorn. They can wipe the traces of me away; they can also geld you if you want. Go, become domesticated, return to making shoes. Those stars will shine on.

—Our cause in this generation, on this globe, is broken, Jaan pleaded. We both know that. What can we do but go wretched, mocked, reviled, to ruin the dreams of a last faithful few?

—We can uphold the truth, and die for it.

—Truth? What proves you are real, Caruith?

—The emptiness I would leave behind me, Jaan.

And that, he thought, would indeed be there within him, echoing "Meaningless, meaningless, meaningless" until his second death gave him silence.

—Keep me, Caruith urged, and we will die only once, and it will be in the service of yonder suns.

Jaan clung to his staff. *Help me.* No one answered save Caruith.

The sky whitened to eastward and Virgil came, the sudden Aenean dawn. Everywhere light awoke. Whistles went through the air, a sound of wings, a fragrance of plants which somehow kept roots in the desert. Banners rose above the Arena and trumpets rang, whatever had lately been told.

Jaan knew: *Life is its own service. And I may have enough of it in me to fill me. I will go seek the help of men.*

He had never before known how steep the upward path was.

> But I pray you by the lifting skies,
>   And the young wind over the grass,
> That you take your eyes from off my eyes,
>   And let my spirit pass.

> —KIPLING

ABOUT THE AUTHOR

A former president of the Science Fiction Writers of America, Poul Anderson was born in 1926, of Scandinavian parents. Married to writer Karen Kruse, they have one daughter and reside in the San Francisco Bay area where he pursues his hobbies of mountaineering, gardening and cartooning.

Mr. Anderson has published over 50 books and more than 200 shorter pieces, the latter in periodicals as diverse as *Analog, Saturday Review, Boys' Life, Playboy* and *National Review*. He is the winner of five Hugo awards and two Nebula awards for his science fiction works. His books for NAL include THE QUEEN OF AIR AND DARKNESS, A KNIGHT OF GHOSTS AND SHADOWS, A CIRCLE OF HELLS, THE HORN OF TIME, THE REBEL WORLDS, THE BY-WORLDER, BEYOND THE BEYOND, THERE WILL BE TIME, and DANCER FROM ATLANTIS.

Great Science Fiction by Robert Adams from SIGNET

(0451)

☐ **SWORDS OF THE HORSECLANS (Horseclans #2)**
(099885—$2.50)*

☐ **REVENGE OF THE HORSECLANS (Horseclans #3)**
(114310—$2.50)

☐ **A CAT OF SILVERY HUE (Horseclans #4)**   (115791—$2.25)

☐ **THE SAVAGE MOUNTAINS (Horseclans #5)** (115899—$1.95)

☐ **THE PATRIMONY (Horseclans #6)**   (112385—$2.25)

☐ **HORSECLANS ODYSSEY (Horseclans #7)** (097440—$2.75)*

☐ **THE DEATH OF A LEGEND (Horseclans #8)** (111265—$2.50)*

☐ **THE WITCH GODDESS (Horseclans #9)**   (117921—$2.50)*

☐ **CASTAWAYS IN TIME**   (114744—$2.25)*

*Prices slightly higher in Canada

Buy them at your local
bookstore or use coupon
on next page for ordering.

More SIGNET Books by Arthur C. Clarke

(0451)

☐ **THE CITY AND THE STARS** (092325—$1.75)

☐ **THE DEEP RANGE** (096215—$1.95)

☐ **A FALL OF MOONDUST** (097955—$1.95)

☐ **GLIDE PATH** (078241—$1.50)

☐ **ISLANDS IN THE SKY** (098234—$2.50)

☐ **THE NINE BILLION NAMES OF GOD** (117158—$1.95)

☐ **THE OTHER SIDE OF THE SKY** (099125—$2.25)

☐ **REPORT ON PLANET 3** (078640—$1.50)

☐ **THE SANDS OF MARS** (111869—$2.25)

☐ **TALES OF TEN WORLDS** (110935—$2.50)

☐ **2001: A SPACE ODYSSEY** (117093—$2.95)

☐ **THE WIND FROM THE SUN** (114752—$1.50)

Buy them at your local bookstore or use this convenient coupon for ordering.

THE NEW AMERICAN LIBRARY, INC.,
P.O. Box 999, Bergenfield, New Jersey 07621

Please send me the books I have checked above. I am enclosing $_____
(please add $1.00 to this order to cover postage and handling). Send check
or money order—no cash or C.O.D.'s. Prices and numbers are subject to change
without notice.

Name_____

Address_____

City _____ State _____ Zip Code _____
Allow 4-6 weeks for delivery.
This offer is subject to withdrawal without notice.